Gently, Jolene

Angela Scipioni

ISBN-13: 978-0-692-23281-1

Cover Art by Pietro Spica
Manarola

Author photo by Mary Ellen Hill

To Andrea, for believing in me

ONE

There was something about the man in the cockpit that gave Jolene the jitters. She was particularly sensitive when it came to pilots, and by the time *Comandante* Adalberto Giacomini finished his welcome aboard spiel, she couldn't shake the feeling that he must be overworked or ill, maybe even drunk or doped up on painkillers. The TransItalia flight had been air bound for close to an hour now, every minute of which she'd spent sitting as far at the edge of her seat as her securely fastened seatbelt would allow, her buttocks clenching each time a ding or a dong sounded in the cabin. Not everyone was aware that the chimes were used to compose more complex messages than "return to your seat" or "fasten your seat belt," but Jolene knew that those two tones were the building blocks of a secret language employed by the pilot and his crew to warn one another of all kinds of dangers they wanted to hide from the passengers. Each airline company devised its own code, and Jolene was still trying to crack the one being used aboard her first Italian flight when another duplet of dings made her spine stiffen and her left eye twitch.

"Here's the story, *signore* and *signori*," sang the captain, tossing Italian in with the English like dressing on a salad. "We're in for a bumpy landing, so no more standing." After allowing himself a moment to chuckle at his little rhyme, he cleared his voice and spoke again. "So be good, *fate i bravi*, and buckle up while we weather the winds. One way or another, we should be on the ground in Genoa in about fifteen minutes. If not sooner."

One way or another? If not sooner? What kind of a pilot would

1

say things like that? Fear triggered anger in Jolene, and nothing frightened her more than feeling helpless. She saw herself storming the cockpit, jabbing a finger in the pilot's face and reminding him that his job was not only to land the plane safely but to keep his passengers calm and comfortable while doing so. She knew that attempting such an action would only get her in trouble, though, since the door would be locked and she would be restrained, her wrists bound in zip tie cuffs or seat belt extensions.

She tried not to think about her father when speculating about what kind of man was at the controls, but it was always his puffy face she envisioned beneath the brim of the pilot's cap; it was always his bloodshot eyes she glimpsed peering at her from behind the tinted lenses of the Ray-Bans perched on his bulbous nose. And it was always his voice she heard, berating her for her fears, saying it was a slap in the face to him, because it was always about him, that the daughter of a pilot hated to fly. In this case, he was right; it was about him, because her lack of trust in him as a father, at home, extended to him as a pilot, in his plane, and by association, to all pilots, flying all planes, in all skies, all across the globe.

Even after her father was stripped of his wings and could no longer pose a threat to her or the unsuspecting passengers he held hostage, the seeds of anxiety he had planted in Jolene by forcing her to fly against her will took root and grew in the fertile soil of a girl's mind writhing with the worms of insecurity, blossoming into a full-fledged phobia by her teenage years. As an adult, her way of dealing with the fear was quite simple: she did not fly. But when taking to the skies was unavoidable, she refused to swallow pills that would lull her into a false sense of security at a time when she most needed to be alert. She had devised other ways of dealing with her anxiety until boarding, marching incessantly through the terminal to keep her body busy while occupying her mind with speculations about the people around her, trying to guess who they were, where they were going, and why. Not one to bolt at the last minute, she always managed to get herself aboard and strapped into her seat, her eyes darting as she evaluated the flight crew, located the emergency exits, and scanned the faces of the other passengers. As the aircraft taxied into position for takeoff and the placidly purring engines were throttled to a diabolic whir, the physical symptoms set in: the dry mouth, the pasty tongue, the sweaty palms, the hammering heart, the spasms of the minuscule muscle at the outside corner of her left eye. During this stage, her sense of impending disaster was exacerbated by the criminal distraction of those seated around her, who were more interested in munching on snacks and settling in for some mindless entertainment than watching the safety demonstrations. Their extreme nonchalance alarmed her, and they didn't seem to realize that it was for their own good when she quizzed them on emergency landing procedures and the proper use of oxygen masks. Some replied with a suspicious stare, others with a nervous giggle, possibly taking her for a lunatic or amateur terrorist, maybe even an undercover investigator from the NTSB. By the time the plane reached cruising altitude, it was not unusual for her to have already interrogated her neighbors regarding their previous experiences with the airline company and its pilots. The fact that no one ever remembered the name of any pilot—not even the one who had introduced himself just minutes earlier, the very same one upon whom their survival depended—always astonished her. But maybe people didn't want to know. Maybe it was easier to trust someone with your life when they remained anonymous, and therefore devoid of human qualities. If people realized that the guy in charge was one of them, they might start worrying about whether he'd gotten a good night's sleep, or eaten a nourishing breakfast, or tipped a glass too many the night before. Or whether he was a right-winger or a left-winger, a child beater or a wife cheater; a religious fanatic or non-believer, a gambler or a meanie. Which brought her back to her father, the pilot. George W. Twyman, that was his name. Instead of letting people assume that the W. stood for Washington, he made it a point to state his name in full whenever he drawled his own introduction: Captain George Wallace Twyman. A name that was impossible to forget, a name that still had the power to make Jolene cringe.

But that was then, it was over, in the past. The last leg of this long trip was almost over, too, thanks be to God. Anyone could remember His name, and He was the One who was in charge anyway, not that lunatic *Comandante* Giacomini. That was what Jolene kept telling herself as she sat strapped in her seat, her eyes squeezed tight as the plane bucked and bounced its way to the ground. When she finally summoned the courage to peek out her porthole, she was horrified to see nothing but jagged mountains and white-capped waters rotating in a nauseating fashion as the plane banked, and no sign of a suitable place to land. The fuselage trembled, slapped by the gusts rushing down the valleys of the Ligurian Apennines to ram the crosswinds blowing ashore from the Mediterranean, pushing and shoving the aircraft like bullies from rival gangs before letting it drop on a runway which, miraculously, had materialized beneath them.

"Welcome to Genoa!" Filippo said, leaning close to be heard above the whining of the plane reversing its engines and roaring to a halt, just as Jolene thought it would skid off the runway and bellyflop into the sea. She was grateful that Filippo had been so engrossed in his complimentary copy of *Il Corriere della Sera* after months of deprivation that he hadn't noticed how petrified she'd been, after doing so well on the overnight transatlantic flight from New York to Rome.

Not wanting to spoil their trip in any way, Jolene had decided to keep her fear of flying to herself, but words were superfluous with a man as sensitive and understanding as Filippo. Back at JFK, when he'd noticed her sitting with her eyes closed, breathing through her nose like she'd learned years ago in the pranayama exercises of her yoga class, Filippo didn't tease her or ply her with stupid statistics about planes being safer than cars. Instead, he'd told her that it was her right to be afraid, that just because millions of people each day paid to get locked up with a bunch of strangers inside a giant metal tube, shooting through the troposphere to the stratosphere then being dumped at far-flung destinations didn't mean that it was normal. He'd walked with her and talked with her as they waited to board; he'd loosened her up with an outrageously expensive martini and entertained her with stories of his childhood in the Cinque Terre. Once on the plane, he'd made sure she was as comfortable and relaxed as possible, then he'd put his background as a hotelier to good use, pretending to be her personal waiter during dinner, extolling the qualities of each menu option, recommending wines, making sure her glass was never empty, until she'd become drowsy. Afterward, he'd tucked a blanket around her legs and stuck pods in her ears, explaining that she'd soon fall under the spell of the hypnotic piano music of Maestro Einaudi, Filippo's favorite Italian composer. Then Jolene had dozed off, exactly as Filippo had said she would, waking just before landing in Rome, convinced that she'd been cured of her fear of flying for good.

"Are you with me, *Splendore mio?*" Filippo asked, tapping her on the head with his rolled-up newspaper. The gesture was playful, even affectionate, but the presence of strangers made Jolene's cheeks flush with humiliation. It was no fault of Filippo's, but the gesture reminded her of the way her father used to discipline the family dog, and sometimes Jolene herself, back in the days when newspapers were thick and inky and delivered to their doorstep each morning. "How stupid can you be?" was what her father the Captain always yelled when wielding his paper club, making both Jolene and the dog cower, regardless of which one he intended to clobber. But this was not her father, she reminded herself. This was a man who did not call her stupid, but "my splendor." And he called her that in Italian.

"Welcome to Genoa, I said," Filippo repeated, prying Jolene's fingers from the armrest and clasping her hands in his. He raised them to his lips, engaging her gaze with eyes so dark and round they made her think of two brimming cups of espresso, with which she hoped to revive herself soon. His whiskers grazed the back of one hand then the other as he kissed them, leaving warm, tingly tracks on her skin. Although she didn't want it to, because she did not want to be reminded of anything else that had come before this precious moment, this time Filippo's gesture made her think of the last guy who had tried to impress her by kissing her hand. In that unfortunate instance, her skin had burned even more, due to a glob of extra hot barbecue sauce ferried there via the guy's greedy mouth, which until a second before had been chomping on Buffalo chicken wings. She could still hear the pig laughing when she thought about it now; she could still feel his greasy tongue licking off the oily orange splotch with a grunt. Shaking the memory from her head, she instinctively wiped the backs of her hands on her jeans.

"Are you feeling okay, *Splendore?*" Filippo asked when she still did not speak, his brow furrowing that way it did when he worried. Filippo's forehead was one of his most expressive features, the place where his strongest emotions were played out, leading Jolene to suspect that his receding hairline was a direct result of his forehead's determination to claim a larger stage for itself. Whether rippling with fleeting concern or creased with deeper troubles, each telltale line was underscored by the thick black brows which stretched out over his eyes when in repose but shot up to form twin arches when provoked.

"Yes. Now I'm fine," Jolene said, sure that she would be, in just a few minutes.

After gathering their belongings, Jolene and Filippo inched their way to the exit of the cramped aircraft, jostled by the elbows and shoulders and cumbersome carry-ons of the other passengers. Finally reaching the door, Jolene paused to breathe in the fresh wind, feeling so giddy with relief that her legs wobbled, forcing her to grab the handrail as she descended the stairs. The feel of her feet hitting the ground fortified her, the sound of her rubber soles squeaking on the tarmac reassured her, confirming that she was no longer a powerless pebble of a person being catapulted through the air. She blinked several times, her green eyes gritty and shocked by the morning light glinting off every surface around her: slabs of granite, panes of glass, panels of metal, stretches of asphalt, and beyond it all, the shimmering blue body of water. Squinting against the sun and wind as her loose hair whipped her face, Jolene shrugged her backpack from her shoulder and fished out her sunglasses. Settling them on her nose, she surveyed her surroundings.

"It's that way, right?" she asked, pointing across the gulf toward a humpbacked mountain jutting into the sea, bathed in the golden September sun climbing in a cloudless sky. Clearly, that direction was east, which meant she could find north, which meant she could find anything. While growing up, Jolene had been constantly prodded by her mother to establish her bearings, so that she would always know how to get where she was going, and how to return to where she had come from. Whether they were out rowing on the lake or cruising the aisles of a supermarket, her mother would only give her directions in terms of east or west, north or south, never referring to right and left like normal people did. "Right and left are relative to a person's position, making them subject to misinterpretation," her mother never tired of repeating. "The cardinal points are absolute. Always pursue the absolute, Jolene."

"That's right," Filippo said, taking her chin in his hand and her mind off the past. "That's the promontory of Portofino, and beyond that…well, you'll soon see for yourself, won't you?"

Overwhelmed by the importance of this moment, Jolene paused to contemplate the view, and her future, in silence. She'd learned enough to know that they would be following the Ligurian coast southeast, toward Tuscany. The map in her backpack was already worn, its creases tearing, its colors smudging, as if she had been wandering around the country for weeks on foot, instead of in her head. Sure, she had done a bit of online research, too, but physical maps were more inspiring, more reliable. You could carry a map in your pocket; you could spread it open and run your fingers over its roads and highways, mountains and lakes, cities and countrysides, while your imagination roamed around all those new places, met new people, grabbed new opportunities, explored less-traveled routes.

Fantasizing about the future had always helped Jolene push back memories of the past, embrace her present, and cultivate hope for brighter days. She had been doing a lot of that lately, ever since one fine June evening on Cayuga Lake, before she even owned a map of Italy. The group she'd been responsible for welcoming aboard the tour boat were attendees of a post-graduate summer session program in hospitality management at Cornell University, and as part of their orientation, they were to be treated to a sunset cruise. Jolene's job was to smile and serve the wine, and although she did not make a habit of flirting while on duty (or ever), she was flattered when the smartly dressed man who looked like he'd stepped out of a GQ ad in his navy deck shoes, yachting trousers, and brass-buttoned blazer, smiled back and thanked her as graciously as if she were the owner of the boat, rather than hired help. By his second glass of Glenora Riesling, the tall Italian was hovering at her elbow, cramping her pouring style as she served other guests, intent on striking up a conversation despite the constant interruptions. His English was passable although a bit quirky, his accent charming, his knowledge of wine-growing in the Finger Lakes region impressive.

Before disembarking, he had handed her an embossed calling card on which his name alone—Filippo Garaventi—announced itself in boldface letters. When the man asked for her name and number, she surprised herself not only by complying but watching to make sure that he got the spelling and number right, as he jotted them down in the leather address book he slipped from his breast pocket. In the days that followed, this debonair Italian did something that no other man had ever done: he outran her fantasies. He phoned before she convinced herself that he'd crossed out her number. He invited her to dinner before she imagined meeting him for coffee. He kissed her over their entrées before she wondered whether his whiskers would feel scratchy. He told her he was in love with her before they made love.

Though profoundly disappointed by her failed marriage to Danny in her younger years, and severely shaken by her disastrous breakup with Evan, Jolene remained a romantic. Sure, it hadn't been easy lately, when the only men she met were so wishy-washy and confused and selfish and petrified of rejection that they wouldn't even use the word "relationship" when referring to ongoing interactions with a woman. But Filippo Garaventi was not that kind of man. He was a man who talked, but not only about himself. He charged through whatever language barriers tried to stop him from expressing his ideas and opinions, picking up the conversation initiated that day on the boat and carrying it on day after day with ease and enthusiasm. He led their discourse through a wide range of subjects, from the philosophy and techniques behind biodynamic wine-making, to the success of Italy's Slow Food movement, to the upheaval in the American political scene, to Brexit and its repercussions on the European Union, to why Jolene absolutely must not miss the Caravaggio exhibition at Milan's Palazzo Reale.

Intrigued by his views, starved for stimulating talk, and eager to practice the Italian she'd learned years ago, Jolene was a keen listener. Up until now, she'd been convinced that she preferred quiet men, but she suspected that was only because she'd never met one with anything original to say. Filippo, with his international education and continental culture, held her spellbound. Between his conversational skills, his impeccable manners and his unabashed interest in her, the hours and days and weeks she spent in his company passed as in a dream. If anyone were to ask her how long they had been together, she would have been shocked to realize that almost four months had gone by since that day on the boat, and even more astonished that it hadn't been longer. Such a perfect balance of passion and clearheadedness, romanticism and practicality, chivalry and hot pursuit, had set her smoldering hopes and flickering fantasies aflame. She'd felt herself drifting effortlessly toward a future together as if she were floating gently down the stream in her mother's old rowboat.

And now she was here, her two feet firmly planted on foreign soil, as the other passengers hurried toward the bus that would shuttle them to the terminal, while she stood looking off into the horizon, immobilized by the realization that the future she had been imagining was no longer a romantic's dream. It was here and now, swirling all around her, blotting out the past. She was incredibly excited, justifiably nervous, and more than a little scared. Her insides were all in a tangle, like the mass of rubber bands she had been surprised to discover inside a golf ball her father had once cracked open in a fit of rage.

Breathe, Jolene, she reminded herself, as she recited her litany of logic. She was here because she and Filippo were in love. Because Filippo was right when he said that at their age—she thirty-eight and he thirty-four—they were both old enough to know what they wanted in a partner. And because he was right about them being a perfect team from a professional point of view. Between their combined studies and experience in food service and hospitality, they could accomplish marvelous things at Locanda Luisa, the hotel in the Cinque Terre that Filippo's family had been running in the same backward way for the past half-century. What was a woman supposed to do when a handsome, sensitive, well-educated Italian man sauntered into her life, laid claim to her heart, offered her a dream job in one of the most spectacular destinations in the world, and proposed marriage on top of it all?

Jolene couldn't help wondering whether her mother would have supported her decision, or discouraged her. She too had moved to a new city for love, then given up her career as a flight attendant when she became pregnant with Jolene. It was unfortunate that her mother's unerring sense of direction failed to make her steer clear of the Captain, but the compass that could deter women from the treacherous course of love had not yet been invented. Jolene's situation was different, though. Filippo had earned her trust, and by his side, she would discover a new world, become acquainted with its people, adopt its customs, master its tongue. She even had a head start on the language, thanks to her high school pal Anna Vigevani, a native of Brescia. Fascinated by the banter of Anna's foreign family, Jolene had striven to understand what they said to one another, a longing that induced her to drop French and take up Italian. Lately, she had been wondering where Anna might be now, but her curiosity was of the vague sort, never compelling enough to make her conduct a search. Maybe she preferred to remember Anna as an exotic sixteen-year-old, just like she herself would rather be remembered as the dewy-eyed daydreamer who hung around their house, her tongue struggling to pronounce the Italian expressions they taught her, her tummy craving the Italian food they fed her, her heart yearning for the Italian affection they bestowed upon her.

"Ow!" Jolene cried out as a pain shot down her elbow to her forearm, making Anna and her parents and the entire city of Chicago retreat to the past.

"What are you doing, *Splendore?* I thought you were right behind me, and when I turned around, I saw you were just standing there, lost in your own little world. What on earth are you thinking about now?" Though he had her attention, Filippo pressed his thumb into her elbow joint a second time.

"Stop that!" Jolene cried, shaking the jolt from her arm. "You promised that my funny bone would be off limits!"

"And you promised that you would always tell me what's on your mind."

He often commented that she had a faraway look in her eyes and asked her what she was thinking, and while his curiosity sometimes seemed genuine, at other times she perceived a hint of irritation that tautened the tone of his voice like a tuning peg, adding an edge of sharpness. Or, in extreme cases, prompted his famous funny bone squeeze.

"Well?" he said, ushering her toward the crowded bus. "Are you going to tell me, or not?"

Jolene stumbled after him, knowing she would not be able to weave together the tendrils of her thoughts, much less bundle them up into a concise answer of the sort Filippo preferred to hear. By now, she knew that if they were in a restaurant, for example, it would be better to say that she was debating over what to order, rather than admit to dwelling on some uninvited random thought that had pulled up a chair at their table and sat down next to her. He was right, of course; she should learn to take control of her mind and focus on who she was with and what she was doing, but keeping the intruders out was no easy feat. Besides, regardless of whether or not he was really interested in her meandering thoughts, sometimes she just did not want to answer. Not to hide things from him, but to keep them to herself, which was different. So many of her nagging notions and resurfacing memories were no more than toxic exhalations from the landfill of her past, and she was determined to keep them buried where they belonged, thousands of miles away, where they could not pollute her new life.

"Nothing, really," she mumbled, stepping aboard the shuttle as the doors nipped at her ankle. Grabbing a pole for support as the bus lurched forward, she glanced at Filippo and was dismayed to notice his lips pursing in that way that made it seem they were being held hostage by the neatly trimmed mustache and equally well-groomed beard that surrounded them. She had seen that look on other occasions, when Filippo was irritated with someone but restrained himself, being too classy to swear, too well-mannered to shout. She had never been responsible for provoking that look before, at least she didn't think so, but she was still learning so much about him. It would take a little time for her to interpret his subtler forms of expression, like the various ways he raised his eyebrows or rolled his eyes, but now that they would be living together everything would be easier to figure out.

The bus jerked to a halt, the opening doors hissing their dismissal. Jolene followed Filippo down the steps and into the sleepy terminal, where a lone red suitcase circled dejectedly around the only baggage claim belt in operation as if planted there to hypnotize impatient travelers forced to endure a long wait. Jolene, too, began staring at the red suitcase going round and round, her bleary eyes struggling to stay focused, her lids growing heavier with each passage. She was startled when a procession of fresh bags began stumbling down the chute and she recognized hers among them, thanks to the braids of green hair yarn she had tied to their handles like her mother had taught her. Before she could make a move, Filippo grabbed the bags, springing to action like a parent dragging a straying child to safety before it could be snatched by a stranger. Gripping a suitcase in each hand, he turned to face her, his lips now spread in a proud grin, as if he himself were responsible for the miracle of their persons and possessions being reunited in the same spot. It gave Jolene a feeling of lightness, almost queasiness, to realize that all she had left in the world was right there, in this one man and those two bags.

Donating all of her clothes to the Salvation Army hadn't been a premeditated gesture of goodwill, nor were her motives for doing so entirely noble. Tackling the daunting task of packing for her overseas move, she had scrutinized each article of clothing to decide whether it should be allowed to continue life with her. It perplexed her that some items seemed so heavy that her arms could hardly hold them up, before realizing that it was the memories attached to certain garments that weighed them down, not the materials of which they were made. They were stitched into the seams of the hiking pants she had worn while exploring the trails of Buttermilk Falls with Evan; they were entwined in the spaghetti straps of the black knit dress she had worn to the opening of their restaurant; they were balled up like tear-stained tissues and stuffed into the pockets of the faded cotton sundress she had worn on the first of many picnics one hot summer with Danny, the boy who had been her sweetheart for longer than he had remained her husband. She became so distracted by the emotions stirred up by every garment, so possessed with unravelling every thread of sadness, unzipping every tragedy, digging into every pocket of disappointment, examining every torn expectation and snagged plan, that the only way for her to get on with the job had been to eliminate every article connected with painful memories, which was pretty much everything. Everything except for a few special items she had wrapped with care and buried beneath the innocuous old clothes and memory-free new clothes that filled her suitcases.

Still staring at Filippo and the bags, she was uplifted by this compact version of Jolene Twyman already taking up less space in the world, already soaring to new heights now that she was finally free from the presences and absences that tethered her to an old identity, to an outdated past, to superseded sentiments.

"I've got everything, *Splendore!*" Filippo said a moment later, hoisting the second of his own suitcases onto the pile in the cart, and already pushing it toward the exit.

"Yes, you do." Jolene smiled, noticing as she followed him that one wheel of the cart twirled around in circles, making it hard for him to steer straight. "And so do I."

The wayward cartwheel wobbled as Filippo pushed their luggage toward the exit, calling unwanted attention to them as they approached Customs. Jolene always got nervous when she was asked to show documents she was sure would be found irregular, or open luggage to display her personal belongings to strangers. Today, she was particularly apprehensive; today, the rest of her life depended on being admitted to Italy with no glitches. When the uninterested officer stamped her passport and waved her through with a cursory glance, Jolene wiped her sweaty palms on her jeans and breathed a sigh of relief. Stepping lightly, she trotted alongside Filippo and the defective cart, noticing that he did not seem to mind the extra work required to keep it on a straight path, as if even this were an opportunity to prove that nothing could slow him down when he had a plan. Thankfully, the terminal at Cristoforo Colombo airport was small and they were soon outside.

"Giobatta!" Filippo cried, consigning the cart to Jolene's custody as he waved, striding toward a wiry white-haired man in a beret standing next to a little green car parked at the curb. Jolene watched the two men shake hands, brush cheeks and embrace. Having been born in these parts, Filippo Garaventi had many people to come home to, and Jolene was looking forward to finally meeting them all. Save for a few photos of himself as a child, Filippo hadn't shown her any of the images she often glimpsed him swiping at on the screen of his phone. The reasoning behind this was that he wanted her to have a fresh impression of the people she would meet, and although she appreciated the concept, not knowing what anyone looked like gave her one more thing to be nervous about. It would have been reassuring to be able to recognize a person or two in Manarola, a town with almost 400 unfamiliar faces, in a country with over 60 million unfamiliar faces. It was an uneasy feeling, for someone who didn't even like going to parties where she didn't know anyone, unless it was a catering job and she was expected to work, not mingle. The thought made her mull over the fact that working a party was actually more enjoyable than attending a party, which made her reflect on parties in general. She was racking her brain trying to remember one party to which she'd been invited in the past five years and had a good time, when something caught her eye: Filippo was waving both arms in the air, calling her over. She gave the lame wheel a kick and pushed the cart to the car, where the first new face to which she could attach a name awaited her.

"Jolene, I want you to meet Giobatta," Filippo said.

"*Piacere, Ciabatta!*" Jolene said, smiling as she shook the man's hand while thinking it odd that he should be named after a type of bread which in turn took its name from the flat "slipper" it resembled.

Giobatta nodded, touched a finger to his beret, and relieved her of the luggage cart.

"It's not *Cia*batta, *Cara* Jo. It's *Gio*batta," Filippo said, standing with her at the curb while the man loaded the car. "Short for Giovanni Battista. John the Baptist was a popular saint around here, so lots of older people were named after him. It's a little outdated now, but don't tell him that." Peering down at her from his six-inch advantage, Filippo gave her a pat on the head, making her feel small in a way she was unaccustomed to. Though he was taller, Jolene was older, and up until today, she had been the one introducing him to new people, showing him new places, telling him how things worked, correcting his pronunciation. Up until today, they'd been playing on her home turf, but now the roles would be reversed. It would be a relief to let Filippo take charge while she settled in, she told herself, to let him do the explaining, while she looked on, listened, and learned.

Not one for dilly-dallying, Giobatta had already stowed the luggage in the boxy Fiat Panda, managing, through a combination of Italian design, creative thinking, and a good deal of pushing and shoving, to make everything fit without Filippo's help. When Giobatta slid behind the wheel, Filippo insisted Jolene sit in the front seat, while he straddled a suitcase in the back, joking that there was nothing he enjoyed more than riding with his knees in his ears. Between the bridges and tunnels followed by more bridges and tunnels of the trafficked A12 highway, Jolene glimpsed the urban sprawl of Genoa, trapped between the Mediterranean sea to her right (south-ish) and the steep Ligurian hillside to her left (north-ish). Once past the city, a succession of towns flashed by in a blur of oranges and greens, pinks and ochers, prompting Jolene to pair them with the names she recalled from her map and now spotted on the exit signs: Nervi, Recco, Rapallo, Chiavari. Smaller clusters of buildings gripped the mountainside, as if fearful of sliding down into the sea, while others huddled around coastal coves, as if jealously guarding sunken treasures. In the first hour of the two it took Giobatta to drive the couple to their destination, Jolene learned that the man was neither an uncle nor an older cousin of Filippo's, but the only driver in Manarola the Garaventi family trusted. Despite her waning alertness and Giobatta's frequent lapses into local dialect, she managed to follow the conversation well enough to learn that this family friend was so reliable that he had been the one to rush Filippo's mother Luisa to the hospital in La Spezia when she gave birth to Filippo.

Everyone who had anything to say on the subject—meaning, Filippo paused to point out to her, virtually everyone in town—

concurred that it would have been impossible for Vittorio, Filippo's father, to accompany the laboring woman himself, when the Locanda was crowded with hungry guests waiting to be served the day's special of freshly caught anchovies, whose silvery little bodies he had painstakingly decapitated, split open, deboned, coated with flour, and had been dipping, one by one, into a skillet of sizzling olive oil, when Filippo's mother's water broke all over the kitchen floor. However, if those same villagers were to be believed, the Locanda was, on the contrary, deserted on the morning mamma Luisa and her infant were pronounced fit and ready to go home. The only baker in town had no doubt as to the veracity of this, remembering distinctly that no orders had been placed for focaccia or rolls or bread of any sort, as Vittorio Garaventi was so notoriously tight-fisted, even for a Ligurian, that he ate stale bread when he had no guests to feed, expecting his family to do the same. The owner of the tobacco shop-newsstand agreed that it must have been so, because the only paper requested by little Lorenzo, Luisa's firstborn who ran the morning errands, was the usual house copy of Liguria's daily, Il Secolo XIX, which each morning was clamped to a wooden rack and placed at the disposal of the regulars who stopped by the Locanda for a chat and a coffee or a nip of white wine. Had there been any lodgers, Vittorio would have been forced to invest in a variety of papers since even back then, anyone who took a room at Locanda Luisa would surely demand a copy of Milan's Corriere della Sera or one of those other big city papers, to read over their morning cappuccino and brioche.

In reality, it was explained, Signor Garaventi's reluctance to drive to La Spezia to pick up Luisa and the still nameless baby stemmed from the fact that the man would have nothing to do with cars. The motives of his aversion went beyond that of avarice, though the ownership of an automobile would doubtless entail a great deal of expense, between the purchase and fuel and upkeep and insurance and annual registration tax. Vittorio Garaventi so detested the sight of those four-wheeled intruders that crept over the hills and descended on the village, hogging up the precious space between the banks of the Rio Groppo and the steep hillside, that he refused to ride in them. He predicted that their numbers would grow, which would lead to the widening of roads and the gutting of mountains and the paving of parking lots, causing more crowding, more noise, more pollution. Cars could do nothing for nature but destroy it, and nothing for him but disrupt the quiet life he had known since his birth in the isolated fishing village of Manarola.

According to Filippo, his father, being a man who refused to adapt his needs to anyone else's schedule, disdained trains, too. As a business owner, however, he admitted that the *Ferrovie dello Stato* played a precious role in bringing in the tourists and their money, an invasion he tolerated as long as he was not denied his inalienable right as a Ligurian to complain about it. In short, as far as Filippo's father was concerned, any man worth his weight in sea salt needed only one other means to get around in the Cinque Terre, besides a set of good strong limbs: his boat. That may well be, except when you have a newborn baby to pick up from the hospital, conceded Giobatta, who then went on to rehash the argument he'd had with Vittorio on the matter. In the end, it had been Giobatta, exasperated by his friend's pigheadedness, who hopped in the car and drove to the hospital. After which Vittorio did not speak to Giobatta until the day of Filippo's baptism, when he began circulating the story of being stuck in the kitchen with the Locanda full of guests, which everyone pretended to believe, while knowing it was not true.

"Let's give it a rest for now," Filippo said when Giobatta paused to let the facts sink in. "I don't want Jolene to get any wrong ideas before she even meets anyone."

Giobatta said nothing more, but judging by the way his Adam's apple bobbed when he swallowed his words, Jolene sensed he was disappointed at being silenced. He concentrated on driving now, his bony fingers gripping the steering wheel, his sharp gray eyes flickering as they blinked away the past and focused on the road ahead. Filippo sighed and leaned back in his seat, whether tired of old tales, weary of his awkward position, or sick of hearing that his father thought his obligation to anchovies more important than attending his birth, it was hard to say. Jolene would have liked to hear more anecdotes about the family, but deferred to Filippo's wishes, knowing that the stories would be more meaningful and easier to follow once she met the cast of characters. Besides, once Giobatta exited the fast-paced autostrada and swerved onto the winding road that led from La Spezia up through the hills and into the heart of the Cinque Terre, the scenery unfurling before her was so spectacular that she wouldn't have been able to speak or listen. No story about people she did not yet know could captivate her attention like the astonishing views filling her eyes with beauty, and her soul with joy.

Motoring amid the sun-drenched hillsides spattered with silvery olive trees, she marveled at the drystone walls snaking across the terraced strips of land strung with gold-leafed grapevines. She gasped at the dramatic vistas of the indigo sea that crashed against the rocks far below, sucking in her breath at every hairpin turn Giobatta navigated by constantly upshifting and downshifting with the assurance of a rally driver, all the way to their final descent to Manarola. It wasn't until he coasted into a parking spot and pulled the handbrake, jerking the exhausted Panda to a halt, that Jolene realized she had lost all sense of direction.

TWO

"Fi-nal-men-te!" A woman's voice rang out over the drumroll of trolleys trailing the trio comprised of Jolene, Filippo and Giobatta as they walked from the residents' parking area to the center of Manarola. Save for rare exceptions, Filippo was explaining, the road running through the village was off limits to motor vehicles, but that didn't really matter since the only place it took you was straight into the sea. Jolene had one ear tuned into what he was saying, while the other was bent on discovering where that voice had come from.

"Ar-ri-voo! Su-bi-too!" the voice sang again, allowing Jolene to trace it to a lady waving from the third floor of a faded pink building. In the time it took Jolene to blink, the woman disappeared, leaving in her place a lace curtain fluttering in an empty window flanked by a pair of green shutters. Before she could ask Filippo whether he knew the woman, she reappeared on the road, wearing a plain white blouse tucked into a knee-length blue skirt. Her attire reminded Jolene of the garb worn by the more modern nuns she had sometimes seen in church during her years as a Catholic.

"Mamma!" Filippo cried when he saw her. *"Splendore mio!"*

It struck Jolene as odd that Filippo would greet his mother with the same term of endearment he used with her, but she didn't have time to decide whether it bothered her; it was all she could do to keep up with Filippo as he dragged her by the hand toward the woman.

"I hardly recognized you with your new hairdo!" he said, dropping Jolene's hand to hug and kiss his mother. "This color is fabulous on you!"

"Oh, well, I don't know about that," the woman said, looking embarrassed, either at the compliment or at the revelation that chestnut brown was not her natural color, while patting her helmet of lacquered hair as if she were still getting to know it, or perhaps feared breaking it. "The village ladies ganged up on me. They said I should look 'presentable' for my son's homecoming. It made me wonder how they normally see me."

Thanks to Filippo's refusal to share descriptions or photos with her, Jolene couldn't know what the woman had looked like before the hairdresser's intervention, but she had been picturing a stone-faced signora dressed in black from head to toe, her gray locks coiled under a hairnet like a snake, ready to lash out at anyone who dared to hijack her son's affection or jeopardize his well-being. The woman before her seemed more dynamic than she'd imagined, the style and shade of her hair were typical of older ladies who got their hair done once a week and didn't like it to be mussed between appointments. Though relieved that the woman did not resemble the Italian mother-in-law of her nightmares, Jolene had to scramble to rethink her approach.

Filippo had told her to "just be yourself and everyone will love you as much as I do," but she didn't even know what that meant anymore. Together with most of her possessions, she had left all the roles that defined that self back in America, making her wonder how Signora Garaventi would perceive her; who she had been expecting, and who she would see. She detested feeling so nervous and unsure of herself, at this age and stage of her life. Hadn't she already been inoculated against the ordeal of parental inspection a couple of decades earlier, the first time Danny brought her home for Thanksgiving dinner, arriving when the Doherty men were already so tipsy on highballs and engrossed in some football game that they barely looked up when Danny sprung the news that they would be married before the Rose Bowl? And again five years later (when she had already been divorced for two), when Evan's parents stopped in for an impromptu visit en route from Schenectady to Niagara Falls to admire their son's new restaurant, and caught Jolene on her hands and knees scrubbing the floors? You would think that by now she would be past worrying about what a grown man's parents thought of her. You would think that by now, after trying so hard to be accepted into the inner circle of the families she'd joined, only to suffer like an abandoned puppy when she was kicked back out into the cold, she'd toughen up a bit. Yet here she was again, with sweaty palms and a quivering smile, hoping she didn't look as haggard as she felt. For the moment, though, Signora Garaventi was still completely taken with Filippo, holding him at arm's length for her maternal inspection.

"Are you trying to grow a beard?" she asked, pointing at the black bristles littering his chin.

"This is a beard," Filippo said, stroking his jaw. "This is how they're worn now, Ma."

"It looks a little, I don't know, frustrated?"

Jolene was pleased that she could follow the exchange in Italian without much difficulty. Despite her nervousness, or perhaps because of it, a giggle escaped her, but she masked the sound with a cough. Jolene herself was of the opinion that there were only two possible advantages to growing a beard: to keep one's face warm in a cold climate, or to elude the slavery of having to shave every day. Filippo's fuzz was too short to provide any insulation, and its upkeep seemed to require constant care. Instead of shaving once a day, Filippo fussed over his facial hair continually, trimming and clipping it each morning, performing on-the-spot touch-ups with the miniature barber's shears he carried in the breast pocket of his blazer, whenever he noticed a whisker out of place.

"I can't exactly afford to look like a hipster, or a terrorist," Filippo said. "Or a Swami, if you can relate to that better. Don't forget, I am a hotel manager."

"How could I ever forget that? You were born a hotel manager." His mother's eyes twinkled as they dropped from Filippo's face and came to rest on his midsection. She gave his tummy a little pat. "At least you've finally gained some weight."

Jolene smiled to herself. She would never have had the nerve to do that, but she, too, had noticed a certain pudginess around his middle lately. His eagerness to explore the Finger Lakes food and wine trails far surpassed his enthusiasm for its hiking trails.

"Four months of American food will do that to anyone," Filippo said. "But how about you? Have you lost weight? Have you been working too hard?" The lines on his forehead rippled with worry as he regarded his mother.

"Well, you know, that's just the way it is toward the end of the season," she replied, waving away his concern as if it were a pesky fly. Then she turned her attention to her son's fiancée, her stare instantly deploying the ball of rubber bands wadded inside Jolene's stomach, where they ricocheted off the walls with an audible twang. Jolene was mortified, but either the woman wasn't close enough to hear the noise, or compassionate enough to pretend she didn't notice. She studied Jolene with eyes the color of a clear lake on a cloudy day; eyes that were neither friendly nor hostile, but as impartial as if they were examining a roadmap or a bus schedule. Then she approached her, extending her right hand.

"I'm Filippo's mother," she said in English. She did not clasp Jolene's hand between hers but shook it. Her grip was firm, her smile unguarded. She wore no lipstick or other makeup.

"It's a pleasure to meet you," Jolene responded in English, partly out of respect for the woman's consideration in speaking her language, partly to dodge the problem of whether to use the familiar tu form or the more formal lei when addressing her. She didn't know what local custom dictated when speaking to one's future mother-in-law; she didn't even know whether to call her Luisa or Signora Garaventi. Hoping for a cue, she added, "*Io sono Jolene.*"

"See, she even speaks Italian," Filippo said. "She's very smart."

"*Bene, molto bene,*" his mother said, scrutinizing Jolene's features.

As she tended to do when embarrassed, Jolene smiled, despite knowing that it would make her cheeks ball up, which would accentuate the wrinkles that had settled in around her eyes and mouth in the latter half of her thirties, with no apparent plans to go anywhere but deeper. The past twenty-four hours of travel hadn't exactly rejuvenated her aspect, either.

"Finally, a grown woman," Filippo's mother said. "You can call me Luisa, *va bene?*"

"*Va bene,*" Jolene said, nodding. "Thank you." With a few words in Italian and a few in English, she had survived the first and most important introduction while laying the cornerstones of her new identity: She was Jolene, a not-so-young American bride-to-be with a nervous stomach. Maybe that was all anyone needed to know, for now.

"You look exhausted," Luisa said. "Why don't you show her to her room, Filippo? We can talk more after you've had some rest. I'll be where I always am. At the Locanda." Jolene wanted to say that she'd love to see the Locanda first, but Luisa was already walking away.

Minutes later the color in Jolene's cheeks was high and bright as she looked over her shoulder at the path she and Filippo had already climbed. Some distance below them, Giobatta emerged from between the colorful dwellings that towered over the narrow passage. With its uneven stone surfaces and stairs, this was not a town for trollies, so instead of dragging Jolene's suitcase, he was forced to carry it, doing so with remarkable ease. Lean and lithe, Giobatta seemed a younger man than suggested by his snowy white hair and leathery skin, but from what he'd said in the car, he must be around the same age as Filippo's father, who had recently turned seventy-five.

"I feel guilty having him lug my suitcase up here, while all I'm carrying is my backpack," Jolene said. She wanted to ask why Filippo hadn't offered to carry it himself, or help load the car at the airport, but she did not want to start questioning everything on the very first day. For the time being, it was best to just observe how things were done, and try not to make any blunders: look, listen, and learn, she reminded herself.

"Don't worry, he's used to manual labor," Filippo called over his shoulder as he trudged on, unfurling a linen handkerchief to dab the perspiration from his face and neck. He was fastidious about personal hygiene, and by now Jolene knew that there were fewer things he found more distasteful than sweat—his, as well as other people's.

"Are we almost there?" she asked, curious to see where he was leading her, wishing he would walk faster.

"Yep!" Filippo replied, coming to a halt so abruptly that she crashed into him. Grinning, he pointed to a door that opened directly onto the footpath.

Jolene stared at the weathered slab of rough wood, thrilled to be at its threshold, anxious to discover what lay behind it. Though old and splintered, to her it was the most beautiful door in the world; to her it represented a new beginning.

"We'll get a new door, of course," Filippo said.

"No!" Jolene cried. "We can restore this one." Many of the doors she'd noticed on the walk up were new, all green and glossy with polished brass knobs, but this one was unique, and it would be a crime to replace it. In the center of the door was a rusty nail; from the nail dangled a chipped shingle of slate. Jolene leaned in close to read what remained of the hand-painted lettering. "Locanda Luisa, Suite 16."

"This is it," Filippo said. "In all its glory."

"You didn't tell me we'd be staying in Suite 16! It reminds me of 'sweet sixteen, never been kissed, always been missed!'"

"What are you talking about?"

"Never mind," she said, smiling as she looked up at him. "I sometimes forget that you've never been a teenaged American girl. But it's a sign, Filippo! It's as if going through that door could take me back to when I was sixteen, all fresh and full of hope that the man of my dreams would one day come along and sweep me off my feet!"

Filippo looked down at her, still looking puzzled, and clueless that a kiss was called for. Not one to insist, Jolene turned her attention back to the shingle, holding her breath as she ran her index finger over the ridges of its cool, unpolished surface. Her new life with Filippo would begin right here, in Suite 16. Never again would she jolt awake in a sweat to find herself alone in her temporary apartment, her temporary job, her temporary life.

"That thing's filthy, remember to wash your hands," Filippo said, taking a single key on a ring from his pocket, while Jolene regarded her smudged finger, appreciating the sight of a little local dirt after all the globetrotting germs she must have been exposed to during the trip. She couldn't wait to shed her travel clothes and throw herself under the shower, then take a look at the other rooms, too. She had talked to Filippo at length about the family business, asking questions, tossing around ideas, and she was impatient to familiarize herself with the property. She could hardly believe she was being given the opportunity to work on such a stimulating project with the man she loved. They'd have such fun discussing the options, drawing up the projects, overseeing the renovations. She was itching to get started.

"So, where are the other thirty-seven suites located?" she asked. There couldn't be more than a few in this small building.

"Fifteen," Filippo muttered, jiggling the key in the lock.

"What?"

"There are fifteen others," Filippo said. "Suite 16 was the last one to be added."

"I thought you said there were thirty-eight suites in all."

"You must have misunderstood. Or been distracted. I said there were thirty-eight beds, in sixteen suites. The Locanda started out with four, right above the restaurant, but then the so-called suites were gradually added on, and those are all scattered around the village," Filippo said, his irritation with the stubborn lock creeping into his voice. He jiggled and turned the key, pushed and pulled the door, but it would not budge.

Jolene prided herself on her memory for numbers, so she was pretty sure she hadn't misunderstood, though Filippo did sometimes manage to confuse her when he was trying to explain things, and admittedly she was sometimes distracted when she was trying to listen. Whatever the case, there was a substantial difference between sixteen guest rooms spread out in the village, and a thirty-eight-room hotel. She wondered what sense it made for Filippo to attend an expensive post-grad course at Cornell to run such a modest operation, but then she reasoned that it was just another indication of how ambitious he was, of how no project was too big or too small for him. Like getting the door open, for example. It wasn't until he began ramming it with his shoulder that the wood finally gave way with a groan, and Filippo burst through, careening across the threshold. In the upset, the old slate shingle was ousted from its nail and sent crashing to the ground.

"Oh, no!" Jolene said, bending to pick up the pieces. "What a shame!"

"Honestly, Jolene! I could have broken my leg and you're worried about that old relic?" Filippo said, though he was already standing in the middle of the room, brushing off his embarrassment at the awkward entrance with the same aplomb with which he flicked a dustball from his shoulder. Then he adjusted his blue blazer, tugging at the hem and cuffs, assuring himself that the middle button was fastened. His composure regained, he made a sweeping gesture with his arm, his stance indicating that he was accustomed to showing grander suites to grander guests. "Now, then," he said, clearing his throat. "I hope you'll be comfortable in your temporary accommodations."

Though Jolene knew they wouldn't be staying in the Locanda indefinitely, Filippo's use of the word "temporary" made her left eye twitch. Peering into the dim room without entering, she waited to see whether he would come back to carry her over the threshold. It seemed like the kind of thing a romantic Italian man like him would do. Instead, he strode toward the window.

"*Bastardo!*" Filippo grunted from the other side of the room, where he was wrestling with the window handle. It was strange to hear him curse for the first time, and in Italian. In a world rife with vulgarity, Filippo's clean language had been one of the qualities she'd first admired in him. In the months they'd been together, she had never even heard him throw in the odd "shit" or "dammit" in an effort to sound less foreign. "*Porca di una puttana maledetta!*" he cursed again. The thin glass panes rattled at the insult, but the window succumbed and flew open. A gust of wind snatched the shutters from Filippo's hands as soon as he unlatched them, slamming them against the facade of the building. The room was inundated with golden sunshine and a briny breeze.

Shelving her threshold fantasy for when they would move into their permanent residence, Jolene dropped her backpack on the floor, stacking the slate shards beside it, and hurried to the window, marveling at the view of the shoulder-to-shoulder rooftops clustered below, of the grapevines stretched across the terraced land on the opposite side of the narrow valley, of the sun spilling its autumn glow over mountains and Mediterranean. It didn't matter that the view was partially blocked by the rooftops, or that the sea could only be glimpsed by leaning out the window. What mattered was that Jolene was in Italy, in the Cinque Terre, in Manarola, looking out the window of her room in Locanda Luisa, where she and Filippo would make their home and livelihood. Jolene cupped a hand over her dumbstruck mouth, tears of joy springing to her eyes.

"Well? Aren't you going to say anything?" Filippo asked.

"It's just that this is all so amazing!" Jolene whispered. "I can hardly believe it's real!"

Filippo put an arm around her shoulders as they stared out the window together. She let herself lean into him, relishing the reassurance she always felt when he locked her into that snug space under his arm.

"Well, it is real, and you'd better get used to it, *Splendore mio*," he said, giving her a squeeze. "This is your room now, and the view is all yours."

Jolene gazed up at him. He looked more handsome than ever, with his face all awash in gold, his brown eyes shining with flecks of a rare amber. "All *ours*, you mean."

"Well, I won't officially be staying here," he said, rewarding her upturned face with a peck on the lips. "This place is still a bit old-fashioned that way."

"Are you saying your mother wouldn't approve of us sleeping together? At our age?"

"No, it's not because of Mamma, it's everyone else. The Garaventis are an important family in these parts, you see. The villagers look up to us, but at the same time, they're envious. And they love to talk. We don't want to set their tongues barking."

"Wagging."

"What?"

"The expression. In English, you set tongues *wagging*, not barking."

"I was explaining something important to you, *Cara* Jo," Filippo said. He always insisted that she correct his English, but it always irritated him when she did. Now that they were in Italy, she thought it might be wise to switch to Italian, so he could do the correcting. Unlike Filippo, she was used to screwing up all kinds of things. A disagreement between article and subject or an improperly conjugated verb were mistakes she could live with.

"Sorry, I didn't mean to interrupt," she said. "But I wasn't expecting to live on my own."

"It's just for a while," Filippo said, pressing the tip of her nose with his index finger, as if it were a reset button used to dispel her disappointment. "We'll be married and living together before you know it. Trust me, I know what's best."

"I'm sure you do," Jolene said, readjusting her vision of the near future, another thing she was used to doing.

"*Permesso?*" Giobatta called from the open door, knocking on the jamb.

"Come on in," Filippo said.

Giobatta entered, deposited Jolene's suitcase on the floor, and turned to leave.

"*Grazie!*" Jolene called after him, but he was gone before she could ask Filippo if it would be appropriate to tip him.

"This room is more habitable than the others, but as you may have noticed, it needs so much maintenance work that it makes more sense to demolish it," Filippo said.

"I'm not so sure about that," Jolene said, but as she looked around for something to praise, her eyes were drawn to the most unpleasant details, the way eyes tended to do, like when you were talking to a woman with a hairy mole on her face. Between the cracked ceiling and stained walls, the pea green floor and cumbersome furniture, the faded photographs of dead fish hanging above the dresser and the vase of fake flowers on the nightstand, it wasn't easy. But there were wood floors you could install right over the tiles, clutter could be eliminated, and it wouldn't take much to plaster and paint everything white. "I'm not saying it doesn't need work, but I can already picture how charming this room could be."

"Meanwhile, you'll have all the essentials for what I hope will be a comfortable stay," Filippo continued, ignoring her comment as he crossed the room. "An *armadio* for your clothes," he said, opening then slamming shut a clothes cupboard, as if he had discovered the putrid corpse of a previous guest inside. "I'm afraid there's not a terrible amount of space."

"It'll be fine," Jolene said, smiling. "I don't have much."

"Of course you have your own private bathroom," Filippo said, pushing open a rather ugly door that would need replacing, then flipping a switch. A neon light flickered on. And off. And on. "*Cazzo!* You'd think they could at least learn how to change a light bulb!"

"Don't let these little things make you so upset, Filippo," Jolene said. "Now that you're back, and I'm here with you, we'll make a list of all the jobs that require attention."

"Yeah, well, it's the people doing the things, or rather not doing them, that upset me," he muttered, his hands at his sides, balled into fists. Jolene wondered who he was referring to, but again deferred her questions.

"You're just tired from the trip, and so I am," she said. "This is a special moment, and we shouldn't ruin it by focusing on anything negative." If she didn't complain about the shortcomings of the room, or harp on the fact that she would be staying there alone, he shouldn't either. "Like you said, it's only temporary, right? And I can certainly change my own light bulbs."

Filippo sighed, relaxing his fists. "You're a gem, Jolene," he said. "And you're right. You must be exhausted. The only thing I want you to worry about now is resting."

"I was thinking we could freshen up, then go for a stroll," she said.

"A stroll? Now? What's the rush?"

"No rush, really," Jolene said, her voice cheerful, though she could already tell that the stroll wasn't going to happen. "I was just looking forward to stretching my legs and having you show me around town. I need to get my bearings, and I can't wait to see where we'll be living and working together!"

"My legs got all the stretching they needed walking up here," Filippo said, shaking out the muscles of one leg, then the other, like he always did before and after a run. "As for the town, you can practically see it all from the window."

Jolene returned to the window and leaned out. "What's that place in front of us?" she asked, pointing to the hillside across from them. "Where I see those people walking?"

"That's Punta Bonfiglio," Filippo said, joining her.

"There must be a gorgeous view of the sea from up there. And look at all those beautiful plants! It's hard to tell what they are from here, but I can see there are even some palm trees!"

"Yeah, people walk up there all the time to look at the view and sit in the garden," Filippo said. "I'll take you there. Just not now, okay?"

"Sure. And how about that, just next to it?" she said, moving her finger slightly while squinting into the distance. "It looks like a gigantic beehive."

"A beehive?" Filippo said, laughing. "That's the cemetery!"

"The cemetery? Oh, so it's all above ground?

"Most of it, except for a few old graves," Filippo said. "Where would you bury anyone here? There's hardly enough room for the living, let alone the dead."

"So those empty holes are vacant slots? Do people reserve them in advance?"

"Honestly Jolene! Do you really have to fixate on the cemetery?"

"No, I was just curious," she said, her eyes already moving on, stopping when she spotted off to the right and a bit higher up the hill, dozens of objects of different shapes and sizes sticking out of the ground, the parts in metal reflecting the rays of the afternoon sun. "What are those things I see, spread all over that hillside?"

"It's just junk." Filippo said, shaking his head, shoving his hands in his pockets.

"You mean like a junkyard? In the middle of the vineyard?"

"People make a big deal about it," Filippo said. "They call it art. But those are all pieces of used plastic and metal that some old guy collects and makes into shapes. Like I said, junk."

"They look like animal shapes. I think I see human figures, too. It looks like some have wings, too, like angels."

"Between now and December you'll see even more pop up. It's supposed to look like a giant Nativity scene by Christmas. People go crazy over it."

"Oh, yeah! I remember reading about that," Jolene said, wondering why Filippo sounded so critical, especially if the project attracted off-season visitors. "What's the story behind it?"

"Another time, Jolene. We just got here and although you don't want to admit it, I know you're exhausted. I want you to rest up and freshen up now, and I'll go do the same. I'll stop by for you at five, all right?"

"All right," she said, as Filippo kissed the top of her head and walked to the door.

"Be ready at five!" he called over his shoulder.

"I will!" she replied, but Filippo was already on the other side.

Now that the options for how to spend her first afternoon in Manarola had been drastically reduced, the idea of stretching out on the bed after a long hot shower held a certain allure. But first she needed more of that window. Leaning out as far as she could, she tilted her face to the slanted sun rays, letting the wind tousle her hair while her lungs drank in the fresh breeze. Though she saw only a corner of the sea, she could hear its waves crashing against the rocks below, and was thrilled at the thought of falling asleep to that sound every night. Inhaling through her nose, she held her breath as long as she could before slowly releasing it, imagining the invigorating sea air cleansing her body of the stale, artificial airplane air.

After taking several breaths, she left the window and went to the bathroom, stripped off her clothes, and let them drop to the tile floor, suddenly feeling too stiff and tired to even consider picking them up. The plastic door to the shower stall shuddered with resistance when she tried to slide it open, but she managed to reach inside to turn on the water. When it became apparent that the spray wouldn't grow any stronger or hotter, she turned sideways to squeeze into the stall, flinching at the tepid trickle of water while wondering whether guests were required to specify their height and weight before being assigned this room. This suite. Suite 16. Smiling to herself, she tilted her head back, delighting in the feel of the fresh water falling on her face and neck, trickling down her back and tummy, buttocks and thighs, dripping over her swollen feet. It was sweet and soft, like the last summer rain.

Jolene couldn't remember lying down on her bed or drifting off to sleep, but she would never forget gasping for air that first afternoon when she jolted awake to find a man's thumbs propping open her eyelids. Seconds earlier, she'd been dreaming of a horrific accident. In the dream she was lying on the ground unconscious while a man knelt beside her, checking her vital signs. But the thumbs holding her eyes open now weren't a doctor's, they were Filippo's, and this was his perverse way of rousing her when she failed to wake up.

"*Ciao, Splendore!*" he chuckled, amused, as always, at her reaction.

"Please, don't do that!" she cried, her heart pounding. She felt crabby and disoriented, and it wasn't until she spotted the photographs of the dead fish that she remembered where she was.

"It's five," Filippo said. As if on cue the church bells tolled, their doleful sound reverberating in the still room. Jolene wished she hadn't fallen asleep. Besides being a waste of time, naps always gave her a headache.

"These are for you," Filippo said, setting a bunch of flowers on her abdomen. Now she really felt like an accident victim: one who hadn't survived. Staring at the bouquet of white chrysanthemums wrapped in cellophane and tied with a bow, she pulled herself up in bed, then stretched and crossed her legs, to make sure all limbs were still intact.

"I wanted to bring you roses, but it's next to impossible to find decent flowers in this place," Filippo added.

"You didn't need to do that," Jolene said, her jaw tight as she fought off a yawn; it would be rude to yawn in the face of a man who brought flowers. The fact was, Filippo had showered her with hundreds of roses since the day they'd met on the boat last June. He'd brought them to her personally, he'd had them delivered to her at work, he'd hidden them in her apartment, he'd left them on the windshield of her car. Jolene had enjoyed the attention more than the bouquets, never having the heart to tell him that cut flowers, especially roses, depressed her.

"They only had these on account of tomorrow being Sunday," he said.

"They're lovely. Really."

"You don't like them, do you? I can't blame you. People only buy chrysanthemums for the dead here."

"Of course I like them, Filippo. They're gorgeous." Jolene said, running her fingers through her hair. It was still damp from her shower, and plastered to the back of her head. Clammy and chilled, she shuddered with another yawn, this one too powerful to stifle.

"You don't look too impressed," Filippo said. "You know my greatest joy is to make you feel special."

"And you do, Filippo," she said. "I'm just groggy. How about you? Did you take a nap?"

"Are you kidding? Mamma kept telling me to go lie down, but every time I tried to leave, she suddenly had one more question to ask me about you-know-who."

"About me?" Jolene asked, tucking the sheet tight under her knees, as if sealing herself inside a pie crust.

"What do you think?"

"It's only natural, I suppose," Jolene said, averting her eyes. The thought of being a topic of conversation made her uncomfortable. "What did you say? I hope you were kind."

"What do you think?" he asked again, placing a finger under her chin and tilting her head so that she was forced to face him.

"Well, I think yes, you were kind." She'd never known Filippo to be unkind, except when he did that eyelid thing to her.

"You think, or you know?" he asked. He was testing her now, playing one of those little trust-building games he'd used to bolster her confidence in him at the beginning, like when he made her stand there, close her eyes, and lean back until she fell into his arms. It had been easy to fall in love with Filippo, but her trust had been broken too often, by too many people before him, for it to follow automatically. The fact that she'd taken the plane and come to Italy with him should suffice as proof that she'd overcome her wariness.

"Look at me, Jolene." Filippo's eyes were so dark in the dim light that she couldn't distinguish the pupils from the irises. "Do you think, or do you know, that I would only speak highly of you to my mother?"

"I know," she said. "I know." Though she still wondered exactly what he'd said to Luisa, she was still too out of it to pursue the discussion. "What I don't know is how you can look so rested."

"Who needs rest? I'm as excited as a little boy at Christmas! Being back here now, with you on my arm and my certificate from Cornell in my pocket makes me feel like Santa just delivered a wagonload of gifts—all with my name-tag on them." He tugged at the sheet Jolene was wrapped in, his eyes now bright with mischief. "Any chance I could sneak a peek at one of those presents?"

Jolene laughed, pinning the sheet down with her hands. "Christmas is still a couple of months away, little boy," she said, but when he kissed her on the mouth, she fell back on the bed and threw the sheet aside, locking her arms behind her head and smiling an invitation.

Glancing at his watch, Filippo sighed. "It's almost five-thirty. Mamma will be waiting."

"Give me three minutes!" Jolene cried. Jumping out of bed, she threw open her suitcase and rummaged through her clothes, searching for an outfit sturdy enough to bear the memories of her first evening in Manarola.

THREE

"*Caffè?*" Luisa asked from behind the bar, her hand already gripping the permanently extended arm of the Cimbali.

"No more for me, Mamma," Filippo said. "I must have had five since we got here. But I'm sure Jolene could use a pick-me-up after her nap."

"Yes, thank you, that would be wonderful," Jolene said, thinking that a jolt of caffeine might alleviate her headache. What she really craved was a hot, frothy cappuccino, but she hesitated to ask. Her mother had taught her to accept what she was offered.

"Come on, speak up! I know you're dying for a cappuccino," Filippo said, poking her in the ribs.

"You're right, I am," Jolene said, smiling. Filippo was always so thoughtful that way, anticipating her every desire as if they'd known each other for years. Whenever they went to the Starbucks in Ithaca, before she could ask for anything he ordered her cappuccino exactly the way she liked it: a double dose of strong coffee with piping hot whole milk, topped off with a generous sprinkle of cinnamon. Luisa moved more swiftly than any barista she'd ever seen, and though the racket she made by banging the filter to empty it then grinding fresh coffee to refill it pained Jolene's throbbing temples, she was fascinated by her sure-handed efficiency, undoubtedly achieved through years of repeating the same gestures over and over again. As Jolene watched her tamp the coffee, secure the filter in place, then hit the brew button in one seamless motion, she wondered whether the woman planned to continue working after the renovations, or was

33

looking forward to retirement.

"So, what will it be?" Luisa asked, holding a cappuccino cup in one hand and an espresso cup in the other.

"Espresso, of course," Filippo replied to his mother, who placed the small cup under the filter just in time to catch the first thick black drop of coffee. "You're in Italy now, *Cara* Jo" he said, turning to Jolene. "You don't want to be caught drinking cappuccino when it's almost dinnertime, like some common tourist. Cappuccinos are for breakfast, for dunking brioches."

Jolene opened her mouth to say that she wouldn't have asked for a cappuccino if he hadn't suggested it, but instead of speaking she blushed. She was glad that Luisa was turned the other way, wiping down the shiny metal surfaces of the Cimbali while waiting for the last of the coffee to drizzle into the cup, and couldn't see her pink cheeks.

"Thank you very much," Jolene said, when Luisa set the little white cup in front of her. It wasn't that she didn't like espresso, there just wasn't much of it. She'd have to sip it slowly if she wanted it to last.

"I'm starving!" Filippo said. "Our last meal, if you can call it that, was on the plane."

Luisa, busy drying glasses, didn't comment. Jolene, her nose deep inside the tiny cup, was concentrating on the heady aroma of the brew, hoping it would clear her head.

"Where's Babbo, anyway?" Filippo asked, drumming his fingers on the bar. "He hasn't even shown his face yet."

"He was here earlier to get things started for tonight. But he had something or other to repair on his boat, as usual."

"And how about Lorenzo?"

"Your brother called to say he got held up with a problem in Genoa."

"Imagine that. Not that it bothers me personally, but how does he expect you to manage without him, on a Saturday night?"

Judging from what Filippo had told her, Lorenzo didn't help with the family-run operation at all. She must have misunderstood. Again. She reminded herself that now was not the time to ask questions, so unless someone spoke to her directly, she would linger over her demitasse in silence, listening and learning.

"Your father and I will do just fine, like in the old days," Luisa said.

"In the old days, you were younger than I am now, and very few people knew this place even existed."

"We can handle it, Filippo. We'll relax tomorrow. Business is finally slowing down on Sunday nights, so I've told your father I want to close the doors to the public so we can all have dinner together and celebrate. After all, it's not every day your son comes home from New York with a girlfriend no one even heard of until two weeks ago."

Jolene's jaw dropped, together with the cup she'd already drained. Filippo had asked her to marry him almost two months ago. Why had he kept it from his family until two weeks ago? And why did she refer to Jolene as his girlfriend, and not his fiancée? Jolene presumed that the distinction was as significant in Italian as it was in English. Fortunately, confusion did not hamper her reflexes, and she caught the cup an instant before it could roll off the bar and crash to the floor.

"Tomorrow evening is perfect," Filippo said, shooting a glance at Jolene. "Hopefully Jolene will be more rested by then. Right, *Splendore?*"

"Right," Jolene said, setting the cup on its saucer and pushing it away.

"*Ehi, allora?*" a man's voice boomed from the doorway.

"*Babbo!*" Filippo cried, jumping in front of the man before Jolene could catch a glimpse of his face. All she could see of him were the two muscular forearms encircling Filippo's torso, and the two hands thumping his back with that awkward sort of roughness men sometimes display when they fear succumbing to emotion. The red hands and particles of dirt under the ragged nails of his stubby fingers told her he was still the working man of Giobatta's anecdotes, and not the distinguished hotelier of Jolene's imagination. Her chest tightened with envy as she witnessed the paternal embrace, and she had to look away. Glancing at Luisa, she noted her expression of placid benevolence as she regarded the reunion from behind the bar, where she continued drying glasses with the striped linen dish towel that seemed attached to her hand. Standing among three Garaventis, Jolene was struck by how ill-equipped she was to fit into this family of strangers, like an understudy called in to play a role she had long coveted but never rehearsed for. Her eyes darted around the room, searching for cues, clues, direction, a back exit.

The neon-lit bar area where they stood was rather small; stuffy rather than cozy, permeated with the odors of strong coffee and house wine and sweat and fish and brine; of lingering cigarette smoke and idle talk; of the dampness that penetrated the thick stone walls and made newspapers stick to the varnished tabletops. She perceived the presence of more males than females, of more locals than tourists, and when her eyes wandered through an arched passage leading to another, larger room she glimpsed empty tables draped in cloths, crouching ghostlike as if poised to frighten off the next invasion of diners. Filippo was right; she could already tell that there was great potential to make the Locanda more alluring to foreigners, but she wouldn't want to alienate the locals, she wouldn't want to forsake the characteristic—

"Where's the girl?" the man called out, cutting short Jolene's musings. Turning to face him, Jolene saw that his eyes were dark and saucer-shaped, like Filippo's, but while Filippo's were often glazed over with the hypnotic veneer that comes from staring at a computer screen for too long, his father's eyes brimmed with a natural brightness, as if they had soaked up an enormous amount of light from the sky and the sea. They twinkled in a different way too. Unlike the fleeting flashes of intensity that brightened Filippo's eyes when he got wind of a rare opportunity or devised a clever scheme, his father's eyes sparkled as though he were anticipating a forbidden pleasure or had recently committed some mischief. He squinted at her as he approached, as if he were focusing on a faraway horizon. Before she could decide how to address him, he gathered her in his thick arms and squeezed her tight, his barrel chest pressing against her thumping heart.

"*Sono Vittorio,*" he said, after stepping back a pace and placing an open hand on his chest, the friendly native greeting the foreigner. His voice was gravelly and determined, its cadence rhythmic, like waves raking pebbles on the beach. "*Capisci l'italiano, no?*"

"*Ci provo,*" Jolene said, disappointed that the hug was already over. "I try my best."

"Good for you. People who don't want to try should stay home, where they can act like they know what they're talking about, and other people can act like they understand them," Vittorio said. "Did you have a good trip?"

"Yes, but it was long, and after we changed planes in Rome, we—"

"Planes! I don't even want to hear about them!" Vittorio said, rolling his eyes the same way Filippo did.

"Me neither," Jolene said. "I hate planes."

"Good, we agree," Vittorio said, with a clap of his hands. "So let's eat. We'll have time to talk later."

"Everything's practically ready," Luisa said, wiping her hands on her apron. "I'll finish setting up while the spaghetti is cooking."

"Can I do anything to help?" Jolene asked.

"You've already done enough," Luisa said. "You got our son to come back."

"Offer Giuseppina a glass of wine!" Vittorio ordered.

"It's Jolene!" Filippo said, but his father had already disappeared down the corridor which must lead to the kitchen. Jolene was curious to see the setup and would have liked to tag along, but having just met the man, she thought it best to wait for an invitation. Vittorio whistled as he went, turning on more neon lights along the way. Jolene detested neon lights, and so did Filippo. Eliminating them was one thing they'd already agreed on.

"Are you switching to wine then?" Filippo said, taking two glasses from a shelf. After holding them up to check for water spots, he placed them on the bar, nudging one, then the other, until they were perfectly lined up.

"Yes, please," Jolene said. The coffee hadn't done much to clear her head; she might as well aim for total befuddlement. "Funny, isn't it?"

"What?" Filippo asked, selecting a bottle from the refrigerated display case.

"When we met, I was the one serving you the wine," she said.

"Yes, and I got knocked out on the spot," Filippo said, turning to look her in the eye. "By the waitress, not by the wine. You looked so sharp in your jacket and bow tie. So professional."

His comment made Jolene wince. She'd never been afraid of hard work, but it hadn't been easy to start taking temporary jobs with caterers and banquet halls when Evan's antagonism had finally made it just as impossible for her to continue working with him at the restaurant as it was for her to live with him. Everything about their relationship had been a drain: on her emotions, on her savings, and on her self-esteem. For several months after their breakup, the idea of dedicating herself to anything or anyone on a full-time basis made her panic. It was then, when she had least expected it, that Filippo had landed in her life like a creature from outer space, speaking to her in an alien tongue whose lexicon contained such words as "love" and "commitment" and "future."

"I'd propose a Cinque Terre D.O.C. Costa da Posa, if I may," Filippo said, turning the bottle to show her the label.

"Lovely! From the Finger Lakes to the Cinque Terre—that's a long wine trail," she said, observing Filippo's panache as he performed the theatrics of opening the bottle, sniffing the cork, and pouring out a taste for her. Coffee still lingered on Jolene's tongue, and she disliked the pantomime of wine-tasting, but Filippo always insisted that she voice her own personal opinion, whether it be on wine or any other subject, which was another thing she adored about him. During her viticulture studies at the community college, she'd learned enough about things like complexity and structure and texture and how to identify hints of this or that in a wine to make recommendations to her restaurant patrons with some degree of authority. But why anyone would prefer the taste of apples and apricots and nuts and spices and cedar and oak and everything but good old grapes in their glass of wine continued to baffle her. Yet now, when she held the glass of Cinque Terre up to the light, she thought of mown hay drying in a sun-drenched field. After swirling the wine around for a few seconds, she passed the glass under her nostrils and took a quick whiff, then dipped her nose into its aromas, so pure and fresh they made her want to run outside and climb the hills, to lie down on that same ground where the grape was grown. Eager to taste the wine, she took a sip, finding it refreshingly natural and crisp.

"What do you think?" Filippo asked. "Be honest."

"I think I'm in love," she said.

"It's not the most complex wine around," he said, topping off her glass and filling one for himself. "But to me, it tastes like home."

"To home," Jolene said, raising her glass.

"Don't forget to pour one for me!" Vittorio called to them, arriving on the scene with a platter of steaming spaghetti buried under a mountain of mussels and clams in the shell. "I hope you like this, Giusy, I mean July, I mean—I'll just call you *Americanina*, okay? Afterward I can grill us a nice fish, or fry up some anchovies, whatever you like!"

The little American. Jolene smiled at already having earned a nickname in the family.

"Let's not overdo it, Pa," Filippo said. "Jolene doesn't want to spend hours gorging herself at the table. She's exhausted." She was actually bouncing back quite nicely by now, but Filippo was right; the pasta would be more than enough. It looked divine.

"I'll take that," Luisa said, grabbing the platter from Vittorio and bringing it to the dining room, then returning to the bar and accepting the glass Filippo had poured for her in the meantime.

"*A casa*," Filippo said, raising his glass.

"*A casa*," Vittorio and Luisa both said, raising their glasses and touching them to Filippo's.

"*A casa*," Jolene echoed, and they clinked glasses with her, too. Taking a sip, she closed her eyes to savor the wine and the warmth rising inside her. Nothing would please her more than to feel that this, a place where family gathered for a meal and raised celebratory glasses of cheerful drink together, could be her home. Maybe if she repeated the word "casa" often enough it would happen. Maybe if she participated in enough moments like these, they would seem less foreign to her. Maybe one day this home would become so familiar, it would be the only one she knew, erasing all the memories she wanted to forget.

It wasn't until she opened her eyes that Jolene realized that the others had moved to the dining room, and she hurried to join them. A table had been set up for the four of them, and Filippo was standing by a chair he had already pulled out for her, seating her with her back to the entrance. Before sitting down, she took a quick tally of the tables in the room, counting a couple dozen, which meant that the Locanda had a maximum capacity of approximately fifty. If the food tasted as good as it looked, she thought, watching Luisa serve the spaghetti then topping off each plate with a generous helping of mussels and clams, business must be brisk.

"*Buon appetito*," Luisa said, when a steaming dish sat in front of each of them.

The few sips of wine had stimulated Jolene's appetite, and she couldn't wait to try the pasta. Years in the restaurant business had dulled her desire for dining out, mostly because it was so rare to find the right combination of wholesome food, a convivial atmosphere, and honest prices. The idea of creating a place where she herself would love to eat was one of the reasons she'd been so enthusiastic about her collaboration with Evan. But it wasn't long before he'd betrayed her, even in this, straying from their original menu of simple fare featuring locally sourced farm products to explore nouvelle interpretations of Old World cuisine. His incursions were predominantly into French territory, where he revisited *patés* and *bourguignons, canards* and *saucissons,* and rendered homage to a battery of heavy sauces whose names never failed to impress the gourmet food and wine junkies who toured the vineyards of the Finger Lakes.

"Around here, Jolene—in places like this, anyway—" Fillipo said, "—one usually responds with '*buon appetito.*"

"Of course! I'm so sorry! *Buon appetito!*" Jolene said. She must focus on this moment and nothing else; she must remember every detail of this first meal in Italy with her future Italian family. Thank you, God, she whispered, then dug her fork into the mound of spaghetti. She felt Luisa's eyes on her as she twirled the slippery strands around the tines, deftly delivering the neatly rolled morsel to her mouth without spattering sauce on herself or anyone else.

"You eat spaghetti like a true Italian, Jolene," Luisa said. "Did your mother cook it for you often?"

"Not really. Not since I was a little girl," Jolene answered. Not since that time when her father, after one cocktail too many, had complained in front of their dinner guests that the spaghetti al dente was so raw it would choke a dog. To prove his point, he had gotten up from his chair and sat the family pup, a rescue mutt who answered to the name SallyAnn, in his place, shoving her drooling snout in the dish. The dog immediately began licking the meat sauce, her eyes darting around the muted table as if to inform everyone that she was only doing as she had been told. Instead of being filled with pasta, however, her belly received a swift kick from the Captain, who snatched the dish away and hurled it across the room, spattering the spaghetti against the fleur-de-lis wallpaper like the blown-out brains of a gangster, while the yelping dog hurried away with her tail between her legs, and Jolene close behind.

"Well, you must have eaten plenty of it elsewhere then," Luisa said.

It still pained Jolene to recall how she and SallyAnn had hidden out under the blankets in her bedroom, the dog whimpering and the little girl sobbing over how unfair life, in the form of her father, was to both of them. Jolene loved her mother, and felt sorry for her, but when she just sat there in silence without standing up to her father, she also hated her a tiny bit.

"Are you with us, Jolene?" Filippo said. "Mamma asked you a question."

Jolene blinked, wiping a tear from the corner of her eye while searching the table for a clue that would lead her back to the conversation. Spaghetti, that was it.

"I'm sorry," she said. "I had something in my eye. "Yes, I got into the habit of eating spaghetti thanks to an authentic Italian, the same person who got me interested in the language."

"Oh? And who was that?" Luisa asked. Although the story wasn't particularly compelling, Jolene thought it a safe one. It would give her the chance to tell them a bit about herself without divulging too many messy details about her family background, which she was not prepared share in Italian, or any other language, at the moment.

"I had a friend from Italy," she began, after taking a sip of wine. "I met her when I was sixteen, the year my father made us move." She remembered the sense of total impotence she'd felt when he made the announcement; she was no longer a voiceless child, but not yet an independent woman. "I didn't want to leave my school, or the few friends I had. And I hated the thought of leaving SallyAnn behind. Even though she was already dead by then, I used to put flowers on her grave and talk to her all the time. Just like when she shared my room." No sense getting into the story of how her father had put SallyAnn down because of her lame hip.

"Wait—you had a sister?" Filippo asked. "You never told me that."

"No, no sisters. Or brothers. I told you I was an only child. SallyAnn was my puppy." Sometimes her memories were so vivid she assumed that anyone near her could experience them the same way she did.

"Oh, a dog." Filippo rolled his eyes. "The way you said it, it sounded like you'd lost a little sister. Instead it was just a dog."

Jolene glared at him, and so did Luisa. Vittorio continued eating, either too interested in the spaghetti, or not interested enough in dogs, to react.

"Anyway, you were going to tell us about your friend, *Cara* Jo, not about your dog," Filippo said.

"I got sidetracked. I'm sorry," she said, wishing Filippo would follow his father's example and just let her talk. "My friend's name was Anna. Anna Vigevani. I met her in Chicago. Her father had just been transferred there, too. We were both new kids at the same high school."

"Wait a minute—Chicago?" Filippo asked, raising his eyebrows.

"Yes, that was where we moved," Jolene said. "Big city, big wind, big water. My mother and I hated to leave our placid little lake for the great Lake Michigan. It wasn't a good place for little rowboats like ours."

"You never told me that, either," Filippo said, switching to English.

"What, that we rowed? Of course I did. I even took you out."

"No, about the rest."

Vittorio glanced up from his occupation of sucking mussels and clams from their shells, his eyebrows arched with curiosity. Luisa patted her lips with her napkin, pretending not to listen.

"Of course I did!" Jolene said. "Anna Vigevani? The one who used to make me listen to CDs of that Italian rapper? That Jovanotti guy? To see how many words I could pick out? Remember?"

"We talked about her, but you never said anything about Chicago."

"We only stayed that one year," Jolene said, lowering her voice. "It didn't work out. But I'm pretty sure I mentioned that." She was in fact positive she had mentioned living in Chicago. It was absurd that he should belabor such an insignificant point in front of his parents, making her look like a fabricator of falsehoods, a concealer of facts. She also thought it rude for the two of them to carry on a conversation in English while sitting at the table with his parents, even though she knew that Luisa, and probably Vittorio, were able to understand; not every word, perhaps, but certainly the terse tone of their son's voice.

Setting his fork down, Filippo tilted his head from side to side, as if he were working out a crick in his neck, the way he did when he sat at the computer for hours: left ear to left shoulder, right ear to right shoulder, left, right, left right. He was a determined man, and strong-willed, and she normally admired those traits in him, knowing that was how he accomplished so much. But now he just seemed pigheaded, and his behavior made her want to press the matter until he conceded that maybe he might have misunderstood something for once. That maybe he didn't always pay as much attention as he should when she spoke.

"Remember I told you how I used to hang out with Anna every day after school?" she insisted, hoping to jar his memory. "And how they had an au pair from Italy who was a fantastic cook? And how they invited me to dinner all the time?"

"Of course I do. I remember everything you tell me, like how you lost touch with Anna after her father was transferred to Singapore. I even offered to do a Facebook search for you, to help you find her."

"Exactly!" Jolene said, smiling with relief. "See how it came back to you?"

"No. You never said you were living in Chicago when you met Anna," he said, wiping his mouth before taking a long drink of water. When the glass was drained, he set the tumbler down with finality of a judge's gavel.

"Well, that part is irrelevant," Jolene said. "It has nothing to do with my spaghetti eating story." Her headache was coming back, and all she wanted was to end the discussion before Filippo tried to convince her that it was all a mistake, that she had never lived in Chicago; or else confess that, for some obscure reason, she had hidden the fact from him.

"Anyway, this Italian girl I was telling you about, Anna Vigevani, became my first best friend," she said to Vittorio and Luisa, switching back to Italian. "We spent every minute we could together." She wished she could have spent all her time at Anna's, a house full of warm and lively Italians who, ironically, engaged in none of the shouting and crying and smashing of objects she was forced to witness at her own house. It was no wonder food tasted better there.

"The pasta I ate at the Vigevanis' was the best in the world," she said. "But that was before I tasted yours, Vittorio."

"Have some more, then," Vittorio urged, grinning as he remixed the food in the platter, the spaghetti glistening in the light sauce, the seafood tumbling over the serving spoon and fork. "Luisa served you first out of good manners," he said, scooping up several mussels and clams as he served her, while Jolene noticed, with relief, that he'd scrubbed his nails clean in the kitchen. "But *beati gli ultimi* when it comes to pasta. The good stuff always ends up at the bottom."

"*Beati gli ultimi*. Blessed are the last. I'll remember that," Jolene said, raising her plate to accept more pasta, as grateful for the distraction as for the food. For the remainder of the meal she would devote all her attention to the plump, orange mussels and the tiniest, tastiest clams she had ever eaten. Meanwhile she would retreat to the sidelines of the conversation, where she would remain an observer of interactions, an assessor of situations, an evaluator of impressions. As if everyone had decided to do the same, the foursome ate in silence until Luisa got up to clear the dishes. Jolene also rose, eager to lend a hand, but Luisa had already hurried off. Vittorio shrugged, motioning for Jolene to sit back down.

"We have to get to work now, but you sit here and relax," he said, pouring her another glass of wine before pulling himself up to a standing position. Unlike Giobatta, Vittorio seemed to feel the weight of every one of his seventy-five years. "*Maledetto* arthritis," he groaned.

"Thank you for the exquisite meal," Jolene said.

"My pleasure, *Americanina*!"

"I have to run up to the house to make a couple of calls," Filippo said, hopping to his feet and waving his cell phone in the air as if it were a press pass to a conference of great importance. "No reception here, in case you haven't noticed."

Jolene hadn't noticed. In fact, she didn't even have a cell phone with her, figuring it would make more sense to buy one locally than to pay for overseas coverage on her cheap old phone with the busted screen. It had been liberating, though a bit unsettling, to drop it into a garbage bin at the JFK security checkpoint, while others tossed their water bottles. Now that she was here, with no one to call and no one looking for her, she was in no rush to get reconnected.

"I'd tell you to come with me, but I know you're exhausted," Filippo said. "Just sit back and relax for a bit, like Babbo said, then I'll walk you up to your room. I'll only be a few minutes."

"Go ahead," she said, but not because she was tired; in fact, the more he insisted that she was exhausted, the more energetic she felt. And although she was curious to see the family home where Filippo would be staying, she was puzzled by his uncharacteristic behavior, and could use a few minutes alone to mull things over. As she sat there sipping her wine and staring at the wall, she concluded that whatever tension she felt between them was due to the grueling trip. Tomorrow, after a good night's sleep, everything would revert to normal, and they could finally start working on all their exciting plans. She couldn't wait.

Satisfied that there was nothing to be upset about, Jolene decided to take advantage of the opportunity to watch the Locanda spring into action for the dinner crowd. Moving to Vittorio's chair, she sat facing the entrance and the other tables, waiting for the show to begin. She'd always had a passion for observing people, trying to guess who they were and what they would do, which was one more reason why she enjoyed her work so much. When a couple walked in the door, she smiled at them as they tried to decide whether they should wait to be seated or just pick a spot. Jolene resisted the urge to ask whether they'd reserved a table, noticing that a cluster of tables had *"riservato"* cards on them. The couple eventually wandered over to a free table, some distance away from the reserved ones, but shortly after they sat down Luisa returned and directed them to another table, right next to the group of reserved tables. As a customer, it annoyed Jolene when a waiter made her sit at a table she didn't like simply because it was more convenient for him, and she hoped Luisa wasn't that type. It was probably because she was on her own tonight, and every step saved was a step earned. Or maybe she was fed up with working; she'd have to ask Filippo about that. She looked on as Luisa took the couple's order for wine and water, rattled off the menu, and convinced them to commit to appetizers, first course and second course in rapid succession, saying it would avoid delays in service, once it got busy. Personally, Jolene always hated to see people order too much food, although it was against the best interests of the restaurant—and a constant point of contention with greedy monsieur le chef Evan. Her recommendation to patrons had always been to start off slow, take the time to savor their food, and pause between courses rather than over-ordering and over-indulging. It sickened her to see half-eaten portions left on plates, and even when her customers reassured her that everything was delicious but they were too full to finish, she cringed when they asked her to wrap up the food for them. It saddened her to imagine the scraps during their trip to the homes of strangers, filling their car with the smells of aromatic herbs and garlic, the filleted sole mummified in congealed butter, the dismembered *coq* drowned in its *vin*, now resting in a polystyrene sarcophagus in the passenger seat, only to be abandoned on a countertop or crammed into a refrigerator next to jars of moldy jam and yellowing mayonnaise and limp carrots and bug-eyed potatoes.

As Luisa returned with a carafe of house wine and a bottle of mineral water for the couple, six more people wandered in, and were directed to tables right next to one another, while the other half of the restaurant remained empty. Only one smartly dressed woman in the company of a younger man said she had come all the way from Milan to eat sardines, not be treated like one, and demanded to be seated at a respectable distance from the other diners instead of at the table reserved in her name. Jolene didn't yet know what was featured on Locanda's menu, but she was willing to wager that the woman would never order a dish like the spaghetti Jolene had just enjoyed. She was the type who needed to be in control of everything, including her food, and would prefer the pliability of gnocchi or the manageability of risotto over unruly spaghetti that would lash out at her pretty silk blouse, spattering it with tomato.

"*Tutti adesso!*" Luisa muttered, hurrying past so swiftly that the tablecloths ruffled in her wake. Jolene knew what it was like when customers came in clusters. One minute you would be killing time filling salt cellars waiting for someone to show up, then as sure as sorbet followed fish, they would all come in at once, demanding immediate attention, and you went from lolling about to moving so fast your own shadow couldn't keep up with you.

It made Jolene feel guilty to see Luisa rushing around while she sat there doing nothing, as if she were here on vacation. She wondered why Filippo hadn't offered to help, what phone calls couldn't wait until the morning, and what was so important to keep her other son in Genoa, with no concern for his mother or father, or desire to see his brother who had just returned after five months abroad. The desire to lend a hand overpowered her when yet another group entered, making it impossible for her to remain seated. Jumping to her feet, she tied her hair back with the elastic band she had the habit of wearing on her wrist, and headed for the door, reasoning that by acting as hostess she could make herself useful while staying out of Luisa's way. Greeting the people crowded at the entrance, she asked whether they had reservations, and led those who did to the tables with cards on them. The remaining couple, a pair of travel-weary Americans clad in hiking clothes, clapped their hands and thanked her when she accompanied them to a free table, too.

Luisa hurried past, glancing at Jolene as she delivered a basket of bread and two plates of seafood salad to a table. Jolene wanted to ask her what else she could do now that everyone was seated, but feared that if she had to keep asking her for instructions she'd be more a hindrance than a help. Surely she could start serving the drinks, she thought. Assuming everyone would want water, she went to the refrigerator, pulling out two bottles of sparkling and two of still, then made the rounds inquiring as to preferences, then opening the bottles and pouring before setting them on the tables, until all the customers were served. Luisa passed again, telling her to grab three bottles of Cinque Terre bianco and one of Ciliegiolo, pointing out which tables to bring them to before scurrying away. Jolene knew where the refrigerator was, and she certainly knew how to uncork a wine bottle. She was sniffing the cork of the cheerful red Ciliegiolo she'd just opened when Luisa flew by again carrying a platter of sliced salami and prosciutto, stopping long enough to mutter, "Just leave it there, they can serve themselves," before disappearing again.

Jolene was trying to help the American couple decipher the menu, which was handwritten, and only in Italian, and which she also was seeing for the first time, when another customer walked in. She made eye contact with the man to indicate she'd be with him in a minute; he was alone, anyway, and probably waiting for someone to join him. While the Americans grilled her with an endless stream of questions about which foods were free of nuts and lactose and gluten, she smiled at the man by the door again, meanwhile hoping that her unfamiliarity with Vittorio's recipes wouldn't cause the Americans indigestion, anaphylactic shock, or worse. The man at the entrance rocked on his heels as he stood there watching her negotiate an order from the couple, rubbing his chin, scratching his head.

"I'm sorry I've kept you waiting," she said to him, hurrying over when she finally freed herself. "Do you have a reservation?"

"No," the man said, folding his arms across his chest.

Though she'd addressed him in Italian, she now wondered whether he might be foreign, not because of any specific trait, except maybe his air of detachment, of not belonging. He certainly didn't strike her as a person on vacation, and if he was, he didn't appear to be enjoying it much. Maybe he was annoyed that his wife or girlfriend or buddies were late.

"May I ask how many are in your party?" Jolene asked, smiling.

"I'll see if I we can accommodate you." Though there were still several free tables, she had no idea how many people Vittorio was prepared to feed tonight. No sense filling up the restaurant if the kitchen couldn't cope.

"There is no party," he replied. "It's just me,"

Jolene decided to go ahead and seat him. He was an attractive man, in his peculiarly unsettling way, and he was all alone in the Cinque Terre on a Saturday night. Maybe his wife had left him, or worse yet, died. She couldn't exactly turn him away.

"Well, if this isn't a welcome surprise!" Luisa called out as she zipped by, leaving an exquisite aroma of pesto in her wake.

"I'm sorry," Jolene said to the man. "I'm new here. I didn't know you were a regular customer. I'm sure we can fit you in."

"Oh, I don't need a table," the man said, but didn't budge.

Jolene continued to smile at him, though she wished he would just come out and say what he wanted. Probably an *aperitivo* at the bar before going to meet someone for dinner elsewhere, or perhaps a cup of coffee or a *digestivo* if he'd already eaten. She'd let Luisa take care of him since they seemed to know each other so well.

"In that case, you'll excuse me then?" she said, as annoyed by his unapproachability as she was anxious to get back to work.

"You're excused," the man said, but as she turned to walk away, he called out to her. "By the way, I'm Lorenzo."

"Lorenzo?" Jolene said, swinging around to face him again. "Filippo's brother?" She felt idiotic for not having noticed any resemblance. Unlike Filippo, who towered over her, Lorenzo stood just a few inches taller than she. His eyes, though brown, lacked the eagerness of Filippo's, their soft shade of almond matching their exotic shape. Strands of gray were sprinkled through the fair, shoulder-length curls that framed the high cheekbones of his tanned face, while Filippo's hair, jet-black, short, and straight, accentuated the type of pallor that comes with management positions, and which the moody sun of a western New York summer hadn't been convincing enough to ease. Though he was eleven years older than Filippo—provided she hadn't misunderstood again—the few lines she saw on Lorenzo's brow appeared to have earned their way there gradually, through years of exposure to the sun and sea and wind, rather than through bouts of worry.

"I'm sorry!" she said. "I never would have guessed."

"Now it's my turn to guess," he said. "You must be Jolene."

"How did you know that?" She doubted he'd seen her picture; Filippo had told her that Lorenzo wasn't good at keeping in touch, and that he was too antisocial to join Facebook like normal people. The negative tone Filippo assumed when speaking of his brother made her wary of being overly friendly, but like Filippo himself said, she should be free to form her own impressions.

"Well, for starters, I can't imagine my mother asking a total stranger to help her out," Lorenzo replied.

"To be honest, she didn't exactly ask me," Jolene said. "I sort of jumped right in."

"And she was okay with that?"

"I guess. Anyway, I couldn't just sit there and watch her run around," Jolene said, brandishing a corkscrew as an excuse to take her leave. "Just like I can't just stand here and talk. There's wine to be served."

Lorenzo reached out to take the corkscrew from her. "I said you were excused. I'll take over now. You must be exhausted from your trip."

"Why is everybody saying that?" Jolene said. "Do I look exhausted?" She didn't know where the edge in her voice had come from, but the instant their eyes locked over the contended corkscrew she realized she was reacting to Filippo, not to Lorenzo. "I'm sorry. But I was actually enjoying myself. Maybe you could show me the ropes?"

"From what I've seen, that would be like trying to teach a monkey how to climb trees," Lorenzo said, relinquishing his hold on the corkscrew and offering her his hand. "Welcome to Manarola, Jolene."

"Thank you," she said, shaking his hand.

Without speaking another word, they turned their attention to the diners. Full dishes appeared and empty ones were cleared; corks were popped and bottles were drained. Luisa, Lorenzo and Jolene waltzed around one another, exchanging glances and gestures, silently conveying appreciation and criticism; curiosity and tolerance; unfamiliarity and routine. More than once Jolene caught Lorenzo flashing a smile at Luisa when they brushed past one another, and for those few seconds his mother's features seemed to soften, the set of her determined jaw relaxing, the veiled blue of her eyes brightening.

Meanwhile, the American couple kept signaling for Jolene to come to their table, where she spent minutes at a time listening to stories, in several installments, of their Italian vacation. They had been to Venice, and to Bellagio, and to Milan, and to the designer outlet mall in Serravalle on their way to Liguria, and after the Cinque Terre they would go to Pisa and Florence and Rome and the Amalfi coast. Jolene tried to act sufficiently impressed, but just listening to them talk about all the gorgeous places they had traveled to, all the amazing sights they had seen, all the exquisite hotels they had stayed at, all the purchases they had made, all the well-planned reservations still swelling their itinerary, made her extremely weary. Over coffee and limoncello they finally asked Jolene where in Italy she had been.

"Here," was Jolene's answer.

"Okay," they both said, bobbing their heads in that way Americans have of nodding approval no one had requested.

"So, where are you going after this?" the woman asked.

"To bed," Jolene said, finally feeling exhausted.

FOUR

Like the beached survivor of a shipwreck, Jolene was sprawled face down on the bed, too weak to claw her way back to the world of the living before another wave could drag her back down into the depths of unconsciousness. As she lay there, she perceived certain faraway sounds: the screeching of seagulls, the calling of voices, the tolling of church bells. At last the sounds joined forces, rousing her from slumber. She blinked, momentarily confused about whose bed she was in, and in whose room the bed was in, and in whose house the room was in. Hugging the pillow to her chest, she rolled onto her back and stared at the cracks in the plaster, wondering how long they'd been there, and what time it might be now. There was no clock on the bedside table, only her mother's necklace watch, which was precious as a keepsake but unreliable as a timepiece, having ticked its final second somewhere over the Atlantic and now sulked amid its puddled chain, wearing an apologetic look on its outdated face.

Jolene stumbled to the window and yanked it open, surrendering the shutters to the wind. Leaning out with her forearms on the sill, the stiff breeze slapped her cheeks the way a barber might pat tonic onto a freshly shaved face. She was suddenly and deliciously alert, reeling with the awareness that yesterday she had awoken in New York and today in the Cinque Terre, the corner of Ligurian coast that was home to five of Italy's loveliest villages, an ocean and six time zones removed from the disappointments of her past.

For years she had focused on consolidating her emotional

51

investments, always buying into someone else's agenda rather than growing her own potential, until she ended up with a portfolio of junk titles: ex-wife, ex-girlfriend, ex-partner, ex-daughter. Craning her neck to stare out at the swatch of sea, she wondered whether her physical distance from the setting of past events would finally enable her to attain the emotional distance she needed to move on. Shifting her gaze, first to the village below, still crouched in the shadow of the mountain at her back, then across the valley and up the steep hills already basking in the silvery light of the morning sun, she felt further removed than ever from the people and possessions she'd once held dear. Whether lost or abandoned, estranged or dead, it seemed they were finally gone from her life for good.

Never requiring much sleep, Jolene had always been a morning person, her thoughts racing to get a head start on the day before her feet hit the floor. To her, there was nothing more inspiring than the limpid light of a fresh morning, while sunsets, however spectacular, spoke of endings, of burnt opportunities and broken promises. Beginnings were what she thought about as she recalled the stunning photographs of Manarola she'd studied over recent weeks, and it dawned on her that many of them must have been taken from the hill in front of her, meaning that she was standing inside the very scene she'd admired most of all. Everything here was on a smaller scale than she'd imagined, but the closeness did not feel restrictive; in fact, it reassured her. She would not need to depend on Filippo to find her way around, nor would she feel the lack of a car; even a bicycle would be useless here. Smiling at an image of herself casually conversing in Italian with the locals, learning their names one by one, family by family, she gazed at the rooftops under which these strangers lived, their slate and terracotta tiles clinging tightly to one another as if to prevent alien attitudes from seeping in.

Jolene was impatient to start meeting her new neighbors and making new friends, now that she'd survived the first round of introductions. Thinking back on the previous evening at the Locanda, she couldn't say what the family thought of her, but she was a believer in the dependability of first impressions, and she'd come away with some that were quite different from what she'd been expecting. It had taken only one bear hug and a taste of Vittorio's cooking to convince her that the man possessed a warm and sensual nature, while in Luisa she'd detected a tightness which she did not believe was entirely due to her character. Judging from the way she treated her family and dealt with her customers, it seemed that an overload of duties was taking its toll, snuffing out the pleasures of daily life. As for Lorenzo, they hadn't spoken after their awkward introduction, and he'd left without saying good night, but he didn't strike her as the shirker of responsibilities or hoarder of maternal favor Filippo's remarks had made her imagine. It was strange to think that these people were Filippo's family, that this was where he had his roots and affections, where he had learned his native language and assimilated a culture that had helped shape him into the man he was. This was where Filippo should feel most at ease and natural, yet he seemed out of phase here, more abrupt and nervous, as if he were a wild fish reeled in from the ocean, now confined to a goldfish bowl.

The shrill caw of a seagull startled Jolene, as the bird launched into flight from a nearby rooftop, circling down to the water. She wondered what the sound communicated to other gulls, and whether they ever misunderstood one another the way humans did; the way she and Filippo sometimes did. She thought back on the little information about his family she'd managed to squeeze out of Filippo: of a father who tested his patience with his backward ways; of a mother who made unfair demands of him while favoring her firstborn; of an older brother who had accomplished nothing in life yet had no qualms about grabbing the attention and merit that were rightfully Filippo's. She reflected on whether she may have misinterpreted his telegraphic descriptions, or read too much into them. It was clear that she must pay more attention when he spoke, and choose her own words carefully, because regardless of which language they spoke it would always be foreign to one of them, making them both susceptible to misunderstandings.

Backing away from the window, Jolene stretched her hands to the sky, then bent down from the waist, tummy tucked in, fingers reaching for her toes. Groaning at the stiffness in her back and hamstrings, she performed a short series of sun salutations on the cold tile floor, making a mental note to find a shop in town that sold yoga mats so she could start practicing again. After taking the quickest shower she could coax out of the ancient plumbing, she dressed and unpacked, feeling like a trespasser of time when she opened the frail doors of the arthritic *armadio*, its joints moaning as she placed her department store clothes in its camphor scented interior. Jiggling open the drawers of a bureau, in whose corners little piles of sawdust suggested the presence of tiny tenants, she found space for the remainder of her things. The top drawer, being equipped with a lock and key, was reserved for the last and most precious items she had buried at the bottom of her suitcase: a parcel concealed inside a woolen Peruvian poncho, a throwback to her mother's make-love-not-war days, with which Jolene would never part, and a leather pouch containing an old soprano recorder. The instrument, hand-carved from maplewood, had also belonged to her mother, in whose hands it had lulled Jolene to sleep on many a restless night. With saintlike patience, her mother had also taught Jolene a few songs, which to this day constituted the entire extent of her repertoire. Maybe she would have the time to teach herself something new, Jolene thought, or even compose her own songs, with so much beauty to inspire her. Another day, she thought, placing the recorder together with the parcel still wrapped in the poncho inside the drawer and turning the key, then storing the key in the travel pouch with her passport for safekeeping.

"There!" she exclaimed, already feeling more settled. Surveying her digs with the benefit of fresh eyes and the morning light, she admitted that this room with its pea green tiles and cracked ceiling, its creaky bed and sunken mattress, its stained walls and rickety furnishings, was not the room she'd imagined. But by now she knew that reality rarely lived up to her fantasies and that sometimes it didn't take much to alter parts of that reality. Like removing the dead fish photographs from the wall, for example, and shoving them under the bed. Looking at the bed, she debated over whether or not she should make it. Since Suite 16 was part of the Locanda, Luisa and Vittorio were probably paying someone, most likely a local woman trying to make ends meet, to tend to the rooms, and that someone might feel threatened or offended if Jolene did her job for her. It was against her nature to leave a bed unmade, though, and in the time it took her to think these thoughts, she'd already smoothed out the bottom sheet, straightened out the top sheet and bedspread, then folded them at the foot of the bed. Like Florence Nightingale, she believed that environments were kept healthy by abundant exposure to fresh air and sunshine, and with the mildew she spotted creeping up the walls, it couldn't hurt to leave the windows open wide. If and when a maid came, she could do the rest, but at least she wouldn't report that

Jolene was a slouch.

Craving some of that fresh air and sunshine herself, in addition to starving for some breakfast, she decided not to wait for Filippo as he'd instructed when walking her home the previous evening, not five minutes after returning from his important phone call and finding Lorenzo at the Locanda. From the outset, Filippo had told her that one of the things that he most admired in her was her independence, and she certainly didn't want to backslide and start relying on him for every little thing. Getting around town couldn't be too complicated; it was only a matter of orientation. To navigate the maze of stairs and pathways, you either walked up or down a level or two, then you either followed the course of the riverbed along the valley inland toward the hills or out toward the sea. Retracing the route she had followed with Filippo yesterday, she soon found herself in the vicinity of the Locanda but realized she did not feel like going in. She was looking forward to joining the family, but first she wanted to get a feel for the village. She needed to stand at the edge of the tiny cove, sniff the salty air, watch the waves crash against the rocks, feel the sea spray on her cheeks.

She had only walked a short distance when the irresistible aroma of coffee grabbed her by the nose and led her to a little bar, whose entrance was flanked by half a dozen outdoor tables. She imagined herself sitting at one of them in just a few weeks' time, waving to new acquaintances who happened by, while she sipped on a cappuccino and read *Il Corriere della Sera* with Filippo in order to improve her Italian, learn more about the country, and keep abreast of current events. It was too soon for her to have any friends to wave at, or to be interested in what was happening anywhere outside of Manarola, but her first authentic cappuccino was long overdue. She entered the bar.

"Buongiorno!" she said, thrilled to be ordering her first breakfast on her own. When the woman behind the bar failed to return the greeting, Jolene decided to skip any attempts at small talk and tell her what she wanted. "*Posso avere un cappuccino, per favore?*" she asked. The only other person in the bar, an elderly gentleman leaning on a cane, glanced at Jolene, then resumed dunking his focaccia in a glass of white wine, tilting his head to one side to catch the dripping bread in his toothless mouth. Looking away, Jolene's eyes landed on a tray of freshly baked breakfast pastries nestled beneath a powdery blanket of confectioner's sugar. Her stomach growled. The woman looked up at her. Jolene blushed.

"*Si serva pure*," the woman said, turning her attention to the coffee machine. Jolene's normal breakfast consisted of oatmeal and yogurt with fresh fruit, but there was nothing normal about today; today there were all those enticing croissants just begging to be eaten. Before serving herself as she had been authorized to do by the woman, she paused to consider whether the croissants were plain or filled, and if filled, whether with jam or custard, though she already knew that knowing wouldn't help, because as soon as she picked one kind, she would feel a tiny stab of regret for not having picked the other. When the woman sat the cappuccino in front of her without asking, regrettably, whether she wanted it sprinkled with cinnamon or cocoa, the need to dunk one of those croissants into its froth became urgent, making her grab one at random. Her first bite into the flaky pastry was bliss, and when, on taking a second bite, her tongue encountered custard filling, she knew she had chosen well. The third bite revealed in full the quality of the cream, which oozed into her mouth with indescribable smoothness and perfectly balanced sweetness. After swallowing the last morsel, she was tempted to grab another one to see whether it might be filled with jam, and if so, whether it could possibly taste any better than the cream-filled variety. It was only by exercising a fair amount of self-control that she resisted the urge, though she did order a second cappuccino, specifying that she would like cinnamon on top. The woman looked at her as if she'd never heard of anyone drinking two cappuccinos back-to-back, and it wasn't until she set a new cup down in front of her that Jolene believed she would satisfy her request.

Resuming her walk with her lips still smacking of goodness, already feeling the rush of sugar and caffeine kick in, she was caught up in a stream of excursionists pouring from a tunnel in the rocks which, according to a sign, led to the train station. Snippets of conversations in various languages floated past her as the tourists charged down the overwhelmed road to the sea, geared up with their hiking boots and backpacks, walking sticks and selfie sticks, cameras and trail maps. A smaller, more somber cluster of Italian ladies headed up the road against the current, staying their course with the expertise of seasoned navigators, spending their words of local dialect with parsimony.

"*Buongiorno, Signorina Jolene!*" someone called out. The voice came from behind her, and it belonged to a man. Fairly certain she was the only Jolene in Manarola, she spun around to see Giobatta maneuvering a gleaming wooden boat on wheels into a parking spot. Filippo had told her that this typical Ligurian boat with points at either end of the hull was called a *gozzo*, but he hadn't told her she'd see so many of them lined up on both sides of the narrow road, squeezing out the pedestrians like the cars did back home. The sight made her giggle.

"*Buongiorno, Signor Giobatta!*" she replied, delighted at having an acquaintance to greet, after all.

"Are you lost?" he asked, braking the boat with his body to stop it from rolling down the slope.

"No, I was just having a look around."

"Are you sure you don't want to head up the other way?" Giobatta said, pointing his chin in the direction the ladies had taken. "You'll be late."

"Late for what?" she asked.

The peal of multiple bells resounded through the village, echoing over rooftops, bouncing off buildings, drowning out conversations. Giobatta pointed an index finger in the air.

"Church?" Her sense of displacement had prevented Jolene from remembering, or even caring, what day of the week it was. Sure, she'd noticed that the atmosphere of the village was laid back, the baked goods in the café plentiful, the number of people with time for a hike astonishing, but she hadn't been around long enough to know how a weekday in Manarola differed from a Sunday.

Giobatta nodded. "First Mass is at nine o'clock," he said, timing his words between the tolls. "Filippo will be there with his family. They always go at nine."

Filippo hadn't said anything about going to church; not yesterday, not in all the time she'd known him. But if he was so concerned about what the townsfolk thought, it made sense that he would want to put in an appearance after months abroad. If he hadn't asked her to join him, it must have been because of his conviction that she was exhausted and needed to sleep in; he hadn't excluded her, he was just being considerate.

Jolene had tried her hand at churchgoing at different times in her life, and for different reasons. Not participating in any kind of structured worship didn't make her feel guilty, but it did make her feel like she was missing out on something. As a girl, she'd listened to her father rant that religion was a crutch for the weak and stupid, while her mother professed herself Presbyterian, though her attendance was erratic, her devotion to church peaking with her husband's devotion to the bottle. Going to church provided an excuse to get out of the house and keep Jolene out of harm's way until the worst of the Captain's nasty Sunday morning hangover wore off.

Jolene's relationship with religion flourished during what should have been her brief engagement to Danny Doherty, who was not exactly a devout Catholic, but who nonetheless crossed himself every time they drove past a Catholic church or cemetery, and who never missed Mass on Holy Days of Obligation: from the Ascension to All Saints' Day, and of course Easter and Christmas and everything in between, he respected them all—all except for Sundays. Sundays, he said, were for the hypocrites.

The Dohertys, for all the bickering that went on between parents and sons, knew how to stick together, and when it was time to plan the first family wedding, there was no doubt in anyone's mind that the nuptials would take place in church. Jolene's objection that she was not Catholic had been overruled; the fact she was fresh out of community college, penniless, and estranged from her father, who by then had left Jolene and her mother in dire straits, was no obstacle. Daniel Sr., aka "Pop" Doherty, would happily foot the bill for everything, including an hour of open bar, provided Jolene would convert to Catholicism.

Having done her research, Jolene had suggested that to get married in the Church it was sufficient for her to agree that she would not encourage Danny to defect from his faith and that she would raise their future children as Catholics, but on the matter of conversion, Pop had been immovable. Jolene just wanted to marry her sweetheart and didn't give a hoot about the reception or the open bar, but not wanting to start off her marriage as the cause of conflict, she had, at last, agreed to his condition. And deep down, a part of her was curious to experience what it would feel like to be a member of something as solid as the Catholic Church.

Jolene hadn't expected her commitment to translate into much of a nuisance or much of a pleasure, but she'd been surprised on both counts. Armed with her Catechism textbook, she'd thrown herself into the pre catchumenate process, attending Mass on Sundays and meeting with the pastor, Father Dwyer. She'd felt awkward at first, since no one she knew ever spoke about God, except to cry out for His help in an emergency, or curse at Him, or blame Him for everything that went wrong. Although she herself had always leaned more toward believing in God than not believing, the first thing she'd learned from Father was that such inclinations were too generic and that a strong framework was required to support her wobbly faith. Eager to learn more, she'd soon found herself looking forward to their meetings, during which she would present lists of doubts to be dispelled and concepts to be clarified. She'd begun sharing her conversations with Danny, who had feigned interest at first, but had soon started complaining that it was bad enough they'd have to take the Pre-Cana course together and had urged her to please just get converted without making such a big deal about it, so they could finally go ahead and get married. Conversion was not to be rushed, though: There had been the Rite of Christian Initiation for Adults to be reckoned with, requiring Jolene to pass through the Rite of Acceptance, then into the Order of Catechumens, then the Rite of Welcoming, then the Rite of Election to the Call to Continuing Conversion until finally, at the Easter Vigil, she had emerged, spiritually mature enough to receive her baptism, confirmation, and first taste of the Holy Eucharist. All that, and she had yet to get married—a plan about which the first seedlings of doubt had in the meantime begun to sprout, for reasons which were later proved to be well-grounded. But by then she was in too deep to back out.

Praying that God knew what He'd gotten her into, Jolene had entered into the sacrament of Holy Matrimony on the first Saturday of the first May of the new Millennium, but that was the last Mass she ever attended with Danny, who for unknown reasons had abruptly stopped going to Church on Holy Days of Obligation. He now preferred to devote his Catholic energies to the practice of procreation, while purposely thwarting its successful outcome, despite Jolene's protests that since he was the one who had insisted on getting married in the Church, he should at least respect his conjugal duty and embrace the idea of fatherhood.

This Catholic God did not seem to appreciate Jolene's wifely efforts as she'd expected, nor did Danny, who had left her to fulfill her newfound Sunday obligation on her own, while he sought his inspiration in the aisles of Home Depot, which he cruised in hot pursuit of one more tool that would enable him to complete the latest of the do-it-yourself projects he had begun and abandoned by the dozens. When a series of stories about child abuse at the hands of priests, followed by others about shady financial dealings at the highest levels of the Vatican flooded the media, shaking the very foundations of her newly adopted religion, Danny's reply had been that being Catholic meant having more faith in the Church and in the infallibility of the Pope than in fake news.

A year later, when Danny had dumped her for the wife of his best friend, the very friend who had been the best man at their wedding, Jolene had felt too embarrassed at having taken part in such a farce to seek comfort in the Church that she had been blackmailed to join. She had pushed for a quick divorce, this time resisting Pop's pressuring, after which she'd dropped her married name of Doherty, returning to her maiden name of Twyman, wishing there were an alternative to being branded by the name of a man. She'd then moved to Ithaca, stunned and alone, and not at all sure whether she still qualified as a Catholic, or had automatically been excommunicated. From that point on it had seemed more practical to her to hash things out with God on her own time and turf, mostly aboard the old rowboat she was fond of paddling close to the shore of Cayuga Lake in silent contemplation, and sometimes singing a tune.

The church bells ceased their clanging, and a voice penetrated her daze. "Go straight up that way," she heard it say. "Then you can take the shortcut up the stairs on your right. If you hurry, you can follow those ladies."

Jolene blinked, surprised to find herself staring at an old Italian man parallel-parking a boat. "I'm sorry, what did you say?"

Giobatta shook his head. "And they tell me I'm hard of hearing!"

"The ladies!" Jolene cried. "Right! I'll follow the ladies!"

If Giobatta recommended she go to church, she'd go to church. Though she hated postponing her walk, she liked the idea of stopping in to say hello to God, to thank Him for bringing her safely to Italy and for giving her one more chance to turn her life around. It would also be fun to impress Filippo and his family by showing up on her own.

"Thanks for the advice, Giobatta!" Jolene said, but Giobatta had already turned his attention back to the boat.

Striding back up the hill, she caught up with the women, who were comparing menus for the Sunday dinners they would prepare after Mass. She was intrigued by one woman's pumpkin ravioli recipe, but put off by another's stewed rabbit. Most of the ladies were compact in stature; some thinner, some heavier, but all looked sturdy, as solid a base for village life as the rocks Manarola was perched upon. Living in such an isolated place, they must have known each other all their lives, and Filippo must know them all, too. Jolene wondered whether any of the women or their daughters had set their sights on Filippo, and how they would react to an outsider stealing away such an eligible bachelor, probably one of the very few in the town's dwindling ranks.

Following the women more out of curiosity than fear of getting lost, Jolene thought of the Italian churches she'd long dreamed of visiting, the colossal St. Peter's Basilica, and the magnificent duomos of Florence and Pisa, Milan and Venice. Yet when she reached the top of the hill, it was the church of San Lorenzo that took her breath away. Standing humbly in the shadow of the stout bell tower that presided over the village below, the church was by far the oldest and most beautiful place of worship she'd ever laid eyes on. Its plain stone façade was embellished with a pointed arch over the portal, and a magnificent rose window above that. The roof was trimmed with delicate stonework as fine as mantilla lace.

With a sense of awe, Jolene walked through the massive wooden door and stepped inside. The smells of incense and candle wax and cut flowers with rotting stems hung in the air, sustained by centuries of whispered confessions and reverence for rites by rote. The pre-Mass hush was broken by the sounds of women's heels clicking and men's soles squeaking and wooden kneelers creaking as they recorded their presence on the ancient black and white marble tiles. On entering, parishioners nodded greetings while touching their foreheads and hearts and shoulders and lips with fingers dipped in holy water. Jolene stood at the entrance searching for a familiar face but found none: no Filippo, no Luisa, no Vittorio, no Lorenzo. The congregation was made up mostly of older women, she noted, though a few were accompanied by even older men, and a handful of others were young enough to have children in tow. She was hoping to hear some inspiring music on the antique pipe organ she spotted, but the church remained silent as the priest made his entrance, followed by two altar boys. When the Mass began, Jolene felt conspicuous standing by the door, as if poised to make a getaway. Genuflecting and crossing herself, she took an aisle seat in the last pew. Not having set foot in a Catholic church since her divorce, she was surprised at how well she recalled the liturgy, and how easy it was to follow its Italian equivalent. Each time the massive door creaked to admit a sliver of the morning sun, Jolene looked over her shoulder in the hopes of spotting Filippo, but it was always another latecomer, or a Sunday hiker wandering in to take a peek.

By communion time she'd given up hope that the Garaventis would turn up, and lowered herself to the splintered wood of the kneeler to pray, while a surprisingly small number of people lined up to receive the host. Thoughts of her mother visited her, as they always did whenever she remained still and silent, making her throat tighten and her eyes sting with tears. Jolene was searching her pocket for a tissue when she felt a hand on her shoulder; turning, she was startled to see Filippo standing behind her. He slid into the pew next to her, squeezing her hand tight while she remained on her knees. It was a comforting feeling, being in church like that together, smelling those Catholic scents, seeing those sacred shafts of colored light stream through the stained glass windows. Still holding hands, Jolene and Filippo stood together, then sat, then stood again, until the final blessing was delivered. That was how it should have been with Danny, all those years ago, but never was.

"What are you doing here, Jo?" Filippo asked, after the priest had led the altar boys through a thick velvet curtain to the vestibule and everyone started leaving. "I came looking for you in your room, but you'd already snuck out."

"I didn't sneak out," she said, following Filippo out the door. "I just woke up early. I needed a cappuccino. Then I ran into Giobatta, who told me your family always comes to this Mass."

Filippo shook his head and smiled. "That's news to me. I ran into him too, when I went looking for you, and he told me that you stopped to ask him where the church was."

"Whatever story suits him best!" Jolene laughed. "I guess he must be concerned for my soul."

"He's not the only one who's concerned," Filippo said, running a fingertip delicately across her eyes. "Were you crying, *Splendore mio*?"

"It's nothing. Don't worry."

"Of course I worry. We're finally in Italy together, and we'll be getting married very soon. You should be happy."

"I am happy," she said. "I was just thinking about my mother. She would have loved it here. She always wanted to come to Italy."

"Then she'd be glad that you're here," Filippo said. "So let's go take a walk and shake off the sadness."

"Yes, let's," she said, instead of replying that grief could not be controlled at will. But it would do her good to think of something else. "Are you going to show me the rest of the Locanda?"

"Not now, Jolene. Today is Sunday, remember? It's a day of rest," Filippo said. "Wait here a minute first, while I go say hello to the priest. He said he needed to see me."

Before she could respond, Filippo had dashed back inside the church. Studying its façade, she saw that there was a date carved in the cornerstone: 1338. She had a system for remembering numbers by associating them with other numbers. It took her thirty seconds to make the connection: when she was 13 her mother had been 38. The same age Jolene was now.

***

Too damn many people out here today," Filippo grumbled, turning sideways to let two couples pass him on the narrow steps.

"Is it always like this?" Jolene asked. After being in Manarola only twenty-four hours, she was already starting to resent the tourists, even though she knew there was but a fine line dividing her from them, and that if it weren't for them, Filippo and his family—and soon she, too—would have to find an alternative way to make a living.

"Weekends are crazy, and Sundays are the worst, especially from April to October. Toward the end of the season, we get these fanatics trying to squeeze in all they can before the rain sets in. As if it won't all be here next year."

"Well, thanks for offering to walk with me," Jolene said. Based on her experience with him in New York, she knew he wasn't particularly fond of hiking. She had surprised him a few times by organizing a day of adventure, selecting some of her favorite Finger Lakes itineraries, even packing a gourmet picnic lunch complete with wine to entice him. Although he always said he was happy to go, his initial reaction lacked the spontaneous eagerness shown on other outings. When they toured the area's well-established wineries, for example, or the innovative craft breweries, hip spirit distilleries, romantic boutique hotels, new age spas or cozy romantic inns; or spent a couple of days in New York, Toronto or Boston, he could never explore enough, taste enough, talk enough. As for the exercise aspect, she knew it was something he preferred to get out of the way first thing in the morning with a good hard run in flat open space so he could move on, guilt-free, to savor life's finer pleasures. From the way he bounded ahead of her now, it seemed like he wanted to get this walk over with as soon as possible, too.

"Stop shoving me, dude!" said a voice behind Jolene.

Her ears winced at the American accent as a trio of soft-bellied youths sporting baseball caps and long baggy shorts from which their sweat-soaked T-shirts hung to dry, rumbled past her in their fluorescent running shoes, jostling one another and nearly knocking her off the steps.

"You're right, it is pretty crowded!" Jolene called to Filippo, once she regained her balance. "We can leave it for another day if you want."

"We'll just take a look at the view, then head back," Filippo called over his shoulder.

"Okay, great!" A grunt escaped Jolene as she heaved herself up another incredibly steep step. She shouldn't have any trouble losing those extra pounds she'd gained since meeting Filippo if she did this every day. To her, walking was a pleasure; no matter how busy she'd be working alongside Filippo, she'd make the time for plenty of hikes.

Observing him from behind, it filled her heart with tenderness to imagine Filippo as a restless young boy with nowhere to run except up and down the vertical hillsides. How many times he must twisted an ankle and skinned a knee! There was something about the range of his movements now, in the way he lunged forward, shifting his weight from one long leg to the other, that suggested his body had outgrown its birthplace, the way a gangling teenager looks awkward curled up in his mother's lap. Filippo's adult body was too tall and bulky to look at home among these narrow terraces, where sinewy grapevines snaked toward the sun among the lemons and olives and minuscule vegetable patches squeezed in between the trees. Everything was planted where it would receive just the right amount of space and soil, sunlight and water, but no more than strictly necessary for survival.

"We're almost there!" Filippo called to her as they rounded a curve, bringing the clustered buildings of Manarola in view to their left, and straight ahead, the open sea. The water was wild today, the sun skipping shards of silver off its surface. It was hard to believe that Filippo had spent his youth fishing and diving off the jagged rocks being pummeled by the waves.

"Punta Bonfiglio!" Filippo announced after a few more minutes, taking her hand. "Well? What do you think?"

"It's breathtaking!"

Filippo smiled. "See that tower over there?" he asked, pointing across the valley to the far end of the village. "And just above that, the tall yellow building with green shutters, between the red one and the pink one?"

"I think I can make it out," she said, squinting as she scanned the colorful conglomerate.

"The top floor of that yellow house is where you're staying."

"Really? That's Suite 16?" she exclaimed. They were standing at the lookout point she'd spotted from the window of her room, the famous belvedere where countless others before her had stood and shot all those photographs of Manarola. From here her lodgings looked like the most charming abode a person could dream of. And it was, really; its soul was there, it just needed a little love and attention, and she was ready to invest plenty of that. After contemplating the storybook view for a moment, she pivoted to take in the stretch of coast to her right, or rather west, or maybe northwest; she was still a little confused.

"And what's that over there?" she asked.

"If you mean that dinky hamlet stuck on the mountaintop, that's Volastra. There's nothing worth seeing there. And if you mean the next village down the coast straight across from us, that's Corniglia. It's the only one of the Cinque Terre that doesn't have direct access to the sea. Once you're there, you're stuck. Even more than we are. You have to walk down hundreds of steps just to reach the train station." Although Filippo was warming up to his role of cicerone, he'd need a few pointers if he were ever to be in charge of promoting tourism.

"They both look absolutely gorgeous to me," she said. "Can you walk there?" Seeing his eyebrows shoot up in alarm, she hastened to add, "Don't worry. I don't mean us, now. But one of these days I'd like to."

"Sure, there'll be plenty of time for that. You can walk to your heart's content here."

"And up there, that's the cemetery I can see from my room, right?"

"Right," Filippo said. "There's plenty of time for that, too. If you know what I mean."

"What a lovely resting place," Jolene murmured.

"I'd rather jump off this cliff right now, than end up there."

"Really? Why? I sense a real communion with nature in this spot. The sea and the mountains, the sun and the sky and the wind, all swirling around."

"All I sense is that I was unlucky to be born here, and I'll be damned if I die here!"

"Filippo! Don't even joke about dying!" she cried. "That's a long way off. Besides, you were lucky to be born here, and you know it." Back in New York, she'd listened with envy each time he spoke of his charming hometown, its mild climate, its spectacular nature, its exquisite flavors, its authentic people.

"Maybe. But the lucky part ended when I was a little kid," he said. "Once I was in high school, I started feeling like I would suffocate. I remember going to bed at night and lying there flat on my back, staring at the ceiling, so convinced it was clamping down on me I could feel it crush my chest. I took the train to La Spezia every morning, and every afternoon, right after school, I took another train back. And then I was stuck here, helping out at the Locanda. Not that there was much else to do. The only kids I could hang out with were the local troglodytes. My parents knew every move we made, and what my parents didn't see, someone else's parents did. There wasn't one place we could go to listen to music, or play soccer, or meet new girls, or sneak a smoke. "

"I still think you were lucky," Jolene said. "The whole outdoors was your playground, and at least you had a family who cared about you, including a brother. I always wished I had a sister."

"If you can call Lorenzo a brother," Filippo snorted." He's eleven years older than me, and he was always so weird, always wandering off on his own. One night, he must have been about fifteen at the time, he never came home. My mother had to round up the whole village to go searching for him."

"How scary! Where was he?"

"They found him up there." Filippo jerked his thumb at the steep hill above the path they'd come from.

"Where that cross is?"

"There are three crosses, even though you can't see them all from here. That's why that hill's called Collina Tre Croci. Lorenzo was curled up in a ball on the ground, and when they woke him he couldn't figure out what the big deal was. All he wanted to do, he said, was to sleep up there by the cross, under the stars."

"Your mother must have been so relieved when they found him!" Jolene cried, imagining Luisa's anguish.

"Yeah, Mamma went to church every morning for a month to light a candle of thanks, even though she's not religious, at least not the kind of religious people around here think is normal. But since Lorenzo happens to be named after the patron saint of Manarola, San Lorenzo got the credit for the happy ending." Filippo paused, breaking into a smile. "But my father beat the crap out of him!"

"Oh, no!" Jolene said, cringing. She couldn't imagine the affable Vittorio beating up on his boy, the way no one could have imagined one of the swellest guys to fly the skies of America taking a belt to her backside. She looked Filippo in the eye. "Tell me, did he hit you, too?"

"No. He never touched me," Filippo said, shifting his gaze to the sea. "And he never hit Lorenzo again either. Mamma would have killed him if he had. She had to whack him with a broom to make him stop that time."

"Worry can make people do things they regret," she said. "All in all, I think your parents provided you with a good home. If they hadn't, you wouldn't have wanted to come back and carry on their work at the hotel."

"If you can even call it a hotel," Filippo said, rolling his eyes. "Every time I go away, I tend to forget what a dive it really is."

"Don't say that!" she cried, wondering what had gotten into him. "What happened to your vision, Filippo? To our vision? You'll see, we'll turn Locanda Luisa into a real jewel. It's just a matter of time, and hard work, but I'll be right here by your side, and I'm committed to putting in plenty of both."

Filippo stared off into the horizon. A thick blanket of clouds had gathered, stealing the sparkle from the waves, muting the vibrant hues of the depths.

"We'd better head back," Filippo muttered. "Looks like rain is on the way."

FIVE

For the second time that day, Jolene decided not to wait for Filippo. It hadn't rained after all, despite his insistence that it would just as soon as the wind died down, but that hadn't happened, either; if anything, the wind had picked up. He'd also insisted on accompanying her back to her room to rest before the family gathering, even though she wasn't the least bit tired. It wasn't until after he'd dropped her at the doorstep, citing a forgotten errand as his excuse for not coming in for a cuddle, that she'd admitted to herself that it would be good to spend a couple of hours on her own. She wanted to process the information he'd shared with her about his family while at Punta Bonfiglio, and revisit the images of Vittorio, Luisa and Lorenzo that had formed, blurred, and reformed in her mind, before seeing them together with Filippo again.

Flipping shut the notebook in which she'd jotted down her impressions of the first morning of her new life, Jolene stood and stretched the stiffness out of her back. She was better at writing than drawing, but she'd also sketched out a renovated version of Suite 16 with a desk and chair in front of the window, thinking that not only she, but anyone spending any amount of time in a room would need somewhere else to sit other than the bed.

Popping into the bathroom, she took stock of her reflection in the bathroom mirror and found her face pale. She wasn't big on makeup, but she didn't want people to keep telling her she looked tired and decided that a touch of lipstick wouldn't hurt. A moment later she was out the door, fighting the uncooperative lock of Suite 16 for possession of the key, when a tickle on her ankles made her jump. Glancing down, she found the wide topaz eyes of a cat staring up at her.

"Why, you sweet thing!" Jolene cooed, crouching to scratch the furry white bib under the cat's chin. The animal was full-grown but scrawny, and she suspected there was little flesh beneath its fluffy coat of variegated fur. "I'll be back soon, kitty!" she said, making a mental note to find something to feed it as she turned to leave, her heart breaking a tiny bit when the cat began trotting after her, then gave up, hopping onto a stone wall where it crouched to watch her walk away.

The unexpected encounter brought a smile to Jolene's lips. She loved cats, but had always been prevented from keeping one of her own; first by her father, whose only use for animals was to kick them around; then by Danny, whose only use for animals was to hunt them; then by Evan, whose only use for animals was to cook them. Having a cat in the neighborhood would bring her good luck, she was sure of it, and the thought cheered her on her walk to the Locanda in the company of her gurgling stomach. Maybe she was more nervous than she thought at the prospect of the family gathering, or maybe she was simply hungry. Filippo hadn't suggested lunch before disappearing on his errand, and she hadn't felt like venturing out on her own again to fight the hordes of tourists swarming the village. She certainly couldn't eat all of her meals out, anyway. An electric kettle was all she needed to be independent. Green tea and fresh fruit would keep her going when she wasn't with Filippo, and would help her shed those extra pounds, too. She added the items to her mental wish list. Yoga mat, desk, chair, kettle, tea.

Instead of taking the direct route straight down the stairs, Jolene continued along the upper level, passing between the narrow rows of houses where an end-of-the-Sunday calm was settling over the village. From a second-floor window, a woman leaned out to rescue the day's washing, twisted and wrapped around the line by the wind. From another open window, one floor below, wafted the herbal aromas of a simmering minestrone. At a third window, on the top floor, a woman stood with cupped hands at her mouth, yelling, "*Luca! Vieni, Luca! Ora!*" Below, a young boy played alone, kicking the daylights out of a soccer ball, making it ricochet like a gunfire off the close walls of the alley. "*Uffa!*" the boy groaned, stooping to retrieve the ball before dragging his feet through the open doorway.

A few minutes later Jolene came upon the church of San Lorenzo, her reliable sense of direction having suggested a new route. A group of giggling Italian excursionists posed for a selfie in the square as the bell in the tower tolled six, then the group hustled down the stairs, backpacks bouncing as they trotted toward the train station. She wondered where home was for them; perhaps Genoa or Florence, or Milan or Turin, or some smaller town in between.

"Jolene!" For the second time that day in a town where she was still a stranger, she was startled to hear a voice calling out her name. Turning toward it, she spotted a man with a little girl straddling his shoulders, heading in her direction.

"Lorenzo!" she cried. "What a surprise!"

"For you, maybe. I'm here a lot." Lorenzo said, his eyes casing the square. "Are you all alone?"

"Yes. I wanted to take a little walk," she said, feeling slightly embarrassed that this was the second time they met, and the second time she was on her own, instead of with Filippo. Or maybe it was Lorenzo making her feel uneasy again, the way he just stood there, unsmiling, looking like he didn't need anything from anybody.

"And who's this young lady?" Jolene asked. Children and animals were always a good diversion when you didn't know what to say.

"This is my daughter, Chiara," Lorenzo said, his hands gripping the pudgy little ankles dangling over his shoulder, his thumbs caressing the soft patch of bare skin between the tiny purple sweatpants and miniature sneakers.

"Filippo never told me he was an uncle!" she said, before it could occur to her that it might be best to leave Filippo out of the conversation until she had a better understanding of the brothers' relationship.

"Me having a daughter doesn't automatically make Filippo an uncle," he said. "Just like it doesn't automatically make me a father. But I try my best."

"That's all anyone can do, right?" she said. "Even Filippo." Filippo didn't need her to defend him, she knew; her response was automatic, triggered by her sense of loyalty.

"Right," he said.

If Lorenzo was contrary, his little girl was delightful. Jolene took one of her hands in hers: it was incredibly small and soft and warm and sticky. Her heart-shaped mouth was puckered in an expression of curiosity and smeared with red, as if she had been eating jam. "*Ciao, Chiara! Quanti anni hai?*" she said, already wishing she hadn't asked the same stupid question adults always asked little children, as if their age was the most important thing about them after their name.

"She just turned four," Lorenzo said, instead of prodding the child to answer for herself. "She's a little shy with new people. Her mother always used to yell at her for speaking to strangers, and it stuck with her."

Jolene's mind whirred, trying to stitch together the image of an adolescent Lorenzo wandering off to sleep under a cross on the hillside, with the image of him taking a beating at his father's hands, with the image of him working alongside his mother at the Locanda, with this latest image of him as a father and husband. She thought it best not to ask him anything about the child's mother, whom Filippo had also neglected to mention, and who could have died or run off with a Frenchman for all she knew. She must make an effort to remember that this was the time to look, listen and learn. And sometimes she learned something wonderful, like that fact that she'd be an aunt to this lovely child. The realization made her smile, despite her irritation with Filippo.

"So where are you headed, all by yourself?" Lorenzo asked.

"Nowhere special," she said, wondering whether he was intentionally emphasizing the fact that she was alone, again. "I was just having a look around before going to the Locanda. I was afraid it might be too early to just turn up there."

"It's never too early. Go down whenever you want, with or without Filippo. Even if the restaurant's closed, the bar is usually open and there's always someone there."

"Thanks. I'll keep that in mind," she said, appreciating the invitation, though she couldn't picture herself hanging around the Locanda with Luisa or Vittorio or even Lorenzo, who was closer to her in age, unless Filippo was there. It was probably just a matter of time, though; soon she'd feel more at ease with all of them.

"I'm going there now," Lorenzo said, already heading toward the stairs. Jolene hesitated a moment before following him. He hadn't suggested she walk with him, but it seemed logical that she should.

"Filippo showed me Punta Bonfiglio this morning!" she called after him as they walked, wanting him to know that he wasn't neglecting her. "What a view!"

"Chiara and I have been scouting out views, too," Lorenzo said.

"I figured as much. I noticed your backpack," Jolene said, falling in step with him as they joined the main road. Despite having shorter legs, he was a faster walker than Filippo. "Where did you go?"

"I didn't have much time, so we just went up to Volastra," he said, repositioning the squirming Chiara on his shoulders. "Besides, this little one can be a handful."

"Oh, I saw where Volastra is! Filippo pointed it out to me. He said there's nothing there, but I'd still like to go sometime."

"Funny. Filippo used to like it up there just fine," Lorenzo commented. "But things change. People change, too, right?"

"Right," she said, not quite sure what she was agreeing to.

***

Scarcely twenty-four hours had passed since Jolene had set foot in the Locanda for the first time, and it already seemed more hospitable to her, even in its deserted state. Today the lighting seemed less harsh, the odors less stale, the atmosphere less fraught with the woes of locals and laden with the expectations of tourists. She knew her tendency to overlook defects increased in proportion with her desire to make them disappear, but today she was already projected into the future, seeing a lighter, livelier environment as soon as she walked through the door.

"And that's all I have to say about it!" Vittorio's voice boomed from the kitchen, segueing into a hearty chuckle, which was joined by another man's hoot. In seconds, the chuckles and hoots crescendoed into a concert of belly-busting laughter, the kind that would infect anyone within its range, whether or not they knew what the joke was about. Its effect was not lost on Jolene, who began giggling, which made little Chiara squeal and clap her hands. Only Lorenzo seemed immune; he just shook his head, as if he had built up a tolerance to such antics.

"You have company!" Lorenzo called out, lifting the laughing child off his shoulders and swinging her around in the air before landing her on the floor. She staggered a moment like a drunkard, then wobbled off to seek out the merriment.

"Hold it right there!" a man's voice called, causing Chiara to scurry back to her father. The voice belonged to Filippo, Jolene was sure of it, but any doubt would have been dispelled a moment later when he appeared in person, dabbing at his eyes with a kitchen towel.

"*Splendore!*" he said, still recovering from the laughter. "How did you get here?"

"I walked."

"Did you have a good rest?" he asked, kissing her on the cheek.

"I wasn't tired," she said, wondering why she should feel so irritated on discovering him having a laugh with his father.

"I was on my way to pick you up, but when I stopped by and saw Babbo was here on his own, I thought I'd give him a hand."

"You could have kept your girlfriend company," Lorenzo said, shrugging off his backpack without looking at Filippo. "Helping out is my job, remember?"

"It looks like you had better things to do, up in the hills," Filippo said. "Besides, it gave Babbo and me a chance to catch up."

"*Mamma!*" Chiara cried, slaloming through the half-dozen legs of the adults blocking her path.

Turning, Jolene saw a woman dressed in black leggings, black boots, and a black sweater, standing at the entrance. With her twig-like legs and shiny black hair, the only dash of color the bright orange gloss on her lips, the woman reminded Jolene of a blackbird passing a bug to her chick, when she crouched to give Chiara a peck on her mouth. Clearly wanting more, the child looked up at her mother, her arms outstretched, her eyes pleading, but the woman in black pulled herself up straight, running her manicured fingers through her thick hair, styled long enough in the front to fall in front of her eyes and mingle with her lashes like a veil. The back and sides of the geometric hairstyle were clipped short, revealing dainty ears whose lobes were weighed down with heavy gold hoops, and a swan's neck that seemed too long for the small, round head it supported. When the woman tossed her head, the bangs fell away from her face, revealing the most striking pair of dark eyes Jolene had ever seen. Jolene was willing to wager that they would be even more beautiful without the expertly applied eyeliner and mascara that magnified their intensity in a way that made it difficult to look at her.

"*Splendore!*" Filippo called, hurrying over to hug the woman.

Lorenzo's wife is another *Splendore*? Jolene thought, her left eye twitching.

"*Ciao, Fil! Bentornato!*" the woman cried, returning Filippo's hug and kissing him on both cheeks, before turning to face Jolene. "So, you must be the lucky girl," she said, extending her hand from where she stood, riveted in place by Filippo's hold on her shoulders and Chiara's grip on her legs. When she moved closer to take her hand, Jolene could detect a trace of cigarette smoke lingering beneath her musky perfume. Though Jolene only used a dab of an essential oil now and then, her nose was not ignorant, and recognized the perfume as one of those high-end scents salespeople always tried to spray you with in department stores. This was not a woman who skimped on her cosmetics budget.

"Yes, that's me. I'm Jolene," she said, shaking her hand. "Nice to meet you." She was tempted to add a fib like, "I've heard so much about you!" or a fact like, "I didn't even know you existed!" but thought the better of it.

"Welcome to lovely Manarola," the nameless woman said, turning to Lorenzo before Jolene could reply. "If my memory serves me right, you promised to have your daughter cleaned up and dressed before the party starts. She's a sticky mess!"

"I know. We came across a bunch of *corbezzoli*," Lorenzo said. "They were so perfect and ripe that we just kept picking and eating, picking and eating. Didn't we, Chiara?"

Chiara clapped her hands, letting go of her mother's legs to twirl around and sing, "*Corbezzoli! Corbezzoli!*"

Jolene had never heard of *corbezzoli*, but assumed it must be a fruit, and wondered what it was called in English; what it looked like and tasted like.

"If she gets diarrhea, we'll know whose fault it is," the woman snapped, before Jolene could ask any of those things.

"She's had diarrhea for the past two days. That's why I let her eat so many," Lorenzo said, sweeping Chiara off her feet and throwing her over his shoulder, making the child squeal as he walked past the bar and up the stairs that must lead to the original lodgings of the Locanda. Jolene hoped to take a peek up there soon, but this was certainly not the time.

"Here we are!" Luisa called from the door, an elderly lady on each arm. When one of them started to stumble, Jolene rushed to help, and the woman latched onto her. Jolene steadied her, patting her hand. She'd always had a soft spot for old folks, especially those who struck her as vulnerable. As a child, she used to fantasize that random old people she saw at the park, or on the bus, or in the grocery store, would turn out to be one of the grandmothers or grandfathers she had never met. She would always run to their aid when they seemed to be in difficulty, helping them get up from a bench, or find the box of pitted prunes they couldn't see on the shelf, or offering them her seat. They would always smile and say something like, "Aren't you a dear!" and when Jolene just stood there smiling back, they sometimes would rummage through their change purse, fishing out a nickel or a dime to give her. But she would always refuse, because she was really waiting for them to say, "Heavens! You're Jolene! I recognized you right away from the photographs your mother sends me!" At that point, they would hug her and ask her if she wanted to go live with them.

"Oh, good. The aunts," Filippo moaned. Jolene glared at him. She didn't know anything about these ladies, but it irked her when people treated the elderly as if they weren't there; as if their ears were deaf, their eyes blind, their minds muddled.

"Where's Lorenzo?" Luisa asked.

"He's getting Chiara cleaned up," the girl's still nameless mother said, sitting down at a table by the bar and crossing her legs, her foot kicking the air.

Luisa looked at the woman as if she wanted to make a remark but said nothing. "Would you help me get them settled then, Filippo?"

Filippo took the second woman off his mother's hands, leading her into the dining room while motioning for Jolene and her charge to follow. The four of them tottered along until they reached a large table, which had been set up in the center of the dining room. Filippo and Jolene settled the ladies into chairs, and the ladies promptly closed their eyes, preparing to doze off.

"Why didn't you tell me about Lorenzo?" Jolene whispered, as they headed back to the bar.

"What do you mean?" Filippo asked, looking genuinely puzzled by her question.

"What I mean is, you didn't tell me that he had a child! Or a wife!" Jolene said, stopping him while they were still out of earshot.

"I'm sure I told you," Filippo said.

"When did you tell me? I wouldn't forget details like that."

"Remember that weekend when we went to that inn on Skaneateles Lake and we had that talk about our families?"

"Of course I remember that," Jolene said. She'd been prepared to bare her soul to Filippo and eviscerate the painful issues which neither Danny, due to immaturity, or Evan, due to self-centeredness, had wanted to help her deal with. She'd been embarrassed about exposing her childhood, and each time she'd opened her mouth to speak but faltered, Filippo refilled her glass with Cabernet Franc, until her tongue grew too thick with sadness and tangled with shame to talk. At that point, Filippo had taken over the conversation, giving her the quickest recap of a family history she'd ever heard, and that had been the end of their big talk.

"I can tell you're a million miles away again," Filippo said, snapping his fingers in front of her face, making Jolene blink. "No wonder you can't remember anything. You're never really with me, are you?"

"Of course…of course I'm with you," she stammered. "I do remember. I remember you telling me about your parents, about how they've been working together at the Locanda for the past forty years, and about how your mother always favored Lorenzo. I would have remembered if you'd told me about his wife. I don't even know her name!"

"You could have asked me."

"How could I have asked you, when I didn't even know she existed?"

"Did it ever occur to you, *Cara* Jo, that you might be too wrapped up in your own thoughts to really hear what anyone else is telling you?"

Jolene's cheeks grew warm, but hers was a flush of frustration, not embarrassment. She did not consider herself above reproach, but in this case, Filippo's comment made her want to scream. In the previous months she'd asked more questions than Filippo was willing to answer, and when he'd joked, in that affectionate manner of his, that she was turning into a pest, she'd finally given up. If it was easier to learn a language when you lived in a place where it was spoken, she reasoned, it was also easier to learn about a person when you saw them in their own environment. Today was proof; today Filippo had finally shared some family stories with her when they were up at the belvedere. Thinking back on that conversation now, it unnerved her to think that maybe Filippo was right. Even while he was describing how he'd suffered growing up in Manarola, her mind had kept wandering back to the trials of her own childhood.

"Don Ludovico is here!" Luisa said, charging into the dining room. "And your father wants to propose a toast." Grabbing Filippo and Jolene by their elbows, she turned to the seated ladies, whose eyes had fluttered open at the announcement. "Zia Marta and Zia Matilde, you two stay right there on your chairs. We'll all join you at the table in just a few minutes." At that, she whisked the couple away.

Vittorio, Lorenzo, and a fresh-faced Chiara, with a mother whose name Filippo still hadn't revealed to Jolene, were gathered around the bar, together with the same priest who had celebrated the Mass that morning, standing, chalice in hand, waiting for the bottle to be cracked open.

"Don Ludovico! How good of you to come!" Filippo exclaimed. "Let me introduce you to my fiancée, Jolene Twyman."

"It's a pleasure to meet you, Giovanna," the priest said, dropping Filippo's hand and clasping hers. "I believe I saw you in church this morning, sitting way at the back. You didn't take Communion."

"I'm happy to meet you, too, Father," she replied, deciding to let him call her what he wanted for now. It was not a good day for names.

"Fiancée?" Lorenzo commented, raising just one eyebrow, the same way Filippo sometimes did. "You mean it's official?"

"Of course it's official!" Vittorio said. "Filippo knows better than to bring a girl back home from America if he's not going to marry her. His father taught him better."

"Babbo's right," Filippo said. "I've finally learned my lesson. Everyone listen up. I talked it over with Mamma, and then with Babbo. I'm happy to say they both approve our plans to get married as soon as possible."

All eyes were on Jolene, as Filippo put his arm around her and pulled her close: Lorenzo's almond-shaped eyes, sparkling with curiosity; what's-her-name's dark eyes, two spheres of glossy onyx; Chiara's child's eyes, half-filled with wonder, half with sleep; Vittorio's sharp eyes, scrutinizing the future on the horizon; and Luisa's blue-gray eyes, too transparent to conceal her skepticism. Lastly, there were Don Ludovico's unreadable eyes, hidden behind lenses that flashed with the glare of neon lights. Jolene blushed again, embarrassed by all the unexpected attention, but above all, feeling stupid: ridiculously stupid. She hadn't realized that there was a parental approval clause attached to Filippo's proposal.

"Jolene has already taken care of the paperwork at her end, now we just have to submit some documents to the American Consulate in Milan," Filippo said. "Then we can publish the banns and set a date! Right, Don Ludovico?"

"That's right. As we agreed, it makes no sense to wait," the priest said, staring at his empty glass. "With a bit of careful planning, we should be able to arrange a December wedding. It's a busy month, of course, but God willing, I'll find a way to squeeze you in before Christmas."

"Christmas?" Jolene parroted.

"I know it seems far away, but it's only three months, *Splendore!* It'll be here before you know it!" Filippo said, stroking the top of her head, though he knew she didn't like it; it made her feel like his pet.

"No, no, it's not that," she said, shaking her head in an effort to knock the hand off. "It's just that for the, you know, the wedding—"

"I know, I know!" Filippo said. "Unlike you, I remember every word you say. We'll keep it small, just like I promised. As you can see, we're a small family."

"No, I meant, you know, about the ceremony—" Jolene insisted. She had to say something to the priest about her ineligibility for a church wedding, but what? How? When? Now?

But Filippo was waving his hand in the air, dismissing her concerns before she could articulate them. "You'll have plenty of time to talk over all the details with Mamma," he said. "And if you need help with flowers or a dress or something, Monica's very artistic. As you know, she's an architect."

Jolene nodded, too dumbfounded to speak, but not to overlook the two important bits of information that had been slipped to her. The mystery woman's name was Monica, and she was an architect. She would never have guessed either.

"Enough talk!" Vittorio said. "Before you women start prattling on about lilies and lace, let's open that bottle!"

"Absolutely!" Filippo said. He was acting more euphoric than she'd ever seen him, uncorking the bottle and pouring with an extra touch of flair, filling the glasses all the way to the brim, chuckling as they bubbled over, dabbing the dribbling Spumante behind everyone's ears. "Porta fortuna! Porta fortuna!" he cried, telling

Jolene it was an Italian custom, that it brought good luck.

Dabbing a bit extra behind her own ears, Jolene asked Filippo to fill two more glasses, which she carried to the aunts, whom she suspected were of sounder mind than most of them.

***

"Oh, hi. Want one?" Monica asked, shaking an after-dinner cigarette from a pack as she stepped out into the cool evening. If she was surprised to see Jolene standing outside, she gave no indication.

"No thanks," Jolene said. "Actually, I do, but I can't. I quit years ago."

"I think about quitting too, sometimes," Monica said, placing the cigarette between her lips, still perfectly outlined a shade deeper than her gloss. Jolene had tried using lipliner once but ended up looking like a psychopathic clown. "Don't get me wrong, I could quit if I wanted to," Monica added. "But I don't want to. Why quit anything that gives you so much pleasure?"

Jolene smiled, sighing. If she had a dime for every time she'd heard her father say the same thing about drinking, she'd be a wealthy woman.

"So what are you doing out here all alone, if you're not smoking?" Monica asked.

"I just needed some air. I've had a little too much food and wine. That fig tart Lorenzo made was amazing. We don't get fresh figs like that back home."

"Not many people can make a crostata like Lorenzo," she said. "But the Garaventis always overdo it when they have the chance to sit down to a meal together. It doesn't happen too often when you're in the restaurant business."

"Don't I know it!" Jolene said. "I was in the restaurant business, too."

"Really? Lorenzo didn't tell me. Not that Filippo tells his brother much, but I would have thought Luisa would mention something like that to him. Lorenzo and his mother are very close, in case you haven't noticed."

Jolene laughed. "I've noticed lots of things. I just haven't figured any of them out yet." Maybe she had been too hasty in judging Monica by her looks, and by her brusque treatment of Lorenzo. He couldn't be the easiest man to live with. "How long have you and

Lorenzo been married?" she asked.

"Married, five years. Together, thirty." Monica said, rolling her eyes.

"Thirty years? That's not even possible!"

"Oh, yes it is. I was only in elementary school when I stole a kiss from him. God, was he a handsome boy! It was my first love affair with an older man."

Jolene was about to ask how many affairs with older men she'd had since then, but opted for a safer question. "You're from Manarola too, then?" she asked. There was an air of sophistication about Monica which had made Jolene assume she was a city woman.

"Oh, yes. I'm a native Manarolese," she said, pausing to puff on her cigarette. "But I only come back when I have to."

"Where do you and Lorenzo live?"

"In Genoa. That's where I studied architecture. It was a real pain in the ass taking the train back and forth every day, but I was determined to get out of here. Now I'm associated with an architectural firm in the city. I even got to work on a project with Renzo Piano," she said, tossing her head back and shooting a sidelong glance at Jolene, as if to gauge her reaction.

"Wow!" Jolene said. The name was obviously supposed to mean something to her, but didn't. She made a mental note to add it to her list of things to look up.

"Do you want kids?" Monica asked.

Jolene was having a hard time keeping up with this woman; in a matter of hours, she'd gone from being a person Jolene didn't even know existed, to being Lorenzo's wife and Chiara's mother, and now her future sister-in-law asking an extremely personal question.

"At one time, I did," Jolene said. "But then I thought maybe it wasn't meant to be. Part of me was always afraid of bringing an innocent child into the world, just so I could screw up its life."

"Yeah, parents have a knack for that," Monica said, sucking the last of the tobacco from her cigarette, before dropping the butt to the ground and stomping it out with her black boot.

"That's just me, though," Jolene hastened to add, not wanting Monica to think she was in any way referring to her or Lorenzo.

Monica remained silent, still grinding the cigarette butt with her heel. Then she looked up at Jolene, the expression in her eyes imperceptible in the dark. "And now?"

"I don't know. I realize time is running out, but we'll see," Jolene said, her chest tightening with the awareness that a decision could not be delayed indefinitely. "In the meantime, I'm awfully happy that I'll be an aunt to your adorable little girl! I hope you bring her here often."

"Oh, you'll get to see plenty of her," Monica said. "I don't have anyone to take care of her in Genoa during the week, so Lorenzo has to pitch in. He picks her up after nursery school and they come down here by train, so he can work evenings in the Locanda. They use one of those rooms upstairs, the ones they never rent out anymore, so he puts her to bed there. The next morning, they catch an early train back to the city."

Filippo had told her that the trip to Genoa took close to two hours each way, due to all the stops along the local line. No wonder Lorenzo seemed withdrawn; he was probably just exhausted. Jolene wondered how they ever managed to spend time together as a family. "That must be hard on all of you," she said.

"It's all about choices. I made it clear I was not going to live in Manarola after getting my degree, but for some unfathomable reason Lorenzo won't leave. He's stubborn. Luisa says he got it from his father."

"Funny, Vittorio doesn't strike me as a particularly stubborn man," Jolene said.

"Vittorio?" Monica tilted her head, studying Jolene. "You really haven't figured much out yet, have you?"

"Maybe we'd better go back inside now," Jolene said, shivering in the chilly wind.

Monica nodded, smiling with her mouth, but not with her eyes. Maybe it was just the effect of her makeup.

SIX

"No! Not my eyes!" Jolene cried, thrashing to shake off the stray cat clawing her eyes out in her dream. She awoke in a sweat to find Filippo kneeling by her bedside, doing that thing to her eyelids again.

"Are you still mad at me, *Splendore?*" he asked, bouncing onto the mattress. He covered her face with kisses, his bristles scratching her chin and cheeks, his hands sliding between the sheets to tickle her ribs in that sensitive spot, just below her breasts.

"Please don't!" she cried, squirming to get away from him. She was in no mood for games or giggles.

"All I wanted was to see your beautiful smile!" he said, relenting.

"You scared me," she said, draping an arm over her eyes. "I didn't hear you come in." As if not being able to sleep with him wasn't bad enough, knowing he could sneak in on her at any time made it even worse. She wasn't with him, yet she wasn't alone.

"By some miracle, I unlocked that damn door on the first try," he said.

"The 'miracle' was me asking your father for some lubricant and spraying it into the keyhole." For a man, sometimes Filippo was clueless when it came to resolving practical problems. Other times, his behavior was very much a man's; for example, when he'd asked her what was wrong at the end of the evening, but didn't press for an answer when she replied, "Nothing!" then let her walk to her room alone, while he continued chatting with Don Ludovico, by then on his third limoncello.

"You haven't answered my question. Are you mad at me?" Filippo repeated, taking her chin in his hand and forcing her to look at him.

"Yes, I am," she said. Anger was what powered the voice she needed to express her feelings, so she'd held onto it all night in bed and wasn't about to let go of it until she'd had her say. But sadly, as soon as she admitted to it, the anger dwindled like a pin-pricked blister. "Anyway, being mad isn't the problem. The problem is, I feel like I'm being left out of some important conversations, here."

"Okay, so maybe I didn't tell Mamma and Babbo everything beforehand, but I didn't want to overwhelm them, you know?" Filippo said, looking her in the eye. "When you spend your whole life in an isolated village, a place where everyone knows everyone else, you feel like any outsider poses a threat. It's only human."

Jolene's home had been her isolated village, and she knew what it was like to feel threatened. Pulling herself up in bed, she prepared to listen to what else he had to say.

"I knew that if I'd called my parents from overseas to say that I planned to marry an American woman they'd never met, they would have been opposed to it, if only out of principle. And I also knew that as soon as they met you and I explained our plans to them in person, they'd see the obvious. So, yesterday after I dropped you off, I had a chat with each of them, separately. They both suggested you'd make a perfect wife for me—as if it were their idea!"

"You could have talked to me about it," Jolene said, annoyed, rather than angry, at the smugness of the smile nestled between those whiskers he was so proud of. "What happened to all your ideas about being open and honest about everything?"

"*Splendore mio*, you were already so anxious about the move and the trip and everything. I didn't want to overwhelm you, either," Filippo said. "I care too much about you. Do you want me to care less? Is that what you want?"

"Don't be ridiculous. Of course I don't want you to care less."

"*Cara* Jo, if there had been any doubt in my mind that someone would try to prevent our marriage, I wouldn't have brought you back here. We could have gotten married in New York. You were the one who wanted to meet my family first, remember?"

That was true. She'd felt it important to see where Filippo came from, who his people were. She was putting everything on the line this time and couldn't afford to make another mistake.

"You could have spared me Don Ludovico last night, though," she said.

"And you could have avoided showing up at church looking all holy on your first Sunday here, if you didn't want him to think you were interested."

"I can be interested in saying a prayer in church without being interested in the whole Church with a capital c, can't I?" she said. "It simply makes no sense to discuss the wedding with Don Ludovico, if we can't get married in his Church."

"Where else would we get married?"

"Filippo, you know perfectly well I was married before. I told you about Danny."

"So? It doesn't count if it wasn't a Catholic wedding."

"But it was a Catholic wedding!" she said.

"But you said you grew up Presbyterian."

"I did. But I converted for the wedding."

"Oh, great! You could have told me sooner!" Filippo jumped to his feet and walked to the foot of the bed, where he stood glaring down at her.

"I did tell you!" she cried. "Besides, you never once went to church in the months we've been together. You claim the Church is a lair of thieves and pedophiles! Your words, not mine!"

"So?" Filippo shrugged.

"So why would you want to get married in a Church you don't have faith in, or respect, or even like?"

"Because it's the only Church we have! It's what people do around here!" Filippo threw his hands up in the air and began pacing back and forth, as if he could dodge the facts by keeping on the move. "And for once—just once!—I'd like my family to do things like a normal family!"

"Well, I'm sorry," Jolene said, shaking her head, wondering what exactly Filippo's idea of a "normal family" was. "It doesn't matter where we are. It can't be done."

"It has to be done. We'll find a way. I'll talk to Don Ludovico."

"I think you'd have to go a little higher up, Filippo. Like the Pope himself."

"Listen, Jo. You were only married for a couple of years, right?"

"Right." A couple of years, a lifetime ago.

"And you didn't have any kids, right? At least tell me you didn't hide that from me too."

"I didn't hide anything from you! And no, of course I didn't have any kids. As it turned out, Danny didn't want them."

"Tombola! Bingo! I'm pretty sure that invalidates the whole thing."

"What do you mean?"

"Leave it to me," he said, bending over to kiss her on the mouth before walking over to the window and throwing open the shutters, to let in the makings of a splendid fall day. "Now, hurry up and get dressed. Jeans, sneakers, and T-shirt."

"What's the big rush?" she asked. She hadn't even had her coffee yet, and she was already exhausted.

"It's time to go get the grapes!" Filippo said.

"Right now?"

"Yes, right now," he said. "Don't you want to go? You've been pestering me for weeks about making it over here in time for the harvest."

Filippo had described his beautiful vineyards in detail, telling her about how they waited until the grapes reached the perfect balance of sweetness and acidity, then family and friends all gathered to lend a hand, picking as many as they could, as fast as they could, before the weather changed. Jolene had been yearning to participate in her first Italian *vendemmia* ever since, and it wasn't only because of her interest in wine. To her, there was nothing quite as inspiring as taking part in a group initiative. Whether it be neighbors digging each other out after a snowstorm, or piling sandbags along the lakeshore during a spring flood, pitching in and doing her share in a time of need gave her a sense of purpose and belonging.

"Of course I want to go!" she said, jumping out of bed. "I just wish you had told me it would be today. I would have been ready!"

"I thought you liked surprises," Filippo said.

"You know I do!" Jolene replied, hopping to the bathroom with one leg already in her jeans, wondering what else he would spring on her before the day was done.

***

Jolene had hoped to set off on foot, but Filippo insisted that they shouldn't waste their time and energy climbing the twelve hundred steep steps to Volastra. There would be plenty of work to do, he said, and it made more sense to ride up on the little green shuttle bus that connected Manarola to the higher hamlet, and walk straight to the vineyard from there, so that was what they did, without taking a moment to stop and look around. After fifteen minutes of trudging uphill, she began to understand Filippo's reasoning, and the strenuous walk heightened her appreciation of what he was telling her about the work required to create the cultivatable terraces. She imagined the backbreaking effort of clearing, filling and leveling the narrow strips of land; of building mile upon mile of dry stone walls to retain the terraces without the use of mortar to allow for natural drainage; of planting and watering and tending tier upon tier of vines positioned to get just enough ventilation to chase away the damp, and all the sun they could soak up to produce the succulent Albarola, Bosco and Vermentino grapes that went into the Cinque Terre Bianco DOC, and the prized sweet Sciacchetrà, made from the first pick of the best grapes. Those, Filippo explained, had already been harvested and were being dried slowly, naturally, into the golden *passito* raisins that would be pressed in another month or so.

"All of this used to belong to the family," Filippo said, making a sweeping gesture with his arm. "But now we only own that part." The parcel of land Filippo indicated was smaller than she'd imagined, covering a rather narrow and almost vertical strip of a dozen meticulously maintained terraces. It wasn't the unexpectedly small size of the property that made Jolene shake her head, but amazement that each weatherworn stone had been hand-picked and fitted into place to make the walls; each pole hewn, each stake planted, and each wire strung with infinite patience and precision by experienced hands. These vineyards were so very different from the ones back home, where the rows were perfectly aligned and spaced widely enough for the passage of mechanical harvesters. There was certainly no room for those huge tractors here; they'd risk somersaulting all the way down to the sea on such a slope!

"What happened to the other section of land?" she asked, pointing to the far side of the hill, where a plot of roughly the same size appeared to have been abandoned, and entire sections of the stone walls were crumbling. The remnants of many vines resisted, but were overgrown and crawling haphazardly, as if trying to outrun the invasive weeds attempting to strangle them. She felt a deep sense of sorrow at the abandonment, and Filippo seemed to share her feelings, judging by the clench of his jaw and furrowing of his brow as he surveyed the land.

"Oh, you, know, the usual awful things that happen with an inheritance," he said with a sigh. "The land got split up at one point, and that half was sold off about fifteen years ago. The person who bought it died a few years later, though, and it was passed on to his two sons. One of them lives in London and one in Milan. They say they want to sell, but they're asking way too much. Not many people want to buy property you can't build on, and not many people are interested in breaking their backs for a few hundred liters of wine."

"But it's so sad!" Jolene said. "It should all belong to your family. You look after it so well!"

Filippo said nothing more; the story must be too painful for him to recall. He simply shook his head and walked away, leaving Jolene alone with her curiosity as she contemplated the astonishing view. The wind had scattered the clouds before dying during the night, and this morning the Mediterranean seemed as calm as Keuka Lake in the dead of summer. Far below and off into the distance, the water glimmered in the morning sun, unfurling its vibrant hues of blue and green like a hand-painted silk scarf. The only blemish on this perfect day was that it was fall and not spring; that she had not witnessed the grapes growing plump and ripening on their vines; that now their leaves were turning yellow and withering; that when they finished cutting away the fruit, their cycle of life would be over.

"Are you with me, *Splendore*?" Filippo called down to her, several steps above from where she stood.

"Of course I am!" she replied. Catching up with Filippo, she was overpowered by a feeling of strong connection with this land, though she'd never set foot on it before. It perplexed her that Filippo had not told her more about the emotional experience of standing high above the sea on this precious soil, limiting his descriptions to the varieties of vines and their yield. If this were her land, she thought, she would never, ever sell it. She would live on it, she would love on it, she would die on it. She imagined spending her days in the little stone house she spotted in a nearby clearing at the top of the hill. At first glance, it seemed abandoned but as they approached, Jolene spotted two bent figures hobbling about in the vine-covered veranda among teetering piles of red crates and straw baskets. When one of the women looked down at them, waving a crooked walking stick in the air, Jolene sensed something familiar about her.

"Do you see those women up there?" she asked Filippo. "They

can't possibly be your aunts, can they?" She couldn't imagine them having the stamina to make the climb.

"They're not my aunts," Filippo said, blotting his brow with a handkerchief. "I just grew up calling them that."

"Who's aunts are they, then?" Jolene asked.

"No one's, really, if you go by bloodline. But Mamma has always treated them as if they were hers. They live in the same old house in Volastra they've always lived in, but they love puttering around in that hole of a *rustico*. They'd crawl here on their hands and knees rather than miss a harvest."

"God love them!" Jolene cried, accelerating her pace. "Hello, Zia Marta! Hello, Zia Matilde!" she shouted, as they reached the little stone *rustico*. "I didn't expect to see you here!"

"We didn't expect to see you, either," Zia Matilde said. Or maybe it was Zia Marta. Whichever aunt she was, the old woman smiled when Jolene kissed her cheeks, her papery skin moist with perspiration. Her puff of gray hair and the old hand-knit cardigan she wore over a faded apron dress smelled of straw and sunshine and wood smoke.

"We especially didn't expect him," the other aunt added, unsmiling, as Jolene brushed her bony cheeks. "But now that you're here, take some clippers and get moving! The others have been here since sunrise."

Looking around, Jolene spotted a dozen or so figures working in the higher terraces. "Are your parents already here, Filippo?"

"Ha!" Zia Marta said, before he could answer. "Luisa can't handle it, poor dear. And Vittorio knows better than to show his face here."

"Lorenzo's the one running the show," Filippo said, rolling his eyes. "It's his moment of glory."

Jolene wondered what the tone of sarcasm in Filippo's voice was about; what it was that Luisa couldn't handle, and why Vittorio's presence would not be appreciated. But this was not the time to ask; this was the time to observe. Besides, she couldn't wait to get started.

"Let's go join the others!" she said.

"No, it's better if we start down there," Filippo said, pointing to the lower terraces, down at the opposite end of the vineyard from where the others were working. "That way I can show you how it's done without too many people around."

Jolene had been looking forward to seeing who else was there, working shoulder to shoulder with them, getting to know them. She also realized that she was a novice, and the last thing she wanted was to get in the way. Filippo's lack of enthusiasm, now that they were here, made it clear that he'd brought her to the *vendemmia* because she'd been asking about it for weeks, and he was making good on his promise.

"Whatever you think is best," she said, grateful to be there at all.

An hour later, Jolene had concluded that the most practical working position, if not the most comfortable, was on her knees, as Filippo recommended. The vines were grown low to the ground, and in some spots she had to lie down on her stomach or stretch out on her back across the width of the terrace to reach the most elusive bunches at the back. Though the setting was bucolic, she perceived a sense of urgency as the people working higher up clipped and gathered and carried away bushels of fruit. Filippo explained that Lorenzo had begun harvesting in the previous days, but today was pick-it-or-lose-it day, as the weather was due to take a turn for the worse tomorrow. Jolene caught on fast and worked quickly, stopping now and then to admire the tight bunches of grapes so swollen with juice that it seemed their pale green skins would burst. After discarding any pieces of rotten or moldy fruit she came across, Jolene carefully placed the bunches into the wicker basket she dragged along with her. Filippo came by now and then, trading an empty basket for her full one, whose contents he transferred to one of the sturdy red crates standing at the end of each row. Jolene was stretched out on her back, her lower lip protruding with the simultaneous effort of reaching a distant bunch while trying to blow a baby spider off the tip of her nose, when she felt a tug on her ankles.

"Hey, you!" she cried, as the hands dragged her forward by her feet, scraping her back along the rough ground until her butt was resting on the edge of the terrace, her legs dangling over the wall.

"Hey, you!" Filippo mimicked in a girl's voice. He was standing on the terrace below the one she was working on, one eyebrow raised in his sexy stare: two for worry, one for sexy.

"I have work to do!" Jolene giggled, sitting up to face the top half of the tall figure silhouetted by the sun. "What do you want from me?"

"A kiss." Filippo plucked a withered grape leaf from her tangled hair, cupped her face in his hands, and drew it close to his.

A kiss was something she could definitely find time for. Apart from the earliest days of their still young relationship, Filippo had never been big on kissing, unless he harbored more serious intentions. Cuddly hugs and affectionate pecks were the daily bread of conquered love, while displays of passion were relegated to the bedroom. Only in bed did he ravage her mouth in that savage way he had, all sharp teeth and stiff bristles cutting and scouring her face raw. They were a small price to pay for a bit of ardor, though, and Jolene had been craving a real kiss. Between the preparations to move, followed by the exhausting journey and the separate sleeping arrangements, they hadn't made love in over a week, and the estrangement had heightened her feeling of insecurity, making her feel less connected to Filippo just when she needed him most. She was in dire need of intimacy, but her urges went beyond the physical. She yearned to feel so full of Filippo that there would be no room for the ghosts of her former selves to haunt her. She wanted to be here, and to be his, just as Jolene.

Filippo also had something more than a peck in mind now. Wrapping his arms around her, he cradled her head in the palm of a hand, fingering the hair tied back in a ponytail, the way he liked her to wear it when they made love. He tugged at the ponytail now, gently at first, then gave it a yank, snapping her head back as she cried out. His lips pressed down on her open mouth, his tongue flicking over hers as he placed his other hand behind her buttocks, pulling her closer. He held her tight and kissed her hard, and Jolene moaned, all her tensions and concerns losing their grip on her, freeing her to slide away to that place where nothing mattered but her sensations. Filippo dragged her to the very edge of the stone wall while Jolene's pulse quickened, her blood hot as it pumped through her veins, making her feel alive, desirable, and full of desire. She wrapped her legs around his waist, her pubic area pressed against him through the denim of her jeans. Filippo swayed his hips slowly at first, inviting her to rub against him, then thrusting his pelvis in time with her grinding motion. Jolene sucked in her breath as a wave of pleasure washed over her, the spasm making her spine arch, her heart pound, her cheeks burn. Tossing her head back, she gazed up at the azure autumn sky, laughing with the pure joy of making love in the open air. There was nothing that aroused her more than nature.

"Why don't we crawl under the vines and fool around some

more?" she whispered in Filippo's ear. "I think I can come up with something you might enjoy."

"Are you crazy?" he said, removing her arms from his shoulders. "Out here in the open?"

"How about if we just lie down for a minute? With our clothes on?"

"The others will be looking for us," Filippo said. "In fact, we'd better go join them now." He kissed the top of her head, tucked in his shirttails, then ran his fingers over his whiskers, as if checking to see whether any new tufts of hair had sprouted while he'd been distracted.

Jolene sighed, sorry that the romantic interlude was already over but grateful for the intense and unexpected pleasure it had given her, and she hoped this was a sign that Filippo might become more receptive to her desire for love in the open air. They didn't have to actually make love, she'd explained to him, just kiss and engage in a little foreplay. She'd rowed him to hidden coves and walked him to remote woods in her crusade to turn him on to the sensuality of the outdoors, but up until now he'd resisted her advances, remaining steadfast in his belief that sex belonged in the bedroom.

"What about these baskets?" she called to him now, but he'd already started up the hill. "Shouldn't we carry them up?"

"Don't worry," he replied. "Someone will collect them later."

Brushing some leaves and twigs off of her clothes, Jolene redid her ponytail, then hurried after him on unsteady legs. She was still too full of afterglow, and the sun was too warm, and the incline too steep for her to ask any more questions. By the time they reached the upper terraces where the others were working, they were both short of breath and perspiring. Jolene stopped to say hello to the first and only person she recognized: little Chiara, who was busy transferring grapes, one bunch at a time, from a wicker basket to a plastic crate.

"Hi there, Chiara!" Jolene said. "No nursery school today?"

"Nope!" the child replied. "I gotta work today!"

"What are you doing?"

Chiara hesitated before answering, as though she were evaluating the risks of revealing the nature of such an important job to someone who was only one notch up from being a stranger. "Counting the bunches," she finally said, then resumed her task. "*Uno, quattro, cinque, due...*" Jolene laughed.

"Oh, good. There's Lorenzo," Filippo said. His brother was walking away from them, toward the far end of the property, bearing a crate of grapes on his shoulder. "I have to go talk to him, but I'll be back soon. You'll be fine here, right?"

Before she could reply, Filippo strode away, now and then raising an arm in greeting to some old men he passed, more a salute than a wave. Scanning the hillside for Monica, Jolene discovered that there were no other women picking grapes, and that the average age of the men was on the wrong side of seventy. They struck her as a happy and healthy lot, though, all lean and limber and looking like they could easily carry on for another twenty or thirty years.

"*Ancora!* I need more!" Chiara said, holding up the empty basket.

Jolene smiled. The sight of a child being entertained by something other than an electronic device was uplifting, though it made Jolene slightly nervous that she'd been left without supervision in a place where it would be easy for her to take a nasty tumble. Chiara shook her basket at Jolene impatiently, letting her know that she was the supervisor here, and that it was time to get back to work. Down Jolene went on her hands and knees again, picking up where someone else had left off, keeping one eye on the little girl while feeling a dozen eyes on her. Those eyes might be dull with age, but they were sharp as needles on her back as she crouched to clip the grapes. Filippo had been right about giving her the chance to grasp the technique before subjecting her to the men's criticism.

"Jolene!" a voice called from behind her.

Butt high in the air, she looked over her shoulder and was embarrassed to find Lorenzo presiding over her backside. "Oh! Hi!" she cried, sliding out from under the vine and hopping to her feet.

"You didn't have to come," Lorenzo said, taking a red bandana from his back pocket and mopping the sweat from his face and neck.

"But I wanted to," Jolene said. "If I'd missed it I would have had to wait until next year."

"Women don't usually help out here," Lorenzo said.

Jolene's face fell. "Filippo didn't tell me that. If I'm in the way, just say the word. I'll go visit with the aunts." She'd be pissed, and think him a jerk, but she'd do what was expected of her. For now, anyway.

"No, you can stay. What I meant was that women don't usually want to help."

"Chiara's a girl and she's here," Jolene said, smiling as she pointed at the child who, in absence of new bunches had transferred half of those already in the crate to the ground, and was busy putting them back again. "*Tre, dieci, uno…*" she counted.

"I thought the *vendemmia* was a family tradition. I was expecting to see Monica, too," Jolene said. "Isn't she here?"

"Monica's in Genoa. At the studio," he said. "Not that she would have helped anyway. It's not her kind of thing."

"I guess it's not for everyone."

"Right." Lorenzo shrugged. "Look at Filippo. How long did he last? An hour?"

"What do you mean?" she asked, glancing around. If Filippo had left her to speak with Lorenzo, and Lorenzo was here, where was he?

"Didn't he tell you?" Lorenzo said.

"Tell me what?"

"He said he had some things to take care of and that he'd be back later this afternoon."

Jolene swallowed, but the lump in her throat wouldn't budge. When he'd said he would be back soon, she was thinking minutes, not hours. What could he possibly have to take care of that was so urgent, and why hadn't he told her about it? She hoped she didn't look as stupid as she felt; she hoped the flush of anger scalding her face would be camouflaged by the effects of the heat.

"So, I guess I'll be taking my orders from you," she said, attempting a smile.

"I don't give orders," Lorenzo said. "But what I suggest is that you come down to the *rustico* with me and Chiara and the rest of us. It's time for some lunch."

"Already? It's barely noon!" Jolene said.

"Meaning that some of us have been working for five solid hours," he said. "*Andiamo!*" he called out to Chiara, who trotted over, as sure-footed as a mountain goat.

Down at the *rustico*, Zia Matilda and Zia Marta (Jolene had remembered correctly; Matilda was the one who smiled, and Marta was the grumbler) had set the weathered wooden table in the veranda with mismatched plates, jelly jars for glasses, and forks so distorted they might have been left over from those experiments in telekinesis that had fascinated Jolene as a child when she saw them on TV. Conservation must be a way of life here, not just an obsession of oldsters who'd survived tough times. Acquiring new things and eliminating the old, even disposing of daily waste, was more complicated than elsewhere. Jolene would be relieved if she was never forced to eat off another plastic plate again.

But as she stood there watching the men taking turns pumping water from a well to freshen up, she was feeling rather like an abandoned possession herself. Could Filippo possibly think that a little smooching among the vines was enough to placate her for his behavior last night, with sufficient credit left over to compensate for today's disappearing act? When the last man in line backed away, shaking his dripping hands in the air, Jolene stepped up to the pump and doused her face and head, hoping the cool water would extinguish the unpleasant thoughts sizzling in her brain. Patting her face with her damp hands, she already felt calmer, as she looked at the little stone house, admiring its simplicity. With a slate roof, wooden shutters, and a rudimentary door, it offered shelter, but little else. Peeking in the open window, she saw that the one-room abode featured a stone hearth and was sparsely furnished with two cots, a small table and two wooden chairs, but there was no sink or toilet, and no lights. Lined up on some shelves built into a niche were a few tin canisters, probably containing staples such as salt and sugar, and a row of mason jars filled with something red, mostly likely tomato preserves. It was clear that the waking hours were meant to be spent outdoors here, working the land and taking breaks in the shade of the cane-covered veranda, and that any cooking was done over an open fire or in the brick oven, with the aid of a more convenient two-ring camp stove on which a large pot was bubbling. She was wondering who, if anyone, had actually lived in this *rustico*, when Zia Marta hobbled over to her, shoving a chunk of stinky goat cheese, a foot-long salami, and a sharp knife into her arms.

"Start slicing!" Zia Marta ordered.

Jolene nodded, relieved to have an assignment. She was good with knives, and in short order had reduced half of the salami into perfect slices of just the right thickness, then attacked the cheese and bread. She felt Zia Marta's eyes on her before she saw them, as she gestured for Jolene to hand over the knife, replacing it with a large fork and spoon.

"Start serving!" Zia Marta said as Lorenzo set down a large aluminum pot which he had carried over from the camp stove. Jolene dished out the pasta, the smell of the simple tomato sauce making her stomach growl.

"Serve yourself now," a man said, approaching her from behind. Turning, she smiled, on seeing that it was Giobatta. As the first person she'd met in Italy, she liked to think that he hadn't only picked her up, but welcomed her, on her arrival. Gesturing for her to sit with him, then pouring them both some white wine from a carafe, he also made her feel looked after.

"This is the stuff from last year," he told her. "This year's grapes are even better." The other men concurred, nodding and commenting as they drank thirstily from their jars. Between sips of wine and mouthfuls of more of the best food Jolene had ever eaten, she answered the few questions the men asked her, spending the rest of the time looking and listening and learning, occasionally catching Lorenzo's eye as he conversed with Chiara, and deducing that although he didn't appear to be Filippo's ideal big brother or Monica's perfect husband, Chiara couldn't ask for a more devoted father.

With some editing, the colorful scene she'd stitched together from Filippo's descriptions of family and townsfolk picking grapes together, talking and laughing and eating and drinking around a big table together like in some movie, was unfolding before her eyes. The only thing missing was the male protagonist.

Hours later, a sense of serenity settled over Jolene as the work in the vineyard drew to a close. The splendid setting and gorgeous day, the repetitive movements and the companionable silence, interrupted only by Chiara who kept coming to visit her, made the hurt Jolene had been harboring seem petty and irrelevant. She'd been looking forward to the harvest, and he'd made it possible for her to participate, so for that she should be grateful. If he couldn't stay, he must have had a good reason, but right now she wasn't even interested in hearing it. Right now her heart was so full with positive emotions that there was no room for the negative.

Transferring her last basket of grapes to the last crate, she smiled instead of groaning as she pulled herself up straight, consoled by the fact that the ache in her back would soon fade, but the memories of this day would be indelible. The golden afternoon drenched the hillside, fashioning haloes around the shapes of the men, rendering them supple and ageless as with one arm reaching across their heads to steady their loads, they carted away crates of grapes on their shoulders, their lengthening shadows trailing them. As Lorenzo approached her, she noticed that he too seemed different in this light, as if he hailed from another time, like a figure in an antique painting who had abandoned his canvas, walking away while his muscles still glistened with the fresh paint strokes of the masterful hand that had designed him.

"That's it, Jolene!" Lorenzo said. "Thanks for everything, including keeping an eye on Chiara."

"It was my pleasure. Where is Chiara anyway? I haven't seen her in a while."

"She's sound asleep in the *rustico*. She's the last thing I have to carry down to the truck."

Jolene smiled. "What happens next?"

"We take the grapes to the wine press down the road. We don't have our own facilities anymore, but I belong to the cooperative."

Despite being filthy from crawling around on the ground, and her hands being sticky and stained, and her nostrils being filled with the cloying smell of ripe grapes, and her muscles and joints aching from all the bending and reaching, Jolene was sorry the day had come to an end. A sigh of regret escaped her.

"Are you all right?" Lorenzo asked.

"Yes, I just wish it wasn't over already!" Jolene said. "I feel like I hardly got to know the grapes, and now they're gone."

"Most growers can't wait for this part to be over," Lorenzo said. "It's a huge relief when you see the grapes through to maturation without losing the harvest to early rains or a fluke hailstorm or some disease. Every time I make it to this stage it feels like a miracle. But I know what you mean. I miss looking after my grapes once they're gone. But then there's the wine to keep an eye on, and remember them by."

Jolene let her eyes wander over the terraces where they had worked one last time, then at the section of abandoned land that was in the shadow, no longer illuminated by the setting sun. "It's too bad about that land," she said.

"What do you mean by that?" Lorenzo asked, the wistfulness gone from his voice.

"About the way it got split up and sold off."

"Yeah, well, Ma did what she thought was right, it was her land,

and I can't hold that against her. What I'll never get over is what happened afterward."

"But wasn't there any way that—" Jolene began.

"Look Jolene, if you want to know anything more about this story, ask Filippo, okay?" he said.

Jolene blushed; she hadn't meant to pry, or offend anyone.

Lorenzo's gaze shifted, looking past her. "Parli del diavolo e spuntano le corna," he said.

"What?"

"It's an expression. Speak of the devil, and out come the horns. Or something like that. Here comes your boyfriend now."

The sunlight was hastening its retreat from the hillside where they stood, taking with it the glow that enveloped them. When its reflection faded from Lorenzo's eyes, they appeared tired and slightly sad. Jolene was tired too, and sad that the sight of Filippo approaching, waving a hand in the air, irritated her.

"I'm sorry Filippo didn't stay to help, Lorenzo," she said. "Brothers should work together at a family harvest."

"He's under no obligation," Lorenzo replied.

***

"You do realize that you embarrassed me, don't you?" Jolene said, flopping down on the bed. She had remained silent during their return to Manarola, trying to hold onto the sense of well-being that had infused her that afternoon as she worked. Filippo didn't seem interested in hearing about her experience, anyway; his chatter was a blatant tactic to prevent her from asking one of the dozens of questions he probably did not want to answer.

"How, exactly, did I do that, when I wasn't even there?" Filippo said, walking over to the window and throwing it open, then leaning out, his back to her. The temperature had plummeted since sunset, and despite the chill of exhaustion, Jolene welcomed the fresh breeze, thinking it more suitable for airing differences than the mustiness that gathered in the room every time she locked it up.

"That's precisely the point! It was the way you walked off without bothering to tell me you were leaving, or why, that embarrassed me!" she said. "If you didn't want to stay, all you had to do was tell me. You should have let me decide whether I wanted to go with you, or stay without you."

"Look, Jolene, some things are difficult for me to explain. I'm coping with a lot of changes right now, too, and I'm only asking two things of you: to understand me, and to trust me."

"But I can't understand what I don't know, and I can't trust you if I keep getting the feeling you're hiding things from me."

Filippo pivoted to face her. "You're right," he said. "I'm sorry. But I was the one who felt embarrassed. There were things I didn't know how to explain to you."

"What things?" Jolene cried, her voice tight with exasperation. "Just tell me, for God's sake!"

"Well, I realized that I may have misled you with all that talk about the family vineyards when we first met. If I gave you the impression that it was a bigger operation, it was only because I wanted to impress you, not deceive you."

"Big doesn't impress me, Filippo. What fascinated me was the idea of your family tending the vines together, generation after generation, and everyone pitching in to harvest the grapes. I even brought up the idea of letting guests at the Locanda participate, remember? Why did you let me run off at the mouth about offering them an authentic family winemaking experience, and so on, and so forth?"

"Then there's the thing about the inheritance," he continued without answering. "It's more complicated than I let on this morning, but I didn't want to bog you down with old feuds that didn't concern you."

"I asked Lorenzo about that," she said.

"You did?" Filippo asked, his eyebrows shooting up. "What did he say?"

"Not much. Just that your mother did what she thought was right, but that he still can't get over what happened afterward. He told me to ask you if I wanted to know more."

"Did he mention how Mamma inherited the land in the first place, or why part got sold?"

"No," Jolene said. "What happened?"

Filippo let out a weary sigh, as if he had already explained too many things to too many people in one day. He didn't speak until after he'd stroked his beard for a moment, like he did when he had a problem to solve.

"The whole thing was my father's fault," he blurted at last, the words tumbling out of his mouth as if they were running away from something. "Babbo couldn't stand the thought of having land to look after. You know how some people get seasick? Well, he gets land sick. The only place he wants to be is out on the water, and the only thing he wants to do is fish. He pestered Mamma until she finally gave into him and sold off that parcel to buy him a fishing boat. He and Giobatta are out fishing practically every day before dawn. I think he'd live on that boat if he didn't have the Locanda, but cleaning and cooking his catch gives him an excuse to spend more time with it. He even talks to those fish more than he talks to Mamma!"

"Why did your mother divide up the land instead of selling it all, if your father didn't want to have anything to do with it?"

"Because the other half went to her precious son," Filippo said. "She made it clear that she would never let anyone get their hands on that."

"Don't you mean sons?" Jolene asked.

"No, I don't. I mean son. Singular. As in Lorenzo. That's the reason I didn't feel like staying there. Those weren't my grapes being harvested. They were Lorenzo's."

"Really?" Jolene said, propping herself on her elbows to listen to his explanation. "Why were you excluded from your share of the land?"

"That's something you'd have to ask Mamma," he said. "She's always treated Lorenzo better than me, and she's always loved him more than me. That's how it's always been, and always will be."

Jolene wished there was one person who would tell her everything she needed to know, instead of bouncing her questions over to the next person.

"But I'll show them both what I'm worth," Filippo continued. "I swear I will. And you'll help me, won't you?"

"Of course I will. And you will show them. We will," Jolene said. "You didn't have to run away, though."

Filippo walked over to her, taking her hand in his. "Please try to understand," he said. "I felt ashamed toward you, and jealous of Lorenzo. I would have ruined your day if I'd stayed."

"I don't care about who owns what, Filippo. What I care about is us. That's what I came here for. Us. Remember that."

It disturbed Jolene that he'd been less than honest, but she was painfully aware of how the way a parent treated a child carried over into adulthood. You could realize it, and live with it, but there was no escaping it. Filippo looked like a little boy now, with those eyebrows sketching sob stories across the vast tableau of his forehead. It was difficult for her to stay angry with that little boy. Especially when he kneeled down on the floor next to the bed and, resting his head in her lap, whispered, *"Ti amo, Splendore.* I'm sorry."

SEVEN

"I hear from Lorenzo that you were a big help with the *vendemmia*," Luisa said, drying a wine glass with one of her ever-present linen towels, then holding the glass up to the light to check for water spots. She rubbed some more, inspected it again, rubbed some more; finally satisfied, she placed the glass next to the lineup on a shelf and set about making the cappuccino she'd been kind enough to offer Jolene. Except for when they were eating, Jolene had never seen her in repose, and even then she always seemed ready to spring to action. Now that Vittorio was getting on in years and Lorenzo couldn't make it from Genoa until the afternoon, Filippo had explained to her that the restaurant was currently only open in the evenings, but Luisa always had her hands full just the same, serving drinks and snacks all day long at the bar.

"I wouldn't have missed it for the world!" Jolene said, welcoming the opportunity for a chat, but at the same time hoping Filippo would turn up before she ran out of safe subjects to talk about. "I've been stiff as a board the past few days, though. I really have to start practicing yoga again."

Luisa set a perfect cappuccino in front of her, then returned to her glasses.

"Thank you very much," Jolene said, admiring the frothy, cinnamon-sprinkled foam that begged to be sipped. In lieu of yoga, a cappuccino could also work wonders for restoring one's inner balance and strength.

"I used to love it, too," Luisa sighed, shaking out her towel.

"What, a cappuccino?" Jolene asked, taking her nose out of the cup and wiping a splotch of foam from its tip.

The quizzical look on Luisa's face told her that she hadn't been talking about cappuccino drinking at all.

"Sorry, I mean, you used to love yoga?" Jolene said. "Really?"

Luisa's stare was still puzzled. She'd got it wrong again. What could this woman who'd spent the last several decades locked up in her Locanda possibly know about yoga?

"Oh...no...wait!" Jolene stammered, realizing she couldn't blow her third chance to get it right. "You were talking about the grape harvest, weren't you?"

"At one time just being on that land used to comfort me," Luisa said, unfazed by Jolene's mental gymnastics. "But I haven't been able to go up there in ages."

"Well, it's definitely strenuous work," Jolene said, twisting to alleviate a kink in her hip, and at the same time prove that she could relate to Luisa's pain.

"Oh, it's not the strenuous work that keeps me away. I've never been afraid of that," Luisa said, taking another glass from the drying rack. "It's too painful in other ways. I still feel the loss."

Jolene was surprised, even honored, that Luisa would confide in her. It was the first time she'd been alone with the woman for more than five minutes, and only because Filippo was late. From her comment, she suspected that Luisa was more attached to the land than either son had let on, but if that was the case, why had she given in to Vittorio and sold half of it off for a fishing vessel? And why had she cut Filippo out of his share of what remained? Jolene's mind may wander off occasionally, but it was present enough to know that these were not questions she could ask her now, if ever.

"I think I can understand that," Jolene said. Recalling the sensations she'd experienced in the vineyard but hadn't yet articulated, she was inspired to share them with Luisa, hoping they would uplift her, too. "I felt a very special sense of privilege up there," she said. "As if dedicating those few hours to the vines and their fruit was a way of honoring the land and the generations of people who had cared for it. Do you know what I mean?"

Luisa nodded, stuffing the dish towel into the glass, turning it round and round and round.

"And even though the work was tiring, it felt as though all the energy I was putting into it was coming back to me, revitalizing me," Jolene continued. "I think I know what you mean when you say the land comforted you, because while I was up there, some things that were really bothering me seemed irrelevant," she added, amazed at how easy it was to talk to her future mother-in-law.

Still silent, Luisa nodded more emphatically, rubbed the glass more furiously.

"It also heightened my awareness of what a delicate balance life is, and how everything can change in an instant. Just like a freak hailstorm can wipe out a year's harvest, any one of us can die before we get to fulfill our purpose."

"There!" Luisa cried, her hands shaking as she held up the glass, now broken in two. "See what happens when you start thinking about certain things?" Throwing her arms in the air, she sent the legless chalice and headless stem crashing to the floor. "See what happens?" she repeated, holding her hand under the faucet, the bloody water splashing the draining rack full of clean glasses.

"Oh no, you've cut yourself!" Jolene cried, the shattered glass crunching beneath her sneakers as she hurried behind the bar to assist her.

"The cut is nothing," Luisa cried, waving Jolene away with her towel. "You can go now."

In her line of work, it would take more than a broken glass to upset Luisa. It must be Jolene's fault; it must have been something she'd said, running off at the mouth like a fool. But what?

"At least let me sweep up," she offered.

"No, no, just go!" Luisa said, staring down at the sink splashed with blood, her jaw trembling as she wrapped her hand in the dish towel.

"Really," Jolene said. "Please let me take care of it."

"No thank you, I said!" Luisa snapped, finally looking up at Jolene, her blue-gray eyes misty. "I just want to be left alone." Then she closed her eyes and rested her hands on her abdomen, the wounded hand cupped in the sound one, and began taking slow, deep breaths through her nose, in and out, in and out.

"Of course," Jolene mumbled, wondering, as she eased the door shut behind her, what she had just witnessed.

After standing outside for a few minutes to see if Filippo showed up, she headed toward the harbor, hoping she'd run into him along the way. As much as she hated to admit it, he was right about the fact that sooner or later she'd have to get a phone. Not that she'd had the opportunity yet; Filippo kept telling her to wait until they could go to La Spezia or Genoa together, where they could buy the phone and whatever else she needed in one trip.

The smell of the tiny harbor hidden among the rocks was already becoming familiar to Jolene's nostrils. As she stood watching the activity below, she caught whiffs of engine grease and diesel fuel and boat paint; of drying fishnets and rocks covered with algae and barnacles. At the south end of the harbor, to her left, was the jetty where the passenger ferry tied up, sea and weather conditions permitting, only long enough for tourists to hop on or off; opposite the jetty, to her right, was a concrete ramp used to launch the smaller boats, and in between the two loomed a modern hoist, a godsend to the owners of the parked crowd of larger craft. A main attraction, at this hour, was the seafront restaurant, whose enclosed veranda and open-air terrace afforded a view of it all. Jolene had talked to Filippo about trying it out some time, saying it would be a good idea to compare prices, service, quality and specialties to those of the Locanda, but he had rejected her suggestion, saying that no one in his family ever took their meals anywhere else in town other than the Locanda. It would look bad if they didn't eat their own food, he said, further baffling her with his comment that they could learn everything they needed to know about the competition on TripAdvisor.

Still seeing no sign of Filippo, Jolene wondered whether he had already discovered his distraught mother, and figured out what was ailing her. Sidestepping a group of tourists, she picked her way to a rock where she could sit in peace and try to make sense of Luisa's reaction. Hugging her knees to her chest, she stared out at the sea to mull over their conversation, but was soon distracted by the tempting aromas wafting down from the restaurant: basil, the king of herbs, mingled in the air with garlic and onion and the smells of fresh fish being grilled, baked, or fried. Though she'd placated her hunger with the cappuccino, her stomach growled its disapproval of her resolve to skip lunch. It was then that she decided that just because Filippo didn't approve of an idea didn't mean it should be discarded. His tendency to jump in and take the lead had gone from reassuring to overbearing in a matter of days, which made her run the risk of becoming passive, and that was a road she never wanted to go down again. She was a grown woman, she knew how to make a reservation, and she had the money to pay for a dinner. She would surprise Filippo and take him to that restaurant to celebrate the day he finally submitted the application for European Union financing that he'd been working on since their arrival. That much she could do, since he wasn't allowing her to pitch in with the paperwork. He'd been devoting hours a day to the project, most of them holed up in his old room at his parents' house, where, he said, he concentrated best, in his own space, at his own pace. Every time Jolene offered to help, he replied that the red tape would be incomprehensible to her; that he just needed a little more time to hunt down the data he needed from the local tourist board, the province, the region, and who knew where else. Surely she could put numbers into a spreadsheet, she insisted, or accompany him when he hopped on a train to queue up at one of the offices whose inefficiency he complained about, but the answer was always the same: Not now, Jolene. Be patient, Jolene.

During this preliminary stage, Filippo was also cautious about involving his parents and Lorenzo, and instructed her not to speak to them about his initiatives. If he didn't succeed, no one would have anything to throw back in his face, but if his project were to be approved, they stood to receive substantial funding for the refurbishing of Locanda Luisa. The time had come to raise the standards of the old-fashioned restaurant and run-down accommodations, in alignment with the expectations of visitors to an internationally acclaimed tourist destination, particularly in light of the Cinque Terre's official status as a Unesco World Heritage Site. In addition, Filippo hinted, it was not unrealistic to think that his success would pave the way for substantial improvements in the village itself, which could lead to further growth.

From her perch on the rock, Jolene had the impression that too many people had already discovered the Cinque Terre as it was. She adored the authenticity of Manarola and had heard that some of the more accessible towns like Monterosso were being over-exploited, now that they offered facilities such as parking for tour buses. She'd told Filippo that whatever the outcome, they must do everything in their power to make sure that the unique atmosphere of this characteristic village would be preserved; that its quirks and inconveniences would not be smoothed over for the sole purpose of attracting even larger masses. That was the thought that gave her the patience to wait it out.

Meanwhile, Jolene had used the time to do some research of her own. She hadn't had the opportunity to talk to Filippo about it yet, but yesterday while he was locked up filling out forms, she had run into Giobatta, and over morning coffee mentioned that she would like to see the other apartments. Happy to oblige—at least he said he was happy, although he didn't smile—Giobatta had taken her on a tour through the paths and alleys of the village, climbing up and down the steps and ramps, cursing under his breath as he jiggled unlabeled keys into stubborn locks, restraining Jolene from pushing open rotten shutters out of fear they would fall from their hinges and crash on the head of an unlucky passerby. By the time they'd visited all fifteen of the other "suites," Jolene could only agree with Filippo that they could not be rented out in their current condition—Suite 16 was a jewel by comparison—but each one of them boasted a certain charm. In each room, she'd paused to pencil some drawings in her sketchpad, which she planned to elaborate on later and study for ideas. By prodding Giobatta for information, she learned that the original floors, trim and window sills in slate were a hundred years old or more, as were the dulled brass fixtures and pocked marble sinks. In one room, she admired a lovely old desk and straight-back chair in Italian walnut, and remarked how she would love to have something like them in Suite 16. Giobatta shrugged his shoulders and nodded, his expression similar to that of an exhausted Ikea shopper too overwhelmed with options to decide anything.

As interesting as these reflections were, however, they had nothing to do with Luisa's behavior, which still stumped Jolene as she sat there on her rock, watching a boat approach under the vigilant escort of a pair of gawking gulls. As the boat drew near, she realized that the man she'd been thinking about was the one at the prow, Giobatta himself, while Vittorio manned the outboard. Though not nearly as large or lovely as the impeccably maintained *gozzo* she'd seen Giobatta fuss over, this one had the same typical keel of the Ligurian fishing boat. She wondered whose boat it was, because if it was Vittorio's, he'd either sold half the vineyard for a pittance or bought the boat from a pirate. She needed to get to the bottom of that story, and when she did, she prayed that she wouldn't end up hating Vittorio for what he'd done, because she really wanted to love him.

When Giobatta tossed some scraps into the air, the seagulls swooped down on them, flapping and cawing. Jolene was curious to see how Vittorio would behave in his natural element, beyond the range of a wife he barely spoke to; of two grown sons who still vied for his attention; of a kitchen where he'd spent his life fulfilling people's orders. When he cut the engine, Giobatta tossed a line to a stubby man with trousers rolled up to his knees who duck-walked down the boat ramp. Jolene couldn't make out what they shouted to one another in Manarolese dialect, but when the arthritic Vittorio hopped ashore with the agility of a teenager, she could tell he was satisfied with the morning's expedition.

"Vittorio!" Jolene called out, waving. "Giobatta!"

"Ah, my *Americanina!*" Vittorio boomed, loud enough for everyone in the vicinity to hear, making Jolene giggle. Standing up, she brushed off her numb butt and hurried to greet him. Giobatta, preparing to land the boat with the assistance of the duck-man, found the time to tip his cap at her.

"Look what I have here!" Vittorio cried, water sloshing in the plastic bucket he toted. "Tonight I make *risotto nero!*"

Peering into the bucket, Jolene saw a bluish blob of slimy bodies entangled in a mass of tentacles. "Ugh!" she gasped, wrinkling her nose and retreating. "What are those?"

"*Seppie!*" Vittorio said.

"Ah, squid!" She'd never seen freshly caught squid, though Evan had gone through a phase of experimentation with calamari. He'd bought them by the bagful, pre-sliced into rings and frozen, taking their restaurant on another detour from the gastronomical journey she'd dreamed of, based on locally sourced farm products.

"Just look at how gorgeous these babies are!" Vittorio exclaimed, raising the bucket and shoving it under her nose. "Look!"

Filippo was right; Vittorio did act besotted with the creatures he'd lured from the sea, and she couldn't insult him by saying how stinky and ugly she found them. She tried to think of them cleaned, cooked and served up in a tasty risotto, and was curious to learn how such a transformation could come about. This was as good a time as any for her first Italian cooking lesson and she was about to ask Vittorio if she could watch him prepare the risotto when he slapped his forehead with the heel of his hand, dropping the bucket to the ground with a splash.

"*Madonna santa!*" he cried, a pained look on his face. "Now that I see you, I'm remembering something I promised him I wouldn't forget."

"Promised who what?" Jolene asked, looking on as Vittorio wriggled his thick hands beneath his waterproof coveralls to search his pockets.

"Here it is!" he said, holding up an envelope. Using his hand as an iron and his chest as a board, he smoothed out the envelope before handing it to her. "You can read for yourself."

"A letter?" she asked, taking it from him. "For me? Where did this come from?"

"Filippo gave it to me. To give to you. To tell the truth, I was supposed to leave it for you at the Locanda before I went out fishing." He shrugged an apology. "I'm old. I forget things."

"Why did Filippo write me a letter?" she asked, too perplexed to open the envelope. Then it occurred to her. Before leaving Ithaca, she had mentioned to Filippo that one downside of going back to Italy with him instead of continuing their relationship long-distance for a spell was that they wouldn't need to write to each other, which in turn meant that she'd have no old-fashioned love letters stashed away in a box, to fondle and reread and reminisce over with nostalgia, five or ten or twenty years from now. Maybe he wanted to apologize in writing for not dedicating more time to her lately, or maybe he simply wanted to tell her how much she meant to him. A romantic letter was just what she needed right now.

"It was still dark out when he left," Vittorio said. "But I always get up early, too. You know what they say, '*chi dorme non piglia pesci.*' How do you say that in English? He who sleeps does not catch fish?"

"'The early bird catches the worm' is close enough," Jolene replied, more concerned with "when he left" part of Vittorio's comment than the adage. "Where did he have to go so early?"

"Milano."

"Milan? He went to Milan without even telling me?" she cried, but as soon as the words left her lips, she regretted showing how unaware of his movements she was, and how upset that made her.

"He did tell you," Vittorio said. "In the letter. You have every right to be angry—but with me, not with him."

Jolene didn't want to be angry with anyone; what she wanted was an explanation. Ripping open the envelope she read: "*Buongiorno,*

Splendore! I'm trying to resolve some problems and the fastest way is for me to go to Milan in person. Catching the early train and didn't want to wake you. See you later. *Ti amo,* Filippo."

With all the fuss Filippo had been making about finding a day to go to Genoa together, couldn't he have invited her to go to Milan with him instead? She certainly didn't mind getting up early; he knew that. She had spent her life getting up early.

"Is something wrong?" Vittorio asked.

Not trusting herself to speak, Jolene shook her head.

"Let me tell you something, *Americanina,*" Vittorio said. "Filippo's the most loyal man you could find." The fact that Jolene hadn't questioned his loyalty made her wonder whether she should, as she watched Vittorio pat his pockets again, fishing out a lighter and a pack of cigarettes with the n logo and brand name "*Nazionali*" stamped on it in blue. After glancing around, he shook out a cigarette and lit up. It was the kind with no filter, and by the way he inhaled, she could tell that smoking was more of a pleasure for him than a habit.

"As for that apartment in Milan, it's caused way more trouble than it's worth," Vittorio continued, dropping his arm to his side, the cigarette cupped in the palm of his hand.

She'd always assumed Filippo had rented a place during the years he'd studied and worked in Milan, but he'd never mentioned it being the source of any trouble. She had no idea what Vittorio was talking about.

"Why do you say that?" she asked, hoping to make him fill in some blanks. "About the apartment?"

Vittorio shook his head, wrinkling his forehead as he took another drag from his cigarette. "Filippo didn't come home to Manarola for a whole year, on account of that apartment. His mother wouldn't speak to him, and neither would Lorenzo. Of course, none of that mess would have happened if Filippo hadn't gotten it into his head to go to university, when there was plenty of work to keep us all busy right here. And as if that wasn't bad enough, he had to go to Milan, when there's a perfectly good university right in Genoa! It was good enough for Monica, wasn't it? And she's a picky one."

Filippo had told her how suffocated he'd felt as a teenager in Manarola, and she could understand why an intelligent and restless young man would want to further his education and experience life in a cosmopolitan city like Milan before being drafted into the family business. But that didn't explain the apartment—or the serious rift it seemed to have caused in the family.

"It took an *Americanina* to bring my son home. Brava!" Vittorio said. "Enough courses! Enough fancy hotels! Enough working for other people! It's time for him to settle down and get back to work, right here where he belongs."

"You were telling me about the apartment?" Jolene said, determined to get to the bottom of at least one story here.

"It's high time he got rid of that place—and everything in it. And I mean everything. Especially now that you're here."

"I'm sure he'll move out soon, now that we'll be living in Manarola."

"Moving out isn't permanent enough. He has to sell that place. You tell him that, too."

"He owns the apartment?" Jolene asked, fed up with fishing; it was time for some direct questions.

"Of course! If he hadn't gotten it into his head that money should be invested in a place you could live in, not in a strip of land you'd never be allowed to build on, the whole vineyard would still be in the family, and so would some of the peace we've lost."

"Are you talking about the vineyard where we harvested the other day?" Jolene asked, more confused than ever.

"That's the only one this family has ever owned. And thank God for that! The ironic thing is, the price of that land has gone way up, whereas he bought the apartment during the real estate boom. With this slump he'll be lucky if he can recover the whole down payment. Who would have guessed that grapes would be worth more than bricks?"

"Wait a minute—are you saying that half the vineyard was sold off to buy Filippo an apartment?" At the risk of Vittorio thinking she was poking her nose into the family's financial affairs, this was a story that she needed to get straight. "I thought you used the money to buy your boat."

"Ha! Now that wouldn't have been fair to Luisa or the boys, would it? Besides, have you seen my boat? Of course, I did have a serious *gozzo* once, one with an inboard diesel engine that purred like a kitty. It could take you to Corsica and back without skipping a stroke, but it was lost in the big flood. In the end, I don't need much these days, as long as it floats, and that little outboard I stuck on there gets me to my favorite fishing spots. Any farther than that, we go in Giobatta's *gozzo*."

"I...um...I must have been confused," Jolene stammered, knowing there was no way Filippo could have said "boat" and she understood "apartment."

"Life is confusing," Vittorio said, pausing to pinch a few stray bits of tobacco off of his tongue. "That whole vineyard story was a huge disappointment for Luisa, particularly because it was her generosity toward Filippo that backfired. She's a fair woman, and only wanted to do what was best for her sons. Both of them. But you don't need to hear all about that again."

Jolene did want to hear all about that, but she just stood there bobbing her head, as if she needed to shake all the new information through a sifter in her brain before she could absorb any more.

"No need to tell them, right?" Vittorio said.

"Tell who what?" she asked, by now too befuddled to worry about pretending she knew what she didn't.

"Filippo, that I forgot to deliver his message. He'd be furious. And Luisa, that you saw me with this." Holding up the cigarette, he took one last puff before dropping it to the ground and stubbing it out with the toe of his rubber boot. "Some quack convinced her it's bad for my heart."

"My lips are sealed," Jolene said.

"So, I'll see you at the Locanda?"

Jolene nodded. "I guess. Later on." It wasn't until Vittorio and his sloshing bucket had disappeared from view that she realized she should have told him to treat Luisa with a little extra kindness.

She stood there for a bit after he left, too dazed and disoriented to know where to go, until she found herself surrounded by a new wave of tourists freshly regurgitated by a ferryboat. She felt like a little girl left out of a playground game as they swirled about her, spinning off into smaller groups according to nationality or the other affinities that had made travel companions out of perfect strangers, laughing and exclaiming and stopping to point at views or pose for photos while moseying from the harbor to the shops where they might be tempted to buy bottles of brilliant yellow limoncello or straw-colored wine, jars of bright green pesto or tiny black olives before departing for their next stop on their Cinque Terre day tour. Instead of actively exploring the hillsides, hiking up and down trails to discover what lay behind a village or two instead of tagging all five, the seafaring tourists hopped on and off the boats calling at Riomaggiore and Manarola, Vernazza and Monterosso, skipping only lofty Corniglia, whose cliffs offered no place to dock. Knowing that it was only a matter of days before the scheduled ferry service would be suspended for the season was of some consolation to Jolene when she finally reemerged on the other side of the human stream. Ducking between two buildings, she trudged up the stairs with heavy feet, Vittorio's words and Filippo's letter shackling her like leg irons. She was angry and hurt that Filippo had slipped away like a thief in the night, and that he hadn't mentioned a word about the apartment. More seriously, he'd lied about the sale of the vineyard and what had been done with the proceeds.

"Hi there, little kitty," Jolene said, pleased to see her newfound feline friend stationed on the doormat of Suite 16. "Are you all alone today too?" The cat yawned, displaying the textured pinks of its ridged roof and raspy tongue, then stood and arched its back, its tail twitching as it rubbed against her ankles. She remembered reading that if a cat greeted you with a quivering tail, it meant that it was excited to see you, and the thought cheered her. She unlocked the door with no problem, but it took a ram or two of the shoulder to separate it from its jamb. As soon as it gave, the kitty trotted inside and hopped onto the bed.

Kicking off her sneakers, Jolene sat on the edge of the bed, holding her head in her hands until the kitty crawled onto her lap, kneading her thighs with its sharp claws and purring a suggestion that they would both be more comfortable if she would lie down. Stretching out with one arm bent over her head, the other stroking the cat, she wondered how many other relevant facts Filippo had distorted or left out altogether. By now she'd begun to realize that many of her expectations had been based on her imagination rather than on information Filippo had provided, but if that information, in addition to being scarce, was defective to begin with, what else could she expect going forward?

Pushing the clinging cat aside, Jolene got up, retrieved the key to the dresser from her travel pouch and unlocked the top drawer, sighing at the sight of her mother's recorder and the poncho-clad parcel. Recorder in hand, she walked to the window and after sucking in a lungful of fresh air, held the instrument to her lips and blew, cringing as her first attempt at playing a C note fell flat. Standing there, she recalled the times when her father was traveling and her mother would play for her, songs like "Down in the Valley" and "We Shall Overcome" and her favorite, because she played it when they went rowing together, "Row, Row, Row Your Boat." After playing a song she would pass the recorder over to Jolene, showing her which fingers to place over which holes, and how to shape her lips to obtain a clean sound. Jolene remembered how it used to comfort her to taste traces of her mother's saliva on the mouthpiece, and feel the warmth left by her breath on the wood. When a seagull landed on a nearby rooftop, she imagined that her mother had sent it to listen, which inspired Jolene to practice, playing up and down the scale until she grew dizzy. Returning the recorder to its drawer, she took out the rolled-up poncho and lay it on the bed.

Lunchtime had come and gone, together with Jolene's plan to fast until dinner. Grabbing the chunk of aged Parmesan cheese and the packet of almonds she'd bought a couple of days ago, she brought them to the bed, together with the Swiss army knife she took from her backpack. The moment she dug into the Parmesan, the kitty was on her lap again, purring and staring at her, as if to politely remind her that twenty-four-month-old Parmigiano Reggiano was best when enjoyed in company. Sharing a morsel or two with the kitty did seem to bring out the cheese's buttery flavor, crumbly texture and perfect degree of sharpness, complemented by the natural sweetness of the almonds. With a glass of that wonderful white wine, the snack could have become a feast, but tap water would have to do. Setting the food on the nightstand, she took a drink, then spent a few minutes observing the cat as it licked its paw and washed its face, reflecting that anyone who shared her bed and food must have a name, cats included. Having discovered that the "it" was a "she" was a start; her name would reveal itself in good time.

"Now that we have a little food in our bellies, let's just stay here and think for a bit," she said, stroking the kitty under its white chin. "We need a little alone time. That always helps."

Picking up the rolled-up poncho, she hugged it to her chest as she stretched out, the cat nestled between her knees. Staring at the cracked ceiling, after a few moments she felt the rhythm of her breath fall in time with the cat's purring, or perhaps it was the other way around. Drifting off to the edge of consciousness, she imagined her mother bending over her, the way she used to when Jolene would wake up crying in the middle of the night and couldn't get back to sleep. When her father was home, her mother couldn't take her back to the big bed, nor could she play the recorder for her, so instead she would tell Jolene a story. It fascinated Jolene the way she could make it up as she went along, always changing the setting and circumstances, but always devising a happy ending for the protagonist, who was always the same: a little girl who could disappear and reappear at will. Her name was Fata Morgana.

"Fata," she whispered, her eyes fluttering open to find the kitty curled up on her tummy, resting her head on the poncho. "That's your name now."

EIGHT

Jolene's step was lighter when she walked back down to the Locanda, later that afternoon. She hadn't napped but had drifted off into that trancelike state, in which the trappings of her body seemed to dissolve, allowing her to float above her physical self, free of weight and worry. It was the type of rest that came after lovemaking, or a cathartic cry, or nodding off with a novel. Refreshed and energized, she felt ready to confront Filippo, confident that every misunderstanding would be cleared up.

"Hey there, Jolene," Lorenzo said from behind the bar when she walked in. Though also braced to face Luisa, Jolene was in no hurry to do so.

"Hi, Lorenzo," she said, smiling.

"I'll bet you'd like a cappuccino," he said, stepping away from the refrigerator he was restocking, his hand already on the arm of the Cimbali.

"Has somebody been spreading rumors about my nasty habits?" she asked.

"*Il paese è piccolo, la gente mormora*," Lorenzo replied.

"The town is small, the people murmur," Jolene translated. "My second Italian adage of the day."

"So, do you want one or not?" Lorenzo asked.

"Um…sure…I'd love one," she said, before she could decipher whether his offer came out of kindness or duty.

As he turned to brew the coffee Jolene stared at Lorenzo's back, recalling how strong and indefatigable he'd seemed the other day, hauling all those crates of grapes around on his muscular shoulders. Today those shoulders appeared slumped, as if they bore the weight of something even heavier. She wondered what, and why, but her musings were interrupted when he turned around and caught her staring. Blushing, she dropped her eyes to the open book that lay face down on the counter.

"*Ossi di seppia,*" Jolene said, running a finger over the faded cover. "Are you reading this?"

"That's a copy I keep here. I pick it up whenever I have a few minutes to spare," Lorenzo said, pouring the steamed milk over the coffee with a surprisingly delicate movement of his hand, designing a flower. He was being kind, she decided.

"I've never read anything by Eugenio Montale, but I read a book by Italo Calvino once in English. The Baron in the Trees. I remember liking his style."

"If you like poetry, you can borrow this whenever you want to. Montale was from Genoa, and he truly captures the essence of the Cinque Terre in this work."

"That would be great," Jolene said, still digesting the fact that he read poetry. She'd never met a man who read poetry, at least not one who admitted it. "I've been wanting to read something in Italian to improve my vocabulary, but the newspaper is so depressing," she added. "It might take me a year to get through a book of poetry, though."

"No rush. Some poems take a lifetime to understand," Lorenzo said. "Cocoa?"

"Cinnamon, please," she said. Lorenzo picked up a shaker and thumped it with the heel of his hand, showering the foam with her favorite spice. Jolene smiled.

"What's so funny?" Lorenzo asked.

"Shhh," she said, placing a finger over her lips. A few seconds passed before she looked up. "Sorry, but I love hearing that sound."

"What sound?" he asked, cocking his head.

"When the powder lands on the foam, all those microscopic bubbles start popping. It's as quiet as falling snow. Do you know what I mean?"

"I do, actually. Chiara always begs for cinnamon on her latte, so she can hear that sound, too."

"Yeah, I guess I'm a little old for that," Jolene said.

"I didn't say that," Lorenzo said, adding, after a pause, "How old are you anyway?"

"Thirty-eight. But you're not supposed to ask."

Instead of saying that he would have guessed younger, thirty-three, thirty-five at the most, Lorenzo resumed his chore, filling the silence with the clinking of bottles. He worked quickly, though, and she was soon wondering what else she could say.

"So, what have you lovebirds been up to today?" he asked, before she came up with anything.

"Not much," she said, staring into her cup. At least he didn't seem to know about her disastrous conversation with Luisa. "Filippo went to Milan."

"Why didn't you go with him?" Lorenzo asked, slamming the refrigerator door and stacking the empty mineral water crates against the wall.

"He had business to take care of," she said. There was no way she'd tell him she hadn't been invited. "I didn't want to hold him up."

"Have you ever been to Milan?"

"No," she replied, watching the clumps of cinnamon turn dark and sink.

"I don't care for cities much," Lorenzo said.

"Me neither, really." There were other places she'd rather see in Italy first, given a choice, but that wasn't the point.

"Unless you like traffic and pollution and unbridled consumerism, you're not missing much."

"Right." That didn't mean she didn't want to visit the city; that she wasn't curious to see the Duomo, or the Galleria, or an art exhibit at Palazzo Reale, or the designer boutiques in via Monte Napoleone. But she wasn't about to tell him that. "I'd rather take a nice walk out in nature than go sightseeing."

"Then you're in the right place."

"As soon as Filippo has a free morning, he's going to take me on a hike," she said, sipping her cappuccino.

"Filippo?"

She glanced at Lorenzo, who was staring at her with one raised eyebrow.

"Yes, Filippo."

"On a hike?"

"Why not? Is there something wrong with that?" she said, tucking her hair behind her ears. She hoped he wouldn't start criticizing his brother, because she wasn't in the mood to defend him to anyone but herself. "I took him on lots of hikes in New York, and now it's his turn. He said we could start out on the Via dell'Amore and go visit Riomaggiore. That's only a kilometer each way, so I guess it's more like a stroll, really. Then he said on another day when he has more time, we can walk the blue trail from here to Corniglia."

"He's planning to take you on the Sentiero Azzurro? The trail along the sea?"

"Yes, he pointed it out to me from a distance, when we were up in Punta Bonfiglio. It looks gorgeous. Very dramatic drops."

Lorenzo laughed. "You'd drop, that's for sure. Right off the cliff. Neither of those trails is even accessible. We were hit pretty hard here between the flood of 2011 and the rockslides of 2012."

"But that was years ago," Jolene said.

"Securing shifting land and making it safe for the tens, even hundreds, of thousands of people that come to trample on it every year is no easy feat, but they're working on it. It seems like every time they set a completion date, we get slammed with another deluge and another part crumbles. The climate hasn't just changed, it's gone crazy. We can't keep up with the erosion."

An image formed in Jolene's mind, of Filippo leading her along a washed-out trail in his double-breasted blazer and tasseled loafers, clasping her hand as they slid off the cliff and into the sea, never to be seen again. It would have made her laugh if she didn't feel compelled to find an excuse for Filippo's ignorance.

"He's been living in Milan and then abroad for quite some time now," she said. "It's only natural that he's not totally up-to-date with current events here in the Cinque Terre."

"Filippo has never been interested in what goes on here," Lorenzo said. "His sights have always been set elsewhere."

"Well, now Manarola is his vision. With all the time he's been spending on his projects to promote tourism right here, I'd think—"

"What projects?" Lorenzo asked.

"I...um...I don't know the specifics, actually," she stammered, hoping she hadn't said too much already. "Filippo's always researching all kinds of things. Has he always been so studious?"

"He's studious all right. He's studied every trick in the book to wriggle out of working, until he could get out of here for good," Lorenzo said, shaking his head. "I'm sorry. Forget I said anything. Old issues shouldn't concern you."

"That's okay," Jolene said, but it was precisely the old issues that continued to prey on her mind. She wished she could squeeze more information out of Lorenzo, and at the same time, she wished she could confide in him regarding Filippo's ambitions. Lorenzo would have to rethink his opinion about his brother when he realized how serious he was about his plans to relaunch the family business.

"*Eccomi!* Here I am!" Luisa called, pushing through the door, hugging two paper bags full of bread.

Jolene hurried toward her. "Here, let me help you!" she said, taking the bags off Luisa's hands, making a loaf slip to the floor in the process. "Oh! I'm so sorry, Luisa!"

Luisa paused, looking straight at her, one eyebrow raised, in the way of the sons she'd passed the trait down to. As she held her gaze, Jolene was thankful to that fallen loaf for prompting her to say those words. Both women knew that they were not only about the bread; that nothing else needed to be said.

"Don't give it another thought," Luisa said, shrugging off her jacket, and patting her head, where the remnants of her hairdresser's handiwork had gone limp, and the swirl at the back of her head had been flattened by her pillow. "People can be so disappointing," she said. "Agostino always made sure we had all our bread by 6 AM. There was none of this running back and forth we have to do with Paolino. If it weren't for the respect I had for his father, I would have changed bakeries last year, when he left his body."

"*Ha lasciato il corpo*" were the exact words she'd used, an expression which was new to Jolene in Italian. Every language had its euphemisms to indicate that a person had passed on without saying the D-word.

"And exactly whose bakery would you switch to, Ma?" Lorenzo asked. "There are only two in town, Paolino's and Sandro's. Sandro hasn't spoken to you since when, 1980?"

"There's too much negativity baked into Sandro's bread, and he knows it. If he wants to use bleached industrial flour and excessive quantities of brewer's yeast instead of sourdough leaven, that's his choice, that's his business. And it's my choice not to buy it." Walking behind the bar, she donned her apron and smiled at Jolene. "Can I make you a cappuccino?"

"I'm fine, thanks," Jolene said. Even she had her limits.

"Where's Filippo?" Luisa asked, her eyes darting from Jolene to Lorenzo and back again, as if she suspected the pair of gagging him and hiding him in the broom closet, or hacking his body to pieces and stashing them in the freezer.

"Seems he went to Milan," Lorenzo said.

Luisa closed her eyes for a moment, then opened them, looking straight at Jolene again. "Be serene. He'll get it all sorted out soon," she said.

When someone told you to be serene and you didn't know why, it usually meant there was a reason not to be. Jolene opened her mouth to speak but was still trying to find the words to ask what it was she should not worry about, when Vittorio burst through the door, whistling a tune that sounded vaguely military, possibly even fascist. On seeing the three of them standing there, his lips lost their pucker.

"What's this? You're having a party, and no one invited me?" he said.

"If we knew where to find you, or if you remembered to carry your phone with you once in a while, maybe we would have," Luisa said.

Jolene recalled how happy Vittorio had seemed aboard his boat with Giobatta, the look of pure pleasure on his face while he sneaked his smoke. She wondered whether all couples grew apart, no matter how much they shared; whether an element of mystery or a fraction of fear of the unknown were healthy for a relationship. She wondered how close she would feel to Filippo in twenty, or ten, or even five years, when he seemed so distant from her today.

"Sorry Pa, no party. I was only waiting for Chiara to fall asleep and Ma to cover the bar, so I could get back to the kitchen," Lorenzo said.

"As long as you stay out of my way," Vittorio warned. "I have fish to clean."

"And I have to finish up the desserts," Lorenzo said.

"Can I help?" Jolene blurted. The idea of handling the slimy squid didn't appeal to her, but neither did being all alone with Luisa, or hanging around doing nothing while everyone else was working.

"I don't really like to chat when I'm doing the pastries," Lorenzo said. "Nothing personal, it just distracts me."

"I was hoping to help Vittorio clean the squid," Jolene said. "If I'm not in the way, that is."

"He has squid?" Luisa asked. "How did you know that?"

"I happened to be at the harbor when he came back on the boat," Jolene said.

"Was he alone?" Luisa asked.

It sounded like a trick question. Jolene looked around the room, trying to read the others' expressions. "No," she said, pretty sure that was what Luisa wanted to hear, besides it being the truth. Vittorio was a seventy-five-year-old in rubber boots and coveralls piloting a *gozzo* that stank of fish: he certainly couldn't be suspected of cruising the coast with a paramour. "He was with Giobatta."

"See?" Vittorio said, rolling his eyes. "I promised I wouldn't go out alone, and I didn't go out alone."

"Oh, all right then. Just go to the kitchen then, the lot of you!" Luisa said. "I need some breathing room."

Lorenzo ruffled Luisa's hair, then dodged the dish towel she tried to whip him with. "You rascal!" she cried, as he danced away.

"You sure you want to do this?" Vittorio asked Jolene, who was right behind him.

"Sure!" she said, more excited at the prospect of finally being admitted to the kitchen than of learning how to clean squid. Filippo kept rebuffing her requests to take a look around, saying that the timing was bad, or that his father was jealous of his territory, or that Lorenzo freaked out when too many people were around.

"Does my son approve of you working in the kitchen?" Vittorio asked.

"I promise I won't disturb you, Lorenzo!" she called to him, as he walked through the swinging doors.

"I didn't mean him," Vittorio said. "I meant Filippo."

Screw Filippo, she surprised herself by thinking, almost as annoyed with him now as she'd been with Evan for hogging their kitchen to himself. It still made her angry, and more determined than ever to try her hand at cooking. "Filippo doesn't seem to be around," she said. "So as far as I'm concerned, he doesn't get to voice an opinion."

"All right, then!" Vittorio said, chuckling. "I could never say no to a feisty *Americanina*!" Taking a large container from the refrigerator, he carried it to the sink and removed the cover, revealing an amorphous blob of tentacled creatures.

Jolene averted her eyes, preferring to take a closer look at her surroundings. Besides some possible code violations, what struck her was the juxtaposition of new and old materials. Stainless steel surfaces gleamed beside aged slabs of marble; indestructible aluminum pots outshone chipped terracotta casseroles; an olive wood chopping block bore scars to which the white plastic boards were immune. As Lorenzo prepared to whip up a liter of cream, she could see why the two men might have trouble working side-by-side in here; it wasn't that the space was small, it was just poorly distributed. She could already envision the improvements that would be made when Filippo got the green light for expansion, but meanwhile, she'd better be careful to stay out of everyone's way, if she wanted to be invited back again.

"Some people wear latex gloves, but I love the feel of fresh fish in my hands," Vittorio began as he scrubbed up, pausing to inspect his nails as if deciding whether to set up an appointment with his manicurist. "Even if these are technically cephalopods," he added, holding one up for Jolene to admire. His eyes shone, as though he were bidding farewell to a loved one.

"Now, let's honor these creatures by treating them right," he continued, drawing Jolene's attention to the position of his hands, close together, one on the head and one on the body. "Just give it a little twist and a tug, like this," he explained, yanking in opposite directions, "and off comes the head!" He held up the two pieces, making sure she took a long look at the tube-like body and the alien-like head, with its trailing tentacles and dripping innards. He placed the tentacled head complete with attached innards onto a cutting board, setting the body on a platter with a reverence that was touching to witness. "See how it's done? Gently, but firmly. You don't want to massacre them."

"Sure" she said, her nostrils twitching. She took her time tying back her hair, then washing her hands, then rolling up her sleeves, before finally picking up a squid. Though she followed Vittorio's example, the squid kept slipping from her hands, escaping decapitation.

"Remember, be firm, but gentle! You want the innards to stay attached to the head!" Vittorio said, tightening his hands around hers, then pulling. "Gently!"

Staring at the head in her hand, Jolene found it difficult to mask her revulsion, but when she heard Lorenzo's laughter above the whirring of his mixer, she grew more determined to master the technique. Vittorio patiently guided her through the procedure a few more times, then instructed her to continue at her own pace, he decapitating five squids for every one of hers, until the tray was empty.

"Bene, bene!" Vittorio said. "Now we reap our reward: black gold, the key ingredient for my famous *risotto nero!*"

Using a paring knife as a pointer, he drew her attention to the cutting board, a loser's battlefield littered with heads and tentacles and innards. "That's the ink there," he said, indicating something that resembled a black vein, and tweezing it out with fingers. It was actually an elongated sac, she saw, as he punctured it with the tip of his knife, then squeezed its contents into a bowl, the liquid tingeing his fingertips a dark purple. "Isn't that a beautiful sight?"

"Um...yeah! Gorgeous!" Jolene said trying to sound enthusiastic. "And you got every last drop!"

"Ah, but there's more!" Vittorio said. "Hidden behind the eyeballs!"

"The eyeballs?" She was beginning to understand why Evan had been content with frozen calamari rings. He was a coward, that was why.

Vittorio smiled at her. "Don't worry, I won't make you do that. Not this time. Let's take a look at the tentacles now."

"Yes, let's." Looking was better than touching.

"You want to chop them off just below the eyes so they stay attached to one another at the top. Then you squeeze here, in the center of the bunch, until the beak pops out."

"The beak?" she said. "I didn't even know they had one!"

"You'd know if you got bit by one! Squid are amazing creatures! Just amazing!" Vittorio said, lining the tentacles up on the cutting board. "Now we give these dangling bits a trim to even the bunch out, and that's it for the head. Now for the bodies. This is the easy part. We don't have to, but we can peel off the skin, just like a banana." he said, pulling away the spotted purplish outer layer. "Then we get rid of the cuttlebone here," he continued, sticking his fingers inside the tube and extracting a piece of something that looked like a plastic quill. "And then we check for any leftovers. You want to take care of that?" he asked, his eyes twinkling.

"Not really," she said, relieved that he hadn't waited for an answer; his fingers were already probing and scraping the inside of the body, reemerging with some slimy goop stuck to his nails.

"Okay, the show's over," he said, discarding all the disgusting bits he had removed and rinsing his hands under the faucet. "Now it's your turn."

This was even more disgusting and complicated than she'd expected, but as her mother always told her, she could tackle any task, if she compared it to rowing a boat across the lake. You couldn't do it in one stroke, but one stroke at a time. Row, row, row your boat, Jolene, she'd sing to encourage her.

"One stroke at a time," Jolene said, out loud. "First the ink, right?"

Vittorio nodded. "First the ink. The bigger the squid, the bigger the sac. Here, try this plump one for starters, it'll be easier for you to get at," he said, placing a head in front of her, combing the tentacles with his fingers as if they were hair.

Her face scrunched up with concentration, Jolene went straight for the sac, plucking it out on her first try. "I got it!" she said, holding it up for him to see, but in her excitement she pinched too hard, puncturing the sac with a nail as it slipped through her fingers and flew into the air.

"Oh no!" she cried. The sac was sailing straight for Lorenzo's bowl of freshly whipped cream!

Horrified, Jolene rushed to Lorenzo's side, immediately joined by Vittorio. All three stared down into the bowl. Though the landing couldn't have been softer, the impact was devastating, the streak of black contaminating the fluffy whiteness like a burst oil pipeline in the pristine Alaskan snow. Jolene's neck sank between her shoulders as she braced herself for the barrage of insults. Maybe Lorenzo would hurl the bowl at her, like a mad chef on one of those cooking shows. Or maybe he'd dump the cream on her head. When she finally screwed up the courage to look at him, he glared at her in silence, making her blush and sweat and feel incredibly stupid for the third time that day. Then Lorenzo did the thing she least expected: he tossed back his head and burst into laughter. Part from nervousness, part from relief, Jolene began giggling too, which in turn made Vittorio chuckle. Soon all three of them were laughing so hard that tears streamed from Jolene's eyes, and when she brushed them away with her fingers, Vittorio and Lorenzo pointed at her, roaring all the more.

"The ink, Jolene!" Lorenzo howled. "You smeared it all over your face!"

At that moment, the kitchen doors swung open, creaking on their hinges. "I'm glad someone's having a good time!" Filippo said, a frown on his lips and Monica on his heels.

"What are you people doing here?" Monica asked Lorenzo. "And what did you do with Chiara?"

"No, what are you doing here?" Lorenzo asked his wife.

"And what are you doing here?" Filippo asked Jolene.

"I don't know what anybody's doing here," Vittorio said, his ruddy cheeks flushed from all the chuckling. "But it's time for you to all clear out of my kitchen! Anyone who wants to eat with the help, meaning me, dinner's at six-thirty, as usual. Now get lost!"

Ten minutes later, Jolene was still in the bathroom, trying to wash the squid ink from her face. By now her cheeks were scrubbed to a bright pink, but the stains remained.

"Since when do I need permission to spend the night with my husband and daughter?" she heard Monica say. She was standing at the foot of the stairs, which happened to be right across the hall from the restroom, meaning that Jolene could hear every word she said to Lorenzo. She wished that they would take their discussion up to their room.

"It's not a matter of permission." Lorenzo replied, speaking in a low voice, but Jolene heard his words through the thin door, too. "It's a matter of routines. And what happens when you upset them."

"You and your boring routines," Monica said. "Other people have a life. Other people have a career."

"By 'other people' you mean you, don't you?"

"Look, I bent over backward to set up my meeting with the engineers in La Spezia instead of Genoa tomorrow, just so I could stay here with you tonight. That way I can grab a train in the morning, and you can keep Chiara here instead of getting up at the crack of dawn to take her to nursery school."

"And the day after that, we'll be back to square one, and she won't want to go to nursery school."

"Well, what I want matters, too," Monica snapped. "I am her

mother, after all."

"Now you remember," Lorenzo said, his voice so tired that it slid under the door instead of passing through it.

Jolene didn't want to hear their argument, she didn't want them to know she was hearing their argument, and she didn't want to come out of the bathroom and risk getting into an argument of her own with Filippo. She didn't want to have anything to do with any arguments, period. She lowered the toilet seat cover and sat down, waiting for the couple to leave.

"There's nothing wrong with my memory, Renzo," Monica said.

Renzo? That was the first time Jolene had heard anyone call him by this nickname. It didn't suit him at all, she thought, wondering whether that was how his close friends called him, or whether the name was a throwback to the time when he and Monica were sweethearts. Or maybe Monica just liked to call him by the name of that famous architect she'd mentioned.

"You're the one who needs to remember a few things," Monica continued. "Like the fact that we had an agreement. I studied in Genoa, like I said I would. I got an apartment in Genoa, like I said I would. I work in Genoa, like I said I would. I took time off to have your baby, like I said I would, even though it meant working like hell to catch up with all the men my age. But I did catch up. Like. I. Said. I. Would. And now I make enough for all of us to live there."

"I'm proud of your achievements," Lorenzo said, his voice free from irony. "I really am. But you know I can't live in Genoa."

"You can't? Or you just don't want to?"

"Sounds like Chiara's awake," Lorenzo said. "I'll bring her down. Unless you want to."

"You go ahead," Monica said. "I need some air."

Monica's heels clicked as she walked away, while Lorenzo's steps fell heavy on the stairs. Jolene wondered whether they were simply going through a rough patch, trying to juggle jobs and the responsibilities of a small child, or whether they were as ill-suited a match as they seemed.

Unlocking the door, Jolene peeked out to make sure no one was around, then threw her shoulders back and headed for the bar, where she found Filippo talking to his mother. He had looked so annoyed when he'd caught her laughing in the kitchen with Lorenzo and Vittorio that she was taken aback when he threw his arms open wide as soon as he saw her approach. Refusing a hug in front of Luisa wasn't an option, but she didn't have to like it, she thought, stiffening as she walked into his arms.

"I missed you, *Splendore mio!*" he said, squeezing her so hard that he lifted her off her feet. "What a long day! I'm exhausted."

"You must have had an awful a lot to do in Milan, if you had to leave so early," Jolene said, wriggling in his arms until she could stand on her own two feet again.

"Yeah, I did," Fillip said, setting her down. "Most of those darn offices close to the public at twelve-thirty, so I wanted to be there when they opened at eight, to take full advantage of the morning."

Jolene nodded, wondering whether he'd also been to the apartment he'd never mentioned, obtained by means he'd lied about, in the city she'd never seen.

"Would you like a cappuccino?" Filippo asked Jolene. "I'll make it for you."

"At this hour?" Jolene said, shaking her head.

"Then how about a glass of wine?"

Jolene nodded.

Luisa sidled down to the far end of the bar to serve a pair of men who had walked in arguing over whose turn it was to pay for their pre-dinner drink of *giancu*. White wine and friendly banter seemed to go hand in hand here, Jolene thought, watching Filippo from the corner of her eye. Maybe a glass or two would facilitate their conversation as well, and as soon as Filippo had measured their doses with the stinginess of a sommelier in a fancy wine bar, Jolene grabbed a glass and swallowed a gulp.

"I know why you went to Milan," she blurted.

"What, no toast?" Filippo said, acting offended that she didn't look him in the eye before taking her first sip, as customary.

"Sorry," she said, banging her glass against his.

"I explained it in the note," Filippo said.

"You didn't tell me everything in the note, though."

"What do you mean?" Filippo asked, the furrows in his brow deepening even as he sipped.

"Your father told me all about it," Jolene said, pushing the words out before she could lose her courage.

"About what?"

"The apartment. You said you got nothing, while Lorenzo was

given a vineyard. As it turns out, you got an apartment," Jolene said.

"That man!" Filippo said. "He's such a blabbermouth!"

"And you lied to my face when you said your mother sold the land to buy your father a boat!"

Filippo sighed, setting down his glass to take Jolene's hand, but she would not release her grip on her glass. "I'm sorry," he said. "I know it was wrong. I didn't know how to explain it, so I said the first thing that came to my mind."

"Really? A lie came to your mind before the truth?" Jolene asked.

"I didn't want to dig up that whole story about the vineyard again, because it makes everyone feel bad. And I had a good reason for not telling you about the apartment."

"There's never a good reason for hiding things, Filippo. Or downright lying. I thought we made a promise to always be open with one another."

"But *Splendore*, sometimes there is a good reason for hiding something. Like when it's meant to be a surprise," he said, this time prying the glass from her fingers and taking her hands in his. "I wanted to wait until there was a solid deal in the works, but if you really need to know now, I put that apartment up for sale. It's only a one-room walk-up, and the seller's market is still soft, but I should be able to get a couple hundred thousand euros for it, which we can use for a down payment on a place of our own here. I've gotten wind of a couple of little places that will go up for sale as soon as the owners die or are forced to move out. One belongs to an old lady who just turned ninety-three; she's a toughie, though. Can you believe she still walks without a cane? The other is owned by a widower; he's only eighty-seven, but he's been going straight downhill ever since his wife passed. Shouldn't be long now."

"Filippo!" Jolene cried. "That's awful!"

"I'm just telling you like it is. Property is expensive here, and things have gotten even tighter since everybody started talking about the Cinque Terre. You need a little insider information, if you want to beat the real estate agencies to the kill."

Once again, Filippo had managed to steer her away from the issue she was hoping to discuss, which was her need for trust and transparency. Talking to him reminded her of those wheelbarrow races she'd participated in a few times as a child, before swearing she would not play again as long as she was expected to be the wheelbarrow. But here she was, with Filippo holding her by the ankles and running wherever he wanted, while she scrambled around on her hands to avoid falling flat on her face.

"That apartment belongs to the past. You are my future, *Splendore*," Filippo said, tipping her chin with his finger and looking into her eyes. "And I'm totally in love with the future."

"Still, you should have told me you were going to Milan, instead of running off like that. Next time—"

"I'll have some of whatever she's having," Monica said, breezing in on a trail of smoke and propping her elbows on the bar next to Jolene. "But don't be so stingy."

"*Subito, Splendore!*" Filippo said, pouring out a generous glass for Monica. The two of them rolled her their eyes when Vittorio's voice boomed down the corridor, announcing that the *risotto al nero di seppie* would be ready in exactly ten minutes, not a minute earlier, not a minute later, and they damn well better be seated at the table when it was.

***

"I'm so tired I almost forgot to give you something," Filippo said, breathing down Jolene's neck later that evening as she jiggled the key in the lock to Suite 16. It was sticking again; she'd have to buy her own can of WD-40.

"Something for me?" she asked, relieved to hear the click before Filippo lost his patience and took the key from her.

"It's something I want you to have, so we can avoid mix-ups like today," he said, setting his briefcase down on the doormat. At Filippo's approach, Fata had vacated her favorite spot and scurried off, jumping to a safer perch on the stone wall. Crouching, Filippo opened the briefcase and ruffled through a stack of folders, then pulled out a small plastic bag and handed it to her.

Jolene peeked inside, finding a box with the Nokia logo on it. "A phone?" She said, her heart sinking. "You shouldn't have." She really wished he hadn't; if she was forced to carry a phone, she should at least be entitled to a trip to the city to buy it.

"Don't get too excited, it's just an old one I had lying around in Milan. But it still works perfectly well for calls and text messages," Filippo said, straightening up.

"Thank you."

"I hate not being able to talk to you whenever I want to. Which is, of course, always." Filippo said, speaking softly as he cupped her chin in his hand and pressed his lips against hers. Though Jolene was still upset, she had never refused him a kiss, and didn't think that turning him away now would be a wise way to end a difficult day. Besides, she was moved by the tenderness of this kiss, and intrigued by a new taste on Filippo's tongue as it probed her mouth, delicately but with a hint of desperation, as if he were trying to reestablish a lost connection; trying telling her he was sorry in a way words could not convey.

"Why don't we go inside?" she said, pushing open the door. "We can talk some more, now that we're finally alone."

Filippo stroked her cheek with the back of his hand. "I'd love to," he said, bending to pick up his briefcase, "but I'm totally exhausted."

"Well then, go get some rest. Next time you have to go to Milan, maybe we can go together, and you can show me around. It would be fun to stay overnight while you still have your apartment. We could make a weekend of it."

"Maybe," he said, pecking her on the cheek. "Good night, beautiful *Splendore mio. Sogni d'oro.*"

"Good night, Filippo. Sweet dreams to you, too."

Instead of going inside, Jolene watched Filippo descend the walkway and disappear from view, then clicked her tongue twice. Hopping down from the wall, Fata slunk toward Jolene, sniffing the air with suspicion. Jolene took a folded napkin from the pocket of her jacket and opened it up, setting before her friend a feast of the tentacles she had picked from her plate of black risotto while everyone else was doting on Chiara. She petted Fata as she ate, then let her follow her inside before closing the door.

Switching on the light, she gasped with joy on seeing the walnut desk and chair she'd eyed in one of the other suites sitting in front of the window. Grinning, she sat down at the desk, running her fingers over the newly oiled wood, her heart swelling with gratitude as she wondered how Giobatta had managed to fulfill her wish. When she stepped into the bathroom and saw her reflection in the mirror, her smile turned to laughter; her cheeks and teeth and tongue were still stained with ink. It would be a while before she'd get close to a squid again.

NINE

Jolene filled her water bottle from the bathroom tap and stowed it in her backpack, together with the notebook and pencil she always carried with her, the Swiss army knife, and what was left of her chunk of Parmesan and packet of almonds, then laced up her sneakers and headed out the door. As often happened the moment she locked a door to leave, she remembered that she had forgotten something. Between the confusing turns of the day and the surprise of the furniture last night, she hadn't even taken her new phone out of the box before going to bed, but thought she should at least plug it in, so it would be charged by the time she got back. Once back inside the room, she was glad for a second chance to leave because there was another thing she'd forgotten to remember: her mother's recorder. Unlocking the dresser drawer, she took the instrument and slipped it inside her backpack. When she left the room the second time, she was again nagged by the feeling she was forgetting something else, but turned and walked away, opting out of a game that could go on all day.

It was early, and the blanket of dampness that tucked itself over the village at night had not yet been turned back by the morning sun, just beginning to peek over the mountaintop. Jolene's plan was to take a stroll and savor her first cappuccino of the day on her own, with no hip-padding pastries or mind-muddling Garaventis to distract her, until her head could clear. Afterward, she would stop by the Locanda to talk Filippo into taking a couple of hours off. A short hike would give them the chance to talk, and a little healthy activity out in the fresh air would do him good. He couldn't jog here, and hunting down documents could hardly be considered exercise. He'd have a hard time refusing her when he saw her dressed and ready to go, and if he did, she would remind him of his mother's comment that he was looking a little pudgy around the middle lately which, by the way, was true.

No trains or boats had yet called to dump their cargoes of tourists, and as she walked along Jolene felt privileged to count herself among the ranks of Manarolans, smiling at the shopkeepers who stared back with suspicion as they hoisted rolling shutters, the rumbling metal discouraging any attempts at conversation. Approaching the café she'd stopped at on her first morning in town, she spotted an elderly man sitting at one of the outdoor tables, struggling to reassemble a newspaper, then giving up and abandoning the pages in a skewed pile, before pulling himself to his feet and doddering away. After having fantasized so often about sitting at one of those tables and reading an Italian paper over her morning coffee, Jolene decided that this was the perfect time to see how it felt. Taking over the man's vacated seat and discarded paper, she glanced at the headlines, while wondering whether she was supposed to go inside to order. In the meantime, she learned that a mayor affiliated with the *Movimento Cinque Stelle* had been accused of nepotism by assigning a public bid to a relative's business, while one of the movement's recently elected senators had allegedly taken a bribe from a banker, causing the representatives of the opposition to lash out that if the M5S did not have a long history of corruption it was simply because it did not have a long history. The controversy had her stomach growling by the end of the article, and when the sour-faced owner of the café came out to take her order, Jolene's resolve to limit her breakfast to a cappuccino was undermined by her memory of the fragrant cream-filled brioche that was its perfect companion. She ordered both.

"You're out early, *Americanina!*" a voice called. Glancing up, she saw Giobatta across the way, juggling a plastic bucket, a pole with a net, and a fishing rod. Vittorio's nickname for her seemed to be sticking.

"*Buongiorno*, Giobatta! I was hoping to see you!" Still clutching the paper, she jumped up and hurried over to him, ready to express her thanks with a kiss on the cheek. Though older, Giobatta was quicker, and managed to fend her off with his pole.

"Thank you so much for bringing me that desk and chair!" she said. "How did you ever get them up to my room?"

"Don't thank me, they weren't mine to give. Seeing as you liked them so much, I went to the Locanda to figure out a way to get them to you. Vittorio keeps telling everyone, 'do whatever you can to make my *Americanina* happy.' Anyway, Lorenzo was all for it. He'd have come to help me himself, but he couldn't get away on account of his little girl, so he rustled up a couple of strapping boys to do the job."

"Well, I really appreciated it, Giobatta. It was so thoughtful, and unexpected." Grabbing him by an elbow before he could slip away, she added, "Come! At least let me buy you a coffee!"

"No, no!" he said, shaking his head, the fishing net, the pail and the rod, until he freed his elbow. "Vittorio gets jealous if I drink anyone else's coffee."

"*Il suo cappuccio, signorina!*" the lady from the bar called to her, setting the cappuccino and brioche down on her table. The woman did not greet Giobatta, who responded by ignoring her, while Jolene began to fear that she herself might be accused of disloyalty by having breakfast there. Gossip traveled in small towns, and she would be mortified if Vittorio felt betrayed. She recalled Lorenzo's comment: "*Il paese è piccolo, la gente mormora.*"

"I only stopped here because I spotted a newspaper and I wanted to practice reading Italian," she said to Giobatta, holding up the paper as proof. "See?"

"There's a paper at the Locanda, too." Giobatta said, squinting at the front page. "And at least it's today's. This one's two days old."

"Well, it's still news to me," she said, feeling the need to defend her actions. "And it still helps me learn new words." But it wasn't just about the news, or the vocabulary, she wanted to explain; it was about the experience.

"Seems to me like you already know plenty of words," Giobatta said. "Go drink your cappuccino before it gets cold." At that, he walked away.

"Thanks again!" she called after him, eager to enjoy her breakfast, although today the cappuccino was bitter, the foam flat, and the brioche stale.

A quarter of an hour later she was already standing at the belvedere of Punta Bonfiglio. Since her walk with Filippo that first Sunday, she'd started coming up each day on her own to meditate and admire the view that no one with half a soul could ever tire of. The little park behind her, with its date palms and olive trees, its clipped grass and white benches, offered a perfect place to sit and read while waiting for the designated time to meet Filippo. Meanwhile, she used the opportunity to study the behavior of the tourists who came and went, sometimes offering to take their pictures, asking the more responsive travelers what had brought them to Manarola; what they liked about it and what they didn't; how long they planned to stay and whether they'd like to come back, then jotting down their responses in her notebook. She was looking forward to sharing the results of her survey with Filippo once she had a larger sampling.

Restless at the prospect of a hike this morning, her legs took her up to the elaborate pink portal that was the entrance to the cemetery. No visiting hours were posted, and the massive iron gate groaned when she pushed on it, suggesting she might be trespassing, but she entered anyway, thinking that this was her morning for breaking rules. Passing a cluster of plain stone crosses tottering with age, she wandered along the wall of stacked tombs, reading the names and dates etched in marble, clicking her tongue at the death of an infant, shaking her head at the man and wife who shared a bond so strong that one had died within weeks of the other. Almost all the plaques featured portraits of the departed in glass-encased ovals, and the somber looks on their now defunct faces made Jolene wonder whether the photographs had been taken in advance with that purpose in mind, or had been chosen because of the air of respectability they conveyed. Jolene studied the faces as if they were kin, speculating on how these people had lived here, how they had died, who they had left behind. Some of them must have descendants who still lived and worked in Manarola; maybe she would even come across some Garaventis; maybe the parents of the dour lady at the café were buried here, together with memories of the giggling little girl she had once been.

Before moving on, she paused to study the words engraved on the monumental marble slab that was also visible from her room. She read the words aloud:

"*O aperti ai venti e all'onde*
Liguri cimiteri!
Una rosea tristezza vi colora

Quando di sera, simile ad un fiore
Che marcisce, la grande luce
Si va sfacendo e muore."

Below the verse were what she assumed to be its title and author:
Liguria Vincenzo Caldarelli.

She understood the words well enough to know that the poem
spoke of death, certainly an appropriate topic for a cemetery, but
poems had deeper meanings, and she wanted to study this one
further. Fishing her notebook from her backpack, she scribbled the
words on a fresh page, then continued her walk along another row of
walled tombs. The votive lights and little bunches of flowers she
noticed, the fresh springs of rosemary or sage tied with ribbons, the
white mums like the bouquet Filippo had given her, were all evidence
that people still visited their dead here. No one she knew back in
America, herself included, went to cemeteries anymore. The old and
infirm considered themselves lucky if anyone visited them while they
were still alive.

A few stone steps took Jolene to a higher level, where a handful of
people had been laid to rest in the ground instead of in the stacks,
some graves marked with simple wooden crosses, others with granite
or marble tombstones. The view from here was magnificent, the vast
sky above and the immense sea below a reminder that while the iron
gates might imprison the bones of the departed, they had no
jurisdiction over their souls. Walking across the lumpy lawn in a
silence broken only by the brushing sound of the overgrown grass
tickling her ankles, Jolene felt sorrow but also peace. She couldn't
think of a more perfect spot to pause and remember a loved one.

Facing the sea, she sat cross-legged on the grass still damp with
dew and tried to pray for her mother, but there were so many things
she wanted to tell her that she could not find the right words. She
thought of the song her mother sometimes played for her at night,
her eyes glistening with unshed tears. Whenever Jolene asked her why
she was crying, she always replied that she wasn't crying, that the
tears in her eyes were liquid love for her little girl, overflowing from
the heart that couldn't contain it all. Seeing her mother's tears always
made Jolene weepy too, but she was never sure whether they were
tears of love for her mother, or tears of sadness for them both.
Reaching inside her backpack, she took out her mother's recorder to
play that same song, surprised by how easily the notes to "We Shall

Overcome" came back to her. She played softly at first, but as her sense of injustice for her mother's unhappy life mounted, so did the intensity of her blowing.

"*Deep in my heart, I do believe, we shall overcome someday!*" Jolene heard her child's voice chant to mother's melody, holding the final note until her breath was spent. Lowering the instrument, she tilted her face to the day's first sun, her eyes closed as she drank in the pure air. It was then that she felt the soft breath on her neck and the gentle touch on her shoulder. A shiver crawled up her spine.

"Oh!" she gasped, whipping around to face whoever or whatever was visiting her.

"I'm sorry!" Lorenzo cried, bending over to pick up Chiara, who had snuck up on Jolene and been bowled over by her reaction. "We didn't mean to startle you."

"I'm sorry, too!" Jolene said, feeling a twinge of disappointment, but mostly she felt awful about knocking the child to the ground. "Are you all right, sweetie?" she asked, but Chiara only scowled at her, then buried her head in her father's chest.

There was nothing ghostlike about Lorenzo's presence either, his legs as solid as tree trunks as he stood over Jolene in the faded jeans he always wore, but he did seem an apparition of sorts, drenched from head to toe in the light of the morning sun. His almond eyes seemed brighter, and his brown hair radiated a golden sheen, without the Locanda's fluorescent tubes glaring down on him. He was standing so close that Jolene had to tilt her head back to see his face, still unshaven, the stubble glinting like flecks of silver.

"We couldn't figure out where it was coming from," he said, tucking a couple of curls behind his ears.

"What?" Jolene asked. She had no idea what he was talking about.

"The music," Lorenzo said, tilting his head, as if straining to hear more.

"Now I'm embarrassed," Jolene said, lowering her eyes. Lorenzo 's feet were clad in the same beat-up sneakers she always saw him wear, except when he was working in the kitchen.

"About what?" he asked.

"About making such a racket in a place where people are supposed to be enjoying eternal rest."

"I don't think anyone here minded," Lorenzo said, setting Chiara down, then crossing his ankles and lowering himself to the grass in one fluid motion, without using his hands for support. "They don't get to hear much music these days. Neither do I, for that matter. I used to love listening to my father play the piano for me when I was little, but no one around here seems to play anything anymore."

It wasn't easy to picture Vittorio's fishy fingers flying over the keys of a piano, but the thought that he had a musical side amused her. She wondered whether he played the classics or jazz, popular songs or his own compositions.

"Don't you play anything?" she asked.

"I wish I could," Lorenzo said, more sadness than regret in his voice, as if playing an instrument was an unattainable dream.

"You could always learn. All it takes is a little time and practice."

"Oh, I know that. I did make a couple of attempts, but first there was Filippo, and then my wife, rolling their eyes and complaining about the noise every time I practiced. It was too frustrating. Musical people should be with musical people, I guess," Lorenzo said. "So, what was that you were playing? An old American folk song?"

"I'm not sure whether you'd call it folk or spiritual or what. It was considered an anthem of the civil rights movement. A protest song."

"And what were you protesting just now?" Lorenzo asked, his arms encircling Chiara, who had settled into the space between his legs.

"Nothing," Jolene said. "I was just thinking about my mother. It was her song, too. Our song. And this was her recorder." Jolene held up the instrument, as if making a formal introduction. Lorenzo nodded in acknowledgement.

"What were you and your mother protesting?" he asked.

"Nothing. Everything." Jolene said, shrugging and shaking her head." That song just made us feel good. It gave us hope."

"I can get that. It made me feel good when I heard it, too. Especially because it was so unexpected," Lorenzo said. After a pause he added, "Would you sing it for me?"

Jolene loved to sing when she was alone, out walking or rowing, riding in the car or pedaling a bicycle, but as a rule, she was not fond of singing in front of other people. Then she remembered that rules were not having a good morning in Manarola. She cleared her voice, closed her eyes, and sang:

"We shall overcome, we shall overcome,
We shall overcome some day.

Deep in my heart, I do believe,
We shall overcome some day."

Lorenzo clapped, holding Chiara's hands in his, which made the child giggle.

"Did you understand the words?" she asked Lorenzo.

"Sure," he nodded. "My parents used to speak to me in English when I was just a baby. I suppose that was what made it easier for me to learn it later in life," he said. "Can you repeat the words again so I remember?"

"How about if I write them down for you?" Jolene said, trying to picture Luisa and Vittorio cooing to Lorenzo in English between piano concerts, as she took out her notebook. Carefully printing the lyrics on a sheet, she tore it out and handed it to him. Lorenzo smiled his thanks, then folded the paper, lifting a hip to slide it into the back pocket of his jeans.

"Now it's my turn to ask you something," Jolene said, flipping to the page with the poem. "I copied this from that monument, and I think I got the gist of it, but I don't want to miss out on any of the meaning."

"Okay," he said. "Tell me what you understand."

"O, open to the winds and waves, Ligurian cemeteries. A rosy sadness colors you when in the evening, like a flower that—what exactly does '*marcisce*' mean?"

"The verb *marcire* means 'to rot.' Like a flower that rots."

"So then: A rosy sadness colors you when in the evening, like a flower that rots? That doesn't sound very poetic," she said. "Maybe we could say 'wilt' instead?"

"Sure, go for wilt," he said, leaning close, his eyes dropping to the notebook in her lap as she noted the words down.

"Okay. So, like a flower that wilts - or maybe 'like a wilting flower' sounds better?" she said, looking up at him, blushing when he raised his eyes to meet hers.

"You have a funny way of holding your pencil," he said.

"What's wrong with the way I hold my pencil?" she asked.

"Nothing. It's just different," he said. It was true. Her teachers had tried to correct her, but she'd persisted in holding the pencil the way it felt right to her. It made her uncomfortable that he would notice, but it also flattered her, in a way.

"So, is 'like a wilting flower' all right with you?" she said, looking down.

"You're the English expert, not me!"

"All right, let's go for: A rosy sadness colors you when in the evening, like a wilting flower, the great light goes '*sfacendo*'? Can you help with that?"

"*Fare* means 'to make' or 'to do', right? And *sfare* is the opposite, same as *disfare*, or 'to undo'. And *sfacendo* is the gerund—no, that's for nouns, right? What do you call the verb form that ends in *ing*? It's been a while."

"Present continuous tense?" she said.

"I think that's it. Like 'we're talking and walking,' right?"

"Right," Jolene nodded. "So what does it mean? The great light goes undoing?" She scrunched up her face. "It doesn't sound right to me. You can't really undo the light, can you? How about, 'the great light fades'?"

"Fades," he repeated. "Yeah, that sounds good."

"Okay. So, the great light fades—and dies?" she said, looking up at him for confirmation before writing the words down. She was getting confused; by the poem, by the translation, by him.

Lorenzo nodded, locking eyes with hers.

"Now I get it. Sort of," Jolene said. "I'm not sure how much I like it though."

Lorenzo shrugged but remained silent, as if he would have liked to defend both the poet and his language, but lacked the necessary conviction.

"We came to visit Nonno," Chiara chimed in.

"That's very sweet," Jolene said, shutting her notebook, relieved to put the poem to rest. "I looked around, but I didn't see any Garaventis buried here."

Lorenzo shook his head. "The only ones in town are still alive and kicking."

"It was Nonno Lani," Chiara said. "The other grandfather. Who did you come to visit?"

"My mother," Jolene said, filing away the information that Monica's father was no longer living.

"Let's pick some flowers for her!" Chiara cried, jumping up. "Where's her grave?"

"She doesn't have one," Jolene said. "I was just visiting her in my imagination."

"Chiara's Nonno doesn't have a grave here either, but we visit him in our imagination too, don't we Chiara?" Lorenzo said.

"Yep!" Chiara nodded. "He's Heaven."

"You mean he's in heaven," Jolene said.

"No, he *is* Heaven," Chiara said.

"You know what I think, you two?" Lorenzo said, standing up in one easy movement, again without using his hands. "I think we've had enough of the cemetery on this fine morning. I also think it's time we treated ourselves to a cappuccino."

"Me too?" Chiara said.

"You too!" Lorenzo said, tossing the child into the air and hugging her to his chest when she landed. "Only without the coffee."

"But that's just latte!" Chiara said.

"Not if you sprinkle cinnamon on top. Or cocoa."

"Can I have both?"

"Yes, you can have both," Lorenzo said, rubbing noses with her, laughing.

"That sounds yummy, Chiara!" Jolene couldn't wait to try it herself. "Can I have both too?"

Lorenzo smiled and nodded, then led the way down the stairs, down the path, through the village, to the Locanda.

Minutes later, Lorenzo was already slipping behind the bar to kiss Luisa, who stood across from the two men drinking white wine from the sturdy tumblers Filippo refused to use, saying they were as thick as a Ligurian's skull. A thin strip of freshly baked focaccia dangled from each man's hand like a lure, glistening with the sheen of extra virgin olive oil.

"*Buongiorno* Stevin, *buongiorno* Giobatta!" Lorenzo said.

"What do you mean, '*buongiorno?*'" Giobatta's crony grumbled, banging the butt of his glass on the bar, nodding for Luisa to serve him another drop. "It may be good for you," he snarled. "Nothing good about it for me."

"Don't get started again, Stevin," Giobatta said. "Unless you want me to explain to our *Americanina* why everyone calls you Stevin '*Menabelin.*'"

The scowl Stevin directed at Jolene told her she'd better stay out of it and keep smiling, which was exactly what she planned to do.

"Don't pay any attention to him," Giobatta said, dunking the tip of his focaccia into his wine. "He's always complaining that everyone's better off than he is, luckier than he is. Always breaking everyone's balls. That's how he got the nickname."

The men refrained from speaking while the Cimbali machine hissed and gurgled, steaming the milk in the pitcher Lorenzo held, while coffee trickled into two cappuccino cups. Lorenzo filled a thick glass with the frothy milk, dividing the remainder between the two cups, then sprinkled all three beverages with cinnamon and cocoa.

"You don't get cappuccino like that everywhere, do you *Americanina?*" Giobatta said, winking at her.

"I have no doubt that the cappuccino at the Locanda is the best in all the Cinque Terre," she said. "And so are the people at the Locanda." Turning to Lorenzo, she added, "I was so distracted up in the cemetery that I forgot to thank you."

"For what?" he asked.

"For letting me use the desk and chair, and for helping Giobatta to get them moved."

"No problem," Lorenzo said with a shrug. "I hate to see old things just sitting there rotting away when they can still be useful."

"Ha! Like me!" Giobatta said, his long ear allowing him to participate in two conversations at the same time.

"Come sit with Nonna while you drink that, Chiara," Luisa said, setting the child's glass of milk and a spoon on a table.

"We went to visit Nonno at the cemetery," the child said, clambering up onto a chair and immediately scooping up some foam.

"That's sweet," Luisa said, visibly moved. She must have been close to Monica's father, Jolene thought. "Remember, you can talk to him anywhere, and he'll always listen."

"Jolene went to visit her mother, too, but she didn't talk to her. She played music to her," Chiara said.

"What a lovely thought," Luisa said, looking up at Jolene. "You'll have to tell me more about your mother sometime. Filippo hasn't been a great source of information."

Jolene nodded, but refrained from commenting on how she herself would have appreciated a little more information from Filippo. She hoped her next woman-to-woman chat with her future mother-in-law would go better than the last one, but she couldn't imagine how a woman like Luisa, living her quiet little life in this peaceful little corner of the world, could comprehend the hell her mother had gone through.

"Speaking of Filippo," Jolene said. "Has he been by yet this morning?"

Luisa nodded. "You only missed him by about ten minutes. He hardly stopped long enough to say hello. He just grabbed a slice of focaccia and ran for the train."

"The train?" Jolene asked.

"Yes, he said he tried calling you but your phone was switched off. He went to pick up some papers he needed from the *Capitaneria* in La Spezia. He said he'd be back by noon, if all goes well."

"The *Capitaneria?*" Jolene asked, wondering what Filippo could possibly need from the Coast Guard. "Why?"

"That's what I wanted to know," Luisa said. "But he said he didn't have time to explain."

A burning sensation in Jolene's chest made her set her cup down. Maybe she shouldn't be drinking a second cappuccino. Or maybe her new bra was too tight. She shouldn't have worn it in the first place, considering she'd put it on to please Filippo. He'd bought it for her at Victoria's Secret, together with a shopping bag full of sexy lingerie, as a surprise. It had made her laugh when he'd told her about his expedition, how he'd browsed the racks with a saleswoman to pick out matching colors and styles. On learning that Jolene was small-breasted, the woman had suggested a push-up bra, and although Jolene agreed that it was flattering, the underwire and padding tended to suffocate her. As soon as she finished her cappuccino she'd go into the bathroom and take it off. It didn't match the underpants she'd chosen to walk in, anyway, and wearing mismatched underclothes always distressed her.

"Is everything all right?" Luisa asked.

"Fine," Jolene nodded, placing one hand below her breasts and covering her mouth with the other to hide a little burp. "It's just that I was hoping to take a hike with Filippo this morning."

"I used to love to hike," Luisa sighed. "That was before I became chained to this place. Now I'm stiff as a *baccala*."

Jolene had a hard time imagining Luisa roaming the hills. In fact, she had a hard time imagining her anywhere else but inside the Locanda, doing anything else besides what she did here.

"Why don't you go with Jolene, Lorenzo?" Luisa suggested. "You're a better guide than Filippo anyway."

"We wouldn't make it very far with Chiara. She stops to talk to every flower."

"Chiara can stay here with me," Luisa said. Turning to the child, she asked, "Would you like to stay here and help Nonna?" Chiara's eyes widened, and she looked around the room at the others, as if she could hardly believe her luck, her spicy milk mustache and impish smile making everyone chuckle. Even Stevin's scowl melted away.

"That makes it easy, then," Lorenzo said.

"Are you sure it's not too much trouble?" Jolene asked, wishing she'd kept quiet and gone off on her own. She felt silly involving the whole family, when all she wanted was to go for a stupid walk with her fiancé.

"No trouble at all," Lorenzo said, placing a hand over his heart and bowing his head. It was a kind gesture, but something about him still intimidated her.

"You people are so polite you kill me," Stevin '*Menabelin*' muttered.

TEN

"Too fast for you?" Lorenzo called over his shoulder. Since they'd set out, Jolene had counted two-hundred-and-something steps before deciding it was a pointless exercise in masochism.

"So far, so good!" she huffed. She was disgruntled at not being in better shape after all the walking she'd done since arriving in Manarola. Even if she hadn't ventured far afield, she must have climbed the vertical equivalent of a skyscraper a day during her exploration of the village, between meetings with Filippo.

"I always come this way, but maybe you would have preferred to take the bus as far as Volastra," Lorenzo said. "I forget how steep a climb this is for people who aren't used to it."

"Filippo made me take the bus the last time," Jolene grunted. She felt compelled to bring Filippo into the conversation, as if by mentioning his name he would be included in the outing; as if it would make her feel a little less guilty about having set off with his brother instead of waiting for him.

"It won't take long. Another twenty minutes, tops."

"No problem!" Jolene said, hoping this hike wouldn't create more problems than it was worth. She wished she'd had a few more minutes to think it over, but by the time she'd returned from the ladies' room, where the removal of her bra had brought instant relief from her chest pains, Lorenzo was standing by the door in his hiking boots, his face freshly shaved and a backpack slung over his shoulder. In her defense, she had phoned Filippo from the Locanda to let him know of their plans, just to make sure he had no objections, but he hadn't answered. There wasn't much to object to, anyway, considering it was Luisa, his own mother, who had facilitated the outing, and Lorenzo, his own brother, who was accompanying her.

Whatever the case, it was too late; she was here now, and she had every intention of making the best of her first Italian hike, she decided, pumping her arms with a burst of energy as she marched onward and upward. Rowing had given her strong arms and shoulders, while her legs and overall endurance had benefited from her habit of walking and biking in all kinds of weather. It annoyed her to feel so short of breath now; to realize that the older she got, the quicker she lost ground.

"Are you okay?" Lorenzo asked, fifteen minutes later. His cheeks were rosy from the climb, but he hardly looked winded.

"I should do this every morning," Jolene panted, her hands on her knees as she joined him in the shade of a massive olive tree. "It would get me back in shape."

"Nah," Lorenzo said. "You don't need to do that."

Jolene straightened up, smiling, half expecting him to say the usual thing, that she looked like she was in great shape, even though she knew it wasn't true.

"You should hike for the pleasure of it," he said, instead. "Besides, why walk up the same stairs every day when there are so many other places to explore? There are simpler ways to lose weight, if that's what you want to do."

Jolene wiped her brow with the back of her hand. She didn't need or want Lorenzo to compliment her, but neither did she want him to agree that she should lose weight. Of course, being used to Monica's birdlike figure, her big-boned American body must seem bulky. Thank God she'd be marrying the taller of the two brothers; Filippo always commented on the handsome figure they cut as a couple.

"I've always hiked for the pleasure of it!" she said, pulling out her map and waving it in the air. "And that's what I plan to do here, too."

"Great. This is the perfect time of the year to get started," Lorenzo said. "It's too hot and crowded in the summer, but by now, if you avoid the weekends, you can often walk all day without running into anyone at all."

"How many people live up here in Volastra?" she asked, taking in the view of the colorful dwellings. They were laid out in a circular pattern, like an old wagon train camp set up to fend off intruders.

"Year-round, only a couple hundred," Lorenzo said. "My grandmother was born here, and so were Zia Marta and Zia Matilde. But the settlement dates back to Roman times. It was the people from up here who later drifted down to the sea and settled in Manarola."

"It amazes me to think of people settling in such a remote place, so many centuries ago. What did they live on?"

"This place wasn't as remote as it seems. It was a strategic location on the old Roman road, and stage travelers would stop here to change horses and rest. Most of the inhabitants were peasants, though, and worked the land. The Romans weren't interested in any place that couldn't produce wine or olive oil, and Volastra had both. There are more olive trees than people here, that's how the settlement got its name."

"I don't get the connection," she said. It was interesting to see how Lorenzo opened up when he explained things, and she appreciated the way he did so, without being pedantic or making her feel ignorant.

"Volastra derives from *Vicus Oleaster*.

"Meaning?" Jolene asked. She recognized the Latin, but like most Americans her age, she'd never studied it.

"It translates to 'village of olives,'" Lorenzo said.

"I see," Jolene commented. "So even in ancient times, the economy was based on food, wine, and tourism."

"That's right," Lorenzo nodded. "I suppose you could say my grandfather was a tourist too, when he met my grandmother. He was passing through in the late 1940s, after the war, when very few outsiders knew about the place except for some poets and artists."

"I'd love to hear more about that. Filippo hasn't told me much about the family," Jolene said.

"Well, he's never been too interested in that side of the family. Maybe you can get Ma tell to you the whole story one day."

"Yes, I'd like that," Jolene said.

"Anyway, getting back to the present," Lorenzo continued, "you'll see there are a few shops and restaurants up here now, and some locals have started fixing up rooms and renting them out to tourists. People like it because you can get here by car, then set out on the higher trails without having to climb up from sea level, like we did."

"According to my map, Volastra is at an altitude of about 330 meters," she said. "That means we've already climbed over a thousand feet! Starting out from here would seem like cheating."

"That was one of the things Filippo liked about Volastra," Lorenzo said.

"What do you mean by that?" Jolene asked.

"Sorry, I meant the accessibility, not the cheating. It made sense, from a business standpoint."

An odd feeling gripped the pit of Jolene's stomach, a strange sinking feeling that was becoming all too familiar, a feeling that she was missing something. The first time she'd asked Filippo about Volastra, he'd brushed her off, saying there was nothing there. And when they'd taken the bus up together, he'd insisted on going straight to the vineyards without showing her around, then disappeared on her. Lorenzo was a direct person, and she thought he'd answer her questions with honesty, but she didn't even know enough to know what to ask. She'd have to go fishing again.

"Well, accessibility is certainly important for the success of any business," she said, hoping to bait him.

"Definitely," Lorenzo agreed. "But it takes more than that. People come to the Cinque Terre for the experience, not for the convenience."

"Of course," Jolene said. "It's all about the experience."

"And for an experience to be positive, it has to match—better yet, exceed— people's expectations. Bringing in a herd of donkeys and then installing a giant hot tub with chromotherapy lights on the terrace right next to their stalls were two contradictory approaches," he said. "You need to decide on an identity, and stick with it."

"Identity is important," Jolene said, wondering what asses and Jacuzzis had to do with anything.

"That's just my opinion, of course," Lorenzo added.

"Of course," Jolene nodded.

"Don't get me wrong, Jolene," he said. "I really care about Filippo. He's a hard worker, and he's come up with some visionary ideas in the past. But if two partners aren't following the same vision, they're headed for disaster."

Jolene's throat was so dry she could barely swallow. Grabbing the water bottle from her backpack, she drank in slow gulps, stalling for time to decipher his last comment. By "partners," was he referring to himself and Filippo, or to her and Filippo? Was he trying to caution her about the endeavors Filippo wouldn't talk to him about, or was he jealous of his brother, as Filippo had always sustained? She needed to know more.

"Yes, you're right," she said. "I've had a similar experience in my business, with my ex-partner. It's important to follow the same vision."

"A simple *agriturismo* would have been perfect here," Lorenzo said. "An authentic Italian farmhouse, where guests could read a book while lying on a hammock strung up between two olive trees, or spend a day tending the vines, or learn how to make limoncello. Even the donkey rides would have been a hit, I'm sure. But drinking wine while taking a soak in a Jacuzzi with flashing lights seems so, I don't know, Californian."

"I see your point," she said, but all she saw were the pieces of a puzzle she couldn't put together.

"Plus, if you try to pass a rustic guest house off as a luxury property, like Filippo wanted to do, you start attracting the wrong kind of tourists, the kind you'll never be able to satisfy. Like those rich Russians who drink all the best Sciacchetrà in the wine cellar as if it were lemonade. Or spit out our wine when they taste it, because they've never been weaned off French champagne. We don't need people like that here. They'd be better off staying in Portofino, or Forte dei Marmi, where they'd find more of their type."

"Right," Jolene said. She'd hadn't been to Portofino or that other place yet, and though she'd met plenty of wine snobs, she couldn't imagine anyone so vulgar. Nor could she imagine what such people had to do with Filippo and Volastra.

"I mean, if Filippo and Wendy couldn't even resolve their own personal problems, there was no way they could run a business together," Lorenzo said. "Either you share the same dream, or you live separate nightmares."

Wendy? Personal problems? Filippo had never mentioned this business, let alone this Wendy. Who was she, and where had she come from? More importantly, where had she gone?

"Look, Jolene," Lorenzo said, placing a hand on her shoulder. "I didn't want to talk about Filippo, but it's no secret that we've had our problems working together in the past. Once he went off to school in Milan, and then abroad, I wasn't good enough for him, and the

Locanda wasn't good enough for him, then Wendy and her guesthouse weren't good enough for him. I can tell you're a good person, and a smart woman. You have the experience, and a natural knack for the hospitality business. That was clear to me from the first time I saw you, when you jumped in to help out at the Locanda. I'm sure the two of you will do great things together. Wherever you decide to go. Whatever you decide to do."

Jolene was more confused than ever, now. Wasn't Manarola where they had decided to go? Wasn't the renovation and relaunching of the Locanda what they had decided to do? From what she'd overheard from Lorenzo's argument with Monica, he had no intention of ever leaving Manarola for Genoa, but from what she'd gathered from Filippo, in addition to not being aware of his brother's vision for the Locanda, Lorenzo was not to be involved in its future. It didn't seem like there was much dream-sharing going on here. All of them seemed to be swinging on separate stars.

"The past is the past, though!" Lorenzo said. "Right now we should be talking about where to go from here."

Jolene was all for bringing the future into focus, and it disturbed her to not be able to speak openly with Lorenzo. She and Filippo had spent many an hour brainstorming, and now she was itching to draw up some concrete plans, but it was imperative that the brothers and their parents sort things out among themselves first. The last thing Jolene wanted was to find herself in the middle of a family feud. *No, grazie.*

"Yes, but you really need to discuss that with Filippo first," she said, promising herself that she would urge Filippo to sit down and talk to his brother without further delay.

Lorenzo laughed. "What does Filippo have to do with our hike?"

"Our hike?"

"Yes, our hike. Where do you want to go from here? That is, if you still want to walk some more."

"Of course I do!" she said, eager to abandon subjects she knew nothing about or wasn't at liberty to discuss. Walking was way better than talking, way less confusing.

"So, we can access several trails from here. For example, we could walk part of the high route that follows the crest, all the way from Levanto to Portovenere," he explained, pointing to the mountainside above them.

"Levanto to the northwest and Portovenere to the southeast," she said, without glancing at her map. "The two gateways to the Cinque Terre, right?"

"Right." Lorenzo nodded. "You have been studying, haven't you?"

Jolene nodded. "I love maps. I like seeing where I've been, and knowing what options I have for getting where I want to go."

Lorenzo stared at her for a moment, his lips slightly parted, as if he were about to say something, but then thought the better of it.

"Why don't we go down to Corniglia?" she suggested. After their conversation she felt like she'd already scaled a mountain, making the idea of a downhill trek more appealing. "I still haven't been there, if you can believe it."

"We could do that," he said. "Unless you want to follow a stretch of the Via dei Santuari, to see the shrine at Riomaggiore. But there's also a beautiful sanctuary right here, too, if you want to take a look. The church of Nostra Signora della Salute."

"Our Lady of Health?"

"Right."

"That's an Our Lady I've never heard of before. Why don't we go see what she has to say, and then decide?"

A short walk took them to a square, where they were faced with a church of exquisite simplicity. As with every beautiful building she'd seen so far, she wondered how old it was. Before she could ask, Lorenzo said, "This church dates back to the 12th century, or thereabouts."

"That's when I should have lived," Jolene said, walking closer. "They didn't go for unnecessary complications back then. Everything was so solid and simple. Just look at this stone."

"That's local sandstone," Lorenzo said.

She ran her hand over the pale blocks of the façade, wondering how many people had walked beneath the arched doorway over the course of nine centuries, how many monumental moments of how many everyday lives had been celebrated inside, how many babies baptized and deaths mourned, how many sins confessed, how many people taken to the grave. All those lives were gone now, but the church stood on.

"What's this style called?" she asked.

"Romanesque," Lorenzo answered, chuckling.

"I'm sorry, that must sound like a stupid question to you, but I don't know much about architecture. I had to ask Filippo the same thing about the church in Manarola."

"I wasn't laughing at you, and there are no stupid questions. It's just struck me as funny. I'm usually the one being lectured on architecture, by Monica."

Jolene smiled. "And just look at that window!" She tilted her head to stare up at the single oval-arched window divided in two by a stone column, centered above the door. "What perfect symmetry and grace."

"It's called a *bifora* in Italian," Lorenzo said, sparing her the need to ask. "You might notice that the window gives it a Gothic touch. These churches took centuries to build, and they often incorporated several different architectural styles. Trends changed over the course of time, just like now."

"Only then everything was more beautiful," Jolene said. "Can we go inside?"

"Of course."

The massive wooden door creaked as they passed through the ancient portal. Jolene dipped her fingers in the holy water and crossed herself, and from the corner of her eye glimpsed Lorenzo doing the same. Once inside, Jolene was almost afraid to move, lest she disturb the solemn stillness of her surroundings. Smooth with age, the black and white marble floor gleamed in the dim light, and she felt slightly ashamed to be standing on such an old and noble surface in her mass-produced rubber-soled sneakers, probably manufactured by Chinese slave workers. There was something to be said for cultures in which the faithful were required to enter places of worship barefoot, she thought. Looking around from where she stood, there was much to be admired in the harmonious simplicity of the intimate interior: the unadorned stone walls with mere slits for windows, reaching up to a plain white vaulted ceiling; the rows of modest wooden pews; the carved confessional booth, where the face of the sitting priest vested with the power to pardon would be hidden by a red velvet curtain, but the repentant sinner must kneel in plain view. The spirituality of this place seemed more tangible to her like this, in its holy emptiness and silence, without a priest leading archaic prayers and a congregation mumbling memorized responses as they sat and stood and kneeled on command. After a few moments, she ventured down the center aisle, stepping lightly on the balls of her feet so her sneakers would not squeak. Spotting a small statue of Mary, she fished a coin out of her pocket and dropped it in the offerings box, where it landed with a metallic echo. She lit a votive candle and placed it in a front-row candle-holder, then crossed herself again before returning to Lorenzo, who still stood by the entrance.

"Was that for something or someone special?" he whispered.

Jolene nodded, wondering how many special intentions she could squeeze out of a one-euro candle. She kept her answer simple. "My mother."

"How long ago did she die?"

"Last year. Ten months ago, actually. It was December."

"I'm sorry. It takes time to adjust. But you never really get over it, do you?"

Jolene shook her head, swallowing over the lump that had formed in her throat. She didn't want to talk about it; not here, not now, not with Lorenzo. "I feel cheated," she heard her voice whisper, disregarding her resolve. "I lost her without any warning. She never told me goodbye. She didn't even want a funeral."

She hoped Lorenzo wouldn't say he knew what it was like, because he couldn't. But Lorenzo said nothing. They stood there for another moment or two, each absorbed in his or her own thoughts, both enveloped in the silence and shadow and lingering scents of centuries-old rites. It struck her as odd that she avoided talking about her mother to Filippo because the few times she had, he'd tried to cheer her up instead of encouraging her to vent her feelings, saying that he hated to see her sad; yet this was the second time in one morning she'd found herself speaking about her to Lorenzo. Sharing her sadness rather than burying it seemed to blunt its sharpest edges.

When they emerged from the dark church she was shocked by the sun's intensity, which seemed to have multiplied tenfold while they were inside. Its heat caressed her shoulders and penetrated her bones, its brightness made her squint.

"I think I'd rather leave the rest of the churches for another day," she said.

"I agree," Lorenzo said. "If you put away your map and trust my lead, I think I know just what you need."

Without waiting for an answer, Lorenzo headed down a path, but not before Jolene could glance at the signposts confirming they had hiked to an altitude of 335 meters, and that Corniglia would be another hour and a half's walk. Next to the signs was a marker, a plain block of sandstone supporting a wrought iron cross. Jolene swiped the stone with her fingers as she passed, whispering a prayer of gratitude for the splendid fall day. Filled with new energy, she set off after Lorenzo, and was soon rewarded with a spectacular panorama of Manarola far below to the east and Corniglia to the northwest, the dregs of doubt and sadness rushing out of her with such force that she felt light-headed as she followed Lorenzo along the mercifully level but perilously narrow path. The only way to safely admire the view of the vine-covered terraces that tumbled straight down to the sea was to stop, and she did so often. The grapes had all been harvested by now, and not a soul could be seen working among the bright yellow leaves waving in the breeze, as if to tell her that they would not be there the next time she passed.

"Sorry for being so slow," she said, catching up with Lorenzo, who had stopped to wait for her. "Everything is so, I don't know, vertical. It makes me a little woozy, but at the same time it exhilarates me."

Lorenzo looked at her but didn't say anything. It was hard to tell whether he got what she meant.

"I mean, walking is exciting here," she said. "Do you know what I mean?"

"Yes, I do," Lorenzo finally said. "Some people feel cramped living in a place like Manarola. But they're the lazy ones. If you want broader horizons, all you have to do is climb. Your whole perspective changes."

"Exactly!" Jolene said. "Every time I turn a corner, I can't wait to see what's behind it. I never imagined all these vineyards hidden away up here! And all these stone walls! There must be miles and miles of them."

"There are. My little piece of land is enough to keep the family in table wine, but it's nothing compared to this. Along this coastline, between Valle dei Pozzi and Posa, you're looking at the best grape-growing spot in the Cinque Terre," Lorenzo said.

"Now I know why it tastes the way it does!" Jolene said, her eyes roving over every curve of the steep hillside, drinking in the beauty.

"What do you mean?" Lorenzo asked.

"The day I arrived, when I sipped that first glass of wine, I could taste all of this, only I didn't know what it was at the time. It was bottled sunshine and sea breeze and shrubs and birdsong and nectar!" Jolene said, closing her eyes, breathing in the air, thick with the resinous scent of the Mediterranean maquis, regretting that she'd arrived in autumn, after the summer sun had left the land parched and the branches brittle. She was already impatient for the spring, for its budding branches and blooming flowers; she could already smell them. "It's absolutely amazing," she whispered.

"Yeah, it is," Lorenzo said, walking away. "But we'd better get moving if you only have until noon."

It annoyed Jolene that he'd interrupted her mood so brusquely, and she wanted to reply that her time was her own today; that just because Filippo had left word that he'd be back at noon didn't mean that she had to be, but she said nothing as she fell in step behind him. Lorenzo remained silent, too, the only sounds accompanying them the crunching of loose gravel, the cry of gulls gliding overhead, the twitter of birds in the trees. At one point, she couldn't resist stopping to look at the sea far below, so blue and calm and inviting, filling her with a sense of urgency that she take her first swim before the weather turned. Maybe that very afternoon, she thought, again hurrying after Lorenzo, because she knew herself, and she knew that she would return by noon, and that she would ask Filippo to go with her, despite the fact that he kept saying that the water was too cold by now, and that one shouldn't go swimming in months with an r. She was already wondering what it would take to convince him, and whether he'd at least take a dip by the rocks he'd jumped off of as a child, when she turned a corner and crashed into Lorenzo, who was standing in the bushes picking fruit.

"Sorry!" she cried.

"Have you ever tried these?" he asked, handing her a couple of bright red berries the size of a cherry.

"No, what are they?" she asked. The berries were plump and warm in her hand, their texture seedy.

"*Corbezzoli*," he said. "The scientific name of the plant is *Arbutus onedo*. In English, it's called a strawberry tree." Jolene studied the shrub-like tree with dark, shiny leaves and little white flowers that seemed to be a favorite with bees, judging from all the buzzing.

"How is it that you know its name in English, when I've never even heard of it?" Jolene asked.

"I have a thing for plants," he said. "And when foreigners ask me something, I like to be able to give an answer."

"Is the fruit edible?"

"You bet. Chiara adores it."

"Oh, I remember! These are the berries she was eating the day I ran into the two of you by the church."

"That's right," Lorenzo said.

"Shall we pick some for her?"

"Better not," he said. "Monica got it into her head that they're bad for her. Besides, they don't travel well."

Studying the perfect shape and color of the crimson spheres, they did feel like strawberries on the surface, as she rolled them around in the palm of her hand.

"Aren't you going to try one?" Lorenzo asked.

Placing a berry on her tongue, Jolene felt like she was breaking the third rule of the day, the lifelong rule she'd learned as a child, to never eat wild berries. Though it may not be poisonous, the berry tasted grainy, and on the sour side.

"Well? What do you think?" Lorenzo asked.

"It's unusual," she said, sniffing a second berry before putting it in her mouth. This one seemed to have a better flavor, now that she knew what to expect. She smiled at the thought of Chiara stuffing the berries into her mouth as if they were candy, and begging her father for more.

"Wait till you try the *corbezzolo* honey I have back at the Locanda. I get it from a local beekeeper," Lorenzo said, popping one berry into his mouth after another, while picking another handful. "Here have some more. They're good for the liver, for the kidneys, for diarrhea, for—"

"I'm fine," Jolene said. "I don't want to overdo a good thing."

As they continued along the path, Lorenzo became talkative again, stopping occasionally to point out a plant or shrub, telling Jolene its name in Italian, Latin, and English. She jotted the names down in her notebook, beneath the quick sketches she penciled as they went along.

"I'm so bad at this!" she said, after botching an attempt to render a rockrose.

"Can I take a look?" Lorenzo asked, coming to stand next to her.

"I'm afraid I wouldn't have made a very good nineteenth-century Englishwoman," she said, frowning.

"Hmm. Try again in the spring," he said. "The five-petaled flowers of the cistus make it easier to recognize."

"Thanks," she said, sighing as she flipped the book shut. "I'll keep it in mind."

"Can I see your other drawings?"

"I don't think you'd be—"

"C'mon, don't be shy," Lorenzo said, plucking the pad from her hands.

"Really, Lorenzo, I'd rather you—"

But Lorenzo was already flipping through the pages, pausing to study the sketches and doodles she'd made of Suite 16, of the bar and restaurant at the Locanda, of the fifteen rooms she'd visited with Giobatta.

"Well, this all looks familiar," he said. "Yet better. No one told me you were an interior designer."

"That's because I'm not," she said. "I was just fooling around."

Closing the notebook, Lorenzo handed it back to her, staring at her in a peculiar way, his eyes not looking into hers but roving over her face, as if he were studying her features for a sketch of his own. Blushing, she dropped the pad and pencil into her backpack and zipped it up, wishing she could ask what he really thought of her ideas, hoping he wouldn't mention them to anyone else.

They walked on in silence until they came upon the tracks of the monorail which prompted Lorenzo to explain that the system had been installed for the transportation of harvested grapes up the steep slopes, as well to facilitate the movement of stones and materials required for the upkeep of the land and its walls. They soon came across a few stone houses in a location called Porciana, also purported to be of Roman origin.

The turns of the trail led them in and out of shaded areas, where a variety of tall-trunked trees offered respite from the sun, which would be precious in the summer months. While the paths around Volastra had been littered with olives, here the ground was sprinkled with the first fallen acorns and chestnuts. Lorenzo told her that the Ligurians had gathered both to sustain themselves when times were tough, and still ground the chestnuts to make flour, which was used in certain types of pasta, like the trofie traditionally served with pesto, and a cake made with pine nuts and raisins, called *castagnaccio*. Re-emerging into the sun, she found that by now Corniglia was not far off, and that here again the olive trees abounded.

"Sometimes I have to pinch myself to make sure I'm really here," Jolene said, admiring the view from the belvedere of Piazza Santa Maria, after they'd stopped briefly to admire the façade of the church of St. Peter, where Lorenzo pointed out the rosette of Carrara marble and bas-relief of a deer, the town's symbol.

"That must be Monterosso I see to the west," she said.

"Yes, from this spot you can see the whole coastline of the Cinque Terre, from Monterosso to Riomaggiore."

"It's so beautiful, beyond words," she said.

"Does that mean you like it here?"

"I love it here. I never, ever want to leave," Jolene said, staring off into the distance. Although Manarola and the Locanda and, she might as well admit it, the Garaventi family itself, weren't quite as idyllic as she'd imagined them, as soon as she pronounced those words aloud, in front of a witness, she realized how fervently she desired to make this place her home. She still had to resolve the issue of the wedding ceremony with Filippo and Don Ludovico, and it remained to be seen how she would fit in with the Garaventi family on a long-term basis; how many of her ideas would be taken into consideration when renovating the Locanda; what exactly her role in running it would be. Filippo had sworn to never take advantage of her the way Evan had, and the fact that he insisted on marrying her was proof of that. Knowing that he'd also failed at an endeavor with the wrong partner, she was convinced that their determination to achieve their common goals would be twice as strong. Filippo just needed to get the technicalities sorted out. And she needed to get to the bottom of that story, too.

"Enjoy it while you can," Lorenzo said.

Turning to look at him, Jolene opened her mouth to ask whether he was referring to the approaching winter or to the work that awaited her, but decided to leave it be. All she wanted right now to was hold onto this magical feeling.

"Just look at that water," she said, gazing down at the sea again. "I wish I could jump right in!"

"Let's go, then," Lorenzo said.

"But it must already be close to noon." She glanced at her wrist, but the only thing there was a scratch from Fata. "Filippo's probably back by now."

"So, do you want to head home?" Lorenzo asked.

"Not really." The thought of leaving now soured her mouth with the taste of anticipated regret. It would be like letting a waiter whisk away her plate in the middle of a delicious meal. Besides, her legs were shaky with fatigue.

"So, do you want to call Filippo and check in with him?"

"I don't have a phone," she said. "Well, I do now because Filippo gave me one, but it's back in my room, charging."

"Here, use mine," Lorenzo suggested, sliding his phone out of his pocket and handing it over to her.

She was already punching in the number she'd memorized, before realizing it belonged to the phone Filippo had used during his stay in America. She felt a bit silly that she hadn't written down his Italian number, a bit dismayed that he hadn't made sure she learned it. "I don't even know his number."

"It's in there, just scroll through the contacts."

Jolene looked at him, waiting for him to reconfirm what he'd just said; Lorenzo nodded. Filippo never let his phone out of his sight, and never suggested that she use it. In fact, she'd never met a single man who told her to browse through the names and numbers on his phone. True, Lorenzo couldn't be clumped together with the men she'd been involved with; he was more like a brother, obviously, since that was what he was going to be, her brother-in-law. Finding Filippo's number, she placed the call, waiting as the phone rang several times before the line went dead.

"No answer," she said.

"Try again."

This time Filippo's phone didn't even ring; instead, she got a recording. "Sounds like it's switched off, or out of range," she said. "It went straight to voicemail."

"That happens a lot when I try to call him," Lorenzo said. "Just send him a message. Tell him we'll be back by two. Three at the latest."

Jolene tapped out the text, then handed the phone back to him.

"Do you feel better now?" he asked.

Jolene nodded, but still felt uneasy at not being able to talk to Filippo directly.

"Good, because I have a surprise for you," Lorenzo said. "Come on."

ELEVEN

Jolene's thighs trembled in time with her clicking knees, as she followed Lorenzo down ramp after ramp of interminable brick steps leading to the two destinations indicated on the signs, one pointing to the station and the other to the sea. With the railway tunnel and tracks visible at their left and the sea straight below, the directions seemed obvious; what she wanted to know was how many more steps one was expected to walk down to get there. It had been nearly two hours since they'd paid their respects to the Madonna in Volastra, and she hoped Lorenzo's surprise didn't entail too much more walking.

"Did you count the steps?" he asked, when they finally reached the bottom of the last ramp, landing in the vicinity of the station surrounded by as many high fences, danger signs, and concrete walls as a military compound.

"I stopped at 200," Jolene huffed.

"That was about halfway. There are 377 of them, plus 33 ramps."

"No wonder my quads are quaking!" Jolene said. She was somewhat disappointed that they had come all that way and bypassed the center of Corniglia completely, but they didn't have all day, and Lorenzo probably planned to take her to one of the next towns for a swim, maybe Vernazza, or Monterosso, where there was a nice beach. The thought of a comfy train seat appealed to her at least as much as the cool drink she'd imagined enjoying at an outdoor café before moving on, especially since the beverage that would lure her all the way back up to town had not yet been invented.

"What time is our train?" she asked.

"We're not taking the train," Lorenzo said. "We're taking a shortcut. Follow me!"

She'd wanted a hike, and a hike she was getting. And steps—this time so narrow and in disrepair that she had to exercise caution while following Lorenzo through a sketchy passage flanked by a jungle of weeds, at the end of which there was not the pristine beach she'd hoped for, but a pitch-dark tunnel.

"Wait—what are we doing here?" she asked, watching him charge ahead.

"Walking!" Lorenzo called from the mouth of the tunnel.

"But this is the end of the path!"

"Officially, yes," Lorenzo said, turning to face her. "But the shortcut goes through the tunnel."

"Through the tunnel? Like the trains?" she asked.

"Don't worry, this tunnel's been out of use for years," Lorenzo said, a note of impatience creeping into his voice. "It's perfectly safe."

"Those signs say otherwise," she said, pointing to the warnings posted at the entrance. "That triangle icon with the exclamation mark means 'danger' in any language!" Jolene didn't mind taking risks, as long as it was her decision; brother-in-law or not, she couldn't just follow a man she hardly knew into a dark and allegedly derelict train tunnel.

"Look, I've been here a zillion times," Lorenzo said. "I could walk to the other side with my eyes closed."

Jolene didn't see much difference between walking with your eyes closed and walking in total darkness, which was sort of what she'd been doing all morning, now that she thought about it. She'd followed Lorenzo wherever he decided to take her, eager to prove she was adventurous and up to the challenge. But who did she want to prove it to? To herself? To Lorenzo? Or to Filippo? Whether or not Filippo minded her taking a friendly walk with Lorenzo didn't overly concern her; in fact, if he felt a twinge of jealousy, so be it. But she had a hunch he wouldn't approve of his brother dragging her through a spooky old railway tunnel leading to who knew where. Maybe Lorenzo wasn't the more cautious of the two brothers, as she'd been led to believe. Just because he stuck close to home didn't mean he didn't take risks; maybe the lack of adventure in his life made him even more imprudent than Filippo, whenever he got the chance.

"For the last time, it's not dangerous," Lorenzo said. "Come on."

Taking her first step toward him, she drew in a deep breath, discovering the answer to her question. She wanted to do this to prove something to herself.

"It'll be worth it, you'll see," Lorenzo said, as they disappeared into the blinding blackness.

Jolene hated the dark, and all the creepy, slithery things that lurked there. Maybe there were snakes and lizards, and even rats and bats, certainly spiders and all kinds of bugs. She hoped to God Lorenzo was at least right about there being no trains.

"Is something wrong?" Jolene asked a few seconds later, hearing him fumble with his backpack as she shuffled along, too terrified to lift her feet.

"Now that I know you'd do it in the dark, I won't make you," Lorenzo said. There was a click, then a beam of light penetrated the pitch-black void ahead of them.

"You could have told me you had a flashlight!" Jolene cried, hating him a little.

"You could have asked," Lorenzo said. She wished she could see his face; if it wore a grin she'd be tempted to slap it.

"How far to the end?" she asked, her pupils giant, her voice small. In some ways, a little light made it scarier, she thought, searching for something familiar in the phantom forms and ominous shadows that lay ahead. In some ways, not seeing at all was better than seeing a little.

"It's only a kilometer," he said. "Without stairs. We'll be there in ten minutes, tops."

"Okay." Ten minutes was nothing. Or an eternity. She was walking so close to Lorenzo that their shoulders kept bumping.

"Why don't you hold onto my arm?" he suggested.

She was still debating over whether the physical contact would make her feel uncomfortable when she stumbled, and would have fallen flat on her face if Lorenzo hadn't caught her. She grabbed his elbow, with no intention of letting go.

"Where will this take us?" she asked, instinctively speaking in a low voice, as if afraid of publicizing their presence to whatever unseen creatures, be they man or beast, that might be poised to pounce on them.

"It's a *SURPRISE!*" Lorenzo shouted, his voice echoing off the crumbling walls and dripping ceiling.

"*AAAHH!*" Jolene screamed, her feet nailed to the ground, her skin crawling with fear.

"I'm sorry!" Lorenzo laughed. "But I couldn't resist. When we came here as kids we used to play tricks on each other all the time. Much worse ones. I guess I've been missing a playmate."

"Well, I don't like that game!" Jolene cried, whacking him on the arm.

"Go ahead, hit me again!" Lorenzo said, gripping her elbow. "Or at least tell me to grow up."

"Yeah, really, Lorenzo! Why don't you grow—oh, never mind. I hate it when people say that."

Jittery with adrenalin, Jolene told herself to keep focusing on the beam of light, to keep putting one foot in front of the other, until she was walking as fast as the conditions allowed. Light, first a glimmer, then a shaft, soon became visible at the end of the tunnel, illuminating the way. Jolene let go of Lorenzo's arm and broke into a run, beating him to the end. The sun had never shone so bright, the air had never smelled so sweet, and Jolene had never received a more precious reward for her courage than what she beheld when she emerged from that decrepit tunnel. Squinting in the explosion of light and colors, her eyes feasted on the sight of the glittering sea lapping the deserted beach below them. She couldn't imagine a more perfect setting for her first swim in the Cinque Terre.

"Oh, my God! This is gorgeous!" she exclaimed.

"I told you," Lorenzo said, tugging her arm again. "Come on, follow me!"

Together they ran, stopping when they reached a steep, rocky embankment covered with scrub. It was true that she was fed up with stairs, but she sure wished she could see some now. "Please don't tell me that's the only way down!"

"It's child's play, for an expert hiker like you," Lorenzo grinned. "It'll be slippery because of the loose gravel, so you have to take it fast. Watch me, I'll go first."

It wasn't a long way down, fortunately, just a treacherous way down, but if this was the only access to that spectacular beach, she would have to give it a go, even if it meant skating down on the seat of her pants. When Lorenzo hopped over a downed chain-link fence and set off on his nimble-footed descent, Jolene was right behind him, her steps tight and light and quick. No problem, she thought, she could do this, her legs scrambling to keep up with her body's momentum, her arms windmilling in reverse to slow her flight. And she could have done it, had it not been for the rock that became dislodged when she stepped on it, making her lose her footing in the sliding crumble of dirt and gravel, careening down the slope with the rubble and crashing into Lorenzo, dragging him to the bottom before finally coming to rest atop of her backpack, her arms and legs splayed like an upturned tortoise on its shell.

Lorenzo was quick to hop to his feet, then to drop to his knees beside her. "My God, Jolene!" he cried. "Are you okay?"

"Um...I think so," she said, the humiliation making her wince more than any pain she might feel. Trembling from the tumble, she couldn't decide whether to laugh or cry, but managed a weak smile. "This isn't exactly what I had in mind when I dreamed of lying on the beach," she said.

Lorenzo didn't smile back. "Can you sit up?" he asked, extending a hand.

"Sure," she replied, pulling herself up without his assistance, then brushing off the skinned knees that poked through twin tears in her jeans. Her elbows and the heels of her hands were scraped, too, along with a couple of knuckles, but apart from that, she seemed all right. "Sorry about wiping you out. Did you get hurt?"

"Hurt, no," Lorenzo said, smiling now. "But you really know how to make an impact on a man." He proffered his hand again, and she took it this time, allowing him to help her to her feet.

"*Owww!*" she yelped, dropping back down to her butt.

"What's wrong?" Lorenzo asked.

"It's my ankle!"

"Let me take a look at it," Lorenzo said, pulling up her pant leg and running his fingers over the ankle, pressing so delicately on each bone that she felt no pain at all. "I don't think you broke anything," he said. "It's probably just a strain, a sprain at the worst. Do you want to try standing again?"

"Okay," she nodded. Whether she wanted to or not, it was clear she would have to try, and succeed, if she ever intended to return home. She was more cautious this time, placing all her weight on her right foot as she stood, but as soon as she tried to shift some weight to her left foot, a stab of pain shot through the joint.

"Ow! Ow! Ow!" she whimpered.

"I'd recommend soaking it right away," Lorenzo said. "Cool salt water is the best, and it just so happens we have lots of it, conveniently located right in front of us. Want to see if that helps?"

Jolene nodded. "Maybe."

Wrapping an arm around her waist, Lorenzo helped her hobble to the shore and sat her down so she could remove her shoes and socks and roll up her jeans. After doing the same, he helped her to her feet again, accompanying her to the water's edge.

"*Ahh*! That feels divine," she said, as the small waves lapped their lower legs. "Though I imagined my first Mediterranean swim a little differently."

"Things tend to turn out that way," Lorenzo said. "Different from how we imagine them, I mean. I wanted to show you one of the most beautiful beaches around, and look at what I did."

"It's my fault. I shouldn't be hiking in these flimsy sneakers," she said, though to be fair to herself, her intentions had not been so ambitious when she'd set out that morning. Yet despite her injury, she was proud of herself for rising to Lorenzo's challenges, and she was grateful that he'd led her to this spot without a single tourist in sight, a spot she would never have discovered on her own. It was so peaceful here, so secluded. If it wasn't for the fact that Lorenzo had to prop her up, she'd be content to stand there for hours, letting the sea bedazzle her with its diamond-tipped waves.

The sound of playful shouts made Jolene turn around, seeing a group of people slaloming down the slope. Though new to the beach and a guest in the country herself, Jolene was irritated at their arrival, as if it were an invasion of her and Lorenzo's exclusive territory. There were only four newcomers, though, and as she watched them spread their towels some distance away, she decided that it might not be so bad if there were a handful of other people around, after all. That way, she wouldn't have to tell Filippo that Lorenzo had taken her to an isolated beach where they were completely alone, which might put weird ideas in his head, brother or no brother. Jolene eyed the two couples as they kicked off their shoes and began undressing with haste, looking eager to jump into the water. She was curious to see, for future reference, how they would change into their bathing suits without exposing themselves, but as each item of clothing was shed and thrown onto a heap, she realized they did not share her concern for modesty. Within seconds, the foursome was hopping over the stones to the water's edge, butts and bellies jiggling, boobs bouncing, dingalings dangling.

"Oh my gosh!" she gasped, tugging on Lorenzo's elbow. "They're all naked!"

Lorenzo smiled. "That's why they came here."

"To prance around naked?"

"No, to swim naked."

"You mean this is a nudist beach?" Jolene asked, dots of anger coloring her cheeks. Was Jolene really still a poor judge of men and their intentions? Was this really just an innocent hike with an impromptu detour, or did Lorenzo have another agenda?

"It's not a nudist beach," he said. "It's just a free beach. People who like to go naked, go naked, and people who don't, don't."

"Do you?"

"Do I what?"

"Like to go naked?"

"Well, that depends," Lorenzo said in a tone he might use to explain something to Chiara. "If I'm in the mood, and I don't spot any jellyfish, I like to swim naked, because it feels natural to me. But I don't strut around naked in front of a crowd, like you see some people doing in the summer, because that doesn't feel natural to me."

Jolene tried not to resent the way Lorenzo seemed to be talking down to her, but mostly she tried not to picture him naked, an effort which hadn't been required of her until he put the image out there. She wondered whether Filippo ever came to this beach, and whether he ever swam naked.

"Could you please check your phone and see whether Filippo has answered my message yet?" she asked, feeling a need to make his presence felt, involve him in their conversation.

"I already have. No news," Lorenzo said. "Look, if you feel uncomfortable here, we can leave."

"Of course not," she sniffed. Apart from the fact that it was unclear to her how exactly she was going to leave when she could barely stand, she had no intention whatsoever of being categorized as a prudish American. Her eyes were riveted, with due discretion, on the four nudists, who shrieked with delight when they dove into the water, swimming out to where the sea was a deeper shade of blue yet transparent enough that she could see their moonlike backsides gliding just below its surface. It only took a few minutes for her to realize that it wasn't shock or curiosity that made her continue to stare at them as they splashed about, but envy.

"How's it feel now?" Lorenzo asked.

Jolene blinked, turning to look at him, wondering how he could read her mind.

"What do you mean?" she asked.

"Your ankle. How does it feel now?

"Oh, right. My ankle," she said, bracing herself as a larger wave hit her above the knee. "Soaking it might be helping, but my jeans are getting drenched, too. And it's hard to stand on the stones with all my weight on the one foot."

Lorenzo tightened his hold on her, sliding his hand up from around her waist to under her armpit. She hoped he couldn't feel the dampness of her perspiration or notice that she wasn't wearing a bra.

"You must be getting tired of holding me up," she said.

"I don't tire that easily," he said.

Jolene tried putting weight on her foot again, but the pain made her wince. Perceiving her discomfort, Lorenzo pressed her against him to offer more support, the tips of his fingers grazing the curve of her breast.

"I was thinking, though," he said, hesitating a moment before continuing. "It would be easier for both of us if you were all the way in."

"What do you mean by that?" she snapped. "All the way where?"

"In the water."

"In the water?"

"Yeah. The element the sea is made of. You do know how to swim, don't you?"

"Of course I know how to swim!" she replied, wishing he would stop trying to confuse her.

"Okay, okay!" he said. "I was just asking. It's just that if you went all the way in, you could take the weight off your foot. You could keep your leg elevated and soak your ankle at the same time."

"Oh, right," she said. "Maybe." It made sense. Except for a realization that was dawning on her now, as she rewound her memory to that morning when she'd prepared her backpack. She could see herself filling up her water bottle, checking to see that she had her Swiss army knife, her chunk of Parmesan, her bag of almonds, and her map, locking the door as she left, then going back for her mother's recorder, but completely ignoring the turquoise bathing suit she'd bought on sale at the Target in Ithaca, which had been sitting atop the chest of drawers where it, too, awaited its first swim. Great, that was the other thing she'd forgotten. Now that she was finally at the beach, she had no bathing suit. But if she discarded Lorenzo's suggestion on the grounds of not having a suit, she would be forced to face the question of whether she herself would or would not swim naked.

"I don't have a towel," she blurted, congratulating herself on finding the perfect excuse. The water might be warm enough for swimming, but summer was definitely over and there was a sharp chill in the breeze blowing in from the sea, not at all pleasant if you were dripping wet. Honestly, even if she had her bathing suit, she wouldn't want to swim if she couldn't dry off. She got goosebumps just thinking about it.

"I always carry one in my backpack," Lorenzo said. "We can share. Heck, you can even have it all to yourself."

"Oh, all right. I might as well spit it out," she said. "I forgot my bathing suit. There."

"Who cares?" Lorenzo shrugged. "No one here would care. I wouldn't care. The question is, do you care?"

Jolene was too nervous to look Lorenzo in the eye, too afraid of seeing another challenge there, or worse, mockery. She stared out at the sea for a moment, debating what to do. She wanted to do what felt right to her in these circumstances, not what Lorenzo would encourage her to do, and not what Filippo would discourage her from doing.

"Are you wearing underwear?" Lorenzo asked.

"Of course I'm wearing underwear!" she cried, turning to face him. Just because she wasn't wearing a bra didn't mean she would traipse around in jeans without any panties. Yuck.

"If you swim in your underwear, I'll swim in mine," Lorenzo suggested.

Instead of answering, Jolene watched the four swimmers flip over and glide across the water in effortless backstrokes, laughing when they joined hands to form a circle, bobbing on their backs. She could imagine how delightful it would feel to float in the sea like that, letting the gentle waves wash away the stickiness from her skin, massage the wobbliness from her tired legs, alleviate the pain beginning to pulse in her twisted ankle.

"Sit me down so I can take these jeans off, please," she said.

Once she was seated, Lorenzo pulled his T-shirt over his head, then stood to step out of his jeans, looking the other way as Jolene wriggled out of hers. She was reassured by the sight of her gray underpants, which were anything but provocative. Chosen for their comfort and practicality during exercise, the chaste cotton briefs with their wide elastic waistband and nonslip legs, also purchased at Target in a convenient 6-pack, covered more skin than the bottoms of the bikini she'd left behind. She considered fishing out the push-up bra she had taken off earlier but decided it would look weird. It was too sexy, apart from being a different color from her undies. Plus, it was brand new, and wearing Filippo's gift in the water would seem disrespectful to him.

The possible reactions of the frolicking foursome didn't concern her, she decided, thinking they were more likely to gawk at her puritanical briefs than at her unremarkable breasts. As for Lorenzo, she trusted him to be discreet, and besides, a man spoiled by the cornucopia of Monica's cleavage wouldn't give Jolene's meager chest a second glance. Thoughts of Monica made her wonder whether she ever swam naked, but being unable to picture her without makeup or accessories, she doubted it. For a moment Jolene considered swimming in her T-shirt, then stopped to asked herself again what she wanted to do. She was pushing forty, after all, and had never swum topless. What better water than the Mediterranean for her baptism? What better place than a secluded beach in the Cinque Terre, nestled in the heart of the Italian Riviera? What better time than now? This could be one of life's more memorable moments in the making, one that she could reminisce about and tell someone about, sometime. She pulled her T-shirt over her head.

Arms folded across her bare chest, Jolene looked at Lorenzo, who was standing with his back to her in his black briefs, gazing at the sea. He had the physique of a swimmer: his legs were strong and his butt tight; his shoulders broad and his back straight. Again, she was struck by the difference between the two brothers: Filippo so lanky, loquacious and cerebral; Lorenzo so sturdy, taciturn and physical. She tried to imagine how she would feel about this topless swim if Filippo were standing at the water's edge instead of his brother, but had a hard time picturing him there, in the powder blue boxer shorts he always wore. It struck her that a man could look so cool and sexy, even dignified, in black briefs, but that a man in any other kind of underwear would always look like a man in underwear. Maybe she could get Filippo to switch.

"Ready?" Lorenzo called.

"I guess!" Jolene replied.

Pink-cheeked, with one arm draped across her chest, she let Lorenzo help her stand and walk to the water's edge, neither of them speaking or looking at each other as they waded in. The water grew deep fast here, and Lorenzo wasted no time diving in, leaving her standing on one leg like a stork. Rather than wait for a wave to topple her, Jolene followed suit, tensing at the impact of the cool seawater, wincing at the sting of its salt on her scraped hands and knees and elbows.

"Is it too cold for you?" Lorenzo called, tossing back his head of wet curls as he turned to check on her.

"Nope!" she cried, knowing she wouldn't admit it even if it was.

"Good! Remember to go easy on that leg. No kicking!" he warned her, before swimming off.

Treading water, Jolene admired the way his body skimmed the surface of the sea, propelled by the swift, neat strokes of someone who must have learned to swim before he'd learned to walk. She wasn't a bad swimmer herself and was disappointed she couldn't take off after him, but just being in the water was pure joy. She loved the way the seawater buoyed her up, unlike the silty water of the lakes back home, where monstrous seaweed reached for her legs like tentacles.

This was definitely different, she mused; this was the Mediterranean. Flipping onto her back, she smiled at the benevolent blue sky, her face basking in the warmth of the sun, her skin tingling with the bracing effect of the water that aroused her senses and tickled her imagination. She thought about coming back here with Filippo, about how amazing it would be to have the whole place to themselves. And if Filippo's face was a bit fuzzy in her fantasies of the two of them swimming naked, what he would do to her when they stretched out on the deserted beach was deliciously clear. Filippo knew what she liked, and after seeing how quickly she'd found pleasure that day in the vineyard, he must finally realize what a powerful aphrodisiac nature could be. This time, they wouldn't be limited to rubbing against one another with all their clothes on; this time they'd be completely naked. Jolene arched her back, circling one arm then the other in a backstroke, imagining the sheer delight of lying nude on the beach, the breeze and the sun caressing her salty skin as his hand slipped between her thighs, making her climax right there, out in the open, in the light of day. And then she would...

"You look like you're enjoying yourself," a voice said.

Jolted by the surprise of finding Lorenzo swimming beside her, Jolene gasped, taking in a mouthful of water. Coughing and sputtering, she curled into a ball.

"You shouldn't sneak up on people like that," she said, as soon as she could speak again.

"I wanted to check on your ankle," Lorenzo said, blinking, droplets of water clinging to his lashes.

"My ankle?" she said. "I don't know. I wasn't even thinking about it until you asked."

"What were you thinking about?"

"Nothing."

"It's not possible to think of nothing."

"All right then," she said. "Have it your way. I was thinking blissful thoughts."

"Blissful thoughts are good," he said, his eyes bright with the reflection of the sun on the water. "I could use some of those, if you want to share."

"Um...not this time," Jolene said, and Lorenzo left it at that. He floated beside her in silence for a while, then sped off in a spurt of strokes and kicks, swimming out, then back, a few times before stopping by her side again.

"I'm starving," he panted.

"And I'm turning into a prune!" she said, fanning her fingers in front of her face, and looking at him through them. "I have some Parmesan in my backpack."

"I grabbed a couple of things from the Locanda, too. Let's get out and have a bite."

Back at the beach, Lorenzo hopped out of the sea ahead of her, returning with a rolled-up towel, then backed into the water again so that she could hold onto his shoulders without being seen as she got out. When he unfurled the towel over his shoulder, she grabbed it, discovering that it was not a beach towel, but a hand towel; draped over her shoulders, it barely covered her breasts.

After sitting, they rummaged around in their backpacks, Jolene setting her cheese and almonds on the stones, happy to have something to offer him, and above all relieved to find that the recorder, which she'd forgotten about, had not suffered from her fall.

"This should still be a decent drinking temperature," Lorenzo said, producing an ice pack from which the neck of a bottle protruded.

"Lorenzo!" Jolene cried. "Were you hiding that from me on purpose?"

"Why would I do that? I just didn't think you'd want to drink before swimming."

"I'm not talking about the wine, I'm talking about the wine cooler!" she said. "It's just what I need for my ankle."

Although the swim had both distracted and invigorated her, Jolene was dismayed to notice that the joint was swelling. She was starting to have serious doubts about her ability to make it back up that slippery slope and through that dreadful tunnel to the train station, and on the heels of those doubts came the worries. Worries about what Filippo would say when he saw her limping. Worries about how to handle what she'd learned in Volastra. Worries about how he'd react to her taking her first hike in the Cinque Terre without him, and her first swim in the Mediterranean, too. Without him. In just her underpants. With his brother.

"I can't believe it didn't even occur to me!" Lorenzo said, slapping his forehead. He slipped the ice sleeve off of the bottle and over her foot, nudging it up to her ankle. "It's not too icy anymore, but it's a perfect fit, Cinderella of the Sea."

There was something so comically ceremonious about the way this man in soggy skivvies slipped the ice pack over her ankle, something so utterly natural about the way he uncorked the unlabeled bottle for them to share, something so celebratory about the way he poured the wine into two sturdy tumblers of the type the old men drank from back at the Locanda, that made Jolene wish she could freeze the time to make the moment last.

"To blissful thoughts!" Lorenzo said, raising his glass in the afternoon sun.

"To blissful thoughts!" Jolene replied, touching her glass to his, blushing a little when their eyes met. She told herself that she shouldn't worry too much about what Filippo thought, because she knew she'd done nothing wrong. Just like she shouldn't worry too much about exposing her American mozzarellas to a little Italian sun, if the towel didn't quite cover them completely.

Neither one of them spoke much as they sipped the cool white wine, consuming their perfect snack of focaccia, cheese, and almonds as they watched the shards of light dancing on the sea. After they'd finished, Lorenzo reached inside his backpack, taking out a leather pouch, from which he removed a book wrapped in plastic.

"Would you think me rude if I read for a few minutes?" he asked.

"Of course not. What could be rude about reading?" she replied. "But shouldn't we consider heading back?"

"I've already considered what there is to consider," he said. "I think we should let your ankle rest a little longer before attempting anything. Besides, it's a gorgeous afternoon. We might not get many more like this before the weather changes. We should enjoy it."

Jolene had been enjoying it. The sun on her face and the wine in her glass had dulled her concerns about the journey back to Manarola and what might await her there. But she knew that the light was quick to fade at this time of year, and that it would take her ten times longer to hobble up the hill than it had to tumble down it. Pretty soon they'd have to get moving. Slipping on her T-shirt, she removed the towel and tucked it under her damp butt, but decided to take a little more sun on her legs before wrestling them back into her jeans.

"What are you reading?" she asked.

"Promise not to laugh?"

"Why would I laugh?" Jolene saw absolutely nothing funny about an attractive man in underpants hugging a book to his bare chest.

"Shakespeare's Sonnets," he said, turning the book around to show her. It was a well-worn copy of a pocket-sized hardcover.

"You're into Shakespeare?" she asked.

"On and off," he replied, shrugging. "I keep this in my backpack, and when I'm out on my own and find a place that inspires me, I like to stop and read for a while. I've been trying to memorize some of the sonnets."

"How did you ever get interested in Shakespeare?" Jolene asked.

"I guess I take after my grandfather. I never met him, but he translated poetry. I studied English literature a bit, in high school. I went to the *liceo classico*, because I already knew I wanted to stay on at the Locanda, and I didn't need physics or calculus for that. Studying the classics seemed like the best way to spend my time in the classroom, and I was lucky enough to have some great teachers. They taught me the difference between studying to pass exams and learning to improve my mind."

Again, Jolene was struck by how unalike the two brothers were, Filippo happiest when his nose was in numbers, Lorenzo when his was in poetry.

"There's something special about this book," Lorenzo continued, flipping it open to the title page. "Look."

"To Luisa, my twin flame," Jolene read, in English. "I can't make out the signature, but I assume it's your father's. How romantic that he called her his twin flame."

"Yeah, it is. My mother always kept this book with her, but she passed it on to me when I graduated," he said, turning the page. "Look here."

"To Lorenzo, our sun/son who keeps the flame burning." Jolene read, these words also in English. It must have been their language of love. "This dedication is signed 'Mamma.' What a touching thing for her to say, Lorenzo." She wondered whether Filippo had ever read that; whether it made him jealous.

"Ma used to read to me from this book when I was small. She tells me that even before I could understand any of the words, the rhyme and meter and the sound of her voice seemed to fascinate me. Kind of like when my father played the piano for me, when I was a baby."

"I'll bet that reading poetry made you a big hit with the girls, back in the day," Jolene said, smiling.

"Not really. The only one I ever tried reading sonnets to was Monica, but she thought they were boring."

Jolene had promised herself to not judge by appearances, but Monica didn't really seem the type to be moved by poetry. She might have inspired a Dark Lady verse or two, however, with those "eyes that were nothing like the sun."

"This book meant so much to my mother that at first I refused to take it," Lorenzo added. "But she said that once the dedication was written it was mine."

"You could pass it on to Chiara, when she graduates from high school," Jolene suggested.

"Yeah, that's what I'm planning to do. But until then I don't want to keep it on a shelf, gathering dust. I want it to still be alive when I give it to her, and the only way to keep a book alive is to read it."

"Do you want to read something aloud?" Jolene asked.

"I'd rather read to myself right now, if you don't mind."

"No, I don't mind," Jolene said. "Would it disturb you if I played the recorder while you read?"

"Nope," Lorenzo said, his book already open, his legs already crossed in the lotus position.

"That's how I keep my mother's music alive, too," Jolene said. "By playing it." Sitting up tall, her left leg with its iced ankle sticking out in front of her, the foot of her right leg pressed against the inside of her left thigh, she took the recorder in her hands and played, not any specific song, just random notes that sounded familiar as they passed through her, before floating out to sea.

***

Being a bother was something Jolene hated even more than owing explanations, and if she hadn't had one worry of each type preying on her mind, the homeward cruise in Giobatta's shiny *gozzo* would have been a sweet red cherry on the day's cake of unexpected adventures.

Sitting with her back to the prow, she left her hair loose, the salt-stiffened strands whipping her face as her gaze lingered on the place she'd left behind rather than contemplating where she was going. Giobatta's practiced hand guided the rudder, his alert blue eyes, shaded by the visor of his cap, scanning the sea. Next to him stood Lorenzo, once again fully clothed but barefoot, swaying on sturdy sea legs. He did not look at Jolene, but past her, toward their destination, his curly locks also blowing in the breeze. Once or twice she sought out his eyes, despite her determination not to, each time being struck with the impression that he had just looked away. The noise of the inboard diesel engine, running at a steady cruising speed, discouraged conversation, in the unlikely event anyone in the trio felt inclined to chat.

Jolene had understood little of Lorenzo's side of the conversation in Manarolese dialect, during the brief phone call he'd placed from the beach, and when he'd informed her that they were to be picked up by boat within the hour, she was surprised to not feel more relieved. Despite the sensation of time standing still while she noodled on the recorder and Lorenzo studied his sonnets, the hour had passed more quickly than any hour of any day she could remember. Then the boat had come, and Lorenzo had ferried Jolene and their belongings aboard, and now they would soon be in Manarola, arriving sooner than she wanted to but later than she'd told Filippo in her message, provided he'd even read it. There wasn't much she could do about any of it now, except hope that he was still away, still unaware of her absence.

By involving a third party in their rescue, Lorenzo had necessarily revealed their whereabouts, which meant that skipping the last part of her story when recounting the day's events to Filippo—not that she was planning to hide anything, anyway—was no longer an option. She had every intention of keeping up her end of their honesty pact, despite all the previously undisclosed facts about Filippo that people kept tossing like so many pebbles into her placid pond of trust. Whether Filippo would be jealous, furious, or worried was anyone's guess, though of the three options, the worried Filippo was the only one she had any experience dealing with, making that the version she would prefer. Not wanting to be caught unprepared, however, she also reviewed her defense, reminding herself that she'd done nothing wrong by taking a hike and a swim with her future brother-in-law, and that she could have just as easily twisted her ankle walking from her room down to the Locanda. However true that may be, the problem was that her conscience test—the one where she put herself in the other person's shoes to see how it felt—said that she would be both furious and jealous if Filippo hiked to a nudist beach and took a swim with, for example, a topless Monica, who was just his sister-in-law, or that Wendy person, whoever the heck she was, which reminded her to keep that name in reserve in the event of a hostile interrogation. Hoping for the best but bracing herself for the worst, Jolene turned around, facing their destination as it neared.

Manarola was even more stunning when approached by sea, its huddle of colorful buildings licked by the fiery tongues of late afternoon sun that set their yellows and pinks and greens aglow. Jolene wished she could remain in the neutral territory of the boat to admire the view for a while, but Giobatta was already bringing the *gozzo* alongside the jetty, and Lorenzo was already tossing the lines to the duck-footed man.

"If I give you a boost, can you manage to pull yourself up there?" Lorenzo asked her.

Jolene nodded. "I have strong arms."

"Good. Hang on to my shoulders until you're ready," he ordered, already grabbing her around the hips and lifting her. When she felt the ledge behind her, she let go of him, using her arms to pull herself up, and sat with her feet dangling, her eyes scanning the harbor as Lorenzo tossed ashore their backpacks. Maybe Filippo had been detained, she thought, relieved at not seeing him, ashamed of her relief. Maybe he hadn't heard about her mishap; or maybe he had, but was waiting for her at the Locanda, knowing she was in good hands. Or maybe he possessed a sadistic vein that had not yet manifested itself; one that wanted to make her squirm, to make her be the one crawling to him.

"Let's get you on your feet now," Lorenzo said, hopping onto the jetty and grasping her wrists. She stood on her right foot as he pulled her up, trying to convince herself that her ankle was already much better. She tried not to wince when she put her left foot down, tried not to imagine herself being escorted through the village like an invalid.

"What a day!" she said, ignoring the pain as she placed her foot on the first of the narrow steps that from the jetty led up to the village.

"Yeah, even if it didn't turn out the way I planned it," Lorenzo said, supporting her from behind as she hobbled up, one step at a time. "But what am I talking about? Nothing was planned, was it?"

"If you say so," Jolene said, already confused about which of her sensations had been real, which imagined, which desired.

"Here he comes," Lorenzo said, pushing her up the last step. No names were needed, and Jolene spotted him too, striding straight toward them on legs that could take him from one end of the village to the other in under a minute. Giobatta, or the duck-man, or some nosy onlooker must have tipped him off that they'd arrived. As he approached, Filippo shook his head, left to right, left to right, like a dog that has fetched a stick it doesn't want to let go of.

"I'll take over from here, thank you very much," he said to Lorenzo, who relinquished Jolene's arm, stepping to the side. He looked away, staring down at the waves washing over the rocks, but he didn't leave.

"*Cara* Jo! Just look at the state you're in!" Filippo said, squeezing her shoulders, his eyebrows and forehead performing their ritual of worry as he scanned her. She cringed to think of how she must look to him, limping along in her in torn jeans, her wild hair spiked by the saltwater. Thank God most of her scrapes were concealed by her clothes.

"I just took a little tumble," she said, reassured by his solicitude. "It's not as bad as it looks."

"My poor *Splendore!*" Filippo said, raising her hand to kiss it, then changing his mind at the sight of her grazed knuckles. "Let me take a look at that ankle," he said, genuflecting, without letting his knee touch the ground. Jolene hitched up the leg of her jeans, revealing the swollen joint protruding above her sneaker. Standing, Filippo threw his hands up in the air.

"I honestly don't know what to say, if this is what happens as soon as I leave you alone for five minutes!" he cried, his concern turning to anger with an abruptness that startled Jolene, making her angry, too. Her first impulse was to tell him that since their arrival in Manarola several days ago, he'd left her alone for more "five minutes" than she could count, and that was without taking into consideration all the solitary nights. But anger could only fuel anger, and she did not want to quarrel, especially not in public.

"Who can I trust to look after you?" Filippo continued. "Certainly not my so-called big brother! Good work, *fratello*. Bravo!"

"Look, Filippo, I'm sorry about what happened. I take full responsibility for it," Lorenzo said, his calm tone of voice making Filippo's sound ridiculous. "But Jolene is not a little girl who needs looking after. She's a grown woman."

"Yes, and she's my woman," Filippo said. "My fiancée."

Jolene glared at him, wondering where this attitude of possessiveness had come from.

"All I wanted to do was take a walk, Filippo," she said. "With you."

"Oh, so now it's my fault because I have work to do," Filippo said. "Unlike some people."

Jolene reddened. She recalled the simple intentions and upbeat mood with which she'd started her day: packing her backpack, taking a stroll through town, drinking a cappuccino, then running into Lorenzo and Chiara at the cemetery before stopping by the Locanda, in the hopes of spending a couple of hours alone with Filippo, clarifying some doubts, learning about his progress, discussing future plans, while getting some exercise in the open air.

"Yes, I was told that something came up," she blurted. "Again. For you. There were things I wanted to talk to you about, though. Important things. At that point, I would have set off on my own, if Lorenzo hadn't gone with me."

Sighing, Filippo rolled his eyes. "You don't know your way around, *Cara* Jo. There are some dangerous trails here. Tourists die every year. Germans. Frenchmen. Even Americans. All it takes is a stumble on the rocks, a slip in the mud, and down you go!"

"Well, I'm still here, as you can see," Jolene said. "Your mother thought Lorenzo would be a good guide. And he was."

"Yeah," he said. "The best, right? Of course Mamma would think so."

Lorenzo opened his mouth to speak, but Jolene silenced him with a wave of her hand.

"He was!" she said. "All I did was twist my ankle, for God's sake! But I learned a lot of interesting things along the way."

"Like what? Where all the perverts hang out?"

"I didn't see any perverts," she said.

"I grew up here, don't forget. I know where you went and I know that beach is where the hippies and the weirdoes go to take their clothes off and worship the sun and dance to the moon and smoke pot and who knows what else." Filippo looked at Jolene as he spoke, though his words were clearly intended for Lorenzo's ears. "It's the last place I'd think of going to for a swim, let alone taking a lady to! I suppose you two thought it was perfectly fine to swim naked, too?"

That answered her question of why she hadn't quite been able to bring the picture of Filippo naked on the beach into focus. It had nothing to do with the style of underwear he wore; it simply couldn't happen.

"Relax, Filippo," Lorenzo said. "Neither one of us swam naked, if that's what you're worried about."

"But I wanted to!" Jolene said, jutting her chin at Filippo.

Filippo stared at her, blinking, as if he were seeing her for the first time. He could think what he wanted to think, but she was only being honest, just like she'd promised. Now it was his turn to do the same.

"When I said I learned a lot of interesting things along the way, I wasn't talking about the beach, Filippo," she said.

"Well, then. Do you care to tell me what you were talking about?"

"Volastra."

"What's so interesting about Volastra?" he asked.

"Lots of things. I learned all about the Roman settlement, for example," she said. "And I saw the sanctuary of Our Lady of Good Health, and learned that it was built in the twelfth century, and that its arched window is called a *bifora*."

"Good for you. But I've heard enough about your escapades. Let's go get you cleaned up," Filippo said, taking her elbow.

"Wait!" she said. "I wasn't done telling you about Volastra."

"I know everything I need to know about Volastra."

"Of course you do," Jolene said. "You're the one who lived there. You and Wendy."

"You *told* her about Wendy?" Filippo said, shoving his face into Lorenzo's.

"You *didn't* tell her about Wendy?" Lorenzo said, pulling back.

Filippo turned to stare at Jolene, possibly trying to decide what to say, possibly waiting for her barrage of questions. But there was nothing else she wanted to know; not in that precise moment when the sun was abandoning them, draining the color from the village and sucking away whatever warmth was left in the air as quickly as if someone had flipped a switch. She shivered.

"I need a hot shower," she said.

"I need to get back to Chiara," Lorenzo said.

"Let's go," Filippo said.

The three of them set off, together but apart: Filippo, dragging Jolene along, faster than she would have liked; Jolene, aching inside and out, refusing to complain about the pain; Lorenzo, catching her eye when she turned to climb the steps to Suite 16 with his brother, raising his hand in a peace sign, before continuing on to the Locanda, alone.

***

"You just sit right there, and let me bring you a nice hot cappuccino," Luisa said to Jolene, after Filippo had escorted her back down to the Locanda, parked her at a table in the bar, and left.

"Thanks. I really appreciate it, Luisa," Jolene said. In the time it had taken her to shower and dress, she and Filippo had barely spoken. The mention of Wendy's name had muted his tongue and dismantled his attitudes, and Jolene had decided not to pursue the matter further while there was so much tension between them. She preferred to dwell on the day's memorable moments while they were still fresh in her mind and a source of joy, rather than harp on Filippo's relationship with a person who was part of the past. The past would always be there, but today was almost over. Sipping on her hot beverage, Jolene wondered when Lorenzo would be down, and how he would act toward her.

"Did Chiara behave for you today?" she asked Luisa. A good way to find out about the father was to inquire about the daughter.

"When it's just the two of us here, that child is the sweetest little angel," Luisa said. "Always trying to help, never fussing or needing entertaining. It's different when her mother is around."

"Where is she now?" Jolene asked. "Chiara, I mean, not her mother."

"They're together. Monica was beside herself when she returned from La Spezia and found that Lorenzo had left Chiara with me. When Giobatta came in and said the two of you were stranded at Guvano beach and he was going to rescue you by boat, she grabbed the girl and hopped on the first train for Genoa. Chiara was in tears, because she wanted to wait for her *babbo* to come back, but Monica wouldn't hear of it."

"Oh, no! It's all my fault," Jolene said, propping her head in her hand, staring dejectedly at her cappuccino. "All I wanted was to take a walk, and look at all the trouble I caused everybody!"

"Nonsense!" Luisa said, taking advantage of the lull in business to sit down with Jolene, her fingers rolling and unrolling the dish towel. "First of all, it was my idea. Second, you are not responsible for the behavior of my son's wife. Or for either of my sons' behavior, for that matter."

"I feel so bad, though." Jolene said.

"The more you go on in life, the more there is to feel bad about," Luisa said. "My advice to you is to just get used to it."

Jolene looked up at her. "My mother used to say the same thing."

"Well, she was right," Luisa said. After a moment, she added, "You must miss her. No one can replace a mother, but if you ever need to talk, between females, I mean, you know where to find me. I'm always here. Always at the Locanda."

Jolene's throat tightened, as she looked into Luisa's blue eyes. She didn't see Luisa as her future Italian mother-in-law, but as a sixty-seven-year-old woman still trying to keep the family going, the business going, herself going. Back in America, sixty-seven-year-old women were just starting to kick back and have fun. Back in America, they joined yoga classes and book clubs, and went on weekend getaways with their girlfriends. She wondered who Luisa's friends were; she wondered whether she would find any of her own here.

"Thank you, Luisa. It's nice to know that." After a moment she asked, "Have you always lived here?"

"More or less," Luisa sighed. "Even though that wasn't always the plan."

"I've often wondered what it would feel like to live in the same place all my life, and to know all the people so well. We moved around so much that my mother never had time to make friends. Neither did I, really."

"I lost my best friend a long time ago," Luisa said, staring down at her dish towel. "Vittorio and my sons and my work never left much time for anything or anyone else. I know a lot of things about the people who live here, and they know a lot of things about me. But that doesn't make us friends."

Jolene nodded. "I know what you mean."

Luisa looked up, smiling at her. "You have Filippo now. He'll be your best friend."

Jolene nodded. She hoped so. That was what she'd always wanted in a husband.

TWELVE

"Just a second!" Jolene called from her bed, hearing the knock on the door. Quick but cautious, she swung her feet to the floor, grimacing as she stood. She scooped up Fata, but the cat would not relinquish the blanket at the foot of the bed on which she'd been snoozing.

"Let go!" Jolene whispered, trying to disentangle the cat's claws without getting any more scratches on her hands. "Keep quiet and come with me, or you'll ruin everything for both of us!"

Fata trilled her annoyance at being dropped on the cold bathroom floor while Jolene shut the door behind them, splashed water on her face, rinsed out her mouth, and threw on her bathrobe. Cracking the door open, she slipped out, leaving the cat behind as another knock came on the door.

"I'm coming!" she called.

Filippo must be determined to stay calm this morning if he didn't even want to struggle with the key. As for Jolene, who had remained awake thinking things over until the wee hours, she had no intention of becoming entangled in a silly argument over a hike and a swim. What concerned her, now that her emotions had settled and her mind had cleared, was the story about Wendy. She needed Filippo to understand that it was his lack of openness about his past, and not the fact that he had one, which upset her. The only way to move forward was for her to be honest, and expect Filippo to do the same. Taking a deep breath, she unlatched the door and turned the knob, ready to greet him with a smile. Standing on the other side of the door she did not find Filippo, but Lorenzo, holding a covered tray.

"I hope I didn't wake you," he said.

"Um...no...I was awake," she stammered, tightening the sash of her robe, while trying not to appear too disappointed or too delighted at seeing him there instead of his brother, not knowing herself which reaction was closer to the truth. "I was just lying there, thinking."

"I'll bet one of the things you were thinking about was a cappuccino," Lorenzo said.

"In fact," Jolene said, smiling, though it wasn't quite true. Cappuccinos weren't the only thing she thought about, despite her reputation.

Balancing the tray on one hand, Lorenzo lifted the corner of a linen napkin, pausing for effect before whisking it away to reveal a plate of fresh figs, grapes, and sliced apples drizzled with honey, a bowl of creamy white yogurt, and a cup covered with a saucer, which Lorenzo now removed to reveal a perfect cinnamon-sprinkled cappuccino. Next to the cappuccino lay a clipping from a strawberry tree, with three bright red balls of fruit still attached to the branch.

"I thought you might want to stay off that foot today," Lorenzo said. Though he smiled, his expression was apologetic. He looked like he hadn't slept too well, either.

"That's very thoughtful of you. This is quite a surprise," Jolene said, then realized it didn't sound quite right. "I mean, I'm not surprised that you're thoughtful. I'm just surprised, period."

"It's the least I could do. As much as I hate to admit it, Filippo was right. I should have taken better care of you."

"I don't need taking care of," Jolene said.

"Yes you do. We all do. Just let me say I'm sorry."

"Well, I'm not sorry," she said. "It was a special day. One I'll remember for a long time. So if I have to accept your apology, you have to accept my thanks. Deal?"

"Deal," Lorenzo said, holding the tray out to her. "Now, can I put this down somewhere before I drop it?"

"Sure, just set it on the bed," she said, blushing when she followed his gaze to the rumpled sheets they both knew were still warm with her body heat. "On second thought, maybe the desk would be better, now that I have one."

"There you go!" he said. After setting the tray down, Lorenzo glanced around the room, frowning at the cracks and stains on the ceiling and walls. "Did Filippo say why he put you here instead of down at the Locanda? Or at the house?"

"For privacy, I guess. And some sense of propriety."

"Propriety, huh?" Lorenzo said. "I see."

"It won't be for long. And I don't mind being on my own."

"Of course," Lorenzo nodded. "Need anything else?"

"No, thanks," Jolene said. "Except to make an apology of my own. I'm sorry if you got into trouble with Monica on my account."

"It'll blow over," he shrugged. "It always does."

As he left, it saddened her to notice a sag in the shoulders which had looked so strong when he swam in the sea, their muscles rippling with each stroke of the arm. She wished he'd brought an extra cappuccino for himself, so they could sit and talk, or even just be quiet together, like yesterday. But it was probably for the best that he hadn't.

***

Lolling about in her bathrobe was not something Jolene had ever had the inclination, or opportunity, to become accustomed to. Relaxing was an activity in which you could indulge when your mind was as clear as your schedule, a combination that had always eluded her. Nonetheless, she had taken her time over breakfast, lingering over her cappuccino for as long as possible for someone who preferred it piping hot, then savoring each morsel of perfectly ripe fruit: the crisp green apples whose tartness was tempered with honey, the plump figs, the sweet grapes, saving the *corbezzoli* berries, which would always remind her of Lorenzo and her first Cinque Terre hike, for last. One slow spoonful at a time, she ate the yogurt, too, then cleaned the bowl with her pinky and let Fata lick it. After that, she spent several minutes contemplating what she could do to combat the mildew steadily scaling the north-facing wall as if it were determined to invade the territory of the water stains spread across the ceiling. When her itch to get her hands dirty with something other than a sketching pencil became unbearable, she went to the window, passing a few more minutes looking out across the valley, today under a low gray sky. Her eyes were drawn to the cemetery, with its rows of empty slots, making her wonder how many deaths, and whose, it would take to fill them, while she tried to recall the words to the poem Lorenzo had helped her translate. Finally flopping down on the bed, she checked the time on her cell phone and saw that it was not yet nine o'clock. She also saw that Filippo had neither phoned nor sent a message. Hanging around and wondering how he would behave toward her today was simply not in her makeup; she would go speak to him in person, and after they resolved their personal issues and cleared up any misunderstandings, she'd share some ideas she'd been developing, and insist that he fill her in on the status of the work he'd been doing without her. She just needed a few more minutes to get centered, to think over her approach.

Resting her back against the wall with Fata nestled between her knees, Jolene picked up her mother's recorder from the nightstand, hoping to replicate the lovely melody she'd improvised on the beach yesterday. Insistence did not equal inspiration, however, and despite several attempts, the tune which had come to her so naturally while sitting by the sea with Lorenzo would not materialize while sitting in her room with Fata. Fed up with the noise disturbing her nap, the cat began yowling in protest, causing Jolene to finally give up. It was then that she heard the banging on the door, as if someone were kicking it. She hoped she wasn't disturbing the few neighbors who were around at this time of year.

"Who is it?" Jolene called, her voice breathless from all the blowing.

"Take a wild guess, *Splendore!*" This time it was definitely Filippo. "Could you please let me in? I can't deal with that door."

For the second time that morning, Jolene detached the disgruntled cat from the blanket and imprisoned her in the bathroom. Limping toward the door, she spotted the breakfast tray sitting on the desk, and decided that it would be best to make that disappear, too. Sliding the tray into the bathroom, she slammed the door shut again.

"What the hell is going on in there?" Filippo called.

"Nothing! I'm coming!" Jolene said, hoping, as she opened the door, that the music had prevailed over the mewing. "I was just playing some—"

"Whatever it was, it sounded pretty awful," Filippo said, standing there with a grin on his face and a tray in his hands. "But maybe you just needed your cappuccino first."

"How sweet of you, Filippo!" Jolene said, about to kiss him on the lips, but made a detour for his cheek when it occurred to her that her breath might bear traces of her previous breakfast. Entering, Filippo bent toward the kiss, then came to a halt in the middle of the room.

"What's that?" he asked.

"What's what?" Jolene said, scanning the room for evidence of Lorenzo's visit; of her clandestine cat; of her scattered thoughts.

"That furniture!" he said, walking over to the desk and setting the tray down on it.

"That's my new desk and chair!" she said. "They don't make them like that anymore. That's Italian walnut, you know."

"Yes, that much I know," Filippo said. "What I don't know is what they're doing here."

"Remember when I told you that I got Giobatta to show me around the other rooms?" Jolene asked.

"Yes, and remember when I told you I wanted to be the one to show you around?" Filippo asked.

"Yes, and remember I told you I just wanted to familiarize myself with the rest of the Locanda, so I could work on a few ideas?"

"Yes, and remember I told you there would be plenty of time for making plans, once I finished working on my applications?"

"Yes…but Filippo? Can we start again, before jumping into that? Didn't you want to know how the furniture got here?"

Filippo sighed.

"Well, when I spotted it in one of the rooms, I happened to mention to Giobatta that I could use a desk and chair here. Not another word was mentioned, but when I came home after dinner last night I found them right here! Polished and delivered to Suite 16! Giobatta took care of everything!"

"Giobatta?" Filippo said, scratching the scruff on his chin. "That's strange. He didn't ask me about moving any furniture."

"He asked Lorenzo, and Lorenzo said it was fine. He even sent some guys to help."

"*Cara* Jo," Filippo said, placing his hands on his hips. "When you need something, I want you to come to me."

"But you were away. Besides, I didn't ask anyone for anything. They just did it."

"Well, you'd do well to remember that Lorenzo does not have the authority to decide what goes where, let alone Giobatta. For future reference."

"I'm sorry. I didn't want to bypass you. Like I said, it all happened spontaneously."

Filippo rolled his eyes and shook his head, looking exasperated at having to deal with a bunch of such inept people; she wondered whether he included her.

"Can I have my cappuccino, now?" Jolene said, determined to keep the conversation calm and stay focused on the topics she intended to broach.

"Of course," Filippo said, lifting half the foam off the cappuccino together with saucer he'd covered it with. "Sorry about that."

"Hey, who am I to complain about room service?" she said, taking a sip; it was already cold.

"I didn't know whether you'd prefer some focaccia or a croissant, so I brought both," he said.

"Yes, I see that. Thank you." The croissant looked delicious, despite the fact that she'd already eaten, but after taking her jeans off on the beach yesterday, and seeing that the hike had not produced any instant miracles on her thighs, she'd decided that she really must cut down on carbs. Lorenzo probably thought so too, considering the healthy foods he'd chosen for her. "Maybe I'll just have the cappuccino for now. I'm not very hungry."

"You have to eat, *Splendore*," Filippo urged. You know how irritable you get when you skip breakfast. Besides, it's cream-filled. Your favorite."

"Not right now, thanks. Maybe later."

"Come on, you love to dunk!" Filippo said, plunging the croissant into the cup and shoving it into her mouth, laughing as she gagged, forcing her to chew and swallow. They'd fed each other like that before, and had even played tasting games while blindfolded, more as a trust-building exercise than for fun, but now Jolene felt bullied, almost violated. Setting her cup down, she made her way to the bed, masking her limp, swallowing her resentment.

"I didn't just come to bring you breakfast," Filippo said, towering over her in his smart blue blazer, while she sat on the bed brushing croissant crumbs from her robe, hoping the cappuccino drooled down its front wouldn't stain.

"You didn't?" she asked, looking up at him.

"No, I wanted to tell you something."

"You did?"

"Yes, I wanted to tell you that you were right."

Filippo was an intelligent man, which was one of the traits that had attracted her from the start. And even if he didn't always understand the workings of the female mind—what man did, really?—he was a man of conviction, and reason. He knew he owed her an explanation about Wendy.

"Well, I'm relieved to hear you say that," Jolene said.

"When you said that we should know what the competition is offering, I brushed you off," Filippo continued. "But I was being pigheaded. So, I'm here to invite you to lunch at that restaurant you've been wanting to try down by the harbor. We could call it a business lunch."

"A business lunch?" Jolene repeated.

"Well, not strictly business, of course. But it would be a good opportunity to talk over some things, without any family around. We haven't had much time alone since we got here."

"I know!" she said, relieved to hear the words coming from him. "That was one of the reasons why I wanted to go walking with you yesterday. So we could talk."

"But I'm worried about that ankle of yours, *Splendore*. I can see it's still swollen, no matter how hard you try to hide it," Filippo said. "Maybe instead of going to lunch, I should take you to the hospital in La Spezia for X-rays. If it were me, I'd see a doctor. In fact, I would have seen a doctor right away."

"I really wish you wouldn't worry so much, Filippo," she said. "The ankle can heal itself. It's the other things that need our attention."

"Whatever you say. It's your ankle. I'll come back for you at twelve-thirty," he said, bending to kiss her hair. "In the meantime, finish your breakfast, and keep that foot elevated as much as possible. Then put on something pretty. I want to show off my beautiful American fiancée."

Filippo was already at the threshold when Fata began mewing. Snatching up the recorder, Jolene blew a lungful of air into the instrument, producing a burst of random shrill notes. Looking over his shoulder at her, Filippo shook his head, a pained expression on his face. As soon as she was sure he'd gone, she opened the door to the bathroom, where she found Fata sitting on the tray Lorenzo had brought, her head buried inside the coffee cup. The cat looked up at her, the remnants of cappuccino foam sticking to her whiskers, acting as though she had no idea who'd been making all the ruckus.

"Come on, Fata," Jolene giggled. "How about some focaccia?"

***

The gray clouds rolling across the horizon like Texas tumbleweed made Jolene grateful that she hadn't passed up the chance to swim yesterday, when the sun had been strong and the sea and wind calm, the contrary of what they were today. Sitting across from Filippo in the glass-enclosed veranda, where the air somehow seemed chillier than it did outdoors, she pulled her sweater tight around her. Gazing out the window down at the boat ramp, she spotted two men talking and gesticulating, quickly recognizing them as Giobatta, wearing his usual boating cap, and Vittorio, sneaking a cigarette. Her musings about what the two were up to were disturbed by the lethargic buzzing of an end-of-the-season fly that finally came to rest on the inside of the window pane, landing on her own ghostlike reflection, in the middle of her forehead, like a winged third eye.

"Perfetto. That will be fine for both of us. Right, *Splendore?*" Filippo said.

Jolene looked up, surprised to see a waiter staring down at her with an expectant look on his pinched face.

"Sure. Fine," she said. After looking forward to dining at this restaurant, she'd missed the waiter's presentation of the day's specials. She was embarrassed at the impression it must give of her, and annoyed at being the cause of her own disappointment.

"And then we'll have the sole *meunière*," Filippo said to the waiter, adding, sotto voce in English, to Jolene, "I know how much you like sole. And that's something we don't serve at the Locanda."

"Yes, but—" she started to say, but the waiter was gone. She wondered what the other choices were, and whether Filippo would be offended if she called the waiter back to ask if it was possible to try something fished from the sea right in front of them and prepared according to local tradition, rather than a bland fish dredged in flour and fried in butter, but seeing Filippo lean back in his chair, looking so pleased with his choices, Jolene smiled back. Today the food was of secondary importance; today her priority was to have those conversations that kept getting put off by Filippo's pressing errands and demanding deadlines.

The waiter returned with a bottle of mineral water, which he opened and poured for them. He next presented a bottle of wine, allowing Filippo to examine the label. Oh well, it looked like she'd missed the wine selection, too. The waiter opened the bottle, sniffed the cork, and poured a splash into Filippo's glass, standing with one arm bent behind the small of his back, while waiting for Filippo to confirm his approval. For a moment, Jolene feared he'd send the bottle back, as he'd done more than once when they'd dined in out in New York, but to her relief he nodded, and the waiter poured for Jolene, then topped off Filippo's. glass. He placed the bottle in an ice bucket, draped a linen serviette over the neck, and with a nod that hinted ever so slightly at a bow, took his leave.

"So far, so good," Jolene said.

"You haven't even tasted it yet," Filippo said.

"I was referring to the service," she said. "Those are the things that can earn you an extra star on TripAdvisor. Of course, the Locanda is a different type of place, with a more relaxed ambiance, but we can definitely bring the level up a notch or two without losing that local flavor, that characteristic—

"God spare us TripAdvisor!" Filippo said. "That's one of the reasons we'll have to change our name from Locanda Luisa and start over from scratch."

"That's your mother's name, though," Jolene said. "Family tradition is something that should be preserved. Family tradition sells. We've talked about this before. You know how I feel. By the way, I think your mother and Lorenzo should be part of——"

"Before my mother it was called something else, and it can be called something else after her. But I didn't bring you here to talk names," he said, raising his glass. "To us."

"To us," Jolene said, touching her glass to his, taking his cue that she was moving too fast; she needed to slow the conversation down if she wanted to keep it on track. It was just that she had so many ideas, so many doubts, so many—

"Well, aren't you going to taste it?" Filippo said.

"Of course," Jolene said, blinking, taking a tentative sip. The wine was chilled to the perfect temperature, and although she would still call its flavor fresh, it was far more aromatic than anything she'd tried since her arrival. "What are we drinking, anyway?"

"If you'd been paying attention, you'd know I chose an excellent Gewürztraminer from Alto Adige."

"Alto Adige?"

"Yes, otherwise known as Südtirol, depending on your point of view."

"Yes, I've heard of the region," she said. "And of the wine, of course." Most of what she'd learned of Italian geography at college was related to which grapes were grown where. Piedmont: Barbera, Nebbiolo, Dolcetto, Moscato; The Veneto: Soave, Bardolino, Valpolicella, Amarone, and so on and so forth.

"I thought you'd like to try something different, instead of the local stuff you've been drinking day in and day out," Filippo said.

"But I love the local stuff!" Jolene said, not quite sure whether he was hinting that she was drinking too much wine, or the wrong wine. She took another sip. "It tastes a little spicy to me."

"That's precisely how it got that name. '*Gewürz*' means 'spice' and Traminer is where it comes from."

"Traminer, let's see if I remember…That's near Bolzano, right?"

"Right, the Italian name is Termeno. Everything has double names up there, in Italian and German."

"Das ist gut," she said.

"I'm glad you like it."

Jolene did like it, but she didn't love it; at least not here, not now. Its tendency to sweetness seemed as out of context by the rugged Manarolan seashore as the sound of its name did; and as the sound of sole *meunière* did. Or maybe it was just her, she thought, staring at the wine she swirled round and round in her glass, losing herself in its deep golden, almost copper color that reminded her of yesterday's late afternoon sun. Maybe it was just that her palate wasn't quite ready to relinquish the memory of the delightful wine Lorenzo had shared with her yesterday. It was the same wine she'd drunk at the Locanda more than once, but there was something about the chilled bottle appearing as if by magic on the beach, about Lorenzo himself, exuding pure physicality as he poured, that had made that wine explode on her tongue, more alive and vivacious than anything she'd ever tasted.

"Where has your mind wandered off to now, *Cara* Jo?" Filippo said.

"What?" she said, looking up at him.

"Your mind, Jo. It's wandering again. Where is it?"

"It's right here," she said. "Along with me. And I want to thank you for bringing me here."

"I know how much you like surprises," Filippo said.

"Yes, I do." There were some surprises she could do without

though, such as the ex-partner-girlfriend, and the failed business venture, and the pied-à-terre in Milan, obtained through the sacrifice of a vineyard. Maybe she should get these topics out of the way first, she thought, so when it came time to talk business she wouldn't have them hanging over her head. "But sometimes, being prepared—"

"Here comes our food," Filippo said, his spine flush with the back of his chair, his napkin across his lap.

Appearing at their table, the waiter announced, *"Insalata di polpo alla ligure,"* placing in front of her first, then Filippo, dishes on which were arranged diced boiled potatoes and chunks of purplish octopus, garnished with tiny black olives and chopped parsley. After offering a drizzle of extra virgin olive oil and freshly ground black pepper to top off their salads, the waiter refilled their glasses and took his leave, wishing them *"Buon appetito."* Filippo had ordered something local as a starter, after all.

"May I make a proposal?" he asked.

"You've already done that," she said. "Remember?"

"Of course. But what I'm proposing now is that we eat first, and talk later."

"Fair enough," she said. "I agree." She'd never tried octopus salad before, Ligurian or any other style, and didn't want her words getting choked by the tentacles. She enjoyed the dish more than she thought she would, finding the octopus meat surprisingly tender and sweet. Their dishes had been removed and their glasses refilled once more, but the sole had not yet arrived, when Filippo cleared his throat.

"Now, let's get down to one of the things I wanted to talk to you about," he said.

"I thought we decided to wait until after lunch to talk," Jolene said.

"I know we did," he said. "But I can't wait." Reaching into the side pocket of his blazer he pulled out a small silk pouch closed with a drawstring. "I know you American women like to seal the deal with something real."

Jolene laughed. "Where on earth did you pick up that expression? Besides, I'm not 'American women,' I'm just Jolene."

Filippo dangled the pouch in front of her, prompting her to cup her hands below it.

"Well then, this is for you, just Jolene," he said, dropping the pouch into her open palms.

"What is it?" she asked, fingering the cream-colored fabric discolored with age, fumbling with the drawstring tied in a double-knot.

"Why don't you open it and find out?" Filippo said.

"That's exactly what I'm trying to do," she said, the abrasions on her knuckles making her fingers stiff as she untied the knot, then held the pouch upside-down and shook it. When a small object tumbled onto the tablecloth, it took her a minute to realize that it was a piece of jewelry.

"A ring?" she whispered. "For me?" The band was made of tiny links, like a chain, and at its center was a square blue stone set on one of its points, offset by a triangular diamond in each of the four corners. She had never seen anything like it.

"Yes, it certainly is a ring, and it certainly is for you." Filippo said, leaning in across the table until their foreheads touched. "It's been handed down in the family, and now Mamma and I want you to have it. I know you're not crazy about jewelry, but I hope you like it."

"Oh, Filippo! I love it!" Jolene cried, turning the ring over in her hand. "I love that it's antique, and I love its geometric look, and the way the stones all fit together like a puzzle."

"The ring itself is eighteen-carat white gold, and the stone in the center is a sapphire. The other stones are diamonds, of course. It was handcrafted by a Florentine goldsmith. I'm sorry there's no certificate, but it's been around for a long time."

"I'm speechless! I honestly don't know what to say."

"You don't need to say anything," Filippo whispered, lifting her chin with his finger and staring into her eyes with that look of pure romanticism she was beginning to fear he'd lost. "You said all I wanted to hear back in Ithaca, *Splendore*, when you said yes."

Tears welled in Jolene's eyes. A ring. A family ring. A family.

"But I don't need this, Filippo," she said. "It's enough knowing that you and your mother wanted me to have it."

"Shall I take it back, then?"

"Don't you dare!" she cried. Even if she didn't need a ring, hadn't ever even thought of needing a ring, she did want this ring. She dabbed at the corners of her eyes with a grazed knuckle. "The fact that it's a family heirloom makes it so special. I can't wait to thank your mother."

"So, can I put it on your finger?" Filippo asked.

"Yes!" Jolene said, her breath catching as he slid it on her left ring finger as far as the knuckle, leaving Jolene to wriggle it over the fresh scab. That old Florentine goldsmith might have made it just for her: it was a perfect fit.

"Don't you want to take a picture of it?" Filippo asked.

"Why take a picture when I can look at the real thing?"

"To show it to people."

"The only people I'd show it to can see it in person."

"Give me your phone. I'll take it."

"The one you gave me doesn't have a camera, remember? Besides I left it back in my room. I figured I wouldn't need it, if I was going to be with you."

"*Cara* Jo, when you say things like that you seem four decades older than me, not just four years. Plans can change, things can come up. You need to stay in touch. What good is a phone, if you don't carry it with you?" he said, shaking his head. "But never mind. I'll take one."

Filippo took his iPhone from his breast pocket and snapped a few shots, but when he showed them to her she was horrified by how out of place the exquisite jewel looked on her disfigured hand.

"My hand looks awful, Filippo! Delete them! Please!"

"It's just for Facebook." Filippo tapped on the screen. "And Instagram."

"*Signori, la sogliola alla mugnaia,*" the waiter said, brandishing a silver platter.

"There, now it's shared!" Filippo said, smirking with satisfaction as he set his phone on the table, then turned his attention to the waiter, who showed them the whole fish swimming in brown butter, before deboning and plating it for them.

Jolene watched in silence, nodding her thanks when the waiter poured more Gewürztraminer. Taking a sip, she glanced at the fish skeleton the waiter whisked away, recalling that soles had both eyes on the same side of their heads in order to watch for passing prey as they lay on their sides, camouflaged, on the seabed. She wondered what it would be like to go through life seeing twice as well when you looked at things from one side, but being totally blind when you tried looking at them from the other.

THIRTEEN

Filippo dropped Jolene's arm, throwing her off balance. *"Grrr!"* he growled, waving his hands in the air like a madman. Fata, found guilty of dozing on the doorstep of Suite 16, scurried away, but not before Jolene could glimpse in the cat's eyes the stare of those accustomed to betrayal.

"Can't you leave her be, Filippo?" Jolene pleaded. "Fata is totally harmless."

"Fata? That mangy cat has a name?"

"She's not mangy. And yes, her name is Fata. Fata Morgana."

"Who told you that?"

"No one. I gave it to her."

"Jolene, I told you, no stray cats. If you start with one, before you know it the place will be crawling with them, all pissing on the door jamb to mark their territory."

"Fata's a female. She doesn't do those things."

"But females attract males."

"Not always." Jolene locked eyes with him before turning her attention to the lock; a jiggle of the key, and the door opened. "Sometimes females chase away males."

"But you're not one of those, are you?" Filippo ran a hand down her back, resting it on her rump.

Jolene had been puzzling over her dessert of deconstructed tiramisù, when Filippo suggested that they postpone the rest of their talk until later, perhaps after sneaking a nap together. Her mood mellowed by all the food and wine and romanticism; her status reconfirmed by the ring, a concrete symbolic of Filippo's commitment and her acceptance into the family, Jolene had left the restaurant both elated and placated, eager for a snuggle and pillow talk which would enable her to definitely shove the ghost of Wendy and whatever she'd meant to Filippo into her mind's attic, where they wouldn't bother her.

The instant they were inside the room, Filippo slammed the door behind them, grabbing Jolene by the shoulders and pushing her up against it. Squeezing her face between his hands, he kissed her on the mouth with the greediness of a starving man, not one who had just polished off a three-course meal complete with wine and limoncello. She was always caught off guard by how quickly he could make the transition from barely touching her one minute to racing over every corner of her body the next, like one of those sports cars that can do 0-60 in under five seconds.

"Can we move to the bed?" Jolene managed to mumble, while clutching his sleeves to avoid sliding to the floor. She needed to take the weight off her foot.

Without detaching his mouth from hers, Filippo dragged her the few steps to the bed, threw back the blankets, and lay her down, then stood to remove his jacket and unbutton his shirt, draping them over the chair. He unbuckled his belt, unzipped his trousers, and stepped out of them, taking care to not let them touch the floor. Though Filippo's passion was quick to ignite, Jolene had never seen it overrule his compulsion for order. Watching him open the *armadio* to hang up his trousers, she hoped he wouldn't notice that the breakfast tray she'd hid in the bathroom earlier was stashed inside, while the one he'd brought her was still on the desk.

As Filippo turned to face her in his powder blue boxer shorts and navy blue knee socks, she again tried to picture him swimming naked with her at the forbidden beach, but the image would not form; it was always Lorenzo she saw standing at the edge of the shimmering sea; it was always him splashing next to her as the cool saltwater lapped at her naked body in the low October sun. She closed her eyes as Filippo approached, her imagination soaring, her skin twitching and tingling with desire, as he lay with her in the bouncy old bed of Suite 16.

***

Jolene jolted awake, feeling sticky and sweaty from sex and slumber.

"Well hello, Sleeping Beauty," Filippo said, buttoning up his shirt.

"I wasn't really sleeping," she said, blinking through the thick fog that clouded her memory of where she was and why.

"That's good, because I've been talking to you for the past five minutes. Before that, I tried to take a shower but it's too frustrating. At least the bathroom light works now. How'd that happen?"

Jolene pulled herself up in the bed and stacked the two thin pillows behind her back, surprised to see a ring sparkling on her finger as she tucked the bedclothes around her legs.

"It was simple enough," she said, twirling the ring, getting used to the feel of it. "I bought a light bulb at the mini market."

"Well, don't go wasting too much of your time and money in this place. I'd demolish that bathroom right now if I had a sledgehammer."

"Granted, the tiles are old and chipped, and it needs new plumbing but that old-fashioned sink and those brass fixtures are worth saving," she said, watching Filippo tuck his shirttails into his trousers then buckle his belt. He'd saved himself the trouble of putting his socks back on by never taking them off. "Anyway, what's your rush?"

"If we want to have some rooms ready by next spring, we'll have to get moving soon," he said.

"I'm dying to talk more details with you," Jolene said. "But that's not what I meant. I was asking why you're in such a big rush to get dressed. Are you leaving already?"

"No. It's just easier for me to talk when I'm wearing clothes," he said. "You do remember we came here to talk, don't you?"

"Of course I do." Jolene placed a hand in front of her mouth, her jaw trembling as she stifled a yawn. She wished they had talked before lunch, before the wine and the ring and the sex.

"So," Filippo cleared his throat, looking as solemn as a clergyman at the bedside of an ailing parishioner.

"So?" Jolene said, pulling herself up as straight as she could while sitting in the bed. If he wanted to update her first, she was happy to let him.

"So, you know how important trust is to me, right?" he said.

"Absolutely," she said. "It's the same for me."

"Good. Because I've thought it over, and I've decided not to get into why you felt it was okay to go frolicking among the hills as if you were co-starring in some Mediterranean version of The Sound of Music with my brother—if he even deserves to be called that. I'll chalk it up to inexperience, and we'll let it go at that."

Jolene blinked, caught off guard by a subject she'd thought was closed, balking at a tone she found insulting. "There's nothing to chalk up to anything, Filippo. We went on a hike and had a swim. That's it. Period."

"Like I said, let's just leave it at that."

"Are you saying you can't trust me?" Jolene said, her head already throbbing.

"No, I'm saying I can't trust him. Lorenzo."

"Why? What has he ever done to you?"

"It's not just one thing. It's a whole lifetime of things," Filippo said, now pacing at the foot of the bed. "Including dragging you up to Volastra and blabbing to you about Wendy. I was going to tell you about her, I was just waiting for the right time. But he just couldn't wait to drive a wedge between us!"

"Filippo, he didn't 'blab' to me about Wendy; her name simply came up when he was telling me about your B&B. He assumed I already knew about both. You can't imagine how stupid I felt playing along, but that's what I did. Out of loyalty to you. And yet you still didn't volunteer any information about her last night. I have neither the desire nor the energy to be jealous of your past, but I do not enjoy looking like a fool. Let's get it out in the open now, so we can put it behind us."

"If anyone here has a right to be jealous of the past, it's me. You were even married, as it turns out." Filippo said. "I wasn't."

Indeed, she thought. And it was thanks to that memorable matrimony that she knew how to recognize a table-turner at work when she saw one.

"There is no 'as it turns out,'" she said, before he could belabor the issue of her marriage. "It was fifteen years ago, and I never hid the fact from you. Why are you bringing this up again?"

Filippo rolled his eyes. "It's just to say, we sometimes make mistakes, right?"

Jolene shrugged. "Right. So?"

"So, Wendy is mine. She's my mistake."

"Did something awful happen between you?" Jolene asked. "Is that why you couldn't tell me?"

Filippo came to sit on the bed. Placing his hand on his knees, he stared at the floor and sighed. "Every ending of every relationship is awful," he said. "I couldn't bring myself to talk about it because it was still so fresh."

"How fresh?"

"This year fresh."

"We met in June, Filippo, and now's it's October," Jolene said. "When exactly did you two break up?"

"Well, you know that before coming to Cornell, I was working in Milan, at the Grand Galleria Hotel. The GM there was the one who suggested I take that management course."

"Yes, that part you told me," Jolene said. "I know way more about your jobs and education than I do about your personal life. It's time for you to fill in some blanks."

"The whole thing in Volastra was a mess," Filippo began, still staring at the floor. "Wendy and I had our differences over the B&B, then the differences became quarrels and the quarrels became arguments, until it got to the point where we couldn't even sleep in the same bed. I couldn't take it, and that was when I moved back to my apartment in Milan."

"I know what that's like, Filippo," Jolene said. "I told you about how I was forced to leave everything behind when I broke up with Evan."

When Filippo glanced up at her with a quizzical expression in his eyes, she feared he might ask her who this Evan was, although they'd spend an entire evening talking about him, and had even driven by his restaurant at Filippo's insistence.

"What happened to Wendy when you left?" she hastened to ask.

"Wendy had to stay on to keep things running. We had debts. She had her stinky donkeys and squawky chickens to take care of, and as if that wasn't enough, she adopted two retired race dogs. Italian greyhounds."

"And you just took off and left her to deal with all that on her own?" Jolene asked. Now that she knew enough about Wendy to be jealous of her, it wasn't happening; what she felt were the stirrings of sympathy.

"What was I supposed to do, take those stupid asses to Milan with me? Wendy was the one who wanted all those animals. She was incredibly childish," Filippo said. "Not that it should have come as any surprise."

"Why? How old was she? I mean, is she?" Jolene asked.

"Now she's twenty-three. Almost twenty-four."

Wendy was twenty-three-going-on-twenty-four, Jolene thirty-eight. Suddenly she didn't feel so sorry for her. If Filippo kept poking around in the embers long enough, he just might succeed in rekindling a spark of jealousy.

"What were you doing with someone so young?" she asked.

"Ten years' difference is no big deal," Filippo said.

"It's not just the number of years, it's the kind of years. The kind that gives a girl time to become a woman."

"As you may recall, you were married at her age, *Cara* Jo," he said.

"Danny and I were both kids. Neither one of us knew any better."

Filippo stood and went to the window, his back to her. After a moment, he turned around and said, "Jo, I had no choice but to go back to Milan. I was offered a good job. After all the money I sank into fixing up that place, which, by the way, we didn't even own, I needed to work. And I needed to get away from here. From Wendy, from Lorenzo, from Babbo and Mamma, from all the nosy villagers who were dying to see us fail. After a few months, when we closed down the business and I got back on my feet again, there was less tension. Things got better. Wendy came to her senses and put her whole menagerie up for adoption."

"What happened to her then?" she asked, again feeling sorry for the girl, imagining the tears streaming down her cheeks as her beloved donkeys were dragged onto a trailer bound for greener pastures, her squabbling chickens caged and handed over to have their necks wrung, and her arthritic old dogs consigned to the animal shelter.

"To who?" Filippo asked.

"To Wendy! What happened to Wendy after she was forced to give up her animals?"

"At that point, she had to leave, too," Filippo said. "The owner decided to rent the place out for the season, seeing as we'd done all that work."

"Where did she go?"

"Well," Filippo cleared his throat. "That was when she came to

Milan."

"To Milan? You mean she came to live with you?" Jolene asked.

"Where was she supposed to go?"

"Home! That's where twenty-year-old girls sometimes go, while they're trying to get on their feet," Jolene cried.

"Not when it's in New Zealand!"

"New Zealand?"

"That's where she's from."

Jolene closed her eyes and took a deep breath. "What's this Wendy doing now, if I may ask?"

"She's doing just what you said. She's trying to get on her feet."

"Meaning?"

"Meaning she's found some work giving English lessons, but she certainly doesn't earn enough to get by on."

Jolene had to ask the question, though she was fairly sure she already knew the answer. "Is she still living in your apartment, Filippo?"

"I couldn't just put her out on the street, could I? Would you respect me more if I did that?"

"That's not the point."

"No, the point is, I'm not the kind of guy who just turns his back on a girl. You should be glad of that."

"Did you see her when you went to Milan?" Jolene asked.

"I had to make sure she was all right, didn't I?" Filippo cried, pacing furiously. "Someone had to stock the cupboards and refrigerator. Someone had to call in a plumber to fix the toilet. Someone had to tell the neighbors to stop putting out their cigarette butts in the potted plants."

"Couldn't she do those things herself?"

"She could, but she doesn't."

"Why not?" Jolene cried, pounding her fists on the mattress.

"Because she's too…vague, I don't know… too spaced out. She's never lived in a big city before. When she starts feeling claustrophobic, she sets off on foot and keeps walking along the canals without paying any attention to where she's going until she's out in the country. Half the time she doesn't even know how to get back home again. When she's hungry she buys one chunk of cheese, one tub of yogurt, one piece of fruit at a time, without giving a thought to what she might need later. If the flusher doesn't work, she throws a bucket of water down the toilet." Filippo sighed, throwing his hands up in the air. "That's just how she is!"

Jolene shook her head, again feeling bewildered and humiliated. The Filippo she'd met in America professed to admiring independence and strength in a woman. He'd repeated over and over what a great privilege it would be to take care of a woman who could take care of herself. Yet at the same time, he'd chosen a partner who was totally inept when it came to handling even the simplest tasks of everyday life.

"She can't be that incapable of surviving on her own," Jolene said. "She managed to take care of herself and the animals in Volastra. She managed to stick it out in Milan for months, while you were away."

"Look Jo, just because she didn't die of starvation while I was away doesn't mean I can abandon her now," Filippo said, sitting on the bed again. "I always hoped that if I wasn't around, she would take more initiative, maybe even meet someone else."

"Do you still have feelings for her?" Jolene asked.

"How can you even think that, *Splendore*? I love you. We're getting married."

"Does she still have feelings for you?" she asked.

"If she does, she shouldn't. It's obvious that we're in different places now."

"Does she know about me, Filippo?"

"What difference does it make?"

"The difference is that if she doesn't know about me, you're letting her live with the illusion that you're still a couple! She still lives in your house, you still provide her with food, you still go see her, you probably even talk to her every day! Of course she keeps hanging on."

"I've been meaning to tell her. I just haven't found the right time, or the right way."

"So you haven't told her!" Jolene cried. "That's just great! You need to tell her now, Filippo. There's no more time, and there's no other way. It's for her own good. And mine."

"I don't want to hurt her unnecessarily. She's totally alone."

"Aren't we all, when it comes right down to it?"

Jolene couldn't move. She hated being naked while Filippo was fully dressed. She hated being in bed while he towered over her. She hated being immobile while he paced back and forth. She hated that she was expected to understand everything when nothing was explained. She hated that she wanted to scream and cry instead of listening to his reasoning. She pulled the bedclothes up over her head, to make Filippo disappear. She felt the bed jiggle as he sat down on the edge of the mattress, and she heard the thump of his shoes on the floor as he put them on, knowing it would be the right shoe first, then the left, as always.

"I'll come by at six-thirty to walk you down to the Locanda," he said, patting her phantom head.

"Thanks, but I can make it on my own," she said, her voice tight with tears, muffled by the sheet. When she heard him open the door, she peeked out from her hiding place and watched him walk out, feeling a twinge of satisfaction that the seat of his trousers was covered in cat hairs.

FOURTEEN

Jolene hobbled down the stairs in the dim evening light, taking care not to stumble on her way to the Locanda. Though she occasionally suspected herself of masochistic tendencies, they were not behind the flutter of pleasure she derived from the pain in her ankle. This pain meant something to her; it was the consequence of a risk she'd decided to take, and proof that yesterday, with its dreamlike memories, had been very real.

Although the strain caused by the jaunt was not limited to her joint—its repercussions having radiated to the relationships between her and Filippo, and between Filippo and Lorenzo, and between Lorenzo and Monica—while hiding under the bedsheet Jolene had reached the conclusion that the whole episode might qualify as one of those blessings in disguise with which her mother had taught her to console herself. Not knowing about a problem didn't mean that it didn't exist, and if she hadn't followed Lorenzo's lead on that hike, she still wouldn't know about Wendy or the B&B in Volastra.

Yes, although yesterday's walk had stirred up some trouble, she decided it was all turning out for the best. Being of a sensitive nature, Jolene cried easily, out of hurt, or sadness, or empathy, or happiness, but she wasn't one to indulge in melodramatic sobfests, and after her stingy supply of tears had dried up, she'd spent the rest of the afternoon in reflection, realizing that not only had she learned some important facts about Filippo's past, she had also gained some valuable insight into his mind, and proof of his character. Considering the matter from his point of view, it was to his credit that despite being displeased that she'd gone off with Lorenzo, he did not press her for every single detail about what she'd said and done with his brother, thereby demonstrating that he was a reasonable man, guided by common sense and intelligence, rather than blinded by jealousy. By overcoming his disappointment in her behavior enough to carry out his surprise of inviting her to lunch and giving her the ring, then retreating to make love and talk about a subject he would have rather avoided, he'd shown that he cared about doing what was right, as well as about making her happy. Wasn't it understandable that he hadn't been able to find a way to tell her about Wendy, knowing how she was bound to react? And wasn't it admirable that he, unlike most men, couldn't simply send the homeless and jobless foreign girl packing, once their relationship was over? Jolene knew what it was like to invest your body and soul in a business tied to a relationship; how it could break your heart and spirit when both failed, how rejected and alone you felt when you had nowhere to go and no family to fall back on. Filippo's behavior showed he was a man with values, one who took his responsibilities seriously.

By the time she reached the bottom of the stairs, her head had cleared, and she felt fortunate to have found such a good, solid man, with such a warm, welcoming family. It was with gratitude in her heart that she spotted Luisa standing at the entrance of the Locanda, having her ear chewed off by another woman whose wagging tongue was unfazed by the weight of the grocery bags hanging from her hands.

"There's our adventuress now!" Luisa called out. "Come on inside, Jolene. Let me make you a cappuccino."

"Ora?" the chatterbox remarked, glaring at Jolene.

Luisa simply shrugged, implying that one must tolerate foreigners and their strange habits. Looking relieved for the excuse to bid the woman a good evening, she hurried to open the door for Jolene and escort her inside.

"Thanks, Luisa. I'm fine," Jolene said.

"Where's that son of mine?" she asked. "Why didn't he come to help you?"

"I don't need any help. Really. Look." Jolene stood up straight, the ache in her ankle undetectable to anyone but herself.

"I know what it's like to be in pain and try to hide it. Maybe you should see a doctor," Luisa suggested.

"That's what Filippo said, but I'm not in the habit of going to a doctor for every little ailment."

"Same here. I've always found that listening to my body and taking care of it with natural remedies is so much better. Filippo, on the other hand, is fond of his doctors. He always has been, ever since he was a little boy. In fact, he was so fascinated with them that I was surprised he didn't become one himself."

Jolene tilted her head. "I had no idea he wanted to be a doctor."

"He didn't," Luisa said. "He just needed to be reassured by someone other than me that he wasn't dying when he had a cold. And he loved it when they dressed his minor injuries or prescribed him medicines. He never really outgrew that. Was he taking lots of medicines in America, too?"

"No," Jolene said, before stopping to consider whether he could have been sneaking pills without her knowledge. It was true that the bargain-size bottle of generic aspirin she'd bought in July had been nearly empty when she'd cleaned out her medicine cabinet before moving two months later. And now that it dawned on her, even the bottle of multicolored antacid tablets, a remnant of the gastric distress caused by her breakup with Evan, had disappeared altogether. Come to think of it, there were those pills Filippo swallowed at mealtimes, too, which he said were nutritional supplements, but who could say for sure? Jolene certainly never checked. "Not that I know of, at least," she added.

"Did he go to the doctor's often, when he was over there?" Luisa asked.

"In the United States, people who are visiting and people like me who are self-employed, together with millions of others, can't afford to go to the doctor's unless they're practically dying."

"I know," Luisa said, sucking in her breath, her face going pale, as if the state of America's public health care system, or lack thereof, affected her personally.

"I'm fine, though, don't worry," Jolene said. "*Sana come un pesce.* Healthy as a fish, as you say over here."

"Of course you're fine. I'm sorry. I was just remembering something," Luisa said with a shake of her head, as if to send the thought straight back to where it had come from. "Now sit down there, while I make you that cappuccino."

Wondering what thought could have disturbed Luisa, Jolene did as she was told, lowering herself into a chair as two tired-looking men, one with a bulbous nose, the other with a hunched back, shuffled in the door. Judging from the chalky patina coating everything from their balding heads down to their thick-soled shoes, she concluded they must be masons by trade. Before the pair could dust off their mouths to speak, Luisa set down in front of them two tumblers filled to the brim with white wine. Their arms heavy with fatigue, the men raised the glasses to their lips, but such an effort was not to be wasted on small sips. After gulping a thirsty draft, the men dropped their tumblers to the bar with a definitive thud, as if laying the last bricks of the day. Observing their silence, Jolene thought that perhaps talking to one another required more energy than they could muster, or perhaps they had nothing left to say after working side by side all day. Or perhaps they were already thinking about the evening ahead of them, of how little they had left to say to the wives who awaited them at home, and who would complain as they did each day about the dust they were tracking into the house the women worked so hard to keep clean. Jolene could imagine the men sniffing the air when they walked in the door, guessing what they would eat for supper. Would they feel reassured by the familiar smells of home cooking, or bored by their predictability?

"Cappuccino with extra cinnamon," Luisa said, setting the cup in front of Jolene.

Jolene smiled her thanks, hesitating until Luisa turned to walk away before adding, "Can you spare a minute?"

"Problems?" Luisa asked, wringing her dish towel as she pulled up a chair.

"No, the opposite. I wanted to thank you for this," Jolene said, placing her left hand on the table.

Luisa sucked in her breath again, her pale cheeks turning pink. Of course she would be appalled to see her precious heirloom on such an unladylike hand.

"Forgive me," Jolene said. "I know my hand doesn't do it justice, with all these scrapes and scratches."

"Broken skin is quicker to heal than a broken heart," Luisa said, staring at the ring as she spoke, then looking up at Jolene. "I'm glad the ring found its way back home."

The comment piqued Jolene's curiosity about the history behind the ring, but it also made her wonder whose heart had been broken, and how that story was connected to the jewel. She was still debating over how to cram her musings into a non-invasive question, one that would not provoke another one of Luisa's strange reactions, when Lorenzo strode through the door, patting the masons on their shoulders, his slaps sending little clouds of dust into the air.

"It's good to see you sitting down for once, Ma," Lorenzo said, greeting Jolene with a nod as he came to stand behind his mother. Placing his hands on her shoulders, he began kneading her neck and shoulders, Luisa's eyelids fluttering at his touch.

"What's that?" Lorenzo asked, stiffening, his eyes on the table.

"A cappuccino," Jolene said. "With cinnamon." She still hadn't touched it.

"Cinnamon has anti-inflammatory properties," Luisa murmured, her head lolling.

"I can see it's a cappuccino," Lorenzo said, abandoning Luisa, chin on her chest, to grab Jolene's left hand. "I meant that."

"Um…it's a ring…an engagement ring," Jolene replied, her eyes lowered, focused on the jewel.

"Filippo gave it to her," Luisa said, her voice strangled by her hanging head.

"I didn't know it was Filippo's to give," Lorenzo said, dropping Jolene's hand.

Jolene's heart sank with the fear that Filippo had committed a colossal blunder by giving her the ring. He'd told her that Luisa wanted her to have it, but even she seemed taken aback at seeing it on Jolene's hand. Could Filippo have coerced his mother into relinquishing something that rightfully belonged to the brother of whom he had been jealous since childhood? Lorenzo was the elder son, and with birth order came certain privileges. Didn't it make sense that the ring should go to his wife, Monica, who would one day pass it down to Chiara? Lorenzo's dismay was understandable; Jolene was little more than a stranger to the Garaventi family, and there was no guarantee that she and Filippo could, or even wanted to, have any children. What business did she have inheriting the family jewel?

"I don't know what to say, it came as a complete surprise to me, too," Jolene mumbled, twirling the ring on her finger, sliding it up to her knuckle. "If there's any problem at all, you can have it back right now."

"No, don't be silly," Lorenzo said. "Someone should wear it. It might as well be you."

Uncertain about what to say or do, Jolene folded her hands in her lap, while Lorenzo resumed his massage.

"This is all wrong, though!" Lorenzo cried a moment later, making Jolene jump. These Garaventis were too unpredictable, too much for her to handle on her own. She wished she'd waited in her room for Filippo.

"You can't be celebrating with a cappuccino!" Lorenzo continued, interrupting his massage again to whisk away Jolene's untouched beverage and dump it down the drain, returning with a stack of three tumblers and bottle of wine. Uncorking the bottle, he poured out drinks for Luisa, Jolene, and himself.

"This is from last year's special reserve," he said, raising his glass. "In honor of my sister-in-law."

Hearing Lorenzo call her his sister-in-law sounded even weirder than hearing Filippo call her his fiancée. This ring on her finger seemed to add a type of gravity to her status, making it more formal, more onerous. Lorenzo and Luisa looked at her expectantly, holding their glasses in the air, but when Jolene raised her arm, it was tremendously heavy, as if she'd spent the day laying bricks with the masons. She smiled, though, her lips quivering when they touched the rim of the glass.

A blast of damp evening air charged into the room as she took a sip of Lorenzo's wine. "*Splendore!*" Filippo called out from the doorway. "What are you doing here already?"

Jolene shivered as he strode over to their table. Armed with reason and goodwill, she'd hacked through her emotions to clear a path to Filippo's point of view, but she had no idea how he would behave toward her after their discussion. And now he'd caught her in another situation he was bound to disapprove of. She set her glass down, smiling nervously.

"I thought we said we'd meet at six-thirty," he said, stroking his whiskers.

"I came a little early. I wanted to talk to your mother," Jolene said.

"We're celebrating," Luisa said, rolling her head in half-circles as if Lorenzo were still kneading her neck.

"Really? What's the occasion?" Filippo asked. He was standing next to Jolene, patting her head in that way of his that made her blink and duck each time he touched her.

"We're celebrating Jolene's engagement ring," Lorenzo said.

"I was planning to tell them about the ring when we were all together," Filippo said to Jolene. "You should have waited."

"I didn't know," she said. She never seemed to know.

"You don't mind if I sit with you, do you?" Filippo said, squeezing a chair in between Jolene and his mother, leaving Lorenzo the only one standing. "After all, this is my party, too."

"Lorenzo, bring Filippo a glass, please," Luisa said.

Lorenzo went to the bar and returned with a fourth tumbler, while Filippo sat frowning at the open bottle. With no label to examine, he had to content himself with sniffing the wine in Jolene's glass.

"You can't stay away from the homegrown stuff, can you?" he commented, wrinkling his nose.

"It's Lorenzo's special reserve," Jolene said. "He opened it especially for me. For us, I mean. All of us."

"I actually had something else in mind for the occasion," Filippo said, pushing back the chair he'd just sat in, hopping to his feet. The swinging doors groaned when he burst through them on his way into the kitchen, where muffled voices denoted a quick exchange with Vittorio, and the groaning had not yet ceased when he charged through them again on his way out seconds later. When he reappeared, he was holding a bottle that looked more precious than any Jolene had ever seen: the glass was gold, the label was gold, the foil seal was gold. Whistling a tune Jolene had never heard before (neither the tune nor the whistle), Filippo stopped at the bar to slide the stems of four flutes between his fingers, before returning to the table.

"I took the liberty of chilling a Luis Roederer Cristal Brut Millesime I picked up in Milan," he said, the crystal chiming as he set the flutes down. "It's a 2000, which I think you'll agree is suited to such a special occasion."

"That's not necessary, Filippo," Jolene said. She didn't know what this particular bottle of French champagne cost here, but back home it went for at least a couple hundred bucks. The price wasn't the point, though. She knew it, and so did everyone else.

"You also said the ring wasn't necessary, but that didn't stop you from taking it," Filippo said, grinning.

Jolene blushed at the comment. It made her feel worse than

embarrassed; it made her feel cheap. Not knowing where else to look, she stared at Filippo's hands as they went through the motions of opening the bottle, not popping the cork as a joyous occasion would warrant, but twisting and trapping it in his hand, so he could satisfy himself with a sniff before serving.

"I would have waited for Pa," he said, tilting the flutes as he poured, a gassy sigh escaping the pale liquid, as if it were relieved to be freed of its long confinement in some dark French cave. "But he's in there gutting fish. I assure you that the stink would not enhance our experience."

"We could have waited till after dinner, when we were all together," Jolene said.

"Too late now!" Filippo said. "Once a bottle of champagne is open, it must be drunk!" He passed a flute to her, then one to his mother, and lastly one to Lorenzo.

"To my beautiful, extraordinary, fiancée!" he said, raising his glass. "Soon to be my wife!"

Jolene didn't appreciate the attention, and she detested Filippo's ostentation. Her smile was stiff as she joined the toast, her chest clenching at the explosion of microscopic bubbles as she downed a gulp of the ice-cold champagne.

The door to the Locanda flew open again, this time by the kick of a high-heeled shoe. Monica entered, a long tube protruding from under one arm, a bulging briefcase weighing down the other. She looked like someone from a James Bond movie, with the way she strode across the room in her stylishly short trench coat, its belt tightly buckled to accentuate her teacup waistline, her shoulders thrown back in an attitude of self-assurance, her thick lashes fanning her fiery eyes as they scanned the room, alighting on the bottle of bubbly.

"Oh goody!" she cried. "It looks like I got here just in time!"

"What are you doing here at all?" Lorenzo asked her.

"Is that any way to greet your wife?" Monica said.

"I could swear you said you wouldn't be coming until tomorrow, that you had work to do."

"In fact, you should consider me here in a professional capacity," she said, sighing as she dropped the tube and briefcase on a chair.

"What professional capacity?" Lorenzo asked her. "And where's Chiara?"

"She was being a fussy pain in the butt, so I left her with my mother in Monterosso," Monica said.

"At that point, you could have kept her on the train for ten more minutes and brought her to dinner here!" Lorenzo said, running both hands through his curls, as if he wanted to pull them out.

"As I said, I'm working tonight," Monica snapped. "You can go get her tomorrow.

"Come on now, don't go spoiling our celebration, you two!" Filippo said, kissing Monica on the cheeks before handing her a flute of champagne. "Bottoms up, *Splendore!*"

"Thanks," Monica said. "What are we celebrating, anyway?"

Jolene's stomach was in knots; she dreaded going through it all again, this time with the person most directly affected by Filippo's gift. She would be mortified if Monica felt cheated out of an heirloom Jolene had not desired; had not asked for; had not even known existed until a few hours ago. Had she rid herself of her old material possessions and the problems they brought, only to be bogged down by new ones?

"We're celebrating the fact that we sealed our engagement with a ring today," Filippo said, handing Monica a flute.

"Is that so?" Monica said, raising her perfectly plucked eyebrows.

"Yes, indeed!" Filippo said. "Show Monica how nice it looks on your finger, *Splendore!* How can anyone see it, if you hide it under the table like that?"

Jolene reluctantly placed her scabby hand on the table, and Monica took it in hers; unlike Jolene's, it was a hand pampered by expensive creams and frequent manicures, despite belonging to the working mother of a toddler; it was a hand suited to fine jewels.

"Oh!" Monica gasped, instantly dropping Jolene's hand, as if it were hotter than its owner's beet red face.

"I'm sorry!" Jolene cried, wishing she could crawl under the table. "I wasn't expecting this. I was as shocked as you are!"

"No, I doubt you could be as shocked as I am," Monica muttered, looking Jolene in the eye.

"I don't know what to say," Jolene said, feeling even worse on noticing that what she saw in Monica's eyes was not the glint of envy, but the gleam of sadness.

"Don't say anything," Monica said. "And all I can say to you is, good luck." At that, she tossed her head, her silky hair shining, the flicker of vulnerability vanishing from her dark eyes, leaving them hard as marbles.

"Thank you," Jolene said, out of politeness; out of a loss of anything better to say.

Luisa looked pained, too, as she leaned in close to Lorenzo, murmuring something which Jolene could not hear. Seeing his mother and brother engaged in a hushed conversation, Filippo sidled up to Monica, also whispering words Jolene couldn't make out, which caused Monica to shake her head, then nod.

"You were supposed to come earlier," she heard Filippo murmur.

"Sometimes you're worse than Lorenzo, you know?" Monica said, unconcerned that anyone could hear her.

"Now that you're here, I want to take a quick look," Filippo said, his voice still low. "But we'll save the talk for later."

"What, are you already tired of celebrating?" Monica said, now grinning.

"This is only the beginning," Filippo said, catching Jolene's eye and raising his glass together with his voice, as if that were enough to make her feel included. "But we can take a break. You'll excuse me for a bit, won't you, *Splendore*?"

"Where are you going?" Jolene asked, assuming she was the *Splendore* he was talking to.

"Just into the dining room. We'll only be a minute," Filippo whispered to her, his back to Luisa and Lorenzo. "Monica has something to show me." While talking to Jolene, he refilled Monica's glass, who picked up her tube and briefcase, her heels clicking as she walked away, as though they were tapping out a message to Jolene.

"What is it that she has to show you?" Jolene asked.

"Just some drawings. She is an architect, you know."

"Drawings? As in blueprints?" Jolene asked. "Of the Locanda?"

"Shhh, let's not broadcast it to the world."

"Why didn't you tell me about it?"

"They're just preliminary."

"Just the same, I'd like to see them too."

"Leave it to me for now, okay?" Filippo said, squeezing her hand. "She was a little thrown off by the ring thing. I know how to deal with her best."

"But this concerns me, too, Filippo. And you should have talked to me about including Monica in our plans."

"Trust me, Jo. All I've ever asked of you is to trust me." At that, Filippo patted her on the head, refilled his flute, and strode toward the dining room.

"Of course," Jolene whispered, trembling with hurt and rage, to Filippo's back.

"Enough lolling around for me!" Luisa proclaimed, concluding whatever she'd been discussing with Lorenzo and pulling herself to her feet. "We have a restaurant to open in an hour, and we still have to eat."

"Tell Pa I'll be in to help him in a minute, okay?" Lorenzo said, also standing.

Jolene wanted to scream; she wanted to cry; she wanted Lorenzo to go away, but he just stood there, staring at her, with her red face and twitching left eye and scabby hands, as if his shoes were glued to the floor.

"What was that all about?" he finally asked.

"I wish I knew," she answered, rising to her feet, too; welcoming, for some curious reason, the pain in her ankle, as if it were a casual acquaintance with whom she'd shared an experience, which, for however memorable, was not enough to make them close friends. Turning away from Lorenzo, she saw the two masons at the bar, taking their leave of Luisa, paying for their wine. Grabbing the champagne bottle by the neck, Jolene limped over to them, pouring the last of the bubbly into their empty glasses. The men nodded at her, chugging the champagne thirstily, as if they hadn't had a thing to drink all day.

Returning to the table, Jolene picked up the tumbler of white wine she'd been forced to abandon in favor of Filippo's Cristal. Lorenzo did the same. After raising their glasses in a wordless toast, Jolene drank, washing down what she could not bring up.

FIFTEEN

Strolling up Manarola's now familiar main road in the crisp morning air, Jolene tuned into the elements that identified the day as a Sunday: the yeasty aromas embodied in the fragrant pastries, more plentiful and extravagant than on weekdays, tempting villagers to splurge on dessert for their family dinners; the peal of church bells ringing louder and longer than on other days, interrupting conversations, recalling obligations; the army of excursionists marching into town from the railway station, counting on the Cinque Terre to provide an adequate return in the form of fun on the few hours they would invest there.

Even Filippo had a certain Sunday-like air about him, with that demeanor of repentance he'd assumed since mortifying her with his champagne toasts and infuriating her with his whispered conferences. He'd outdone himself to make amends yesterday, unrolling the blueprints on the bed of Suite 16 to show her that they weren't anything new, just the layout of the kitchen, restaurant and bar area in their current state, upon which Monica had made some notes and doodles. He'd acted interested when she showed him her own drawings of the other suites, too, and had even promised to walk her through the rooms again, maybe even the ones at the Locanda, which she hadn't seen yet, because Giobatta didn't have the keys to those, but not today, another day soon, so that she could explain in words the ideas that her amateurish drawings could not quite convey. Most important, he'd apologized, saying that he tended to be overly enthusiastic and overly protective toward the people and things he cared most about, that was just how he was, though he could try to change for her, if she really wanted him to, which led her to reply that she wouldn't want him any other way.

It was because of this that she was able to take Filippo's arm as they strolled, surprised to see yet another side to him as he paused to greet the people they encountered, affably inquiring about their families and remarking how good it was to be back. Judging from their reactions, she deduced that they, too, were taken aback by Filippo's chatty cordiality, and might speculate among themselves as to whether he was running for some public office.

"Piacere!" Jolene limited herself to saying each time Filippo, speaking enough for both of them, introduced her as his *"fidanzata americana"* to a shopkeeper, or to an ex-schoolmate pushing a baby carriage, or to an old friend's sister walking a dog. If the sight of Filippo stopping for a gab sparked some smiles and raised a few eyebrows among the people they encountered, hearing him casually mention the fact that he was engaged, and that his fiancée was American, generated genuine interest. The same people Jolene had smiled at, without reciprocation, when venturing out on her own, now shook her hand with a mixture of curiosity and warmth.

Between Filippo's revised attitude, and all these new acquaintances finally extending a welcome to her, Jolene was more convinced than ever that this village she'd known nothing about until a few months ago had always been destined to be her home. Yet what were the chances of her ending up in Manarola, of all places? And what were the chances that she should meet Filippo, of all the people she could meet, aboard a tour boat in the middle of Cayuga Lake, of all the Finger Lakes, of all the lakes in the United States? Wasn't this a sign that she should learn to trust fate (or God?) and accept some good fortune (or blessings)? She'd thought so, since her very first day here, which was why every time she walked up to Punta Bonfiglio to admire the panorama, she recited a little prayer of thanks for the miracle that had delivered her to a place where she would be safe from her past. And whenever she strolled up from the belvedere to the cemetery to play a tune to her mother, she felt closer to her than she'd ever felt since losing her, possibly even before that. And when she stared across to Corniglia clinging to its cliff, her mind was inundated with scenes from her hike, with its breathless climbs and shaky-legged descents among the withering vineyards and aromatic maquis, concluding with her sensuous soak in the sea. Her soul felt light then, and every nerve in her body buzzed with the sensation that many more magical moments awaited her in these "five lands" that were her new home.

"Jolene! Watch your step or you'll wind up with a broken ankle, instead of just a strain!" Filippo cried, tightening his grip on her elbow as she stumbled over a curb. "You need to pay more attention. What were you thinking about? Did you even hear what I was saying?"

"Of course I heard you," she said, having been distinctly aware of the words streaming from his mouth and swirling around her ears while her mind, through no fault of its own, had wandered elsewhere.

"What do you think, then?" he asked.

"About what?"

"About what I just told you," Filippo said, rolling his eyes. "Do you agree?"

"Um…yeah…I guess. Sure," she said, hoping that this was one of the times that agreeing was better than admitting she had no idea what he was talking about. "Whatever you think is best."

"Fine. That's what I was hoping to hear," Filippo said, his voice trailing away, as if even he was weary of its sound. He should realize that when he talked non-stop, like this morning, it wasn't easy for her to catch every word of what he said, what with trying to remember people's names, and constantly switching back and forth between English and Italian. And maybe he did confuse her when he talked. Maybe she did tune out sometimes. Maybe she had been retreating to a corner of her mind to avoid conflicts for so many years that she didn't even realize she was doing it anymore. In the time it took those thoughts to run a lap around her brain, they reached the square in front of the church, the bells tolling nine.

"What are we doing here?" Jolene asked, as the people milling about filed into the church.

"It's Sunday, Jolene," Filippo said. "And this is our church."

"You didn't tell me we were going to church," Jolene said, unprepared for further contact with Don Ludovico. "You told me we were going for a walk."

"Your ankle is still recovering, *Splendore*," Filippo said. "And may I mention that when you went for a walk with Lorenzo you visited a church? Or don't you remember that part?"

"Of course I do, but it wasn't for Mass, it was—"

"It isn't for Mass this time, either. Rather, not only for Mass, I should say. And did say. To you. On our way here. Right?"

Jolene looked at him; at the expectant smile, at the inquisitive brows arched over the searching eyes, all waiting for her answer. With all the things he'd told her, all the names she'd learned, all the people she'd listened to and all the questions she'd been asked, she must be overwhelmed.

"Right," she said. "Let's go in then." At least the only person she would have to listen to was the priest, and the only answers she would have to give were printed in a leaflet.

Taking her arm, Filippo led her into the church, its hush like balm to Jolene's ears. She'd already slipped one leg into the first available pew at the rear of the nave, when Filippo tugged her away, escorting her to an empty front row, nodding and smiling at people on both sides as they walked up the aisle. He looked very much the part of the future bridegroom, she reflected, and this ancient, intimate church would be the perfect venue for a Catholic wedding, but Jolene felt awkward and conspicuous marching in like that, a divorcée on Filippo's arm. Was it embarrassment at having all those eyes on her? Or concern about how people would judge her, now that they knew she was here to stay? Did they think she looked too old to marry Filippo? Too unattractive? Too foreign? Doubt by doubt, her heartbeat accelerated, until her spiraling anxieties were shattered by the jangling of the altar bells. The priest entered, and the Mass began. Picking up the leaflet she found on her seat, Jolene focused on the celebrant's words and read along with the congregation's responses, but their voices were weak and disjointed, and she did not want to be part of their unintelligible drone. Jolene stood and sat and kneeled with rest of them.

At Communion time, she refused to follow Filippo to the altar, remaining on her knees with her head in her hands to pray the only way she knew how, by closing her eyes to distraction and opening her mind to inspiration. She began by thinking back on her time as a practicing Catholic, wondering whether Danny had returned to the fold of the faithful; whether he had any children, or ever regretted not having had them with her. She thought about how ill-equipped twenty-year-olds are to make decisions that affect the rest of their lives, and those of others. Then again, maybe that was the beauty of youth, that irrepressible drive that made you dive headlong into life without weighing the consequences of your choices. Maybe it took a degree of recklessness to bring another life into the world, at any age, with the planet's population nearing eight billion, devastating its continents and oceans and atmosphere, fouling whatever limited resources it didn't hog up. Were you really better equipped at thirty to know what would be best for you? Or at forty, or fifty, or beyond? Did there come a time when you stopped basing decisions on a desire for growth and your greatest goal was avoiding past mistakes? Jolene hadn't yet reached the part of her prayer where she talked to God, when Filippo tapped her on the shoulder. Raising her head, she noticed that everyone else was standing, and scrambled to her feet just in time to receive the final blessing,

"*La Messa è finita, andate in pace.*"

"*Rendiamo grazie a Dio,*" the congregation mumbled, crossing themselves as they hurried off, already thinking of dinners and soccer matches.

When Jolene turned to leave too, Filippo held her back by the elbow. "He said to wait here," he whispered.

"Who said what?" she asked, glancing up at the ceiling, as if she may have missed a direct order from above.

"Don Ludovico. He said to wait for him here, so we can have that talk."

"What talk?"

"I knew it!" Filippo said, his church voice cracking.

"Knew what?"

"That you weren't listening to me on the way here! *Cara* Jo, we have some important decisions to make. You've been complaining that I leave you out of things, yet you don't participate when I give you the chance. You really do need to focus more."

"You're right, Filippo," she said. "I'm sorry. I'm just feeling a little confused with all that's happened lately."

But that didn't change the fact that she had no desire to meet with Don Ludovico—or any other priest, for that matter. It was a gorgeous fall day, and it looked like a sizable portion of the planet's billions intended to invade Manarola before nightfall. Maybe the hike had stimulated her craving for adventure, or maybe Filippo's claustrophobia bug had bit her, but this morning Jolene had the itch to get out of town. There were so many places to explore, and they didn't need to go far; even Riomaggiore would do. Better yet, maybe they could borrow Giobatta's car and take a drive to Portovenere, if Filippo wanted to use her ankle as an excuse to avoid walking. From there they could hop over to the island of Palmaria on the ferry boat to take a look around. It was Sunday, after all. They were free, after all.

"Confused or not, please don't make me look bad by acting like you don't know what's going on," Filippo said.

But she didn't know what was going on, and now Don Ludovico, liberated from the brocaded vestments of Mass, was approaching them, a sense of purpose billowing his plain black frock as he walked.

"You remember my fiancée, don't you, Father?" Filippo said to the priest.

"Indeed I do," Don Ludovico said, clasping her hand. "And I've heard a lot more about you since last we met, Signorina Giovanna."

Jolene's left eye twitched; the fact that he got her name wrong again did not bode well for the importance of her voice in whatever was to be discussed. And the fact that he'd heard a lot more about her made her wonder what, exactly, he'd heard and from whom. That she drank too many cappuccinos and too much wine? That she played rebel music in the cemetery? That she went on adventures with her boyfriend's brother? That she swam naked?

"Please, be seated," Don Ludovico said, making a sweeping gesture at the empty church with his hand, the star of the show offering them the pick of any seat in the house.

Jolene sat back down in the pew next to Filippo, while the priest sat in the pew in front of them and crossed his legs, his arm draped over the smooth wood backrest, his torso half-turned to face them, half-turned to face the altar, as if he were seizing the opportunity to contemplate his stage from the perspective of his audience.

"Now, if we want to hold the wedding ceremony between the Feast of the Immaculate Conception and Christmas, we'll need to move things along," Don Ludovico began, looking at Filippo as he spoke.

Move things along? Was that what they wanted to do? Jolene tried to catch Filippo's eye, but he was too busy bobbing his head at the priest. Yes, that was apparently what they wanted to do. But the Feast of the Immaculate Conception was not nine months before Christmas, which would make it next March, because it didn't have anything to do with the conception of the Baby Jesus by in the womb of the Virgin Mary by the hand (or whatever) of the Holy Spirit. The Immaculate Conception, which allowed Mary to be born free of original sin, was celebrated just seventeen days before Christmas, in December. That much she knew, just like she knew December was just around the corner.

"We must make a concerted effort if we intend to achieve that goal," Don Ludovico continued, his eyes moving from Filippo to Jolene. "You are aware of the obligation to attend the pre-Cana course before the marriage can be performed?"

Now Jolene was nodding. She knew about pre-Cana, too, and had already fulfilled her duty, though she was quite sure it was only valid for the one wedding. It wasn't like a driver's license, which you could use with any car once you passed the test. It was a moot point, anyway. She'd already pointed out to Filippo that there was no way the wedding could be performed in the Catholic church; surely he must have referred such an important detail to the priest.

"It's a seven-session course, so it takes some time to complete," the priest continued. "We in Manarola fall under the diocese of La Spezia, and I'm afraid the last course of the year has been concluded. There won't be another one until after the holidays, in January."

"Yes, Father, I'm aware of that," Filippo said. "Our first choice would of course have been to fulfill our obligation here, in our own diocese." Pulling his Moleskin planner and Mont Blanc pen out of his breast pocket, he consulted his notes, then cleared his throat, adding, "I've done some research, and discovered a couple of alternatives. One is an online prep class, which can be taken anywhere, anytime. It's offered by an organization based in America, but it's widely recognized by Catholic churches throughout the world."

"An online course?" Don Ludovico looked positively aghast, as if Filippo had suggested emailing him the Holy Eucharist.

"Yes, to accommodate those couples who live in different places or have conflicting work schedules and can't attend at the same time," Filippo said, clearing his throat again. "Modern couples face modern challenges."

"Undoubtedly. However, one would think one would find the time to devote to one's spiritual future as a couple," Don Ludovico said, staring at Jolene.

"Yes, Father," she said. "One would."

Nodding, Filippo winked at her; at least she'd gotten one answer right.

"That's why another organization has developed a full immersion weekend course for couples," he said. "There are some perfectly convenient dates available, right here in Italy." Filippo reached into his pocket again, this time pulling out a few folded sheets of paper. When he opened them, Jolene could see they contained a printout from some website. Granted, she might have a few holes in her memory, but her brain wasn't made of Swiss cheese. She definitely would have remembered if he'd shown her information about a pre-Cana course. She held her hand out to take the papers, but acted an instant too late; they had already been placed in the hands of Don Ludovico. Like everything else, apparently.

"Um-hmm," the clergyman nodded, tilting his head back to read through the lower half of his bifocals as he leafed through the sheets. "Yes, I've heard of this organization. It wouldn't be my first choice, mind you, but this will satisfy your requirement."

"Thank you, Father. That's wonderful news." Filippo grinned. Turning to Jolene, he squeezed her hand and said, "Next month, we go to Asti!"

"Asti?" Jolene bit her tongue to stop herself from asking whether it was that same Asti whose famed Spumante occupied the lower shelves of liquor stores across America. She wasn't about to feed any rumors about her propensity for wine-drinking.

"Yes! We leave on a Friday and come back the following Monday. I've already signed us up."

"But Filippo!" Jolene said, trying to send him a signal with the nails she dug into his hand. Spumante aside, she didn't have anything against taking a little trip to Asti, nor did she object to the idea of exploring their spirituality as a couple. What bothered her was the way he was putting her on the spot in front of Don Ludovico. What was the use of keeping up this farce, when they both knew Jolene was not eligible to remarry in the church?

"You know how I detest dilly-dallying, Jolene," he said, freeing his hand from her grip. "That'll be one less thing on the list." As if to demonstrate his point, he crossed out something on his agenda and scribbled in something new.

"But Don Ludovico!" Jolene appealed directly to the priest now. "I was married in the Catholic Church once before. I've tried telling

Filippo this can't be done. He won't listen to me, but he has to listen to you!"

"Now, now, one thing at a time, Signorina Giovanna," Don Ludovico said, removing his glasses and massaging the indentations on the bridge of his nose. He took a linen handkerchief out of his pocket, huffed his breath on one lens, then the other, then proceeded to polish them before speaking again. "Filippo has told me all about your unfortunate previous experience with the sacrament of holy matrimony."

"The sacrament wasn't the problem, it was the husband! I'm divorced!" she cried. "I can't get married here. I can't even receive Communion here!"

"Now, now," he repeated. "Be patient, and listen. I've known Filippo's family for many years. I've watched Filippo grow up into a fine young man, and I know how important it is for him to set things right with his birth family, as it were, by marrying in the Church and by raising his own family in the Church."

Jolene opened her mouth to speak again but didn't know how to respond to the comment about Filippo's future family. Every time she tried to broach the subject of children he sidestepped the issue, refusing to reveal whether, and how badly, he wanted them, insisting that the important thing was to be together. But what if, once they were married, he felt a burning desire for that family Don Ludovico was so sure he wanted to raise in the Catholic Church? What if Jolene was past her reproductive prime, and couldn't get pregnant? What if she no longer felt such a pressing need for motherhood, even though she'd now found the perfect candidate for fatherhood? She wasn't so naïve as to think that everything would fall into place as soon as they were married.

"Our Holy Father is going to great lengths to bring his prodigal children back home," Don Ludovico continued, the multiple minuscule reflections of votive candles flickering in his shiny lenses, obliterating his eyes. The effect was eerie, distracting Jolene, who was forced to focus on his mouth instead. His well-defined lips were plump, perfect for eating, for catching the juices of meats and sopping up sauces. "It so happens that quite recently, His Holiness has made it simpler for Catholics to obtain an annulment, so they may remarry in the church and thus be spared the sin of adultery. His reasons are amply explained in the two *motu proprio* documents he issued on the subject."

"Isn't that wonderful news, Jolene?" Filippo said, squeezing her hand so hard she winced, his cheeks glowing with pride as if he, and not the Holy Spirit, had guided the Pope in his infallible decision.

Don Ludovico, stimulated by Filippo's enthusiasm, began expounding on these first changes in such matters in three centuries. Jolene, in the meantime, was visited by recollections of the only person she'd ever met who had been entangled in annulment proceedings. Molly, one of Danny's devoutly Catholic aunties, had requested an annulment from the good-for-nothing husband who'd walked out on her. Once, at a gathering of relatives whose tongues had been lubricated by a few drinks, stories had slid off of them, shocking Jolene with accounts of exorbitant sums of money worming their way from the family's pockets up through the ranks of the clergy, and of reluctant witnesses being forced to testify regarding painfully intimate issues. The proceedings had dragged on for so long that they outlived the auntie, who had continued to count her blessings every morning and every night, even though these did not include the possibility of marrying the kind man who looked after her and her children with love and generosity, but was never granted live-in privileges.

"Did you hear that, Jo? It's in the bishop's hands. If he says your marriage wasn't valid, it wasn't valid. The bishop is the judge!"

Jolene recalled the man Molly had loved, too, a tall, thin fellow, with gentle manners and a soft voice. His name was Jeremy something. Maher, that was it, Jeremy Maher. She shook her head, tears welling in her eyes as she remembered how desperately he had wept over the coffin of the woman he'd loved as his wife.

"Did you hear me, Jolene?"

She looked at Filippo, panic pounding in her chest. She knew she would miss something important once she started thinking about dear Auntie Molly, and how unfair life (and the Church) had been to her, but how was she supposed to switch off her thoughts? How? Her ears, like antennae, searched for a signal, capturing some words they found suspended in the rarefied air of God's house.

"The bishop is the judge," she repeated, wiping her damp palms on her knees.

"Yes. And all he needs to do is examine the evidence that proves your marriage wasn't valid, and it will be as if it had never taken place!" Filippo said.

"We have to prove that my marriage wasn't valid?" Jolene asked.

There were many events in her life which Jolene wished had never taken place, starting with, in her darkest moments, ever being born. But was it really possible to undo what had been done? Shouldn't people be held accountable for their decisions? She and Danny had been in love; they hadn't been forced to marry, they'd wanted to.

"Of course, you will need to provide the proper documentation, but based on the *Mitis Iudex Dominus Iesus*, and what Filippo here has told me in our previous meetings, it is safe to say that the matter can be resolved in a timely fashion by His Excellency the bishop himself, with no need for a second ruling."

"What previous meetings? What proper documentation?" Jolene asked, by now unconcerned about masking her bewilderment. Her eyes darted from Filippo to Don Ludovico and back to Filippo, but neither man answered. Don Ludovico shook his wrist until the sleeve of his cassock revealed the luminescent face of a bulky sports watch, glowing green in the dim light of the deserted church.

"I'm afraid I must run now," he said. "I've been invited to Sunday dinner and I don't like to keep my gracious hosts waiting. Or the *tagliatelle al sugo di cinghiale* they have promised me." With twinkling eyes and parted lips—whether in anticipation of the noodles with wild boar sauce, or with satisfaction at having contrived a viable plan was unclear—Don Ludovico stood to take his leave. Filippo also rose, but Jolene just sat there, dazed. Filippo nudged her, and when she still refused to budge, he pulled her to her feet by the elbow.

"She has an injured ankle, Father," he said. "Please forgive her."

Don Ludovico nodded his understanding, while Jolene wriggled free from Filippo; gripping the back of the pew in front of her, she watched her knuckles turn white.

"Filippo has all the details, Signorina Giovanna. Perhaps you will find the whole process more understandable if he explains it to you in English," Don Ludovico concluded.

Turning his back to Jolene, Filippo said something she couldn't hear as he clasped the priest's hand in both of his, then Don Ludovico swished his way back to the sacristy, his hand reaching beneath his frock to the pocket of his black trousers.

"It's Jolene," she murmured, but he was already out of earshot.

Her marriage had been dead and buried for years, and she would play no part in exhuming it so that someone could declare it had never existed. Jolene's head ached at the thought of Filippo struggling to translate page after page of Catholic jargon into something she could understand. But the throbbing in her head could not match the thumping of her heart, pulsating with indignation that these two men had been confabulating about her, deciding what about her life was valid, and what was not, while she wandered around Manarola like the village idiot.

SIXTEEN

After the meeting with Don Ludovico, there was no trip to Riomaggiore or Portovenere, nor was Jolene in the mood to even suggest one. Filippo, however, was in ebullient spirits as they walked down to the Locanda, and if he noticed her stunned silence he did not remark upon it. On their arrival, they were greeted by a frazzled Luisa, in dire need of help with a group of thirty-eight American women touring the Unesco world heritage sites of Liguria and Tuscany, who were due to arrive by train within the hour. There was no trace of their reservation, allegedly made by email four months earlier, and while Jolene wondered how such an oversight could have possibly occurred, she knew that this was not the time to review records; this was the time to act. To make matters worse, Lorenzo had agreed to spend the Sunday in Genoa with Monica and Chiara, and would never make it back in time to help, provided Monica would even stand for it. As a result, Filippo was being asked to assist Vittorio in the kitchen, while Jolene would give Luisa a hand in the dining room. Whether Filippo was feeling happy about the prenuptial arrangements, guilty toward Jolene, or relieved at Lorenzo's absence was hard to say, but his enthusiastic attitude took everyone by surprise. Cheerfully exchanging his blazer for an apron, he rolled up the cuffs of his monogrammed shirt and whistled his way to the kitchen.

Jolene, eager to make herself useful and in no hurry to get into another discussion with Filippo until she'd had time to think things through, welcomed the opportunity to spend an afternoon at work, knowing that her mind did a better job sorting things out while her body was busy elsewhere. Setting the tables, greeting the guests, as always at ease on the serving end of the spoon, she was bolstered by Luisa's nods of appreciation, while the ladies' curiosity encouraged her to expound on the dishes they were enjoying, her colorful explanations in much appreciated English a hymn to both Vittorio's cooking and the quality of the ingredients employed. After spending an overwhelming two days in the Uffizi Gallery in Florence, which had allowed them to marvel at only a fraction of the masterpieces on exhibit, the women were primed for relaxation and soon grew chatty. Flushed with the wonders and wines of the Cinque Terre, one of them asked Jolene how she'd landed a job in this corner of paradise. When Jolene confided that she was engaged to one of the owners' sons, the news was passed around the tables along with the Parmesan, making the women titter with delight. Jolene was prevailed upon to show everyone her ring, and despite her initial embarrassment, she was not immune to the twinges of pleasure she felt at their unmasked admiration of the jewel's unique style and history. Twinkling eyes admired Jolene as she flitted from table to table pouring wine, replenishing bread baskets, swapping empty plates for full ones, and answering a barrage of questions.

By the end of the meal, the women had elevated Jolene to the status of heroine, seeing in her the impulsive romantic they all yearned to be, instead of the dedicated professionals they all were, who would put everything on the line for love. When the women begged to meet her husband-to-be and the tall, trim-bearded Filippo stepped out of the kitchen in his apron, charming the ladies by greeting each one individually and offering the entire group a glass of Sciacchetrà on the house, Jolene was struck with the uplifting realization that her future vision of the two of them working harmoniously together was no longer a fantasy, but a fact. Did she realize how lucky she was? the women asked her with envy. Did Filippo have any available brothers? they asked him with a giggle.

After the group cleared out, Filippo and Jolene, by then exhausted, agreed to retreat to their respective rooms for showers and a rest, neither calling the other for the remainder of the day until dinnertime, when they agreed to skip the family meal at the Locanda, Filippo with the excuse of getting a head start on some paperwork he needed to submit on Monday, Jolene with that of resting her ankle, puffy from overexertion. As a result, she had gone to bed too early, and even after the tiring day, even after spending two hours reading the Calvino book Lorenzo had loaned her, even after counting down from nine hundred and ninety-nine to zero four times, then repeatedly reciting the good night prayer she used to say with her mother, sleep still refused to come. Tucking the blanket around Fata, a foreigner to the affliction of insomnia, she dragged herself out of bed, stumbled to the bathroom, and splashed cold water on her sleep-deprived face.

Some fresh air might help, she thought, pulling open the window and pushing out the shutters. With the sun still abroad brightening faraway horizons, the moon waned to the point of oblivion, and the stars too lofty to penetrate the low clouds pressing down on the village, the only light tempering the darkness was the glow of the lampposts. The temperature had dipped since sunset and the dampness had risen, but Jolene liked the feel of nighttime on her face as she tuned her ears to the heaving sea, instinctively adjusting her breathing to the cadence of the waves breaking on the rocks. The solid buildings huddled in the dark below; within, their inhabitants slumbered. The scene struck her as eerily silent, unbearably dead. Stillness was the opposite of what she needed when her thoughts ran amok, running to places she preferred to avoid; what she needed was action, and she knew where to find it.

Yesterday morning, after a similarly sleepless night, Jolene's thoughts were still bouncing back and forth between the engagement ring drama and Filippo's dismissive treatment of her when the first light crept into her room, giving shape to the water and mildew stains on the walls and ceiling. At that moment it became clear to Jolene that unless she pushed back, she too, ran the risk of being overtaken. A sense of urgency filled her, making her spring from the bed, determined to prove something to someone this morning, if only to make a point, if only to herself.

The last person she would approach for the supplies she required was Filippo, who would only tell her not to waste her time and energy fixing up a room he intended to demolish. Bypassing him and going to Giobatta or Lorenzo was also out of the question, considering how furious Filippo had been about the episode of the borrowed furniture. While mulling over how she could procure what she needed, she'd walked down to the harbor for a cappuccino, happening upon the two masons with whom she'd shared Filippo's expensive champagne, already slinging mortar in Via Belvedere, where yet another building was being converted to accommodate tourists. She'd waved at the men, who greeted her so warmly that she was inspired to inquire where in town she might obtain some whitewash. The words were hardly out of her mouth when the man with the bulbous nose called out, *"Ehi, Dumitru, portami quel mezzo sacco di calce!"* at which point one of the more lowly workers stopped shoveling debris into a wheelbarrow, shuffled over to a lean-to where the supplies were stocked, and carried over to the hunch-backed man a half-full bag of lime. The three men gathered around Jolene, explaining in a mixture of Italian, Manarolese, and Romanian, exactly how much water she should add to the powder to obtain the desired consistency. She had already thanked them and was on her way when Dumitru came running after her, handing her a paintbrush, stiff-bristled but still perfectly usable, which she'd been forced to stash in the *armadio* together with the lime, when Filippo had turned up on her doorstep unannounced, armed with apologies on his lips, and Monica's tube under his arm.

The sun had set twice since then, and Jolene was itching to get started. She could be sure no one would barge in on her at this ungodly hour, and digging into a project with immediately visible results would give her a sense of accomplishment. Stepping away from the window, she threw on a pair of jeans and a T-shirt, deciding that it was a perfect time to whitewash the walls.

Recalling the masons' instructions, she measured the white powder into the bucket Giobatta had slipped her on the sly to place under the leaky sink, and gradually mixed in the water using a wire clothes hanger, settling on a slightly thicker solution for better coverage. Dipping the brush into the whitewash, she unleashed her doubts and frustrations on the walls, dripping and splashing as she painted up and down and back and forth in great sweeping strokes, her ever-changing stances as she reached and squatted and stretched offering new perspectives of the problems preying on her mind.

"This wall's for you, Wendy!" she whispered to one of her nocturnal brain worms. Slapping her brush over the ghosts of the picture frames she'd removed days ago, she imagined she was blotting out Wendy's presence in Filippo's life, while in reality she'd been convinced to accept it. She'd allowed Filippo to persuade her that keeping Wendy, his so-called "mistake," in his apartment was fair and just; that buying groceries for her, fixing toilets for her, and paying bills for her was fair and just. But was it fair and just for Filippo to turn around and expect Jolene to repudiate the first man she'd ever loved, the man she'd married? She'd desired that marriage; she'd made her mistakes in it and learned from it, and it was part of who she was. She could not and would not espouse the view that her bond with Danny had never existed in the eyes of God, when it had most definitely existed in hers.

These thoughts accompanied her to the north wall, where, together with the heaviest mildew stains, Jolene took on the Catholic wedding conundrum. As she slopped whitewash over the speckled surface, she theorized that a power play, rather than religious fervor, was behind the whole scheme. Don Ludovico was using Filippo to weasel his way into a non-religious family with whom he was friendly but over which he had no control, because their relationship was conducted on their turf and terms, not his. Yes, that was it, the priest was behind it all. Tomorrow she'd tell Filippo to be careful; to extricate himself from the man's grip before he dug his claws in any deeper. There would be no annulment, and there would be no Catholic wedding.

With aching arms and a clearer head, Jolene soon found herself surrounded by four whitewashed walls. A second coat would be needed, and so would a ladder if she wanted to reach the upper walls and ceiling, but for now she was satisfied, and tired enough to grab a few hours' sleep. Shedding her clothes, she flopped down on the bed next to Fata in her underwear, feeling a pang of self-pity that her closest confidante and bedfellow was a stray cat. If only she could confide in someone who knew her and cared about her, someone who would reassure her that she was doing the right thing, or shake her by the shoulders and tell her to wake up. But who could she turn to here, in a foreign country, where everyone was either a stranger or a relative of Filippo's? Dragging herself back out of bed, she stumbled to the dresser, unlocked the top drawer and took out her mother's rolled-up poncho. Hugging it to her chest, she lay down again. Fata, always content to curl up in company, crept onto Jolene's shoulder, draping herself over her collarbone, purring in her ear. The sound was soothing, and a sense of calm soon settled over Jolene, allowing her to finally drift off to sleep.

Row, row, row your boat, gently down the stream!

It was her mother's voice she heard in her sleep, floating across the water to the ears of a younger Jolene. The gawky girl that she'd been stood on the muddy bank, peering out to the middle of the lake, where she spotted a woman in an old rowboat.

"I'm over here, Mom!" Jolene called, waving her arms in the air, but the woman rowed and sang on, oblivious to her shouts.

Row, row, row your boat, gently down the stream!

"It's me, Mom! Jolene!" She cried louder, trying to jump as she waved, but her sneakers were mired in the ankle-deep mud, and the woman kept rowing away, her strokes gentle but steady, her voice sweet but strong as she sang.

Row, row, row your boat, gently down the stream!

Jolene's hands shook as she unlaced her shoes, her feet finally free to dive into the lake, swimming as fast as she could, while the woman and her voice receded into the distance.

Row, row, row your boat, gently down the stream!

Head down, arms circling, legs kicking, Jolene swam without pause, finally coming up for a lungful of air as a mighty wave, bigger than any wave ever recorded on any lake, engulfed her. An eternity later she reemerged, sputtering and gasping, her eyes scouring the lake, her ears straining to hear the song, but the boat and the woman who rowed it were nowhere in sight.

Jolene jolted awake, panting and entangled in the bedclothes she'd been trying to swim through in her dream. Fata, a safe distance from the frenzy, sat at the foot of the bed staring at Jolene as she flung aside the pillows, sheets and everything in between, and swung her feet to the floor. Picking up her mother's pendant watch from the nightstand, she checked the time; unsurprisingly, the hands were exactly where they'd stopped somewhere over the Atlantic. Yearning for a physical connection with the mother who'd left her behind, she slipped the necklace over her head, feeling the cool weight of the metal against her skin. Opening the nightstand drawer to check the time on her phone, she discovered it was just past five. A sudden chill made her wonder why she'd gone to bed with the windows and shutters wide open, and it wasn't until she stood and looked around her that she recalled her whitewashing folly. She went to the window, hugging herself against the cold, and looked out, walking her eyes up the path to Punta Bonfiglio and the cemetery, following the splashes of light from the lampposts. The lowest layer of clouds had lifted enough for her to make out the string of lights of the railway station in Corniglia, and those marking the endless ramps of steps she had walked down with Lorenzo. Farther along the coast, to the northwest, was the orange glow of the Monterosso seafront, a metropolis compared to Manarola. With each landmark she recognized, her breathing grew more regular, her realization that she was standing on solid Italian ground, and not drowning in an American lake, more concrete.

Apart from exhausting her, Jolene's dream had left her with a sense of abandonment and frustration. If only she could have reached her mother; if only she'd had a boat of her own, she would have rowed like she'd never rowed before to catch up. Fondling the necklace with her fingers, she was puzzling over what message her mother might have intended to send her, when a vibration came from the nightstand, signaling the arrival of one on her phone. As she hurried to pick it up, an eerie feeling came over her, a shiver running down her spine like that morning in the cemetery, when she'd felt a child's breath on her neck and thought…

"*Buongiorno, Splendore!*" she read. "Paperwork done! Grabbing the 5:20 to Milan! If I'm back early enough maybe I can take you to La Spezia! Glad you have a phone now so I could let you know in person! *Ti amo!* F."

Filippo had done it again! He'd gone off on his own, only telling her when it was too late for her to question him about the motives of his trip, too late for her to insist on going along to learn something about how such matters were dealt with in Italy. Running after him was as futile as trying to swim after her mother, she knew, and besides, she had no desire to go visit his so-called ex-girlfriend, which was certainly on his agenda. But like the Jolene in her dream, she couldn't just stand there and watch, either. The 5:20 to Milan wasn't the only train calling at Manarola; there were plenty of them, including one bound for Genoa every hour, and on one of those would be Jolene, she decided, throwing the stupid phone back in the drawer and slamming it shut. She'd spend the day exploring the city, seeing some sights, buying the things she needed, then return to Manarola when she was good and ready. Maybe she'd even find someone to repair her mother's watch.

Making a decision always calmed Jolene's nerves, while at the same time making her anxious to implement it. Both she and the room were a mess from the whitewashing, though, and she'd have to clean up before she could go anywhere. But before she could even consider doing that, she'd need some coffee. Stepping into the jeans she'd dropped on the floor, she rummaged through her tops, discarding the lighter ones in her search for something warm. The first sweater she came across was the fluffy pink pullover Filippo had picked out for her one day in Canandaigua, saying he adored the sensual feel of it, insisting that she looked particularly pretty in pink, despite her conviction that it didn't suit her coloring, taste, or personality. She recalled how he'd run his hands over her arms and back when she'd tried it on, how her mind had flitted away from the department store dressing room and made a beeline for Italy, imagining where she'd wear the sweater, what they would be doing when she wore it, and, when he would try to slip it off of her, how they would giggle when her head got stuck in the tiny neck hole which had earned it a spot on the clearance rack. Deciding the sweater would do for now, she stuck her head through the hole, tugging until it popped out on the other side.

While sitting on the bed to lace up her sneakers, she spotted a fringed swatch of brightly striped wool sticking out from the tangle of sheets. Freeing her mother's Peruvian poncho, she slipped that over her head, too, then evicted Fata, and set off in search of a hot cappuccino. As she stole through the sleeping village, she smelled no aromas of coffee brewing or bread baking, only the ever-present traces of brine and algae and fish swirling on the breeze. Where there were fish, there were fishermen, though, and they drank their coffee early, Jolene reasoned, stepping up her pace as she headed for the harbor. Not even there, however, did she see any signs of life, but knowing it couldn't be long before someone stirred, she decided to sit on her favorite rock while waiting for a light to appear, a shutter to open. Crossing her legs, she sat up tall, drinking in the invigorating air, watching the waves chase each other in and out of the tiny harbor in a foamy frenzy.

"Ah! I see Manarola has a *Sirenetta* now too!" a voice boomed in the semi-darkness behind her. "Just like Copenhagen!"

"What?" Jolene cried, so startled that she nearly fell off her rock.

"The *Sirenetta*, the little mermaid!" the man said, chuckling that hearty chuckle she knew could only belong to one man.

"Vittorio!" she cried. "You scared me to death!"

"Not any more than you scared me!" Vittorio said. "What are you doing down here at this hour?"

Jolene shrugged. "I couldn't sleep."

"I haven't been able to sleep for over forty years," Vittorio said. "It seems like a waste of time, when I could be fishing."

"You're going out fishing?" Jolene asked. "Now?"

"As soon as Giobatta gets here," Vittorio said.

"What are you going to fish for?"

"Squid."

"Oh, no!" Jolene laughed, recalling the mess she'd made of cleaning the squid, how the ink sac had flown from her hands and made a nosedive into Lorenzo's whipped cream.

"What's so funny about that?" he asked.

"I was thinking about our cooking lesson," Jolene replied. "I was a disaster."

"You'll get the hang of it," Vittorio said. "Hey—why don't we make a date for this afternoon? I have a feeling I'll haul in a good catch. It's the perfect time of day, perfect time of year, and I know the perfect spot. If Giobatta ever gets here, that is."

Jolene hesitated, not wanting to tell Vittorio that she didn't know whether she would be back from Genoa in time. He was certain to ask why she was going to Genoa, and who she was going with, and all kinds of questions she didn't want to answer.

"Ah, here he comes now!" Vittorio said, waving at the stooped figure shuffling toward them.

"No, that can't be Giobatta," Jolene said, climbing down from her perch. But it was Giobatta, she could see, as soon as he came a little closer.

"No fishing for me today, Vitturin," he muttered, shaking his head.

"Why? What's the problem?" Vittorio asked.

"Ah, just some sort of virus," Giobatta said, coughing; a phlegmy cough that twisted his face into an expression of disgust. "I went to visit my sister in La Spezia, and she was sick. It would be just like her to give it to me."

"Why'd you get out of bed then, you fool?" Vittorio said. "You should have called me."

"I did call you. God knows where you left your phone this time."

"Damn thing!" Vittorio said, rolling his eyes and looking annoyed, as if it was his phone's fault for not following him wherever he went. "Must be in my cook's pants."

"Lot of good it'll do you there," Giobatta managed to say, before a coughing fit wracked his body. Jolene moved toward him, fearing he might lose his balance, but he waved her away.

"You worry about what will do you good," Vittorio said, "and let me worry about what will do me good. Now go on home."

"That's what I intend to do," Giobatta said. "As soon as you promise me you won't forget your promise."

"Which promise is that?" Vittorio asked.

"Don't play dumb with me!" Giobatta said, his steely eyes fixed on Vittorio as he expectorated into a handkerchief.

"I wish you people would stop treating me like an old man!" Vittorio said.

"I'm the last person who would treat you like an old man. If you were old, that would make me old," Giobatta said. "All I'm telling you is that I made a promise to Luisa, like you did, and I'm holding you to it."

"Okay, okay, I heard you," Vittorio grumbled. "Now go back to bed."

"Can I walk you home, Giobatta?" Jolene asked. The man stared at her, his eyes blank, as if he didn't recall ever meeting her.

"I don't go places I can't get to on my own," he said. Walking away, Giobatta pointed a finger at the sky, as if invoking God to witness his words. "*La promessa!*" he called out, coughing, while off to the east, a blade of red cut through the leaden horizon.

"Damn Luisa and her promises!" Vittorio muttered, pulling out a pack of the cigarettes Jolene had already caught him sneaking more than once. He shook one out and lit it, shooting her a glance that dared her to object.

"Didn't you just promise not to smoke?" she asked. She didn't want to get on Vittorio's wrong side, but neither did she want to be in the position of knowing he wasn't keeping his word and hiding the information.

"No one expects me to keep that promise," he said, picking a fleck of tobacco from his tongue. "He was talking about another one, the promise about not going out in the boat alone. Giobatta always comes with me. Sometimes we go in his boat, and sometimes in mine."

"Isn't there anyone else who can go with you?" Jolene asked, wondering whether he ever took his sons fishing. Filippo had never indicated a passion for fishing, nor did he seem the type, though who was she to know? It was easier to picture Lorenzo fishing, but when? Most days he never arrived from Genoa until late afternoon, leaving very early the next morning.

"You like fishing?" Vittorio asked.

"Me?"

"Yes, you! Who else is here besides you and me? The mermaid?"

"I like boats," she said. "Mostly I like rowing."

"You want to come with me?" Vittorio asked.

"Well, I'm not really dressed for the boat," she said, knowing it was an excuse, but also knowing it was true.

"What are you wearing under that striped contraption?"

Jolene lifted a corner of her poncho, revealing her fluffy pink sweater.

Vittorio guffawed; he obviously did not share Filippo's taste in ladies' wear.

"Take that blanket off, and you can throw my slicker on over that pink thing," he said, already thrusting his jacket at her. Before she could consider how to beg off without hurting his feelings, he'd pulled the poncho over her head, rolled it up, and stuffed it in the duffel bag slouched at his feet.

"But what about you?" she asked, reduced to the status of onlooker watching her obedient arms slip into the slicker before she could stop them.

"I have my coveralls, and I'm roasting as it is in this turtleneck," he said. "Zia Matilda knits them faster than I can wear them out, and she always makes the necks as tight as a noose!" Running his fingers under the double layer of cable-stitched yarn encircling his neck, Vittorio stuck out his tongue, as if he were choking.

"I know the feeling!" Jolene giggled. "The neck of my sweater is too tight, too!"

"So, are you in?" Vittorio asked, the look of expectancy in his eyes melting her heart. She was genuinely touched by his invitation; so touched, that she knew her plans to go to Genoa wouldn't make it as far as the station. A boating expedition would be more of an adventure, besides being a good way to bond with Vittorio. And it would also send a signal to Filippo; a signal that some people wanted to include her, not exclude her, and that she had better things to do than wait around for him to maybe take her to La Spezia.

"There's just one more thing I really need," she said, zipping up the slicker.

"What's that?"

"Coffee. Where can I get a cup at this hour?"

Vittorio reached into the duffel bag again, this time pulling out a thermos. His eyes twinkled as he unscrewed the cap, waving the thermos under her nose.

"Mmm! That smells heavenly!"

"It's black," Vittorio said, pouring out a small dose for her.

"That's just what I need!" Jolene said, sipping the hot, strong liquid.

"Good. That's all you get for now," Vittorio said, putting the thermos away. "I'm a little embarrassed, though, *Sirenetta*."

"Embarrassed? Why?"

"That I can't take you out on a finer vessel. We'll have to go out in my little tub this morning," Vittorio said, pointing to the beat-up boat she'd seen him in the other day, equipped with a small outboard engine and a pair of mangled oars that looked like they'd been wrested from the jaws of a shark.

"I like your little tub," Jolene said. "It reminds me of an old rowboat my mother used to have, and the song we used to sing when we went out in it."

"What song was that?" he asked.

"I promise to sing it for you, if you're promising more coffee."

"Now that's a promise I can keep," Vittorio said. "But first you're gonna have to help me push this thing down the ramp. I don't know where everyone is hiding this morning, but they can't all have the flu."

Vittorio loaded the duffel bag, bait, tackle box and bucket into his boat as he spoke. Jolene slipped off her sneakers and socks and tossed those inside, too. Giddy at the prospect of another unexpected adventure, she rolled up her pant legs and helped Vittorio slide the boat down the ramp and into the water. Her jeans wicked the water as she waded in, Vittorio holding the boat steady as she hopped aboard. Manning the oars, she turned the boat around and brought it alongside the jetty, so Vittorio could jump in, immediately performing mysterious and manly miracles on the old outboard which sputtered to life as they set off toward the new day.

SEVENTEEN

Splashes of color appeared across the gray sky, a stroke of violet here, a touch of indigo there, while streaks of rose oozed through cracks in the dark clouds stacked along the horizon. God was a more gifted painter than she, Jolene reflected, and He had a far richer palette.

Motoring slowly along in the little boat, another of Jolene's talents was put to the test that morning when Vittorio reminded her of her promise to sing for him. His eyes twinkled as he made her repeat Row, row, row your boat, gently down the stream! several times before finally joining in, his Italian tongue tripping over the numerous r's as they chanted their mantra to the new, albeit sunless, day.

"You prefer to steer, or bait the lines?" Vittorio asked, interrupting their chorus mid-verse.

"Bait the lines? Me?" Singing together as they put-putted out to sea was so pleasant that she'd forgotten the purpose of their expedition.

"Yes you, *Sirenetta!*"

Jolene liked her new nickname even more than she liked *Americanina*, and both were preferable to Filippo's *Splendore*, which was starting to get on her nerves.

"I don't know," she said, regarding the sea with suspicion. "I'd rather you steer."

"Well then, I'll tell you how to bait the lines," Vittorio said. "You can't just sit there looking pretty and singing songs if want to be part of my crew. Do you or don't you want to be part of my crew?"

Jolene wished there were a third option. Handling whatever stinky bait Vittorio had brought was bound to disgust her, maybe even make her sick, but a quick survey of the sea, so dark and deep and unpredictable out here in the open, told her that despite all her experience rowing on lakes, she'd feel safer with Vittorio at the helm.

"Where's your pole?" she said, unzipping her borrowed slicker and tugging at the tight neck of her sweater, suddenly too warm, too scratchy.

Vittorio shook his head. "No poles on my boat," he said. "Poles make me nervous, except when I'm fishing off the rocks. Out here I like to stick to my old system." Reaching into his tackle box, he pulled out a block of cork with a nylon line spooled around it, and handed it to her. The line was fitted with a series of sinkers and beads and other doodads she didn't know the names of.

"Now, take one of these," he said, dipping into the box again and producing a long steel pin with a crown of hooks at one end. "But be careful not to stick yourself!"

It felt good to know he was looking out for her safety, but even without his warning, Jolene would have exercised caution on taking the pin between her thumb and forefinger; those hooks looked like they could cause some serious pain.

"Some people rub anchovy grease or pig fat on the line, but we've got some irresistible bait here," Vittorio said. "Grab yourself one of those little bogues or sardines, whatever inspires you, and stick the pin right through it."

"Like this?" Jolene asked, scrunching her nose as she stabbed the fish in the head, voodoo style.

"No, not like that!" Vittorio chuckled. "You've got to slide it through lengthwise, from the tail to the head, so its mouth ends up by the hooks. That's where the squid will grab it."

As much as Jolene didn't want this job, she wanted to do it right. She wanted to earn one of those nods of approval her own father had been so stingy with. She took another stab at it.

"That's the way!" Vittorio said. "Now attach the hook to the line there, but be careful not to get it all tangled up!"

Determined to make Vittorio proud of her, Jolene handled the line with patience, completing the task without a snag. When she glanced up at him he nodded, handing her another line wound around another cork block and another hook. She repeated the operation.

"We've each got about a hundred meters of line to work with," Vittorio explained. Squid stay close to the bottom and come up to feed when something catches their eye, so the trick is to attract them. This here's one of my sweet spots because there's a good current, but that's between you and me, you hear that? Giobatta's the only other living soul who knows about it."

"It'll be our secret," Jolene said. "I promise."

"Do you want to troll along nice and slow, or do you want me to cut the engine and we can drift?" Vittorio asked.

With no other boats in sight, Jolene loved the idea of drifting slowly in the pale morning light, just she and Vittorio and the waves that rocked them in their little tub. "Let's drift," she said.

For several seconds after Vittorio cut the engine, the air resonated with the memory of its sound, then silence settled over them, delicate as a veil. As she watched Vittorio sink his hook over the back of the boat, his thick hands unwinding the line from the cork, she tried to visualize those same calloused fingers caressing the keys of a piano to lull little Lorenzo to sleep, but nothing about the scene would come into focus: not the tired Luisa as Vittorio's young wife; not the rugged Lorenzo as a squirming infant; not the pragmatic Vittorio as a sensitive musician; not the piano or the house it was in, to which, with one excuse or another, Filippo had still not taken her.

"You go ahead and drop your line on that side of the boat," Vittorio instructed her. "And I'll stay over here."

Abandoning her unformed fantasy, Jolene sank her hook into the sea, feeling clumsy as she flipped the block of cork to feed out the line, hoping she wouldn't drop the whole contraption into the water; hoping more that she wouldn't catch anything. After baiting up and sinking a couple more lines, Vittorio relaxed, looking as comfy as if he were sitting on a sofa, with one arm draped over the engine, and the other jigging the lines now and then. The silence between them was amiable, natural, as the waves lapped the hull, gurgling with discretion.

"You want one?" Vittorio asked, after a bit, shaking a cigarette from the pack and holding it out to her. She admired his knack for juggling so many things at once, an ability which served him well both on his boat and in his kitchen. It was obvious that he hadn't needed her help baiting up while he steered, but she was glad he'd asked for it; touched that he'd taken the time to teach her.

"No thanks, I don't smoke," she said, half wishing that she could puff on a cigarette with him now, if only out of complicity, but the early hour and the rolling of the boat made the temptation easy to resist. "I wouldn't mind some of that coffee you promised me, though."

"Help yourself," he said. "It's in the sack."

Though not as adroit at one-handed tasks as Vittorio, Jolene managed to procure and pour the coffee without incident. "Ah!" she moaned, her eyelids fluttering as she sipped. "Coffee never tasted so good!"

"You know what I like about you, *Sirenetta?*" Vittorio said.

"No, what?" she said, smiling at the thought that there was something he liked about her, besides giving her nicknames.

"You know the meaning of pleasure."

"You think so?" she asked, cocking her head, but she knew he was right. Most of the time she liked that about herself, too.

"Yes, I do. You were really tasting that coffee."

"I adore the taste of coffee," she said, refilling the cup and passing it to him. "Though I do need the caffeine this morning, too."

"I've noticed the way you eat, too," Vittorio added. "Without gobbling the food up, but without pushing it around on your plate as if you didn't know what to do with it. I'm a cook, remember, and I can tell that you're thinking about what you're eating, wondering how it was made, singling out the ingredients, savoring every bite. Now Monica, she's a different story," he added, rolling his eyes. "That girl picks at her food like a sparrow. No bread. No pasta."

"That's how she stays so trim," Jolene said, wanting to demonstrate her loyalty toward her future sister-in-law, while at the same time envying her figure. Jolene had accepted her own body type by now, though, and she wasn't about to give up so many of the foods she loved for the sake of squeezing into a smaller size. For the most part, she ate well and exercised regularly, and if her butt didn't look good in tight pants, too bad for the pants; they could go stuff themselves with another pair of buns.

"Trim?" Vittorio said. "I can hardly stand to look at those skinny little stick-legs! I don't understand where Lorenzo got his taste in women, but we all know it wasn't from me. Of course, there are lots of things I don't understand about Lorenzo."

"What else don't you understand about him?" Jolene asked. If

Vittorio was inclined to talk, she wouldn't be the one to shut him up. She still had too much to learn about this family.

"Well, for one thing, why he won't budge from this place," he said. "Now that Filippo's back, and you're here with him, he should step aside and go live with his family in Genoa, where he belongs, instead of making everyone do all that running back and forth. Don't get me wrong now, no matter what anybody may think, I've always loved him every bit as much as I love Filippo, but hanging around here all the time isn't good for him, or his marriage."

Vittorio's need to emphasize the fairness of his feelings made it clear to Jolene that he had a favorite son, and that it was Filippo.

"Filippo was always interested in the finer things in life," he continued. "While the other kids craved bread and Nutella at snack time, he begged for smoked salmon on toast. It's no wonder he went on to learn all about fancy foods and luxury hotels."

"He certainly is knowledgeable," Jolene said, recalling their discussions while visiting the wine cellars of the Finger Lakes region. She had listened in awe, impressed not only by the wealth of information at his fingertips, but also by the sensitivity of his palate when he cited the shortcomings of the Rieslings and Chardonnays and Cabernets that were building up quite a reputation for themselves nationally. In recent days, she'd reluctantly concluded that Filippo was actually a bit of a wine snob, as prejudiced against the up-and-coming New York State wines as he was against those so arduously produced in the hills that were his home.

"Knowledgeable—and ambitious," Vittorio said. "Can you imagine how much more popular Manarola would be if they put in a couple of public elevators so tourists wouldn't have to trudge up and down all those stairs? And how about the idea of a panoramic cable car that would take them straight up to Volastra?" Vittorio squinted as he spoke, as if he could already see the transformation taking place. "Filippo says people will try to stop him if they get wind of his projects, that's why he wants to keep everything hush-hush for now. He just has to find the right funding, you know? He needs backers that share his vision."

"But this is a national park! A world heritage site!" Jolene cried, appalled that Filippo could possibly be serious about such absurd ideas, shocked that he hadn't discussed them with her, angry that he'd shared them with Vittorio after swearing her to secrecy. "They would never allow any of that here!"

"Well, that depends, doesn't it?" Vittorio said. "There's lots of money to be made, and money can close lots of eyes. I'm not saying that's good, mind you, I'm just saying that's how it works. Filippo reckons the Cinque Terre could be more...what was the word he used? Posh, that was it. Like five Portofinos, or five Porto Rotondos, all lined up along the coast. *Boom boom boom boom boom!* And he's determined to make Manarola the best of them all. *Cinque Terre, Una Regina.* That's his slogan. But I'm not telling you anything you don't already know."

"Five Lands, One Queen?" Jolene repeated, cringing. "His slogan?"

Vittorio grimaced, then burped. "Darn coffee gave me heartburn."

"I think it's those ideas that give you heartburn," she said. "You didn't even want a road here. You don't even drive a car."

"Now, don't get all worked up, *Sirenetta*. Things happen slow in Italy, if they ever happen at all. Between the two of us, I don't buy into those ideas either, but I have to give Filippo credit for thinking big. That's something I was never able to do. If we want to keep my son here, we have to encourage him. Me, you, our family—even the priest."

"All we ever talked about was coming here to live, fixing up the Locanda, renovating the suites, and working together to make the place as charming and as hospitable as it can be! That's been our dream, our plan!" Jolene blurted, relieved to finally confide in someone. "Filippo never mentioned any of those other schemes to me. But then again, I seem to be the last one to know lots of things these days!"

"You've got to understand Filippo," Vittorio said. His expression was pensive, his explanation slow to form, as if he himself was trying to make sense of his son as he spoke. "That brain of his is constantly churning out so many new ideas that he may not even remember what he did or didn't tell you, or me, or his mother. My son is restless, he gets bored with routine. That's why he keeps going away. But just because he doesn't like hiking or fishing or wine-making doesn't mean he can't be happy in Manarola. He can find all the new challenges he wants, right here. And if he doesn't step forward and develop this place, someone else will. In the old days it was the Milanese buying us out. Next it'll be the Chinese."

Jolene loved Manarola the way it was, tucked among its protective hills; she loved having her breath taken away by its steep stairs and paths, and by the views those climbs earned her. Her left eye began twitching at the thought of even more people, more cars, more boats, invading it. Then her fingers began twitching, too, jerking the line they held. Or was the line being jerked by something else?

"I think I caught something!" she cried, her pulse quickening, the nylon cutting into her fingers.

"Stay calm now," Vittorio coached her. "Start reeling it in, nice and steady, and keep it on the jig. Those hooks aren't barbed, so until it's in the net, it's not yours."

"Will you do it for me?" Jolene said, holding her line out to him.

"No, no, you can do it!" Vittorio said. "I'll be ready with the landing net. Just remember, we have to grab it, not pull it up. It might just be hanging on by its arms and tentacles, and those can snap right off! You could still lose it!"

If the effort it took her to wind in the line was any indication of the squid's size, she thought, it must be a monster of the abyss. Then she saw it! No more than a glimmer in the water, at first, then the sleek brown body with all those tentacles appeared, clutching the bait as if it were its last meal. Which it was.

"Oh, no!" she cried, torn between shame and pride. She wished the cephalopod would flail and fight like a fish instead of passively hanging on while she dragged it to its death. Let go! she willed the squid, as Vittorio prepared to scoop it up in his net. Do something! And then it did do something, as soon as it hit the air. It fought back the only way it knew how, by spouting seawater and squirting ink, dousing its predator and her fluffy pink sweater.

"Good catch, *Sirenetta*!" Vittorio laughed, his eyes shining. "I was just going to mention you should watch out for that!"

Startled and speechless, Jolene stared down at the front of her sweater, wondering how much Filippo would like it—and her—now.

"Here you go, bait up again," Vittorio said, handing her back the line after finishing off her catch and dropping it into the bucket of seawater.

"Do I have to?" she asked. She'd proven to both of them that she was capable of catching a squid if she wanted to, but now she was even less sure that she wanted to. Though there had been that special look of fatherly pride in Vittorio's eyes, which she wouldn't mind seeing again, and she had felt a sort of animalistic thrill which she wouldn't mind feeling again. Flushed and sweaty, she took off the slicker and flung it aside. The fate of the fluffy pink sweater had already been sealed; she'd let it face the battle and go down in glory.

"Of course you have to, *Sirenetta*!" Vittorio said, but she was already taking a sardine from the bait box, already sticking the pin through it, already dropping it into the water.

"I think I have a bite, too!" Vittorio cried. "*Whoa whoa whoa!* Here it comes, here it comes!" His thick-skinned hands wound in his line effortlessly, catching the squid in the net and throwing it into the boat in one fluid motion.

"Oh, no! I've already got another one, too!" Jolene cried, her heart thumping, her palms sweating. Remembering Vittorio's advice about keeping it on the jig, she fought the impulse to reel it in as fast as she could.

"Hold on tight!" Vittorio reminded her. "Here, grab the net! I've got another one!"

"I've got it, Vittorio! I've got it! Ooh, this is a big one!" she cried, thrilled and proud and pumped with excitement.

"Oh, and be careful not to—"

"Don't worry! I've learned my lesson! It's not gonna get me this time!" she cried, braced to dodge another shower as she scooped up the squid on her own.

"*Oowww!*" she wailed. "It bit me! That beast bit me, Vittorio! It won't let go!"

Vittorio was by her side in an instant, taming the tentacles that terrified her and stabbing the squirming squid right between the eyes. "That was the other thing I wanted to warn you about!" he said, detaching the slain creature from Jolene's hand. "Let me have a look."

"Don't worry about me now!" Jolene said, clutching her hand to her chest, wanting to be brave, yet alarmed at the amount of blood oozing from the deep cut in her finger. "Go get your squid first!"

"I'll teach you to mess with my *Sirenetta*!" Vittorio cried, juggling his multiple lines. Squid were splashing to the surface everywhere, their tentacles whipping, their ink spraying as Vittorio pulled in one after another, until the boat was invaded with the alien-looking creatures. There might have been ten of them, or a hundred, or a thousand; whatever their numbers, their writhing bodies would have had the same horrifying effect on Jolene. Soaked and soiled and bleeding, she clung to her seat, kicking her bare feet in the air.

"Kill them, Vittorio!" she urged. "Kill them!"

Moving silently, swiftly, expertly, Vittorio wielded his knife, stabbing every single one of them in the head until their squirming ceased, then tossed them into the bucket.

"Whew!" he huffed, his face flushed a deep red from all the excitement and exertion. Then he chuckled, releasing his hearty, barrel-chested laughter into the morning air. "First time I ever went fishing with a mermaid!" he howled. "You bring good luck, *Sirenetta.*"

The sight of Vittorio in such a state made Jolene laugh too, but when her gaze wandered over the aftermath of the battle, from the bloodied floor of the boat, to the bucketful of lifeless bodies and stilled tentacles, her smile faded. Now that the squid were all dead, she was mortified by how badly she'd wanted to see them that way.

"Let me see that hand of yours," Vittorio ordered, leaning over the side of the boat to rinse his hands, then drying them on a rag.

"Is it bad?" Jolene asked, holding out her finger.

"It's a pretty nasty bite," he said, taking her hand in his. "I'll bet it smarts."

"Yeah, it does," she said, her voice small.

"You might need a stitch or two," he said, looking dismayed, as if he'd misplaced his suture set. "Wouldn't you know it? My first aid kit is on the *gozzo*, like everything else."

Jolene preferred not to think about what Vittorio would have done with his first aid kit, but the look of concern in his eyes as he held her hand in his was already making the pain subside, at least a little bit.

"Saltwater's a good disinfectant, though," he said. "Lean over here!"

"Ouch!" Jolene cried as he dipped her hand into the sea. "That stings!"

"That's good. It means it's effective."

Jolene tried not to squirm as he held her hand in the water. First her ankle, now her finger. Whatever the injury, the sea seemed to be the cure-all.

"There we go, *Sirenetta,*" Vittorio said, after a moment. "Now we'll just wrap it up." Reaching under his coveralls, he extracted a fairly clean handkerchief from a pocket and wrapped it around her finger to stem the bleeding. "You just hold it there like that, okay?"

"Okay." Jolene nodded, looking up at him. Their eyes locked.

"I've always wanted a kid like you," Vittorio said, his voice thicker than usual, softer than usual. "A smart and sweet little daughter."

"Too bad I'm already thirty-eight years old!" Jolene said, giggling to hide how touched she was.

"I could still be your father."

"Yes," Jolene said. "I'd like that."

Vittorio nodded, clenching his jaw.

"Is it all right if I sit up at the prow for a few minutes?" Jolene asked, sensing that he needed a breather from the intimacy. She could use a few minutes to distill her own feelings, too. "I love looking out at the sea."

"Me too," he said. "Let's do that for a while. Let's just sit and look out at the sea."

Jolene swung her legs around, hopped over the seat and straddled the prow of the boat, dangling a leg over each side. The blaze of dawn had been short-lived, the tongues of pink fading to purple then disappearing behind the clouds that loomed low and gray. The motion of the boat disturbed her less in this position, and a sense of serenity settled over her as she admired the melancholy beauty of the overcast morning, knowing that Vittorio's paternal eyes watched her back, protecting her. A whiff of tobacco tattled that he'd lit another cigarette, but she did not turn around. One of these days maybe she might talk him into quitting. But not today; not now.

After a spell, it occurred to her that Filippo must be wondering why she hadn't answered his text message, something she couldn't do even if she wanted to because her phone was back in her room. He'd probably assume she was sleeping in, which she never did, or ignoring him out of spite, which she also never did, then put any worries about her out of his head until lunchtime, when he'd send her another message. He had a way of compartmentalizing his thoughts like that; the only way he got anything done, he said, was to focus on the business at hand, and put everything else out of his mind until the appropriate time.

Glancing over her shoulder, Jolene smiled on discovering that Vittorio's protracted silence was not due to the chain-smoking of secret cigarettes or the contemplation of the morning seascape. With his left arm hugging the outboard, his right arm dangling over the

back of the boat, and his chin resting on his chest, he had drifted off
to sleep in the gently rocking bosom of the sea, reminding Jolene of a
little boy who refused to rest until he crashed from exhaustion. A
little boy who'd gotten his way this morning by charming her into
coming on the boat with him despite the fact that she had other
plans, then making her fish with him despite the fact that fishing
disgusted her. He'd certainly had a good laugh at her expense, too,
she thought, looking down at her ruined sweater. Maybe it was time
to test his sense of humor; maybe she should even things out a bit
and play a little joke on him, too, she mused, the idea already forming
in her head. First she would bait up a line and place it in his hand,
being careful not to wake him. Then she would jig it up and down
until she got a nibble. She could already imagine the startled look on
his face when he jolted awake to find a squid on a line he didn't
remember casting, and how he'd scramble to reel it in. After they had
their laughs they'd better head for home though, she thought, staring
up at the sky. It seemed to be growing darker instead of lighter, as if
it had changed its mind about facing a new day and had rolled over
and gone back to sleep.

Discarding the makeshift bandage that impeded her gestures,
Jolene baited a line with the last of the sardines and slipped it through
the fingers of Vittorio's right hand with such stealth that he didn't
even flinch. Trying not to giggle at her own cleverness, she held the
cork in one hand, jerking the line in Vittorio's hand up and down
with the other, but after only minutes she grew impatient. Nothing
was happening; the squid had either gotten wiser or gotten lost. Or
maybe it was the boat that was in the wrong place now, she thought,
noticing that they'd drifted quite a distance from the point where
they'd begun fishing, which shouldn't come as a big surprise,
considering how the wind had picked up. The sea was unpleasantly
choppy now, too. Maybe this wasn't such a good time for a childish
prank, after all, she decided. Jolene had been caught in a sudden
storm or two, a terrifying experience even on a little lake, and not one
she'd want to repeat on the Mediterranean.

"Vittorio?" she said, speaking softly to avoid startling or
embarrassing him, now that the joke was off. Meanwhile, she
removed the line from his hands and set it aside.

"You fell asleep, Vittorio," she said, a little louder.

Vittorio did not stir. He was an early riser, and must be used to napping, she thought. She wouldn't be surprised if he slept better in his beloved boat than in his own bed; maybe he and Giobatta both dozed off when they fished together, as older folks tended to do. He looked so peaceful right now that if it weren't for that growing sense of foreboding caused by the lowering sky and rising sea, Jolene wouldn't have had the heart to disturb him. But with no anchor dropped and no engine running, it wasn't the best time to be floating adrift.

"Vittorio," she said, tapping on his arm. "The weather's changing. I think we should go back."

But Vittorio was so sound asleep that he didn't hear her. "Wake up, Vittorio!" she called, shaking his shoulder. He could probably sleep the morning away if she let him.

Squatting down in front of him, Jolene grabbed both of his shoulders. "Vittorio!" she cried. "Wake up, Vittorio!"

The wind riled the water, and whitecaps skipped around the ungoverned little boat, taunting Jolene, making her queasy. Cupping Vittorio's lolling head in her hands, she tilted it back, bringing him face to face with her.

"Vittorio!" she screamed.

Vittorio was leaving her no choice. If he refused to open his eyes for her, she would open them for him, the way Filippo did when Jolene wouldn't wake up. Maybe it was a game Filippo had invented as a child, to rouse his father from his deep sleep. Yes, that would explain the origin of that dreadful torture. Using her thumbs and index fingers, she propped one eye open, then the other, waiting for his reaction.

By now Jolene's hands were shaking, her shoulders were shaking; the boat was shaking, the sea was shaking. How could Vittorio not feel all that shaking? How could he not wake up?

EIGHTEEN

There had to be an explanation for Vittorio's refusal to wake up, apart from a desperate need for sleep. He could have fainted, for example. Yes, that must be it. That turtleneck he'd complained about definitely looked like it was obstructing his airflow, especially with his head hanging over his chest like that. She needed to free him from that wooly noose immediately, with or without his cooperation, and to do that, she needed a knife. Not imagining she might need one to hunt down a cappuccino, she'd left hers back in her room, but she'd seen Vittorio use a knife to slay the squid. Plunging her hands into his pockets, she fished out a half-empty pack of cigarettes, a lighter, a tin of Calabrian licorice, a crumpled kerchief soiled with engine grease, and a key, before her fingers finally found the smooth wooden handle of the Opinel. She flipped open the blade.

"*Scusami*, Zia Matilde," she muttered, her hand shaking as she cut through the tight cable stitches, exposing the stubbled skin of Vittorio's throat. "There! Now you can breathe!" she cried, sucking her words in with a gulp of air, as if to demonstrate how it was done. "It's your turn now! Come on! Take a deep breath!"

The fact that she had to tell him to breathe was not a good sign, nor was his refusal to act on her instructions. Maybe she should slice the sweater open completely, she thought, exposing his chest. Maybe the shock of fresh air would revive him. Maybe he'd wake up and start yelling at her for trying to freeze him. Gripping the knife firmly in her fist, Jolene began slashing through the wool, but between the shaking of her hand and the sharpness of the blade and the bobbing of the boat, Vittorio's neck got gashed in the process.

"*My God, my God, my God, Vittorio!*" she cried at the sight of the bright red blood dripping from the cut, trickling down his neck to his undershirt. Kneeling before him, she watched in horror, paralyzed with the fear that she'd hit his jugular vein. At that moment, a shaft of sun, slicing through the gloomy sky, glinted off the blood-tipped blade in her hand, before disappearing behind the curtain of clouds again.

"How could I?" she wailed. "How could I stab a man?" Horrified, she flung the knife into the sea, leaning over the side of the boat, retching and shaking and scrubbing her murderous hands in the seawater. She needed to snap out of it, she told herself, splashing water on her face; she needed to get a grip.

Screwing up her courage, she turned back to Vittorio. Sopping up his blood with the same bandage he'd made for her, she took a closer look, realizing, with immense relief, that the deadly gash was no more than a nick, and that she'd bled more from her squid bite than he was bleeding from his stab wound. As reassuring as that may be, however, the fact remained that Vittorio was still not breathing. If he was going to be that stubborn, she decided, she'd have to try something else. Tugging on his feet, she slid him unceremoniously to the floor of the boat.

"I'm sorry, Vittorio!" she cried, when he banged his head on the way down. "That must have hurt like hell! Come on, scream at me! Go ahead, swear at me! *Please?*"

But Vittorio did not speak or scream or swear, nor did he cooperate in any way as Jolene wrestled his bulky body into a supine position on the floor, his legs sticking over the side of the boat. Pulling back the flaps of the rent sweater, she paused to pray over his blood-stained undershirt. "*Help me, God!*" was the best she could do, what with her mind so occupied trying to recall the first aid techniques she'd learned years ago. Since then, she'd applied the Heimlich maneuver only once to dislodge a chunk of unchewed steak from a gluttonous guest's gullet, but had never been called upon to perform CPR. Seven minutes, that was one detail she remembered. That was approximately how much time you had to revive a person before brain damage set in. Taking a deep breath, Jolene pushed up the sleeves of her pink sweater and set to work.

Placing the heel of her left hand in the center of his chest and her right hand on top of her left, she began the compressions, hoping her memory would fill in some more gaps as she went along. There had been a strange suggestion of the instructor's, she recalled, something about a song. Humming helped, that was what he'd said. Yes, and the song he recommended had seemed off color for circumstances necessitating CPR because of its title; yes, the title, but what was it? It was coming to her now, yes, that was it! It was "Another One Bites the Dust," but it wasn't the title that mattered, it was the beat, because it marked the time for the correct number of compressions per minute. With the bass line throbbing in her head, Jolene got down to the life-saving business of pressing and pausing to the beat of the song: (*another one bites the dust*), and press and pause and press and pause (*and another one gone*) and press and pause (*and another one gone*) and press and pause. After several minutes of pressing and pausing she stopped to check for a heartbeat, feel for a breath, but could detect neither. She picked up the beat again, pressing and pausing, pressing and pausing, until, at last, she collapsed on Vittorio's chest, herself breathless from her efforts.

"*Please, Vittorio!*" she pleaded, but his lungs refused to breathe and his heart refused to beat and the song began to fade, and the only sounds left were those of the waves slapping the hull of the powerless boat and the gulls cawing their mockery as they circled above.

Reaching beneath her sweater, Jolene rubbed her mother's pendant between her fingers for comfort, not needing to look at its stopped hands to experience the feeling of time standing still. Vittorio could ill afford her paralysis, though. For him, each passing moment was precious. She needed to call for help. Now. But how? She'd heard Vittorio tell Giobatta that he'd left his phone in his cook's pants, and Jolene, idiot that she was, had left hers in her room, despite promising Filippo she'd always carry it with her.

"Help!" she cried to the pitiless sky, staring down at her with its great gray grimace. "*Aiuto!*" she shouted to the sea swirling around her, so foreign and menacing, so dark and nervous, so devoid of other boats on this gloomy, end-of-the-season Monday morning, except for a massive cargo ship piled high with containers, miles and miles away. Grabbing Vittorio's duffel bag, she turned it upside down, frantically searching for something louder and stronger than her voice; for the emergency flares or whistles or horns or anything boaters in Italy used to signal distress, but all she found was the empty coffee thermos, a half-full bag of saltine crackers, and her mother's Peruvian poncho.

How could a man who spent so much time out at sea be so lax about safety? Even if he'd planned to go out in Giobatta's boat, even if hadn't intended to drift so far from shore, how could he have been so careless? How could he do this to her? But even as this thought formed, so did other, more troublesome thoughts; thoughts about what she'd done to him. About how she'd turned her back on him precisely when he'd needed her most. About how she'd been so lost in her sea-gazing, so absorbed in fancying him her father that she hadn't even noticed that anything was amiss. About how long he might have been slouched over like that, gasping for air; about how he might have cried out to her, choking and in pain; about how he might have reached out his hand, desperate for help, but she couldn't be bothered to turn around and take it.

Her head pounded and her stomach lurched and her chin quivered with self-recrimination, but this was not the time for despair. This was the time to keep her wits about her and get Vittorio ashore immediately.

Jolene knew how to pull a starter cord and wouldn't have been overly intimidated by the 25-horsepower Johnson Evinrude if she hadn't witnessed firsthand all the tinkering it had taken Vittorio to coax it to life; but she had. Staring at the old outboard with a defiant look in her eyes, she gripped the handle of the starter cord and pulled as hard as she could, praying for a miracle. The engine seemed bored by her effort, though, mumbling a response that was something between a grumble and a snore. Jolene tried again, and again, each time pulling harder, so hard she thought she'd dislocate her shoulder; but the engine would not be cajoled into starting.

"Come on, you can do this!" she cried, as much to the engine as to herself, ripping the cord out as hard and as fast as she could, over and over, her heart skipping a beat when the engine finally rewarded her efforts with a cough. "Yeah!" she cried, bolstered by the promise of success. "We can do this!" She pulled on the cord again, incessantly, furiously, sensing that the engine was on the verge of sputtering to life. It was then that the cord snapped, making her lose her balance and keel over backward, knocking over the pail of squid as she fell.

"*Noooo!*" she screamed, scrambling to her knees amid the sloshing squid, staring in disbelief at the amputated section of cord dangling from the handle in her hand, the remainder of which had been sucked back into the mysterious inner chamber of the Evinrude. "Damn you!" she shouted, flinging the useless handle into the sea, pounding her fists on the useless piece of machinery until its plastic casing cracked. "And damn you, too!" she cried, kicking at the tentacled creatures floating around her bare feet. "It's all your fault!" Frantic to rid the boat of the squid, she began scooping them up in the bucket and jettisoning them overboard, two or three or five at a time, attracting the sharp-eyed gulls that screeched and squabbled as they swooped down for a free meal.

Desperate and exhausted, Jolene collapsed to the floor of the boat, curled up next to Vittorio, and cried. After a few minutes a strange calm settled over her, calling her to action. Pulling herself to her knees again, she stared down at this man, who with his bloodied chest and boot-clad feet sticking up in the air, reminded her of a gunned-down outlaw, whose sea was his Death Valley, and whose beat-up old boat the horse that would carry him home.

"I'll take you home, Vittorio," she said, wiping a sleeve of her pink sweater over her eyes. "But not like this." Folding his legs, she gathered them close to his body, pulling together the two halves of the slit sweater to cover his chest, then opened up her mother's Peruvian poncho and tucked it around his torso, leaving exposed only the part of his legs that wouldn't fit, and his head, because to cover it would have been an admission of something worse than defeat.

Now she must row. She would row faster and more furiously than she'd ever rowed before, she would make that heavy wooden boat glide right over the waves, all the way back to Manarola. Pulling herself up on the seat, she grabbed the beat-up oars and dug them into the water, her feet straddling Vittorio's inert form as she leaned into her movements: reaching and pulling, reaching and pulling, reaching and pulling, the repeated mechanical actions releasing her mind from the need to think until her body got the job done.

Crying and rowing were often close companions, she reflected, caught up in a flash flood of memories that swept her back to the past, to those days when her sobbing mother would drag Jolene from the house, clasping her hand as they ran down a grassy slope to the rowboat that would carry them away from the weathered shingles of their modest Cape Cod, and from the angry man ranting within. Seeing her mother cry filled Jolene with an unspeakable terror, and it wasn't until the house receded from view that she would finally seek her mother's gaze, hoping her tears would have dried by then. Nodding silently, her mother would invite Jolene to share her bench, squeezing her child's narrow hips between her warm, fleshy thighs and wrapping her long-fingered hands around hers. Jolene loved the feel of her mother's warmth on her back; of the soft curves of her breast and belly against her spine as they rowed together; of the strength she felt coursing through her arms; of the marvel that their power could take them as far as they wanted to go.

"In order to go far you have to be strong, Jolene," her mother would say, whenever she turned the oars over to Jolene. "Strong, but gentle."

What Jolene wanted more than anything else was to be strong. Strong enough to defend herself and her mother from anyone who tried to hurt them or bully them. Those words of her mother's always made Jolene want to act instead of hiding; to scream instead of crying; to pour every ounce of her energy into her bony shoulders and scrawny arms, making them row more furiously than they'd ever rowed before.

"Gently, Jolene! Gently! If you want to go far, you have to go gently," her mother always reminded her, when Jolene's muscles grew too shaky and weak to row another stroke. "Remember the words of our song," her mother would say, helping her with the oars as she started to sing, and then Jolene would know that the crying was over and the anger was spent, and that they would always have each other, and their song.

"Row, row, row your boat, gently down the stream!" her mother would sing, always beginning alone, but after the first verse Jolene would join in, too, repeating the same line over and over again. Sometimes they played that silly game where they left the last word off each time, until they pared it all the way down to "Row, row, row" then "Row, row," then finally "Row," which sounded so weird they always burst out laughing. Jolene hadn't even known that the "Merrily, merrily, merrily" part existed until a schoolmate told her. She'd run all the way home that day, excited to share the discovery with her mother, only to find out that her mother knew those words too, but said they must wait to sing them. "Wait for what?" Jolene had wanted to know, flushed from her dash home, disappointed at delivering stale news. "For the time to be right," her mother had replied, smiling her usual calm smile, with the usual twitch at the corners of her lips. Since that day, Jolene had begged her to add on the new verse every time they sang the song in their rowboat, but her mother always shook her head and said, "Not yet."

A clap of thunder made Jolene snap out of her reverie. She raised her eyes to a livid sky, hearing the first plump drops of rain plunk on the boards of the boat before feeling them on her face. Despite the wind and the waves, she was rowing at a good clip and hated to break her pace, but knew she should cover up before she got drenched. Retrieving Vittorio's slicker, she put it back on and zipped it up to the neck, pulling the hood over her head. Reaching down between her legs, she rearranged the poncho so that it would shield Vittorio's face from the rain. Shivering, she rubbed her palms together and grasped the oars again, ready to race the rain.

Gently, Jolene, she told herself, plunging the oars into the choppy water. *You've got to row, row, row your boat. Row, row. Row.*

NINETEEN

At last Manarola was near enough for Jolene to see how many villagers had opened their shutters to this dreadful new day, and how many seemed to know better. Half-asleep and half-deserted, tuckered out by the seasonal comings and goings of strangers, the village would not welcome back this American woman with her cargo of tragedy, and it would not be prepared for the departure of one of its four hundred native souls. Vittorio Garaventi would be deeply mourned and sorely missed, and who would be blamed for this atrocious loss? Jolene. Jolene Twyman. She was the one who would be blamed. By Luisa. By Filippo. By Lorenzo. By Don Ludovico. By the entire village.

"First you have to get there, Jolene," she grunted, forcing herself to keep rowing. Glancing up now and then, she blinked at the familiar landmarks as they came into view, as amazed to see them still standing as if she were returning after a devastating earthquake: the stout tower with its ringing bells; the heavenly belvedere with its blooming gardens; the scrappy sculptures of metal and plastic waiting to announce the birth of Christ; the monumental stone eulogizing Ligurian cemeteries; the cemetery itself, with its vacant sepulchers waiting to be filled by the soon-to-be-dead. Would Vittorio's body be slid into one of those slots? Would she visit him there and play her recorder for him, like she did for her mother? Would she be able to stay on in Manarola, after what had happened? Would Filippo still want her to?

Row, row, row your boat, Jolene, she urged herself on, instead of imagining the faces of Luisa and Lorenzo and Giobatta and all the others hurrying down to the harbor when they caught wind of the news, and then Filippo's face when he arrived from Milan, and then all of their eyes staring at her, accusing her. *Row, row, row your boat, Jolene,* she repeated, instead of rehearsing an explanation of how she'd gone out for a cappuccino and ended up in a boat with Vittorio's lifeless body. Her shoulders were shredded with fatigue and her hands were on fire, but she could not rest until she cleared the rocks and entered the harbor safely. For a split second, she was tempted to abandon her oars and let the waves slam the boat against the boulders of the seawall, like they threatened to. Maybe it would better for people to think that Vittorio had drowned; maybe it would be better if she drowned, too.

"*Paaaaa!*" Jolene heard a shout, carried to her on the wind, followed by another, more feeble voice calling, "*Vitturiiiin!*" Glancing over her shoulder, she spotted two figures standing in the square above the harbor, waving their arms in the air. It didn't take long for her to recognize Lorenzo and Giobatta, the two men who had already delivered her to safety once, and even less time for her relief at seeing them to be crushed by her burden of dread. She must reach them, though, she must deliver Vittorio to their hands. With a pounding heart and a heaving chest, she navigated the churning water, finally guiding the boat into the harbor and toward the jetty, where the men gestured for her to dock instead of attempting to land at the boat ramp.

"I'm so sorry, Vittorio," she cried, her head bent beneath the hood of his slicker as she glanced down at his covered body, aware that their time together was almost over. "I really wanted to be your daughter."

Deftly maneuvering with one oar then the other, Jolene managed to steer clear of the rocky outcrops in her path and bring the boat alongside the jetty, where Lorenzo already stood waiting. Jolene tossed him a line, and he quickly tied the boat up, whipping his head around for a double-take of the face peeking out from under the hooded slicker. Frozen, Jolene watched his features register his shock, then recognition, then bewilderment.

"Jolene?" Lorenzo said, blinking. "What are you doing alone on Pa's boat in this weather? Are you crazy? Are you all right?"

Jolene felt her entire body shutting down in fear; her stomach clamping shut, her lungs and heart clamping shut, her jaw clamping shut. Only her eyes remained open, stunned and staring.

"Where's Vitturin?" Giobatta wheezed, arriving on the scene and looking equally perplexed to see Jolene on the boat; equally alarmed to see her alone.

Jolene's eyes darted from Lorenzo to Giobatta to the floor of the boat. She was unable to speak, unable to breathe.

"The last time I saw Vitturin he was with you!" Giobatta said. "That's what I told Luisa when she called around looking for him!"

"Where is he, Jolene?" Lorenzo asked. "Where's Pa?"

"I don't know how to…what to…" Jolene stammered, her eyes lowered, her body sinking deeper into the slicker.

"What's going on, Jolene?" Lorenzo cried.

Jolene's tongue was too tied to speak the unspeakable words; her hands were too shaky to pull back the poncho and reveal Vittorio's face. But then they did.

Lorenzo looked down at his father's still form. "Pa! What are you doing, lying there like that?" he cried.

"He's not lying!" Jolene blurted. "He's…he's *dying*…or…or… *dead*!"

"Dead? What are you talking about?" Lorenzo cried, hopping into the boat and kneeling beside the body. Pushing aside the poncho, he slapped Vittorio's cheeks, he put his ear to his chest, he felt his neck and his wrists for a pulse, his actions spinning a final, fine thread of hope for Jolene to cling to. But instead of getting up and running for help or calling for an ambulance or telling her that she'd been mistaken, or hallucinating, or crazy, Lorenzo remained sickeningly silent as he observed his father's ghostly pallor, his blue lips, his slit sweater, his bloodied undershirt, his gashed neck.

"What the hell happened, Jolene?" he cried. "For God's sake, what *happened?*"

When Jolene looked up, it was to Giobatta that she found her eyes drawn. When he met her gaze, his eyes held no questions or accusations. They were damp and resigned, like a miserably drizzly day.

"He really wanted to go fishing," Jolene mumbled. "But since he couldn't go alone and Giobatta was sick, he asked me." She stared down at Vittorio's expressionless face, recalling how quickly the look of disappointment in his eyes had vanished, replaced by a sparkle of joy, the instant she'd agreed to go with him. "So I said yes."

"You can't be telling me that this was a fishing accident, Jolene!" Lorenzo cried. "Was he attacked by someone?"

"No!" Jolene moaned. "It was me!"

"You attacked him?"

"No! That's not how it went. No one attacked anyone. There wasn't a soul out there except for us," Jolene said, her voice tentative, as if she needed to reassure herself of the story as she told it. "We were just drifting along, fishing for squid."

"And?"

"And I caught one right away, but I wasn't very happy about it, because I made a mess of things again, with all that squirting ink and all, but Vittorio was so proud of me," Jolene said, spitting out her words in a nervous stream.

"And then?" Lorenzo said.

"And then Vittorio caught one, and then I caught another one, but I got bit, and then Vittorio kept on catching them, one after another. They were biting so fast they were practically flying into the boat. He was having a grand time, laughing so hard he couldn't catch his breath," Jolene said, clamping her mouth shut before it could spew out more nonsense. "Well, not literally, you know, it's an expression."

"No, I don't know, Jolene! What I do know is that I don't see any squid on this boat!" Lorenzo said, waving the empty bucket in her face. "Now tell me what happened to Pa!"

"Nothing happened," she said, wishing she'd never set foot on this boat; wishing she could get off it before she puked again. "I was looking the other way, and when I turned around, he was like that."

"What do you mean, 'he was like that?'" Lorenzo cried. "One minute he was fishing, and the next minute he was cut up and bleeding and…and…*dead*? While you were turned the other way? On this tiny tub of a boat? And you didn't even *notice*?"

"No, I didn't mean to say he was how he is now," Jolene said, clasping her hands to stop them from shaking; wincing at the rawness from her rowing, at the throbbing from the squid bite. "I meant to say that I was sitting with my back to him, and when I turned around, he was slouched over. I thought he was sleeping."

Lorenzo raised a single eyebrow, staring at her, waiting for her to continue.

"I tried to resuscitate him!" she cried. "I tried so hard! I slit open that stupid turtleneck that was strangling him! I wanted to help him breathe, but my hand slipped! I know, it looks awful, but it's only a nick, and I freaked out when I saw the blood, too, believe me, especially when I realized he didn't even flinch, and that's when I started to panic. I did CPR on him for as long as I could! I kept trying and trying, but nothing I did helped. Nothing!" Jolene wailed, but she didn't want them to see her cry. She wanted them to see how strong she was. Wiping away her tears with the backs of her hands, she breathed in, using all her will to push back the sobs before they could overcome her.

"*Vieni, Americanina*," Giobatta said, extending a hand to her. "Let's get you out of that boat."

Jolene's chin quivered as she looked up at him. "You saw him earlier, Giobatta, right? He seemed fine, right?" she asked.

"Same as every morning," Giobatta said.

"I shouldn't have gone fishing. I didn't want to go fishing," she muttered. "All I wanted was a cappuccino."

"It was bound to happen, sooner or later," Giobatta said. "Now take my hand and hop up here."

Before Lorenzo could offer to help, Jolene was already out of the boat, standing on the jetty, her legs wobbly as she grew accustomed to the feel of solid ground beneath her bare feet.

"Here, you'd better take these," Lorenzo said, tossing her the soaked sneakers that had walked her off the plane in Genoa the day of her arrival. How she wished she'd turned them around and made them march aboard the first flight back to America!

"I'm so sorry, Lorenzo," Jolene said, gazing down at him. "What can I do?"

"You've already done enough," he replied, pulling the poncho over Vittorio again. "I'll fetch Dottor Costa. The last thing we need now is for those volunteer ambulance people to speed down here with their blaring sirens and flashing lights. It's too late for them to do anything but draw a crowd."

"I came back as fast as I could!" Jolene said, uncertain of whether Lorenzo was accusing her of the same things for which she already blamed herself. "I called for help but there was nobody around for miles! We didn't have phones! And the outboard broke down! All I could do was row, so that's what I did!"

"You're a strong girl, *Americanina*." Giobatta said, nodding at Jolene before turning to Lorenzo. "You run ahead, Lorenzo. We'll wait here for you."

"I'll be right back, but don't say anything to anyone, in the meantime," Lorenzo warned, already out of the boat and on his way. "Word travels fast here. We can't let it reach Ma before I do."

But the ambulance did come, blaring its siren and flashing its lights; and so did Luisa, and so did Don Ludovico, and so did the villagers, first in a trickle, then in a stream, all swirling around Luisa, cutting off Jolene's access to her. Eyes stared, tongues clicked, heads shook, hands made signs-of-the-cross, while Jolene stood off to the side, her teary eyes lowered, her aching limbs trembling, her overtaxed heart quivering with fear at the appearance of two armed officers in uniform. If Jolene did not collapse when they approached her, informing her that they'd been dispatched from Riomaggiore to investigate the case, it was partly thanks to Vittorio's stiff slicker which she still wore, zipped all the way up to her neck, propping her up.

She needed to talk to Filippo, she needed him here desperately, immediately, and so did his mother and brother and everyone else, way more than that stupid girl in Milan needed him. But how could she go call him when the first *carabiniere*, the older one she mentally referred to as Carabiniere Uno, wouldn't stop talking to her in his approximate English, asking questions and making comments that confused her jumbled thoughts as she repeated her squid story? It wasn't until she noticed the younger *carabiniere*, Carabiniere Due, jotting down the mumblings dictated to him in Italian by Carabiniere Uno that she feared she was being interrogated.

Meanwhile, Dottor Costa and Lorenzo and Giobatta and Luisa conferred with one another, reaching the unanimous conclusion that Vittorio's ailing heart must have finally failed him. This news was not given to Jolene directly, but through Carabiniere Uno, who nonetheless expressed reserves about abandoning other avenues of investigation that would take into account highly suspicious details such as the obvious stab wound on the victim's neck, the violent manner in which said victim's torso had been denuded, the tampering with and destruction of the outboard motor at the hands of the foreign woman who had essentially held the victim hostage on his own boat. To Jolene's relief, as the more reasonable Carabiniere Due timidly reminded his colleague, it was their job to gather the physical evidence, record the witnesses' testimony, and file their report. It was the duty of the coroner, and the coroner alone, to establish the official cause of death.

While Vittorio's body was being photographed by Carabiniere Uno, first on the boat then off the boat, Lorenzo said that it was his duty to inform Filippo of what had happened, and that no one else should speak to him before he did. Jolene's initial surge of cowardly relief at not being allowed to deliver such devastating news soon turned to frustration when each of Lorenzo's attempts at getting through was thwarted. Out of range or switched off, engaged or ringing endlessly, Filippo's phone seemed determined to elude Lorenzo and the bad news he bore. Jolene regretted that she wouldn't be by her fiancé's side when he received the shattering news of Vittorio's death, just as she was sorry to see that Lorenzo's wife was not by his side in his moment of need. Though he appeared calm and efficient as he dealt with the doctor and the carabinieri, all the while keeping a vigilant eye on Luisa, she knew he must be suffering terribly inside. She wished she could speak to him and to Luisa in private; she wished she could beg for their forgiveness, but the fact that they did not seek her out could only mean that she was the last person they'd want to talk to.

At last Vittorio was whisked off to La Spezia, accompanied by Lorenzo and more flashing lights and screaming sirens, while the villagers, craning their necks to stare at the ambulance until it sped out of view, crossed themselves again. Left with no dead body on which to focus their morbid curiosity, their next best option was the remaining victim (or perpetrator?) of the morning's tragic fishing expedition: Jolene. She didn't need to hear what they were whispering behind their cupped hands to feel their hostility; she didn't need to look into their eyes to know she would not see sympathy there, but judgment.

Stuck standing there on her own under vigilant eyes of the carabinieri, Jolene wondered whether it was ever possible to refrain from observing the people around us, no matter how grave the circumstances, unless we were blindfolded, like a condemned prisoner standing in front of a firing squad or with a noose around his neck. In need of distraction, Jolene did not resist her natural curiosity which prompted her to examine the assembly of villagers standing in front of her, larger than any she'd seen so far, including at Sunday Mass. The majority seemed to be made up of older women, and as Jolene's gaze, careful to avoid accusatory faces, roamed over their sensible-shoed feet, she imagined how many bore the discomfort of bunions and callouses and hammertoes to stand in support of Luisa and her family. From their shoes, her eyes ventured up to the simple house dresses the ladies had been caught in when receiving the news of a death; to the crocheted shawls and hand-knitted sweaters they clutched to their sagging breasts, as if to shield their weary hearts from the pain of another loss. While these women murmured their comments and dabbed at their eyes, the men drifted along the jetty toward the sea, where they stared silently into the nothingness, some smoking, all looking glum. Nothing could replace their lost companion, but once they got over their initial shock, Jolene imagined they would behave like men everywhere, disrupting their normal routine to indulge in a drink or two over shared anecdotes about Vittorio, unanimously agreeing that he was as good a man as they came, a hard worker and a good family man, really, and didn't deserve to die. Men and women alike displayed a reluctance to move away from the scene, though nothing had actually happened there. It was merely the place where the before had collided with the after, and the inevitable proved it could only be postponed for so long.

Watching the individuals spin off occasionally to regroup in new clusters, Jolene had the impression that nothing could break the bonds that held them together. It was the wizened women, however, who struck her as the unifying force of the village. Most of them must have been born amid the winds of war, enduring hardships and isolation. Later, these women must have been the pioneers of local tourism, squeezing the first liras from adventurous travelers, selling them the fruit of their family's labors, serving them meals at their tables and letting them sleep in their beds for rent.

Still in her sixties, Luisa was younger than most of those present, and hadn't seemed to have many friends up until now, only friendly customers. But now she was a widow; now she would be entitled to the solidarity and protection of other women as she lived out the remainder her days in Manarola, where the routine of work, children, and grandchildren would keep her occupied. One lady dragged over a chair from the bar for her to sit on in case she felt faint; another delivered a glass of strong liquor for her to sip on, to alleviate her shock. Huddled around her, these women formed a formidable barrier that defied trespassing. Not even Jolene's sympathetic gaze could break through to Luisa; not even a silent nod to tell her how sorry she was could escape interception in the short distance that separated them.

The carabinieri, also reluctant to leave the scene despite the fact that the body was gone, latched onto Jolene but seemed to have run out of questions. It wasn't until she heard the sound of violent coughing that Jolene relocated Giobatta, who sat alone on the concrete ledge, not far behind her, with his head drooping and his elbows resting on his knees. His uncharacteristic slump suggested that he was fed up with this village and its chatter, fed up with friends who displayed a total lack of loyalty by dying on him, fed up with a body that no longer behaved the way he wanted it to. Jolene hurried over to him, helping him to his feet and offering to accompany him home.

"You stay here, Miss!" Carabiniere Uno ordered.

"But this man is ill!" she cried. "He needs help getting home."

"Don't worry, *Americanina*," Giobatta said, already walking away. "I'm used to making it on my own. Good thing, too."

"What is it that you still need from me, anyway?" Jolene asked Carabiniere Uno, whose suspicion was making her nervous, and whose insistence on speaking to her in English was driving her crazy.

"We need identity document to fill up in the form," the officer said. "I accompany you to bring your passport."

All I wanted was a cappuccino, Jolene thought, her head hammering. She wished she'd stayed in bed with Fata that morning. She wished she'd never come to Italy at all.

TWENTY

Jolene trudged up to Suite 16, her shoulders sagging, her legs dragging, Carabiniere Uno nipping at the heels of her squishy sneakers. Though chilled to the bone she was in a sweat, having remained zipped up in Vittorio's slicker to hide her dirty clothes from the prying public eye. She longed to strip down, toss that jinxed pink sweater into the garbage, then stand under the shower for as long as it would take to scrub away the stink and stains of her battle with the squid. Nothing would ever be able to cleanse her of her guilt or sorrow, though, or of the touch of death.

Setting aside her personal reasons for being upset at Filippo's absence, Jolene could not stop worrying about him being on his own at a time like this. Until you lost a parent, you couldn't foresee the effect it would have on you. Emotions ran amok, spanning the gamut from love to hate, grief to anger, desperation to relief, shock to acceptance, regret to resentment. But most devastating of all was that numbing sense of loss; that ultimate, irreversible gesture of abandonment, when the all-powerful parent walked out on you for good, leaving you fatherless or motherless for the rest of your life. Jolene hoped that Lorenzo had finally gotten through to his brother and that he had broken the news gently, omitting most of the details about her own involvement in the tragedy. There was no sense making him worry about her on top of everything else. Besides, Jolene wanted to be the one to relate the events to him, in person, in her own words, and to tell him all the good things his father had said about him before he died.

Reeling with shock and exhaustion, Jolene could hardly think straight by the time she stopped in front of her door, the panting *carabiniere* bumping into her like one of those wind-up toy dogs that keep yapping and walking until they hit a wall. It disturbed her to feel him standing so close behind her as she retrieved her key from her pocket, his moist breath making the fine hairs on her neck bristle, tempting her to pull Vittorio's hood back over her head. She wondered whether his closeness was intentional; whether it was meant to intimidate her. What it was doing was making her so nervous she couldn't open the door.

"This door is a little temperamental," she said, jiggling the key in the lock.

"Let me do it," the *carabiniere* said, pressing even closer, but Jolene had no intention of relinquishing her key. It was her key to her door, to her legitimate place of residence, and she would be the one to open it. Once she did, she would show him her legitimate passport to establish that she was a legitimate citizen of the United States of America, and not some undocumented migrant who made a habit of rowing around with dead bodies in her boat.

"Step aside, miss!" he barked. "I do it!" This time it sounded more like he was issuing an order rather than offering assistance, but that couldn't be legal, could it? Jolene pushed back, trying to shake him off.

"*Meeoooow!*" came a cry from above. Spinning around, Jolene spotted Fata, legs splayed as she swooped down like a superhero cat from her favorite hideout atop the stone wall. Crash landing on the man's shoulder, she dug her claws in, fastening herself to his uniform.

"*Ayyy! Aiuto! Aiuto!*" the *carabiniere* cried, frightened back into speaking Italian, his dark eyes flashing with the universal language of terror.

"Fata Morgana!" Jolene exclaimed, shocked at her mild-mannered companion's aggressive behavior.

"*Toglimi quel gatto di dosso!*" the carabiniere cried.

Jolene was quick to react and was already trying to separate the cat from the man, but Fata was a feral feline, and not inclined to abandon her prey without a fight.

"Now!" the paralyzed *carabiniere* cried, daring only to move his eyes, their whites showing as he attempted to identify the aggressor perched on his shoulder.

"Fata, be a good kitty and let go of the nice man," Jolene cooed.

"*Mmmeeoowwmm!*" Fata growled, glaring at her.

Sweat pearled on the officer's brow; Jolene began to panic. What if the cat gouged his eyes out, or shredded a vein with her claws? She could already see the blood squirting from the man's blinded eyes and ravaged neck; she could already imagine how the *carabiniere* would accuse her of using the cat as her weapon; of how this aggression, on top of the priors he suspected her of committing that very same morning would further compromise her shaky standing. She could already envision this leading to an arrest, and the arrest leading to a horrifically biased and never-ending trial at the mercy of the Italian justice system, while Jolene wasted away behind bars.

"Now, now, behave like a good kitty, and come with me," Jolene pleaded, straining to keep her voice calm. She hoped that speaking to the cat in English would settle her down, like it normally did. Fata's ears twitched twice, which usually meant that she'd received Jolene's message, but did not wholly agree with it.

"Fata honey, you're Italian too," Jolene said. "You should know that the job of this *carabiniere* is to protect us, not hurt us."

Arching her back, Fata hissed a warning in the carabiniere's ear that made him blanch. Then she cocked her head at Jolene. That usually meant that she was surrendering to Jolene's wishes, albeit reluctantly. Jolene ripped Fata off the man's shoulder before she could change her mind, at the same time stripping him of his epaulet, which remained ensnared in the cat's claws.

"Humph!" the *carabiniere* sighed, trying to mask his evident relief, while Jolene kept her eyes lowered and Fata in her arms, allowing him a moment to recover.

"Is that cat belonging to you?" he barked at her. His tone was so ferocious that Jolene refused to look at him, let alone answer.

"*Signorina!*" he cried. Jolene raised her eyes, silently watching the officer square his shoulders, straighten his jacket and reposition the epaulet, still dangling by a thread. "I must to ask you again! Is that cat belonging to you?"

Now that the danger was over, Jolene realized how absurd this scene actually was; how ridiculous this *carabiniere* looked, with his chest puffed out with authority, his cap askew and his face pale because of an encounter with a cat. A cat! He looked so comical in fact, that Jolene, already on the verge of hysteria, did not trust herself to speak. This was no time for her to start laughing in the face of justice.

"For the last time!" the *carabiniere* cried, his anger mounting now, inflaming his cheeks, making the veins in his neck protrude. Jolene hugged Fata tight, grateful that those juicy blood vessels were at a safe distance. "Is. That. Cat. Belonging. To. You?"

"Well…" Jolene said, wanting to give an honest answer since she was talking to an officer of the law. "I don't really believe people can own animals. Certainly not cats."

"You know what I ask!" he said. "Answer the question. Is this animal living on your premises?"

"Actually, it's more the other way around," Jolene said. "She was here before I was. So I'd be the one living on her premises."

"I don't care who is first here, but that animal—" he sputtered, pointing at Fata without looking at her directly "—that animal better stay out of my way or I will write another report! Assaulting a Public Official! Obstruction of Justice! These are Offenses Punishable by Law!"

Fata's ears remained pressed against her head during the barrage of potential indictments. With her mouth half open, her tail twitching, her eyes unblinking as she stared at the *carabiniere*, she looked like she was casting some ancient Italian cat curse over him. Jolene wanted to have nothing whatsoever to do with such serious sounding accusations, though it was unclear whether they would be lodged against her, or Fata.

"Look, miss," the *carabiniere* said, "I have more important things to do than stand here with you and your cat! We have a dead body to deal with! Now open this door and show me your passport!"

"What do you want me to do with Fata?" Jolene asked.

"Get rid of that animal! *Now!*"

Jolene hurried to the stone wall. "You're free to go!" she whispered to Fata, standing on tiptoe to release her on the highest section. "Now scram!"

Wishing she could do the same, Jolene turned her attention to the door, determined to get rid of the *carabiniere* without further delay. Another jiggle of the key followed by a butting of the shoulder convinced the door to comply, but when it finally opened, Jolene was overcome with shock and confusion, as if a good friend had slapped her in the face. Inside this room, which couldn't be hers, dresser drawers gaped, spilling someone's underwear and socks and shirts, though if she looked closely, some of those items did resemble some of hers. The bed, not unlike one where she vaguely recalled crashing for a few hours of fitful sleep, was a mess, its linens more mangled than in any bed she had ever slept in. Why would anyone pummel the pillows or wring the sheets that way? Why would anyone bury books and bags and tissues and God only knew what in the tumbled bedclothes? Afraid of what else she might see—of what the *carabiniere* might see—Jolene's eyes surveyed the room with caution, widening at the sloppy whitewashing job that had left streaks on the walls, spatters on the furniture and puddles on the floor, mortifying her with memories of the brush-wielding insomniac who had occupied the room last night.

"I'm…um…sorry about the mess," she stammered. "I left in a rush this morning."

The *carabiniere* stood at the threshold, arms akimbo, rocking on the heels of his shiny black shoes as he scanned the room, nodding. The door remained ajar, probably due to some regulation that prohibited him from being in a woman's room alone with her.

"I do not care about how you keep your house," he said, but made no secret of his disgust. "The only reason I come here is to document the details of your identity. The sooner you show your passport, the sooner I leave."

"I'll only be a second," Jolene said, already savoring the relief she'd feel when she could slam the door behind him and lock it. "It's right here."

Crossing the room, she picked up her backpack, knowing exactly where to find the passport, which she always kept in the inside zipper pocket. Except, evidently, when she didn't. The reason she'd chosen this particular backpack was that it had so many secret compartments, which now meant that she'd have to check them all.

"I know it's in here somewhere," she said, opening zippers and snaps and Velcro strips, while reminding herself that she could never find what she was looking for when she was nervous. She must remain calm; she must breathe in, and breathe out; breathe in, and breathe out.

"Signorina Twinings!" the *carabiniere* called. He had stepped into the room now, and was standing by the bed.

"Yes?" she replied, not bothering to correct him. He'd get the name right when he saw it on her passport.

"What is that?" he demanded, pointing at the bed.

"It's my bed," she said, embarrassed that a stranger would imagine her sleeping in such a mess; that he would imagine her in bed at all. "As I told you, I left in a hurry this morning."

"I meant that!" he said, moving closer, pointing his finger at the large Ziploc bag sticking out from under a pillow.

"Oh, that," she said. "Um…it's nothing."

The *carabiniere* glared at her, just long enough for her heart to start banging against her ribs, just long enough for a fresh stream of sweat to start trickling down her spine. When he had her where he wanted her, he tugged on a corner of the bag, tweezing it with his thumb and index finger, like they did on crime shows to avoid leaving prints, exposing it on the bed.

"Nothing, you say?" he asked, raising his eyebrows.

"Nothing of interest to you," Jolene said, angry at this violation of privacy. "It's personal."

"A personal possession, is it then?" he asked, picking up the bag now, holding it along one edge using only his fingertips, and dangling it in front of her.

Jolene's mind raced, searching for the most honest answer she could possibly give, but she knew that no matter what she said, it would be the wrong thing, because the wrong thing happened to coincide with the truth.

"I said it was personal," she said. "Not that it was a possession. I don't own it."

"Enough of this playing with the words!" the *carabiniere* yelled. "Tell me this now: Was that bag was in your possession when you entered Italy?"

"Um, yes," she nodded, recalling her relief when she'd sailed straight through the green "Nothing To Declare" lane at the customs checkpoint, well aware that she was taking a risk, one that she was hiding from Filippo. Miraculously, no dogs had sniffed her out. No one had opened her suitcase. No one had stopped her. No one had asked any questions.

"Signorina Twinings, you have recently arrived from overseas. You are in possession of some unidentified powdery substance in a plastic bag, but you deny owning it. If it is not belonging to you, who is it belonging to?"

"It isn't belonging—I mean, it doesn't belong to anyone! I'm just holding onto it."

"And what exactly are you planning to do with it?" he asked, switching the language of interrogation to Italian; he clearly wanted to keep the upper hand.

"I don't know yet," she said.

"I must insist that you identify this substance for me," he demanded, holding the bag just inches from her face.

"But I can't!" Jolene cried, fighting the urge to snatch the bag away from him.

"But you must!" he insisted. "Don't pretend you don't know what it is! You brought it into the country! It was on your bed!"

"It was on my bed because I couldn't sleep last night. I needed it."

"How much did you take?"

"I didn't take anything!" she cried, her voice excessively shrill, she knew, but she was exasperated. This man had been on a mission to nail her for something, anything, from the moment he'd laid his eyes on her. "I only needed to hold it."

"Or maybe you just needed to smoke it!" The *carabiniere* posited, pointing at another object his sleuth's eye had spotted on the nightstand, even as they spoke. "Is that what you used?"

"What?" she said, thoroughly confused. "That's a recorder. It's a musical instrument."

"I know what a recorder is!" the *carabiniere* said. "It's just a different kind of pipe, after all. Easily modified for illegal uses by plugging up the holes and adding an attachment!"

Jolene just stared at him, dumbfounded that he could possibly think she'd sniff, smoke or otherwise use for recreational purposes the contents of the bag. Yet she knew she must say something or her silence would be interpreted by this idiot as an admission of guilt. But if she did explain, and the explanation made him feel like a fool, as it was bound to do, it would anger him all the more, which would certainly lead to more problems for her.

"Tell me, Signorina Twinings," he began, his voice calm as he started in on her again. "Were you in an altered state when you convinced Signor Vittorio Garaventi to go out in the boat with you this morning?"

"No!" she cried. "And I didn't convince him, he convinced me!"

"Do you deny knowing that the victim was in poor health?"

"Yes! I mean no! He seemed fine, like always!" she said, alarmed that "Signor Vittorio Garaventi" had suddenly become "the victim."

"Were you taking advantage of said victim and using his boat to explore the coast?"

"No!"

"Were you scouting for some secret cove, perhaps?" the *carabiniere* asked, the dawning of some far-fetched idea brightening his eyes. "A safe spot you could return to when it was time to hand over your goods to your contact?"

"No! I'm not handing anything over to anyone!"

"Who is your contact?"

"I don't have any contacts!" she cried. "I don't know what you're talking about!"

"Signorina Twinings, what exactly were you doing out in a boat with a sick old man before daybreak?"

"We were fishing!" she said, relieved to finally be asked a question she could answer.

"Yet no fish were found in the victim's boat!" the carabinieri said. "You don't find that strange, considering the victim's reputation as an excellent fisherman?"

"We fished for squid! We caught lots of them! See, I have proof!" she cried, unzipping the slicker and thrusting out her chest to display her fluffy, ex pink sweater, now spattered with squid ink and, well, quite a bit of blood.

"I see your proof, all right!" the *carabiniere* said, his smug grin turning Jolene's legs to jelly. Moving calmly, deliberately, he set the bag on the nightstand next to the recorder, then began pacing, rubbing his chin in ominous silence. She could almost hear the cogs in his brain click with the effort of churning out some cockamamie plot. Then he approached Jolene, lowering his face to her chest for a closer look.

"Plenty of proof!" he sang, victorious, as he straightened up, pointing a finger in her face. "Now I suppose you are going to say you don't own this sweater?"

Jolene shook her head, her left eye twitching. "The sweater's mine," she said. "But it was a gift. I hate pink."

"And how about these highly unusual stains on your sweater?" he asked. "What can you tell me about them?"

"That's ink you see. It came from the squid we fished," she said.

"Signorina Twinings, I presume you are aware that ink is not the only stain on your sweater. What can you tell me about the others?"

"Well, actually, they're blood stains," she said. "It's my blood. One of the squid bit me. See?" She held up her finger as proof, but was dismayed to see how small and insignificant the cut looked now that it had stopped bleeding. It was inflamed, and it still hurt like hell. Not that he would give a damn.

"Interesting, considering there were no squid on the boat, either. Did they jump off the boat and swim away after you caught them?"

"That's ridiculous!" she cried. "The seagulls ate them."

"The seagulls," he nodded. "I see."

"Yes." Jolene closed her eyes, recalling the disgust she'd felt when she'd fallen to the floor of the boat, with a whole bucketful of tentacled creatures slipping and sliding all around her. "I couldn't stand looking at them or touching them. It was their fault if the vict—I mean Vittorio— got so excited his heart gave out."

"Signorina Twinings," the *carabiniere* said, looking into her eyes. "I am going to ask you a question about that blood and I am warning you to be careful how you answer. Do you understand?"

"Yes," Jolene said, thinking maybe she shouldn't answer at all. She'd listen to the question, then decide.

"Are you quite sure that if we have this sweater of yours analyzed—which, I assure you, we will—that none of the blood can be traced to the victim?"

"Well, you see..." she began, thinking that maybe she should consider a little lie after all, for the sake of simplification, but knowing that she was a terrible liar, that her face would turn red, that her palms would sweat, and that she would start stammering. No, she would tell him the truth; it wouldn't be anything he didn't already know. "Actually, no. I can't say for sure that it's all my blood. There was that accident, you see. You know, the one with the knife."

"Yes, we all heard about that accident," the *carabiniere* said. "But based on what I'm seeing here, I suspect you may not have shared the whole story. It looks to me like you and the victim engaged in a struggle."

"No! There was no struggle!" Jolene cried. "I was trying to help the victim, I mean, Vittorio. I wanted to—"

"Stab him? You were trying to help the victim by stabbing him?"

"No, I told you before! It was an accident!"

"I demand that you hand over the weapon to me," the *carabiniere* said, holding out his hand. "Now."

"What weapon?"

"You know what weapon! The knife!"

"You can't call it a weapon if it wasn't used to attack anyone!" Jolene protested. "It was just a pocket knife!"

"Enough of your stupid word games! This my language, and my job, and I know what I am talking about! Hand over that knife!"

"I don't have the knife!" she shouted. "It fell into the water! The knife fell into the water!" But no, she'd thrown the knife into the water; why did she say it had fallen? To prove to herself that she could lie, after all? She could already feel her face turning a deeper shade of red.

"You stabbed the victim, then threw the knife into the sea, didn't you? Isn't that what happened?" the officer asked.

"I didn't stab anyone! Certainly not on purpose!" she cried, recalling her desperation on seeing what her hand had done, her revulsion at seeing it hold the tainted blade. "But you're right, okay? After the accident, I threw the knife into the sea. I couldn't bear the sight of it!"

"So everything you couldn't bear the sight of, you threw overboard? Were you planning to do the same with the victim's body?"

"Of course not!" Jolene cried, fighting back tears. "Please! I told you how it went. I have nothing else to say."

"Very well," the *carabiniere* said. "Is that your final version of the story, then?"

"It's not my version of the story. It is the story. It's the truth! It's like I said earlier. Vittorio couldn't breathe! His turtleneck was too tight! And he's not a victim! He just—died!"

"These are all very interesting developments indeed," the officer said, whipping out his cell phone. "Stand still, right there where you are," he ordered, then began shooting a series of photographs of her chest, from every imaginable angle, bending and squatting as if he were a fashion photographer and she a top model. After pocketing the phone again, he checked that the brass buttons of his jacket were properly fastened, then he tugged on the cuffs of his sleeves, readjusted his cap, and threw back his shoulders.

"Signorina Twinings!"

"Please stop calling me that!" she snapped, her nerves frazzled. "My name's *Twyman*, Jolene Twyman. Twinings is a brand of tea!"

"Until you locate that alleged passport of yours, we don't have any proof of that either, do we?" The *carabiniere* rocked on his heels again. "So I strongly suggest you find it. Now. Then you'll all come with me. You. Your passport. Your sweater. And your stash." He made a sweeping motion with his arm, encompassing the entire room and its contents in the gesture, looking as self-satisfied as if he had single-handedly busted a drug ring made up of one American woman and one Manarolan cat. She half expected him to pull out a roll of crime scene tape and seal off the whole mess.

Jolene was fraught with helplessness and anger. If only she could find the damn passport, maybe she could convince him to just leave her alone. She'd hand it over to him as assurance that she wouldn't flee the country; she'd even let him lock her in Suite 16 and take away the key. Her hands trembled as she held her backpack upside down and shook it, watching its sundry contents rain to the floor. Kneeling, she rummaged through her journal and notebook and pens, her sketchbook and pencils, her packets of tissues and tubes of lip balm, the vials of lavender and tea tree oils (which she hoped he wouldn't spot) and her Swiss army knife (which she hoped he wouldn't confiscate). How could her passport not be there? How could she have misplaced it? She was assailed with doubts: about her memory, about her sanity, about why she was always called on to prove something to someone. This was the first time her identity had been questioned, though, and it wasn't a pleasant feeling at all. It was the stuff nightmares were made of.

A buzzing sound coming from the opposite side of the room made her glance up. She brushed away a few tears before the *carabiniere* could see them, but he wasn't looking at her. He was looking at the nightstand, the source of the sound.

"That's my phone," Jolene said. "It's inside."

The buzzing persisted, resonating in the wooden drawer.

"Can I answer it?" she asked, jumping to her feet.

The *carabiniere* nodded, his half-smile indicating the anticipated pleasure of standing close by and making her sweat it out while carrying on a conversation with her contact, or whoever he thought it was, while not letting on that The Law was onto her. When she tried to open it, the drawer stuck, of course, like the door and the windows and the shutters and everything else in Suite 16. Jolene was used to these tugs-of-war but was so jittery that when the drawer finally gave, she keeled over backward, overturning the nightstand.

"The evidence!" the *carabiniere* cried, scooping up the Ziploc bag and recorder before they could fall to the floor, while Jolene tumbled onto to the bed, holding the drawer to her stomach, hoping the caller wouldn't hang up.

"Pronto!" she cried, as soon as she got her hands on the phone. "Hello!"

She pressed the phone to her ear, squinting at the poor reception, then sighed with relief on recognizing the voice at the other end. "Filippo! Finally!" she cried. "Have you spoken with Lorenzo? He's been trying to call you all—"

"Lorenzo's a royal pain-in-the-you-know-what. He can wait. I've been in meetings all morning. The bank. The accountant. The freaking consulate."

The bottom dropped out of Jolene's stomach. He didn't know anything yet, and she was not prepared to handle such a delicate conversation; not now, not in her state, not under strict surveillance.

"Filippo, you really should talk to Lorenzo," she said, her voice cracking. "He has something important to—"

"Everything's always so important to Lorenzo. He never learned to prioritize." Filippo sighed, adding extra emphasis to make sure she'd pick it up no matter how bad the connection, then resumed talking before she could get a word in. "Honestly Jolene, it's almost impossible to get in there now, even when you have an appointment."

"What are you talking about?" she asked. "Get in where?"

"Are you even listening to what I'm saying? The consulate. Your consulate. Of the United States of America. They treat everyone like terrorists. Even when you wave a U.S. passport under their noses."

The lesser problem elbowed its way to the forefront of the conversation, while the question of informing Filippo of his father's death was put on hold. "Wait—did you say a U.S. passport?" she sputtered. "Whose U.S. passport?"

"Whose passport do you think I would show to those goons so they'd let me pick up your documents for you?" Filippo said. "You do remember we need to have your birth certificate and your marriage certificate and your divorce decree translated and stamped and notarized before we can get married?"

"What?"

"Let me take it back a step, Jolene," he said, his voice tight with irritation. "You do remember we're planning a wedding, don't you?"

"Of course, Filippo. Of course!" she cried, burning with impatience. "Please, just tell me one thing, though! Do. You. Have. My. Passport?"

"Yes, I have your passport. I told you I was taking it from your backpack the other day when we went back to your room after lunch. After I gave you the ring. Or don't you remember that, either?"

Of course she remembered that day, the lunch, the surprise, the lovemaking, but she didn't remember him saying anything about him taking her passport. He must have taken it while she was dozing.

"But you can't just take away my identity like that, Filippo!" she cried.

"Your identity? What are you talking about?"

"That passport says who I am!" she said. "It's the only proof I have! I'm a foreigner here, remember?"

"Last time I checked, you didn't need a passport to buy a cappuccino in Manarola," Filippo said.

"There are other things I might need a passport for!"

"Like what?"

"Like if a *carabiniere* asks me for it!"

"Why on earth would a *carabiniere* ask you for it?"

"If he needed to fill out a report, for example," Jolene said, "and if in order to fill out the report he needed the details of my document."

"Exactly what kind of a report would this *carabiniere* need to fill out?" Filippo asked.

"The report of what happened on the boat."

"What boat?"

"The boat I was on this morning."

"What were you doing on a boat this morning?" Filippo asked, sounding more annoyed than curious. "Whose boat?"

"Your father's boat," Jolene said. "I was with your father, Filippo." It was then that the sob came, one great, heaving sob, so strong that she couldn't hold it back, so strong that it pushed out the words she couldn't bear to say. "*And now he's dead!*"

The *carabiniere* took the phone from Jolene's hand before she could drop it. "Pronto!" he said to Filippo. "Pronto!" Then he looked at the phone, shook it and pressed it to his ear again before turning to Jolene. "This is dead too."

TWENTY-ONE

The Alfa Romeo they rode in was dark blue, with red lightning bolts painted on its sides and a blue light flashing on its roof. The vehicle pressed its nose to the ground, gobbling up the asphalt as it sped toward La Spezia, the pair of carabinieri sitting up front and Jolene strapped in the back. Each harrowing twist and hairpin turn, each pump of the gas pedal and stomp on the brakes, heightened Jolene's fear about how this thrill ride would end.

She knew, or was pretty sure anyway, that she could have refused the so-called *invito* to go down to the station, and insisted on staying behind in Manarola. After all, she hadn't been placed under arrest or formally charged with any wrongdoing. But after Carabiniere Uno, her interrogator, had summoned Carabiniere Due up to Suite 16, and the two had conferred outside her room, mercifully without Fata's interference, Carabiniere Uno had announced that the Ziploc bag, together with Jolene's pink sweater, with or without her inside it, were being seized and taken down to headquarters. Jolene was fairly certain that they'd have to obtain the Italian equivalent of a warrant to confiscate her personal belongings, but the pained look on Carabiniere Due's face suggested it would be best for her to comply with his colleague's invitation and go along voluntarily. They did not deny her the right to contact Filippo, but her attempts to call him back and explain the situation had been in vain; she kept getting the message that his phone was either out of range or switched off, an inconvenience he always blamed on the endless succession of tunnels along the train line from Milan, which is where he must have been for the past hour, already speeding home aboard a *frecciarossa*. As for Lorenzo, she presumed he would be tied up for a good part of the day, between the hospital and the morgue and whatever formalities sudden death implied in Italy. Besides, he hadn't shown any concern for her feelings or well-being, and the last thing she wanted to do was involve him in another drama brought about by her own stupidity. Luisa, meanwhile, in addition to her own grief, had an entire village of mourners to contend with, and could not be imposed upon for guidance.

That had left no one, *nessuno, ninguno, personne,* to whom Jolene could turn for moral support—except for the bag itself, now in Carabiniere Uno's clutches. Seeing him gloat over his "find" was intolerable, and that was what made Jolene decide, in fact insist, on accompanying them. She would rather go to jail than surrender the bag to strangers.

Like the waves of nausea that hit her at every curve, her bravery was fickle, though, surging and receding, surging and receding. One minute, she was confident that everything would be clarified by the afternoon, with Filippo already rushing back from Milan with the passport that would prove her identity as a full-fledged citizen of the United States of America. Once that matter was settled, Carabiniere Uno could finish filling out his report, and meanwhile Jolene would take Filippo aside and tell him about the bag. She could already see the deep furrows of concern forming across his forehead, and just below the furrows the stitching of his eyebrows, and just below the eyebrows the rolling of his eyes. Imagining Filippo look at her that way made her cringe, but she knew she would only have to endure it for a moment or two before he figured out a way to resolve her predicament. Filippo was loyal; he was smart; he was Italian; and from what he'd told her of his recent activities, he was quite an expert at cutting through red tape.

Yet the following minute, her blood ran cold as she recalled a much-talked-about case in Perugia, where an English exchange student had died in mysterious circumstances, and some fellow students, including a young American woman, had been arrested for her murder. The investigation had dragged on for years, and the American had been put on trial, found guilty and incarcerated. Her name, Amanda something, popped up now and again in the news as the months then years went by, until she was ultimately acquitted on appeal. Jolene had no idea whether she was guilty or innocent, but what if something like that happened to her? She couldn't imagine the autopsy showing that Vittorio had died of anything but natural causes, but then again she never could have imagined him dying at all that morning. And whatever the outcome, the problem of the bag remained. Could she be put in jail for smuggling it into the country? How serious an offense could it be?

The dreamy coastal scenery, with all its silvery olive groves and terraced hillsides and roiling seas, failed to distract her during the hair-raising drive to La Spezia, but the drastic change in her surroundings as they arrived in the city hit her like a slap in the face. The port with its massive military vessels and container ships and ferry boats docked beyond the tall steel fence blocked the view of the sea beyond; the overpasses and underpasses and intersections with their honking cars and roaring scooters and stinky trucks and double-parked vans obstructed the view of the hills in the distance; the gray concrete buildings with their gray offices and gray apartments and gray shops obliterated whatever zest the city whose name translated to "The Spice" may have claimed for itself. The Alfa Romeo, with the added effect of a siren, zipped through the traffic, eliciting the stares of everyone they passed and a fresh flurry of fear in Jolene's breast.

***

Lacking the strength to sit up straight, Jolene slouched in one of the plastic chairs lined up by the door, wondering how to stop the twitch in her left eye, which apart from being annoying, might be interpreted as a sign of guilt. She didn't know what to do about her head, either. It was unbearably heavy, but she resisted resting it against the wall behind her, where a telltale strip of greasy-gray indicated that many other heads of many other unfortunate suspects or witnesses or victims before her had previously lolled there. Pulling Vittorio's slicker tight around her, she recalled that it was equipped with a hood, which she presently pulled over her head, finally leaning back to let the wall take over the task of holding her up.

After Carabiniere Uno had announced the plan to haul her down to headquarters in La Spezia instead of going to the local station in Riomaggiore, stating that the potential international ramifications of such a suspicious case warranted the involvement of his superiors,

284

Jolene had attempted to negotiate ten minutes of privacy in order to shower and change. Carabiniere Uno, however, appeared to be quite keen on bringing her in looking exactly how they'd found her at the scene that morning—with the unexpected bonus of the previously concealed sweater.

A shower and clean clothes were not foremost in Jolene's mind as she sat waiting, wondering what would become of her. She was fortunate to understand enough Italian to grasp what was going on, but at the same time, she appreciated the advantages of being less than perfectly fluent. It allowed her to ask for questions to be repeated, and to stall for time before providing answers, and to pass off her state of befuddlement as confusion over the meaning of words. Most interestingly, it forced her to become more attuned to the non-verbal forms of communication in which Italians were so well-versed. Jolene had been observing the signals exchanged by her two carabinieri all along, and now at headquarters, out of earshot but within sight, as they conferred with two more uniformed men behind a low partition, she tried to decipher who would decide what with regards to her fate. Carabiniere Uno, who was doing most of the talking, seemed to be concluding a presentation of his findings for the benefit of his superiors. Carabiniere Due, while standing at attention by his side, unwittingly sent out a series of signals—the scratching of his beaklike nose, for example, and the pursing of his thin lips—which could indicate, Jolene believed, a certain degree of embarrassment for his colleague's zeal. He did not speak unless spoken to, and each time Carabiniere Uno solicited his backing, his responses were monosyllabic, accompanied by a nod or shake of the head. With no discernible forewarning, the two men were suddenly dismissed, but not before Carabiniere Uno was reprimanded for the indecorous manner in which a mangled epaulet dangled from the shoulder of his jacket. As the men walked toward her, Jolene pulled herself up tall in her chair, trying to look more confident than she felt about the possibility of her imminent release and return to Manarola.

Carabiniere Due did not slow down when he reached Jolene, but simply touched his fingers to the brim of his hat as he passed, averting his eyes. "*Addio*, Signorina Twinings," he said, striding out the door.

Carabiniere Uno, in no apparent hurry, stopped in front of Jolene, looking her in the eye. "The bag remains here," he said, smiling.

"And what about me?" Jolene asked.

"You remain here, too. The *brigadiere* has some questions for you," he said, cocking his head toward the men remaining in the office. One was standing, flipping through papers and dictating as he paced, while the other pecked at a computer keyboard with his index fingers. "They'll keep an eye on you until your alleged boyfriend brings in your alleged passport." At that, Carabiniere Uno also touched the brim of his cap and walked out, the reinforced metal door latching behind him with a definitive click.

Of all Jolene's nightmares, not being believed was one of the worst, and the fact that neither she nor the carabinieri had been able to contact Filippo at the number she'd given them did not exactly enhance her credibility. She glared at the cell phone in her hands, worrying that he didn't answer, or call, or at the very least reply to her text messages. She hit the redial button again, her pulse quickening when she heard a ring at the other end instead of the usual voice message. On the second ring, she jumped to her feet, poised to summon the *brigadiere* as soon as Filippo answered. On the third ring, she heard a pause, then static, then silence. Then her phone died. It was an old phone, Filippo always reminded her, and should be charged all night, every night, regardless of how much she used it, but for some reason, she neglected to plug it in when she went to bed. Maybe it was because of the way he said it, as if she couldn't remember without him reminding her, or maybe it bothered her that he wanted to be able to reach her at all times even though he could rarely be reached. Or maybe it was just because the only outlet was on the other side of the room and she wanted to keep the phone nearby during the night in case Filippo called or texted her, but inside the drawer where its electromagnetic radiation (Filippo said she was paranoid) wouldn't disturb her sleep. It angered her to admit that he was right (about charging the phone, not about the radio waves), though the malfunctioning device wasn't the only cause behind the rage bubbling up in her chest. She was dying to hurl the stupid phone across the room, the same way she had thrown the stupid knife and the stupid squid into the sea; she was dying to watch it smash against the concrete wall, then crash to the floor in a million pieces. So irrepressible was this urge that her arm wound up for the pitch, without her telling it to, but she made her other arm grab it when she saw the carabinieri's eyes on her. All she needed now was for them to peg her as a crazy lady prone to violent reactions. One who might, in certain circumstances, even stab her future father-in-law.

Trembling with frustration, she forced herself to sit back down, letting the phone slip through her fingers and drop to the floor. It took more than a tumble to wreck an old Nokia, though. Looking up to make sure she wasn't being watched, Jolene began stomping on the phone with one foot, then the other, then with both, until she felt that justice had been served. Her lips were parted, and she was panting slightly, feeling an odd warmth spread through her as she sat there staring at the phone, lying face down between the feet that had destroyed it. After cooling down a bit, she picked the phone up, turning it over in her hands, the blank stare of the smashed screen making her feel rather heartless, but liberated.

TWENTY-TWO

Just as dawn had seemed late in breaking, dusk seemed to be falling early. The gray light slipping through the barred windows of the carabinieri headquarters on that dark October day was already fading, taking with it the vestiges of Jolene's courage. Exhausted, hungry, and chilled to the bone, she prayed for something to happen, anything. As if on cue, a harsh buzz reverberated through the waiting area, making her jump in her seat. An instant later one of the officers emerged from behind the partition, sweeping by her on his way to the door, paying her no more heed than he would have paid to a dust bunny. Speaking into the intercom, he requested the party at the other end of the line to state his name the purpose of his visit. Shooting Jolene a glance as he listened, he hung up the receiver and pressed a button, activating another buzzer. The lock unlatched. The *carabiniere* opened the door. Jolene jumped to her feet. Filippo had finally come for her!

"What in the name of God is going on here?" the familiar voice called from the corridor.

"Ciao, Lorenzo," the *carabiniere* said, extending a hand. Lorenzo stared at the hand for a moment before setting down a bag, then finally shook it, while looking in Jolene's direction.

"Ciao? Is that all you can say?" he replied, now staring at the *carabiniere*, his eyes as wild as his curls.

"What do you want me to say?" the *carabiniere* snapped, then seemed to immediately regret his tone. Placing a hand on Lorenzo's arm, he gave it a squeeze. "Hey, I'm sorry about Signor Garaventi.

He was a great guy."

Lorenzo blinked, as if he couldn't quite place the name, or understand why the *carabiniere* should be sorry. Then he turned to Jolene.

"You're shaking," he said, without greeting her.

"Did Filippo send you?" Jolene asked.

"Filippo? Who can talk to Filippo? Maybe you, but not me."

"No, I couldn't reach him, either!" Jolene said. "Do you think something awful has happened to him?"

"I honestly can't imagine any more awful things happening today, Jolene," Lorenzo said. "He'll turn up sooner or later. He always does."

"But how did you know I was here?" she asked.

"After I finished at the hospital, I was walking over to the station to catch a train back home," he said. "Those two carabinieri from this morning recognized me and pulled over to ask if I needed a lift. They told me you were here, but wouldn't tell me why. They said it was confidential, that there was an ongoing investigation or some bullshit like that. What's going on, Jolene?"

"I'm waiting for Filippo to bring me my passport," Jolene said. "They want me to prove who I am!"

Lorenzo turned to the *carabiniere*. "You mean to tell me you're detaining this woman because she couldn't show you her passport?"

"We don't want her here, Lorenzo," the officer said. "The guys from Riomaggiore dumped her on us."

Reaching into the back pocket of his jeans, Lorenzo took out a beat-up billfold. "Here," he said, handing his identification card to the *carabiniere*. "We've known each other since elementary school, but you go ahead and take down my details anyway. Jolene is family. I'll vouch for her."

The *carabiniere* held the ID card in one hand, tapping it against the open palm of the other. "It's not only on account of the passport, Lorenzo," he said. "I like to think those colleagues of mine wouldn't drag her down here just for that."

"What do you mean?" Lorenzo asked, alarm flickering in his tired expression. It had broken her heart to see the disbelief in those eyes when she'd uncovered Vittorio's bloodied body. What would Lorenzo think of her now, when he heard about her alleged struggle with Vittorio and her admission that she'd thrown the knife overboard. Would he, too, doubt her story?

"Come with me," the *carabiniere* said, taking Lorenzo by an elbow and leading him off to the side. Standing with his back to Jolene, he spoke to Lorenzo in a low voice, but Jolene was able to catch a few words. "... new guy in Riomaggiore ... found in her room ...unidentified substance ... almost two kilos ... refuses to cooperate..."

"What's this story about the bag?" Lorenzo asked, walking the few steps back to Jolene.

"They wanted to take it from me!" Jolene cried, wishing she didn't sound like a child refusing to relinquish a bag of candy.

"What's in the bag, Jolene?" Lorenzo asked.

"I can't say," Jolene said, her eyes downcast, spotting the shards of her ex-phone on the floor.

"You can't because you don't know, or you can't because you won't?"

Jolene looked up. "Because I won't."

"Why not?"

"Because I'm afraid."

"Jolene, did you smuggle something you shouldn't have into this country?" Lorenzo asked. "Was it Filippo's idea? Did he make you do something you didn't want to do?"

"No! Filippo didn't even know about it!" she cried. "I was afraid it could get me in trouble, but I had to bring it! I had no choice!"

"Jolene, you have to tell me what's in the bag!" Lorenzo demanded, the day's strain adding an edge to his voice. "If you don't, they'll have to keep it and get it analyzed. It's your call."

Jolene looked at the *carabiniere*, rocking on his heels as he waited. She wondered whether they all did that.

"You can trust me, Jolene," Lorenzo said, speaking in a softer voice. "I'm here to help you."

"It's my mother!" she blurted. There, it was out. She already felt calmer. She'd take whatever punishment she had coming.

"Your mother?" Lorenzo asked.

Jolene nodded. "My mother's ashes are in that bag."

"You put your mother in a plastic bag?" the *carabiniere* exclaimed, a look of horror on his face.

"It's not like it's her body!" Jolene cried. "Only her ashes. The urn was too bulky, and it would have tipped everyone off right away."

"You can't just put the ashes of a Christian in a flimsy storage bag and take them wherever you want to!" the *carabiniere* shouted.

"It's not a flimsy storage bag!" Jolene cried. "It's a heavy duty Ziploc bag! They're very sturdy! My mother used them for everything! She loved them!"

"This is unbelievable!" the *carabiniere* cried, throwing his hands up in the air. "Unbelievable!" After rubbing his chin for a moment, he shook his head and ordered, "Come with me! Both of you!"

Escorting Jolene and Lorenzo to the office behind the partition, he made them wait while he went to see the *brigadiere*, who was talking on a mobile phone while doodling on a scrap of paper, glancing up long enough to wave him away.

Leading them to a second desk, the *carabiniere* indicated two plastic chairs slightly cleaner than those in the entrance. "Sit there," he told them.

"I'll stand, thanks," Lorenzo said, his jaw clenched, his arms folded across his chest. Jolene did as she was told.

"So this!" the *carabiniere* began, picking up the Ziploc bag from his desk and holding it in front of Jolene. "This is your mother in here?"

Jolene nodded.

"I need a yes or a no, please."

"Yes," Jolene swallowed. "That's my mother."

"Was your mother an Italian citizen?" he asked.

"Obviously not!" she answered.

"Nothing here is obvious, miss," the *carabiniere* said. "Yes or no, please."

"No! She was American."

"Was she an Italian resident?"

"No! She lived in Little Falls," Jolene said. "That's in Herkimer County. But she didn't always live there. Before that—"

"If I want to know every place she ever lived, I'll ask you!" he snapped. "Now stick to my questions."

"Hey, take it easy on her, would you?" Lorenzo said. "It's been a rough day for everyone."

"Did you make arrangements with an Italian cemetery for the custody of her ashes prior to importing them?" the officer demanded, ignoring Lorenzo.

"No!" Jolene cried. "I don't want to put them in a cemetery. My mother hates—I mean hated—cemeteries. I think she would have liked the one in Manarola, though. Of course, I had no way of knowing that before I got here."

"Of course!" the *carabiniere* said, rolling his eyes. "I suppose it would be useless for me to ask you to produce her mortuary passport?"

"Her mortuary passport?" Jolene repeated.

"Yes, her mortuary passport! You must have the death certificate and the *nulla osta* from the proper authorities in order to bring a dead person's ashes into the country!"

"But I don't have any of those things!" Jolene said, her eyes darting from one man to the other.

"*Fantastico!*" the carabiniere said, shaking his head. "How can we be certain that this bag contains the remains of who you say it does? We don't even know for certain who you are. We need some *proof* here, Signorina!"

Now neither one of them had an identity. What did it matter, anyway, when neither one of them had ever really fit in anywhere? Why should Italy be an exception? Maybe they'd both be expelled, Jolene thought, burying her head in her hands.

"Listen, Renato," Lorenzo said. "At this point, the ashes are here and there's nothing we can do about that. Why don't you just give this girl her mother back?"

"The guys from Riomaggiore brought this bag in on the suspicion it contained drugs, Lorenzo," he said. "I can't just release it without a lab analysis."

Lorenzo glanced at the *brigadiere*, still chatting on the phone. "Do you really want to look that stupid to the guys at the crime lab?" he asked the officer, lowering his voice. "It would take a fool to mistake ashes for drugs!"

"You never know," the officer said. "There's all kinds of new substances coming on the market all the time. And did you see how fine that powder is?"

"Yeah, I see that," Lorenzo said. "They must do good work over in America."

"Oh, they do!" Jolene looked up, chiming in. "There's a really good crematory in the Finger Lakes. It was highly recommended to me." Both men stared at her, neither commenting.

"Whatever the case, my hands are tied," the *carabiniere* said. "Once a file is opened, it's opened."

"Well, then find a way to close it, Renato," Lorenzo said. "I have a grieving family to get home to. The Milan-Inter derby starts in an hour, and I'm sure you and the *brigadiere* would rather watch the soccer game than waste your time writing up such a complicated and useless report."

The *carabiniere* puffed up his cheeks, then sighed. "Step over there with me a minute," he said to Lorenzo, nodding at the *brigadiere*, who had finally terminated his call.

Jolene remained in her seat, watching as the *brigadiere* stood and shook hands with Lorenzo, who listened, occasionally interrupting, while the two men, occasionally gesticulating, explained things she could not hear. It was unbearable to watch them haggling over her fate while she just sat there, powerless. She'd been naive, that was all, and she was prepared to pay the consequences if she'd done something wrong. But she couldn't let them send her mother off to some forensics lab; she simply wouldn't allow it. Folding her hands in her lap, she bowed her head. We shall overcome, Mom! she whispered. We shall overcome!

"I think I have something else of yours," Lorenzo said. Retrieving the bag he'd walked in with, he pulled out the Peruvian poncho, unfurling its bright stripes in the gray office. "It made it onto the ambulance with Pa, but I sure as heck never saw him wear it."

"Oh, Lorenzo! Thank you!" Jolene cried, her chin quivering as her fingers ran over the coarse wool. The poncho was damp and stank of the day's awfulness, but Jolene was grateful when Lorenzo slipped it over her head and settled it over her shoulders.

"Now I'll take you home," Lorenzo said.

"Now I'll take you home," Jolene whispered, clutching the bag to her chest.

TWENTY-THREE

Jolene had never traveled by train before. Back where she'd grown up and spent most of her thirty-eight years, trains were expensive, inconvenient and unreliable. Planes (when they couldn't be avoided) were for long distances, then came cars, then bicycles, then her feet and, of course, rowboats, which were for pleasure; or rather, used to be. As she sat waiting for the La Spezia-Sestri Levante *regionale* train to depart, her hands bubbled with blisters, her shoulders stiff with soreness, her heart aching to the point of numbness, Jolene doubted she would ever want to board a boat again.

Lorenzo, sitting across from her, stared out the window, absorbed in thoughts of his own. It occurred to Jolene that if she hadn't twisted her ankle that day on their hike, her first Italian train ride would have been quite different. She and Lorenzo would have been sitting together, like now, but they would have been chatting about their impromptu outing, possibly sharing a laugh over the terror Jolene had felt while walking through the abandoned tunnel. During the three-minute ride back home from Corniglia her eyes would have been glowing with the breathtaking views of her first authentic exploration of the fabulous Cinque Terre, her skin tingling with the salt of her first Mediterranean swim, her face rosy, from the sun and the wine, but also from the shyness she'd felt around Lorenzo.

Or her first train ride might have been with Filippo, as it should have been, if he'd invited her along on one of his trips to Milan. Or, she might have taken her first trip by herself, as she'd planned to do that very morning if she hadn't run into Vittorio down by the harbor.

Right now, she might be traveling in the opposite direction, returning to Manarola enriched by the sights she'd seen in Genoa, satisfied with the supplies she'd purchased. In addition to the items on her list, she might have picked up a little gift for Luisa, and Vittorio might still be there to greet her and offer her a glass of white wine when she walked into the Locanda, weary but content, on her return. Then, when Filippo sauntered in, brimming with accounts of all he'd accomplished in Milan, he might raise an eyebrow or two on learning that she'd gone to Genoa on her own, and remind her of the dangers of venturing off into an unfamiliar city without checking with him first.

A whistle blew. The last of the stragglers hopped aboard, the doors slid shut and the train pulled out of the station. Movement was good, Jolene thought, it always jostled her thoughts from their well-worn grooves and gave her the impression that she was not only going somewhere, but getting somewhere. She wondered where the other passengers were directed, why they were still in a hurry now that they were on the train. Bumping and banging their bags and bundles against any obstacles in their way, they pushed past, shouting into their phones, broadcasting dates and demands and excuses for all to hear. Didn't they know that all that planning was utterly pointless? That everything could change in a heartbeat? We were all so clueless when it came down to knowing what was really important, she reflected, turning to look out the smudged window as the train rumbled along, now and then glimpsing snatches of the ominous sky and churning sea flashing by between tunnels.

"Here we are," Lorenzo said, standing as the train screeched to stop. He hadn't spoken a word to her during their brief journey, but she wasn't surprised or offended by his silence.

"Already?" she remarked, amazed at how much quicker the journey was by train than by car, disappointed that it was already over, nervous about what lay ahead. It was only a short walk from the station, and she could hurry past the people they'd meet along the way in the hopes that no one would stop her, but the real challenge for her would be entering the Locanda. There she would be confronted with the ordeal of facing Luisa, with whom she had not yet spoken; and Filippo, who certainly must have arrived by now; and Monica, who would also be there; and probably even little Chiara, who'd just been deprived of her only grandpa. Then there might be the aunts, and certainly the priest. Jolene had been the last person to see Vittorio alive, she'd been with him when he'd died, and anyone who was close to him would expect, understandably, to hear the whole, tragic story straight from her mouth. It filled her with dread to think of all those people hanging on her words, pressing her for details, making her relive every agonizing minute of the ill-fated expedition.

"Aren't you coming?" Lorenzo called over his shoulder.

With leaden legs, Jolene dragged herself after Lorenzo, barely clearing the doors before they slid shut, a guillotine cutting off her last chance to escape. She remained on the platform for a moment after the train pulled out of the station, staring out at the open sea, breathing in the fresh air with the heightened awareness that came with the loss of freedom, however temporary. On noticing that Lorenzo was gone, she hurried down the stairs, holding her bag against her chest, nestled between her mother's poncho and Vittorio's slicker, catching up with him halfway down the pedestrian tunnel that led to the exit.

Judging from his long, quick strides, Lorenzo was as anxious as she was to avoid contact with the few people they encountered along the way. He didn't stop until they reached the Locanda, when he turned to look at her directly for the first time since La Spezia.

"Are you okay?" he asked, placing a hand on her shoulder.

"I guess," she said, but she wasn't, and his touch made her eyes well with tears. "I mean no, really. I've been feeling numb all day. And detached, in a way, as if I were watching all these awful, absurd things happen to a stranger."

"Yeah, sometimes you just have to go through the motions and do what you have to do, until you come out at the other end."

"Before we go in, Lorenzo, I need to tell you how sorry I am," she said. "We haven't really had the chance to talk."

"You don't need to tell me anything, Jolene. And there's no need to talk."

"I know Vittorio wasn't my father," she continued. "But I imagined he could be, in a way. I didn't realize until today how much I still needed one."

"I know exactly what you mean," Lorenzo said, clenching his jaw, moving his hand to the door handle. "You ready to go in?"

Jolene wished she could take a few more minutes to prepare

herself, but she nodded. Filippo would be waiting, and now that she was once again able to put things in their proper perspective, she was more concerned about consoling him than complaining to him about his infuriating unreachability. The flood of relief she'd felt when the carabinieri had released her to Lorenzo's custody, still wearing the befouled sweater they had no intention of analyzing, had been so great that it had swept away the anger she'd been feeling toward Filippo. This was no time to argue, she knew, this was the time to stick together, to mourn together.

When Lorenzo pushed open the door, the reality of greeting Filippo while looking and smelling so bad, with traces of his father's blood on the very clothes she wore, hit Jolene full force, sparking a sense of shame, more than embarrassment. Her top priority was to hug Filippo, though, to see with her own eyes how he was coping, before she could even think about going to her room to wash up. Yet as soon as she crossed the threshold she hesitated again, unable to move forward. The Locanda was teeming with all the townsfolk they hadn't encountered along the way, its air dense with the odors of perspiration doused with cologne, of cigarette smoke mingled with alcohol. But it wasn't the presence of those smells that overwhelmed her; it was the absence of other smells, so close to dinnertime, that came as a shock. There were no onions or garlic sautéing, no minestrones simmering, no sauces bubbling, no seafood stewing in Vittorio's deserted kitchen, to fill the Locanda with their tantalizing aromas.

"Everyone's here but him," Lorenzo said.

Jolene stared at him, astonished that he'd read her mind.

"He would have been in his glory, cooking for such a crowd," she said.

"Pa? Yeah, he would have," Lorenzo said. "But I was talking about Filippo."

"Oh," she said. "Well, I'm sure he's here somewhere. You go on ahead, I'll have a look around."

Shrugging, Lorenzo dove into the crowd, enduring the barrage of hugs and questions and comments, while Jolene stood on tiptoe, trying to locate Filippo. He didn't appear to be at the bar or behind it, where people seemed to have been serving themselves, nor was his head visible above the others. As she moved forward, Jolene was relieved, but also a bit saddened, to discover that apart from a few stares, people were ignoring her, no one volunteering information as to Filippo's whereabouts despite the fact that she was obviously looking for someone. He was probably in the dining room, she thought, peering past the archway into the semi-darkness, where she glimpsed Luisa sitting in a chair. Of course, it made perfect sense that Filippo would hold vigil with her there, where it was quieter. Jolene felt nervous as she approached, wishing she'd been able to have a word with Filippo alone before facing Luisa, wondering whether she would find her hostile, or distant, or distraught; hoping she could find the right words to say to her. Zia Marta and Zia Matilda were sitting in there, too, she now saw, but the other chairs were empty. For an instant, Jolene considered turning around, but it was too late; the women had already spotted her. Clutching her mother tight for courage, she headed toward them.

"You poor child!" Luisa cried, surprising Jolene by rushing at her with outstretched arms. Her unexpected show of affection jolted Jolene out of her numbness, making her release the tears she'd been holding back, now running down her cheeks and dampening Luisa's hair as Jolene embraced her awkwardly with her free arm. Zia Marta and Zia Matilde looked on, nodding wisely, as if dying was the one thing you could expect a person to do, sooner or later, and know you wouldn't be disappointed. After a few moments, Jolene's silent sobs subsided enough for her to speak. She pulled back from Luisa, using a corner of the poncho to wipe her tears.

"Luisa, I'm…I'm so sorry," she stammered. "I never would have gone along with Vittorio if I'd even remotely imagined that he could have…that something like this could have happened."

"There are so many things we would never do if we knew what could happen, Jolene. Most of life, in fact," Luisa said, her eyes red-rimmed, but the irises a clear blue. "I'm only going to tell you this once: It wasn't your fault."

"Do you really believe that?" Jolene sniffed.

"Yes, I do. I know that," Luisa said. "Vittorio's been unwell for some time now, but he never wanted to give up who he was or what he did. We all have choices, and he made his. He moved on while doing something he loved, in the company of someone he loved. What more could a person ask for?"

Luisa's words soothed Jolene like a balm. She wasn't hated; she was loved. More importantly, she was forgiven.

"How did it go at the hospital?" Luisa asked, abruptly turning her attention to Lorenzo, who had just walked into the room.

"I took care of everything I could for now," Lorenzo replied, wrapping his mother in a hug, his generous arms including Jolene in the gesture. It felt so good to be included in their love, in their family, and she was sorry when he broke the embrace to speak again. "But like I told you over the phone, I really do need to talk to Filippo. Where is he?"

"He's up at the house," Luisa said. "He insisted on looking for some papers he said would be needed for the formalities. He doesn't deal well with public displays of emotion, as we all know."

"Yes, we sure do," Lorenzo said, glancing at Jolene, his sigh indicating that his well of tolerance was running dry.

Maybe they all knew, but she didn't know. She and Filippo had slept at romantic inns, and enjoyed sumptuous dinners, and visited countless vineyards together, but they'd never shared an experience that could remotely compare to the death of a father.

"How did Filippo take the news?" she asked, her voice shaky. "Is he all right?"

"He'll be fine," Luisa said. "He's coping the way he always does. On his own."

Jolene didn't want to hear that Filippo was coping fine on his own. She didn't want to think that he bundled her up with the rest of the public to whom he did not wish to display his emotions. No, she was not at all relieved to hear that he was handling it; she was disappointed, even slightly offended.

"Um, did he ask about me?" she said. "I haven't talked to him all day."

Luisa cocked her head, looking perplexed. "Well, yes, he did ask where you were when he got here," she said. "I told him that last I knew, you'd gone to your room."

"My room?" Jolene felt the blood rise from beneath her sweater, travel up her neck and spread across her cheeks. She was ashamed that anyone, Luisa above all, could have thought she was hiding out in her room all that time, even though she'd wanted to, in her initial state of shock. And what about Filippo? Had he cared enough to check?

"Ah, splendid! You're all here!" Don Ludovico called out, his frock sweeping the floor as he sailed into the room, bringing smiles to the lips of the aunties, dispensed from rising on account of their infirmities. Joining Luisa, Lorenzo, and Jolene who stood in a loose circle, the priest arranged his arms in such a way as to touch all three, in a sort of laying of the hands. "I've already spoken with Filippo, and the rosary's been arranged for tomorrow evening," he announced. "And the funeral for the day after tomorrow."

Filippo couldn't be so withdrawn after all, if he'd taken the initiative to make these arrangements. Then again, it seemed nothing could hold him back when it came to working out details with his good friend Don Ludovico. Jolene clamped her mouth shut before she could say something she'd regret, noting an awkward silence between Luisa and Lorenzo, too, as the two of them locked eyes. Then Luisa nodded, and Lorenzo cleared his throat.

"We appreciate your efficiency, Father," he said. "But I believe we can do without the rosary."

Zia Marta and Zia Matilda, who had probably been rehearsing for hours, froze with their beads in their hands, pricking ears which seemed to hear perfectly well.

"Whatever do you mean, 'we can do without the rosary?'" Don Ludovico asked. "And who, exactly, is 'we'?"

"When was the last time you saw Pa in church?" Lorenzo asked.

"All the more reason!" Don Ludovico said. The aunts nodded.

"But there's no body to pray over, Father," Lorenzo said. "It's at the morgue in La Spezia. They decided not to perform an autopsy after all, but the best we can do is bring it straight here for a service if we can arrange something for tomorrow afternoon."

"Well, certainly, if he had died at home with his family, where he should have been, sound asleep, instead of running off on a boat with a...with a..." Don Ludovico sputtered. "What I mean is, the vigil could have been held right there. At home. With Vittorio laid out in his own bed."

"Don Ludovico," Luisa said. "The last thing Vittorio would have wanted is a bunch of people hanging around his bedside reciting the rosary. And quite honestly, the idea of displaying the body he left behind in our bed for people to gawk at and weep over doesn't exactly appeal to me, either."

Jolene agreed. She didn't think she'd ever be able to sleep in a bed where a dead body had lain. Furthermore, she shared Luisa's idea that Vittorio's spirit was already elsewhere, and admired the way she stood up to Don Ludovico. She'd have to ask her for some tips when her turn came.

"But my dear ones, think of what it would mean to deny Vittorio a rosary!" Don Ludovico cried, working from the diaphragm to project his voice to a wider audience. At the bar, heads turned, necks craned, curious to catch the theatrics. "You mustn't only think of yourselves. You must think of the friends and relatives you would be depriving of the opportunity to gather in prayer in preparation for the funeral and burial. And above all, you must think of Vittorio's soul, which must be prepared for its homeward journey to our Almighty Creator." Upon concluding, he stared purposefully at Luisa, then Lorenzo, deeming even Jolene worthy of a quick glance in his canvass for support. When no one uttered a word, an expression of alarm crept into his features.

"Of course we'll have a proper Catholic funeral?" he asked, directing the question at Luisa.

"Yes, we'll have a Catholic funeral, Father," Luisa said. "That is, if you'll extend him the courtesy. But no rosary. Vittorio wouldn't like it one bit."

"What about all those devoted parishioners gathered over there? Doesn't it matter what they would like? Or what *God* would like?" Don Ludovico cried, raising his hands to the ceiling, imploring Someone to listen to reason.

"Why don't we do something everyone would like, including Vittorio?" Jolene heard herself ask. "And God too, I think." No one was expecting Jolene to speak up, least of all Jolene herself. But she'd been visited by a thought—she might even call it an inspiration—that she wanted to share. She didn't have all the details yet, but if everyone stopped staring at her, she felt sure they would come.

"Well, what I was thinking," she began, focusing on Lorenzo, who raised an eyebrow in encouragement, "was that I could go see what's in the kitchen and rustle up a hot meal for everyone. And before we eat, Don Ludovico can lead the rosary, right here at the Locanda."

Don Ludovico ran two fingers between his jowl and Roman collar, pursing his lips as he pondered the plan. Luisa nodded. Lorenzo smiled. The aunts bobbed their heads, looking a bit lost.

"That's genius!" Lorenzo said. "I'll help. We'll cook together."

"And I'll set up the tables," Luisa said. "It'll be good to have something to do after moping around all day. Being the recipient of so much sympathy is positively exhausting."

"Wait, wait, wait!" Don Ludovico said, pushing the air down with his hands. "Not so fast! As you pointed out, there's no body to pray over!"

"We don't need Vittorio's body," Luisa said, placing a hand over her heart. "We have his spirit. And it just spoke through Jolene."

The aunts crossed themselves. Don Ludovico took off his glasses and polished the lenses on a sleeve of his frock, while running his tongue over his lips. Perhaps he was already wondering what might be in the pantry.

"Very well, then," he said, returning his glasses to their proper place, then looking through them and down his nose at Jolene. "Giovanna's idea might be an acceptable compromise."

Emboldened by the unanimous approval of her suggestion, Jolene cleared her throat. "Excuse me, Father," she said. "It's Jolene."

"What is?" he asked.

"Never mind," Jolene sighed, shaking her head.

"We'd better get to work!" Lorenzo said, grabbing Jolene's elbow with such force she nearly dropped her bag.

"Hold on!" she cried, lowering her eyes to her midriff. "I need a few minutes to… um…freshen up, you know…"

"Of course, I'm sorry!" Lorenzo said, slapping his forehead. "Come on upstairs. You can take a shower in my room."

"I wouldn't want to impose," Jolene said. She'd been wanting to see his room, and the others at the Locanda, but today was not the day, this was not the time. Though she did need the shower.

"Don't be silly. No imposition. Monica keeps some clothes there, you can throw on something of hers."

"I wouldn't want to impose on her, either."

"Don't worry, you won't," Lorenzo said. "She's not here."

Jolene couldn't imagine squeezing her butt into any of Monica's short skirts or tight pants, but knowing that a shower and a safe, if temporary, resting place for her mother were both within her grasp made Jolene feel that she just might survive this day. It wasn't until the hot water was streaming over her sudsy head, coursing down her aching body, and ferrying the dreadful day's dirt down the drain that she wondered whether anyone had called Filippo to notify him of the program. She heard herself groan, but didn't know whether it was because she was enjoying the shower, or fretting over Filippo.

TWENTY-FOUR

"Do you see what I see?" Lorenzo whispered, peering into the shadows.

"Yes, and would you please turn the light on?" Jolene murmured.

The neon tubes flickered to life, illuminating the stove and sink, the refrigerators and freezer, the shelves stocked with canned goods, the slouched sacks of flour.

"Crazy how your mind can play tricks on you, isn't it?" Lorenzo said, squinting at the harsh light.

"I know! I could swear I saw Vittorio bent over the sink, cleaning fish!"

"And there he was. For a minute, anyway." Lorenzo took two aprons from a hook and handed one to Jolene.

It shouldn't come as a surprise if she was hallucinating. At Lorenzo's insistence, she'd helped herself to Monica's line of expensive bath products, and although her appearance and odor were greatly improved after her shower, luxuriating in all that silky suds and steaming hot water had exacerbated her physical and emotional exhaustion. After her night of insomniac whitewashing, followed by her catastrophic morning at sea, followed by her one-woman rowing regatta, followed by her afternoon of surreal drama, courtesy of the carabinieri, it was all she could do to stay on her feet. But on her feet she would stay, because cooking a meal for Vittorio's family and friends would be her small way of honoring him. Passing the apron strings through the belt loops of Lorenzo's cargo pants (she hadn't even tried on anything of Monica's), she tied the knot around her waist to hold the trousers up, leaving the bib hanging, like Lorenzo did. Lorenzo had offered her a belt, too, but like the pants, it was too big, and the one he'd found in Monica's drawer couldn't quite complete the journey around Jolene's waist, no matter how much she sucked in her gut.

"Thanks again for the clothes," she said, raising her arms to tie back her damp hair, her aching muscles appreciating the loose fit of the black cotton T-shirt. She'd hesitated to put it on when she noticed that the tags were still attached and recognized the trademark Armani wings stamped across the front, but Lorenzo said it didn't matter that he'd never worn it because he never would; he had no intention of becoming a walking advertisement for anyone. Once she was cleaned up and dressed, Jolene remained with the problem of her sneakers, which were still damp and stinky. Monica's shoes were two sizes too small and, except for a pair of flip-flops, all high-heeled, while Lorenzo's were way too big. But now she spotted a suitable solution, right there in the kitchen.

"Do you think he'd mind?" she asked Lorenzo, her heart breaking a bit more as she pointed to a pair of Crocs guarding the door, waiting for their owner's feet. Though white, they were dulled by the patina of grease that settles over anyone or anything that spends any amount of time in a professional kitchen.

"No, not at all," Lorenzo said. "Go ahead."

Jolene's legs shook as she slipped her feet into the clogs while Lorenzo looked on in silence. Size-wise, she came close to filling Vittorio's shoes, but standing in for him at his stove was another story altogether. When Lorenzo's gaze crossed hers, they both sighed, but an instant later he was springing to action, rummaging through the refrigerator. He took out a large container, inviting Jolene to peek inside, and when he cracked the lid open, the heavenly scent of fresh basil was so powerful that it made her swoon.

"Pa's famous pesto," Lorenzo said, uncovering the tub full of bright green sauce, its slightly coarse consistency proof that he'd ground and blended the basil and garlic and pine nuts and cheese and oil by hand rather than tossing all the ingredients into a food processor. "I saw him make it yesterday."

Jolene bent over the container again, filling her nostrils with the aroma of Vittorio's culinary legacy, so fragrant, so alive. Recalling his comments about liking to watch her eat, the knots in her stomach relaxed, making her painfully aware of how utterly empty it was.

"Are you okay?" Lorenzo asked, when she failed to straighten up.

"Just a little woozy," she said, gripping the counter. "I just realized I haven't eaten all day."

"Same here," Lorenzo said. He'd taken a shower while Jolene dressed, and although he looked somewhat revived, the pallor of exhaustion was visible just below the surface of his suntanned face. "But first things first," he added, with a clap of his hands. "The pasta cooker is on the blink again, so I'll put some pots on to boil. In the meantime, why don't you take a look around and see what else inspires you?"

Minutes later, four banged-up aluminum pots were huddling over four gas fires like four old bums warming themselves at the corners of an intersection. Though she'd never spent as much time experimenting in the kitchen as she would have liked to, Jolene had a few standards to fall back on, and thought that something zesty would revive the mourners and offset the sadness of the occasion. The spicy tomato sauce recipe that Anna Vigevani's mother had taught her to make as a teenager would be a good contrast to the pesto, both in color and in flavor, she thought, and the decision was clinched by the not irrelevant fact that, like any respectable Italian kitchen, Vittorio's had a plentiful stock of peeled plum tomatoes. Armed with a can opener, Jolene began cutting into the lids of the tins.

"I'll be back in a minute!" Lorenzo called, the door swinging behind him.

Her injured finger and tearing eyes made it necessary for Jolene to exercise extra caution as she chopped the red Tropea onions, and she was so absorbed with her task that she didn't notice Lorenzo's return until he spoke.

"Well?" he said, from behind her.

Turning, she saw that in his hands was a tray, and on the tray was a bottle of white wine, two tumblers, and a basket of focaccia.

"Dry throats and growling stomachs are a distraction to cooks," Lorenzo said. "Pa's words, not mine." Setting the tray down, he uncorked the bottle. "You seemed to enjoy this the last time."

Jolene nodded. The last time, to celebrate her new ring; and the time before that, on the beach. Both times were a lifetime ago.

"To Vittorio Garaventi," Lorenzo said, raising his glass.

"To Vittorio," Jolene said. She liked the solid sound of their thick tumblers touching; she liked to think that she and Lorenzo shared the same type of sturdiness. Bringing the glass to her lips, she took a sip, savoring the crisp coolness of the wine as it slid down her parched throat.

"You'd better have some of this, too," Lorenzo said, offering her the focaccia.

"Thanks," she said, moaning softly as her teeth sunk into the perfect combination of crispy and doughy, oily and salty; reaching for another slice before the first one had cleared her throat; washing it all down with a thirsty gulp of wine. Lorenzo laughed at her greed, though he'd already wolfed down several slices of focaccia himself, and drained his glass as well. He poured more wine for both of them.

"I'd better finish making my sauce before I keel over, and drag the tomatoes down with me!" Jolene said, giggling at the mental image that formed of herself, passed out on the kitchen floor in a pool of red liquid, finally nabbed with a knife still in her hand.

"I'm feeling a little tipsy too!" Lorenzo chuckled. "I can see myself swimming with you again, this time on the floor, in a pool of pesto!"

The thought made Jolene giggle more, which in turn made Lorenzo laugh harder, their exhaustion finding release in giddiness, their tension in hysteria. Within seconds, they were both doubled over, whopping uncontrollably.

"Is it too much to ask for a little respect?" Filippo boomed, bursting into the kitchen, the doors swinging behind him. "I could hear you laughing from the bar! And so could everyone else!"

"Filippo! Finally!" Jolene cried, dabbing at her eyes with the corner of her apron as she ran to hug him. "How are you?"

"It was nice of you two to fill me in on your plans!" he said, brushing her arms away while glaring at Lorenzo. "He was my father, you know!"

"I tried calling you all day, Filippo!" Jolene cried. "And so did Lorenzo. You have no idea what we've been through!"

"What you've been through?" he shouted, his eyes darting from one to the other. "I can assure you that being out of town when you find out that your father has died in mysterious circumstances, then being stuck in a tunnel on a train with mechanical problems is a hell of a lot to go through!"

"What mysterious circumstances?" Jolene asked. "Who could

have told you that when no one could even reach you?"

"Some people know when it's important enough to keep trying! And to be there to console a person in grief! Like your priest, for example!"

"Don Ludovico told you?" Jolene cried.

"Ah, so here they are!" Monica called, pushing open the still swinging doors, her heels clicking as she entered the kitchen with the pep of a tap dancer flapping in from the wings. Head held high, she jutted her jaw out at Lorenzo, then at Jolene, then at the bottle of wine, as if her chin were equipped with a hidden lens she was using to photograph all the incriminating evidence. "Having your own little party, are you?"

"Oh yes, we've been having a real blast!" Lorenzo replied. "Poor Ma has been stuck here all day entertaining the people who were supposed to be consoling her, with no one around to help!"

"And where were you two, if I may ask?" Filippo said. "Off on another one of your hikes?"

"Can we cut the irony, please?" Lorenzo cried, slamming the counter with his hand. "For your information, I spent the whole day in La Spezia. Someone had to take care of arrangements for Pa!"

"And someone else was hauled off by the carabinieri like a criminal because another someone else took off with her passport!" Jolene cried, startled by her own tone of voice.

"Was that before or after you stole my husband's clothes?" Monica asked, jabbing a sharp nail at Jolene's chest, before turning to Lorenzo. "I bought you that T-shirt for your birthday! And in case you don't—"

The blaring of a musical ringtone interrupted Monica's tirade, prompting a frantic search through her leather satchel until her hand reemerged with a phone. Turning her back to the others, she plugged her free ear with a finger and began shouting into the phone that this was not a good time, no, not a good time at all, though the party at the other end must have thought otherwise, judging by the number of times she was forced to repeat herself.

"I can't believe this! This is just awful!" a female voice cried out, accompanied by another groan of the swinging doors. A big-boned girl with a headful of blonde spikes entered the kitchen, her pierced nose dripping, her blue eyes swollen and rimmed with red as though she'd been crying for hours.

"*Oh, Lore!* I'm so sorry!" the girl wailed, ripping a paper towel off the roll on the wall as she rushed toward Lorenzo. The moment she draped her arms over his shoulders, she began sobbing so desperately that her spikes shook all the way down to their roots. Who could she possibly be? Jolene wondered. Watching the way Lorenzo ran his hands gently up and down the girl's spine to console her, she also wondered why their intimacy should disturb her so much when it didn't seem to bother Monica, who was still on the phone, or Filippo, who was edging closer to Jolene. Of course, the Garaventis must have slews of relatives and family friends Jolene had never heard of. All kinds of people you hadn't seen in years turned up when someone died.

"Listen, why don't you give me the ring?" Filippo whispered to Jolene in a voice barely audible above the girl's sobbing and Monica's shouting.

"The ring?" she asked, genuinely perplexed. "What are you talking about?"

"I'm talking about the engagement ring!" he cried, sotto voce. "What other rings are you wearing?"

"But Filippo…" Jolene began, too bewildered to speak. Could this really be happening? Could he really hold her responsible for his father's death? Could he simply call everything off, right then and there, in the middle of the kitchen? She'd been having some misgivings of her own, it was true, but they were both too emotionally charged right now to make rash decisions. "But…are you sure?"

"Please, Jolene. Don't go making a big deal about it in front of everybody," Filippo said, holding out his hand. "Just give it to me."

"But it is a big deal! To me, anyway!"

"All I'm saying is that you shouldn't be wearing a valuable piece of heirloom jewelry in the kitchen!"

"You mean you're not asking me to give it back to you for good?"

"Honestly, *Splendore!* Sometimes I wonder where you get your ideas!" Filippo said, shaking his head. "I'm just suggesting you let me hold on to it for you before you damage it, or worse."

Jolene's hands, greasy with olive oil, shook as she removed the ring, which slipped off too easily. Filippo was right; she was lucky it hadn't slid right down the drain! Relieved at having been spared yet another disaster, she dropped the ring into his open palm.

"Don Ludovico is waiting!" Luisa called out, pushing through the doors to the crowded kitchen. "The rosary is about to begin."

Filippo clamped his fist shut, shoving his hand into his pocket. Walking over to the blonde girl, he pried her off of Lorenzo. "Come on, now," he said, snatching another paper towel as he dragged her out the door. "Pull yourself together."

At last Monica stopped shouting into her phone and dropped it in her bag. "I want that T-shirt back," she hissed to Jolene over her shoulder as she followed Filippo and the blonde girl out the door.

"It looks like things are a little behind schedule in here," Luisa said, her hands on her hips as she faced Jolene and Lorenzo. "You two had better let the others worry about Vittorio's soul while you take care of feeding their bodies. They'll be ready to eat in half an hour, and then we can send them on their way."

Turning to leave, Luisa glimpsed Jolene's feet. Her eyes were damp when she looked up at Jolene and Lorenzo again. "Thank you. Both of you."

At last, the doors stopped swinging and Lorenzo poured them each another glass of wine. Jolene fired up the skillet, and when the olive oil was warm she tossed in the chopped onions and several cloves of crushed garlic. The soft sizzling sound was reassuring, instantly filling the air with enticing smells. Although she was extra careful when pouring in the tomatoes from those unwieldy jumbo cans, her blistered hands made her clumsy, and some juice splashed onto the Armani T-shirt. Good thing it was black.

Jolene went about her work in silence, taking a sip of wine now and then, as Lorenzo walked from the pantry to the refrigerator to the counter and back again, slicing dried swordfish and tuna, prosciutto and salami, opening mason jars of anchovies and olives and artichokes preserved in olive oil, and arranging everything on platters for the antipasto.

The water in the pots rolled to a boil. Don Ludovico's voice, squandered on such a small venue, resounded throughout the Locanda as he led the rosary, carrying his words down the corridor and into the kitchen so that not one pair of ears would be deprived of prayer. When it was the mourners' turn to recite their response, the very walls reverberated with the love of an entire village, and its faith in itself to carry on. Jolene had not yet learned the Hail Mary in Italian, but she listened to the words of the prayer, and understood.

Santa Maria, Madre di Dio,
Prega per noi peccatori
Adesso, e nell'ora della nostra morte.
Amen.

TWENTY-FIVE

Jolene had to admit that Filippo, assisted by the blonde girl, did a laudable job managing the dining room. Despite Luisa's protests, Filippo had convinced his mother to remain seated throughout the meal and allow herself to be waited on like a proper neophyte widow, instead of running around and serving others as if it was just another busy mealtime at the Locanda. Though Jolene noticed the pained look on Luisa's face as she endured the kindness, she concluded that grief was not its only cause. Aggravating her weariness was Don Ludovico, seated at her right, bending her ear with his ministrations, combined with the insistence of the two aunts, seated at her left, that she repeat every word being said, complaining that their hearing was impaired by all the background noise.

Though by now it was clear to Jolene that Luisa was not rigorous in her practice of the Catholic religion, observing her tête-à-tête with the priest made her wonder whether she actually considered Don Ludovico a spiritual leader at all, or simply treated him with the same respect and tolerance she'd bestow upon any other stalwart member of the community, like the mayor, or the postman, or the garbage collector, who was just trying to do the job he was hired for.

Meanwhile, the packed dining room proved that Jolene's idea was greatly appreciated by those villagers who were able to linger after the rosary, now speaking softly among themselves at tables of four or six as they ate, their eyes darting furtively around the room as if trying to discover the hidden motive behind a free meal. Jolene wondered how many of these accidental diners had ever ventured past the bar area into the restaurant; how many had ever brought their families in for a meal; how many of their offspring, now grown up and living elsewhere, had returned to treat their parents to a dinner here. Though she'd thought of Giobatta often as she worked, it wasn't until Jolene saw the entire assembly seated that his absence became conspicuous. On asking Luisa whether he was still home in bed, she was distressed to learn that his condition had worsened. His fever had spiked, and his sister had come in from La Spezia, insisting on driving him back to the city to see a specialist.

Surveying the room as Filippo and the blonde girl made their final rounds to offer a *bis* (seconds) or a *tris* (thirds) on the pasta dishes, Jolene was pleased to observe the contented looks on the faces of their guests as they leaned back in their chairs with their hands laced over their full tummies, and had no doubt that Vittorio, wherever he was, must be looking down on them all, his eyes twinkling with satisfaction. Lorenzo, who had come to stand beside Jolene, smiled wistfully, probably thinking the same thing.

"Where's your mother going?" Jolene asked him, watching Luisa rise from her table and steal away on tiptoe, so as not to disturb Don Ludovico and the aunties who appeared to have talked themselves to sleep.

"Home," Lorenzo said.

"All alone? Will she be all right?"

"She can't wait to be all alone. She's planning to sneak out the back door."

Before Jolene could decide whether she should follow her to make sure she really was all right, Filippo walked up to them.

"Babbo would have been so happy to see a full house sharing a meal in his honor," he said, looking uncharacteristically relaxed, especially in view of his previous attitude. Maybe he felt more at ease relating to these people in a professional capacity, Jolene thought, rather than subjecting himself to their embarrassing hugs and sweaty handshakes and sentimental platitudes. After all, that was who he was here, a Garaventi, a member of the family who'd owned the Locanda since before he was born.

"Yes, he would," Lorenzo said. "It was Jolene's idea, you know?"

"That was so *brilliant* of you, Jolene!" the blonde girl said, her rosy lips quivering, her blue eyes brimming as she grabbed Jolene by the wrists. She spoke good Italian, but with a foreign accent Jolene did not have the ear to identify.

"I didn't know Vittorio for as long as I'd have liked to, or as well as I'd have liked to," Jolene said, her heart heavy with regret for what could have been. "But it just seemed right to me."

"*Absolutely!*" the girl said, her grip on Jolene's wrists tightening. Though the feeling was disturbing, almost like being handcuffed, Jolene said nothing, knowing she must be overreacting due to her recent run-in with the law.

"Forgive me, Jolene," Filippo said, clearing his throat, still immersed in his role as the courteous dispenser of hospitality. "I should have made a proper introduction sooner, but you know what they say. Customers first! Wendy, this is Jolene. Jolene, this is Wendy. Now if you'll excuse me a moment, I have something important to tell Mamma and I must catch up with her before she gets away from me!"

"*Wendy?* You mean…" Jolene started to ask him, but Filippo was already hurrying away.

"I think I'll go check where Monica is," Lorenzo said, following his brother out of the dining room.

"Actually, I started going by Windy when I got to Italy, just for a change, you know? For a new start, you know? It made me think fresh and free, you know?" the girl said, her full attention focused on Jolene. "But Filippo said it wasn't a real name and never really warmed up to it, and people here just don't get it. You speak English though, right? You get how by changing one vowel, the whole meaning changes, right?"

"Right," Jolene repeated, too confused by Wendy's unannounced appearance on the scene, by her laid-back attitude, by her overall quirkiness, by her unrelenting grip, to say anything else. Nonetheless, the girl seemed to be taking Jolene's presence extremely well, possibly proving that Filippo had been right about taking his time to break the news of their engagement to her.

"*Awesome!* I'm Windy to you then, if you don't mind," the girl said, giving Jolene's wrists another squeeze.

"Whatever!" Jolene said, deciding that being nice was one thing, but being trapped was another. Using a self-defense technique she'd learned in high school, she raised her arms then quickly lowered them, twisting them down and out, at last breaking free. Her abrupt action startled the girl, leaving her wide-eyed and open-mouthed.

Seconds later, a new smile lit up her face as Filippo walked back in.

"Let's all sit and eat now!" Filippo said, directing the women to the family's usual table.

"Come on, Jolene!" Windy said, taking Jolene's elbow. "Sit next to me!"

"What a great idea!" Filippo said, pulling out chairs for Jolene and Windy, then swiftly sliding a third chair in between theirs and sitting himself down in it.

Lorenzo, returning with the beverages and bread basket, freed his arms in time to hold out a chair for Monica, who hurried in on his heels with the annoyed purposefulness of a busy woman who was late for a meeting she had neither the time nor the desire to attend.

"That child will be the death of me!" Monica moaned, pulling up her chair. "She refuses to settle down and go to sleep."

"Chiara's upstairs?" Jolene asked, the blood draining from her face. "In your room?"

"Of course she's in our room," Monica snapped. "Where else would she be?"

"Of course," Jolene said, trying not to panic at the thought of what an unattended, restless child could do with a bag of ashes. But no, she was being ridiculous. Lorenzo had stashed them in a garbage bag, together with her soiled clothes, in the closet. Even if Chiara climbed out of her cot, she wouldn't dare open the closet. Little girls didn't like dark closets. Little American girls, anyway.

"Is she afraid of the bogeyman?" Jolene blurted.

"What?" Monica asked, looking at Jolene as if she were insane.

Windy, seeming to have a knack for it, did Jolene the favor of drawing the attention to herself as she stuck her nose into the platter of pasta, inhaling so intensely that her nostrils caved in. "Oh my God, how I miss this pesto!" she cried, reaching across the table to take Monica's plate with one hand while scooping up a generous spoonful serving of pasta with the other.

"No, no!" Monica cried, placing both hands over her plate. "None for me!"

"Pity you never tasted the pesto Vittorio used to make with the basil I grew up in Volastra, Jolene," Windy said, leaning across Filippo to serve her the food Monica had refused. "We were a great combination, me and Babbo," she continued, sniffing and shaking her spiky head. "A little more?" she asked, batting her blue eyes at

Jolene; Jolene nodded. The more confused she felt, the hungrier she got, and there was plenty of extra room in Lorenzo's pants.

Silence fell over the group as Lorenzo opened a bottle of Cinque Terre Bianco and poured for everyone. Though they had food on their plates and wine in their glasses, they did not eat or drink, but sat there staring at what they'd been offered. Jolene wished there were a way to eavesdrop on each person's thoughts at that moment, and wondered whether they should say some sort of prayer, but felt awkward suggesting it. Bowing her head, she asked Vittorio to keep an eye on them all, wherever he may be, then raised her glass.

"To Vittorio," she said.

"To Vittorio," Windy chimed in.

"To Vittorio," Lorenzo said, standing as he raised his glass in the air.

Filippo, then Monica, rose to their feet too, then person by person, table by table, everyone in the Locanda stood. "To Vittorio!" they chanted. "To Vittorio!"

Don Ludovico, roused by the commotion, pulled himself up from the table. Though groggy, he responded like a true pro, taking his cue from the roomful of parishioners gathered around him.

"*Nel nome del Padre, del Figlio e dello Spirito santo*," he said, his open hand designing a cross the air. "May he rest in peace. Amen."

"Amen!" rang out the voices from every corner of the room.

Glasses were drained and chairs were dragged over the floor as people began taking their leave. Filippo and Lorenzo and Jolene and Windy and Monica sat back down and began eating in silence, save for Monica's crackling and crunching as she ripped open package upon package of pencil-thin Torinesi breadsticks and munched them nervously.

Glancing around the table now and then, Jolene tried to steal a look at Windy, but Filippo kept leaning forward, blocking her line of vision. Perhaps it was just that the day's events were too atrocious to leave any wiggle room for other negative feelings, but apart from her initial (understandably unpleasant) surprise at finding herself face-to-face with Filippo's ex, Jolene wasn't experiencing the gut-wrenching jealousy she would have expected. It was a relief to get their relationship out in the open and to find that meeting Windy was far better than brooding over her. By withholding information, Filippo had left Jolene with no alternative (other than to not think about the girl at all, which would have been impossible for any woman in her position), but to rely on her own imagination, which worked day and night, conjuring up images of a conniving snip of a girl who feigned helplessness in order to wrap Filippo around her little foreign finger and keep him there. The unconventional young woman sitting at their table seemed to possess an unusual combination of toughness and sensitivity, determination and spontaneity, and Jolene was curious to learn more about her, maybe even hear her version of what had happened in her relationship with Filippo. She clearly wasn't his type, anyone could see that. She was more Lorenzo's type, if anything. And that, for some inexplicable reason, was what bothered her most. That, and Monica's incessant crunching.

TWENTY-SIX

On the morning after the longest day of her life, Jolene lay flat on her back, her arms and legs splayed. Snatched from the comfort of sleep by a needle-sharp pricking in her chest, she opened her eyes to find Fata staring at her through slit lids, kneading her bosom and purring contentedly.

"Ouch!" Jolene cried, detaching the cat from her. "As if my heart hasn't been tortured enough." Rolling over, she closed her eyes again, hoping for a few more hours of respite from reality. She was just beginning to drift off again when a knock came on the door.

"Jolene?" said a muffled male voice. She pulled the blanket over her head. She wouldn't answer; she couldn't. There were three more raps.

"Are you there, Jolene?" called the voice, now loud enough for her to recognize it as Lorenzo's.

Sighing, she threw aside the blanket and the cat and grabbed her robe.

"I'm coming!" she called, tiptoeing to the door in her bare feet. Fata materialized between her ankles, almost making her trip, and darted out the door as soon as Jolene cracked it open, ears pricked, tail twitching, primed for a morning prowl.

"Hi," Jolene said, hiding behind the half-open door.

"Hi," Lorenzo said. "I hope I didn't wake you."

Running a hand over her disheveled hair, Jolene shook her head, wishing she'd told him to wait while she at least washed her face and brushed her teeth. Unshaven and rumpled, Lorenzo looked pretty rough around the edges himself, though, particularly his eyes. Red-rimmed and glassy, they seemed to have sunk so far into their sockets that they might disappear altogether. It pained her to look at them.

"I was awake," she said. "But I didn't want to be."

"I know what you mean."

"It's those first thirty seconds or so, you know? When you have a vague feeling that something awful has happened, then you remember what it was. It's like getting punched in the stomach."

Lorenzo nodded. "Yeah, at least I skipped that part."

"Don't tell me you've been up all night?"

Lorenzo nodded. "It was a tough one," he said, rubbing his chin. "Monica doesn't handle these situations well."

"I'm sorry," Jolene said, but her sympathy was for Lorenzo.

"She freaks out when life interferes with her plans. The only thing that calms her down is talking, and every talker needs a listener." He shook his head a few times, as if to unplug his ears, the way he'd done when emerging from the sea after their swim. "So, can I come in a second?"

"I'm sorry, of course," Jolene said, opening the door, though she wasn't keen on letting him get a full view of her, or her room, in their present condition.

"I thought you'd want your things," Lorenzo said, holding up a black garbage bag as he entered.

"God, yes! The bag! Thank you so much!" Jolene said, taking the bag from him and hugging it to her chest. The plastic hissed, leaking the stink of fish that clung to her soiled clothes. She never wanted to see, let alone wear, those clothes again, and felt awful that her mother, even in her current state, had been forced to share their hiding place. "I was terrified something would happen to it."

"The bag was in my custody," Lorenzo said. "What could happen?"

"I don't know, but lately it seems like everything that can go wrong, does." Jolene shrugged. Lorenzo nodded. "I'm sorry I can't even make you a cup of coffee," she added, after a moment.

Lorenzo's eyes left her face to glance around the room, as if to check whether she was telling the truth or might possibly be concealing a pot. The change in his expression told her he was shocked by what he saw.

"What the hell happened here?" he asked.

"I…um…I suppose you mean the walls and all that?" Jolene asked. She should have cleared it with the family before painting, she knew, but her plan had been to keep it secret until the job was finished and the room cleaned. Everyone would have been so impressed; everyone would have praised her initiative. According to her plan, at least.

"Yeah, the walls and all that," Lorenzo said. "That's what I mean."

"Well, it's kind of a complicated story," Jolene began, still clutching the garbage bag to her chest. "But not really, I don't know. I just wanted to freshen up the room, and I got my hands on some whitewash, so then the other night when I couldn't sleep—God, was it only the night before last?—I got up and started painting but it was dark and I was agitated and I made a mess, and then I went out looking for coffee, and that's when I met Vittorio. And it's all my fault! I should have stayed in my room where I belonged! I should have left well enough alone!"

"No, no, no, Jolene," Lorenzo said, prying the garbage bag out of her arms and setting it on the floor. "Don't even go that route."

Fighting back tears, Jolene pulled her robe tight, wondering how she would ever be able to forgive herself. Lorenzo reached out a hand, as if to touch her, but ran it through his tangled curls instead.

"I should go," he said, shoving both hands into his pockets.

"Yeah, I guess," Jolene said.

Lorenzo turned on his heels to leave, but stopped, facing her again. Jolene's heart skipped a beat when he looked at her with those sad, sunken eyes. She felt a desperate urge to hug him, but was afraid he wouldn't want her to, and more afraid that he would.

"Listen, I was just heading down to the harbor for a breath of air and a cup of coffee," he said. "Do you feel like coming along?"

"Uh…I wasn't expecting this," she stammered. "What I mean is, I'd need a minute."

"Yeah, well, I'm sorry for barging in so early, but I wanted to bring you the bag before anyone starting asking questions. Go back to bed. Or meet me there, if you like."

"Yeah, I'd like that," she said, watching Lorenzo's back until he shut the door behind it.

It never took Jolene more than a few minutes to get ready—until that morning. Now it seemed like the faster she moved, the longer she took. Her toothbrush flew out of her hands, landing in the toilet; soap attacked her eyes, temporarily blinding her; no matches were to be found for any of her socks, and her shoelaces were all in knots. When at last she was ready to leave, she took a look around, vowing that after one quick coffee she'd come straight back to her room to clean up the mess. Pulling the door behind her, she hurried down the steps that led to the path that led to the road that led to the harbor.

The air that morning was moist and salty, heavy with the sea. The clouds were of the stratified sort that hung around looking gloomy, too belligerent to budge, too miserly to rain. Watching the waves hurl themselves against the rocks, she thought of her tendency to beat herself up, knowing that it was useless, that it would only wear her down. Life threw itself at you, and you had to push back, not waste your time wondering what you could have done differently. Lorenzo was watching the sea, too, she noticed. He was easy to spot, the lone occupant at the cluster of outdoor tables huddled in the early morning chill.

"Sorry it took me so long," Jolene said, sitting down across from him.

"Funny, I was just going to ask how you got here so fast," Lorenzo said. He'd waited for her to order and now waved at the man puttering about inside the deserted restaurant, who responded to Lorenzo's gestures by nodding and disappearing from view. Noticing the upturned chairs can-canning their bare legs above the tabletops, Jolene wondered whether the restaurant was closed for the day, or for the season. It seemed like months had passed since Filippo had brought her here to give her the ring, and now her finger already felt bare without it.

As they waited to be served Jolene sensed that Lorenzo wanted to ask her something, now that they were alone and sharing a quiet moment. Perhaps he'd ask her to go over what Vittorio had talked about in the boat, curious to know whether he'd mentioned him, and what he might have said. She'd have to be careful about how to phrase things, even if it meant leaving out some comments that if taken the wrong way might make him feel bad.

"Did I get it right?" Lorenzo asked, breaking the silence as the man placed a cappuccino laced with cinnamon in front of Jolene and a double espresso in front of him.

"Perfect," Jolene said. "Thanks."

"One never knows with you," Lorenzo said, tossing back a gulp of steaming coffee. He drank it black, with no sugar. Like Vittorio.

Jolene's nose was in her cup, her upper lip already dipping into the foam, when he spoke again.

"How did you feel when your mother was cremated?" he asked.

Jolene sucked in her breath at the abruptness of his question, inhaling so much cinnamon powder that she began coughing and sneezing and sloshing the cappuccino all over the table.

"I'm sorry!" Lorenzo cried, mopping up the table with his napkin. "Wrong approach."

"Don't worry," Jolene sputtered. "Just give me a second, okay?" No one had ever asked her that before, not even Filippo. They sat in silence for a moment as she delved into her memory, slowly sipping what was left in her cup.

"My mother didn't regain consciousness after her stroke," she began, at last, preferring to look out at the sea rather than at Lorenzo's suffering eyes. "Each day that passed without any improvement reduced the chances that there ever would be any. After about a week they said that although she was breathing on her own, she couldn't swallow food or water and that I should decide what to do. What kind of a thing is that to ask a person? What did I know? But mom had always told me that if there came a day when she couldn't at least sit up in a chair, have a bowl of chocolate swirl ice cream, and read a book, she'd rather die. It wasn't about the ice cream, of course, but knew I had to respect that. In America, they don't keep patients who are never going to recover in the hospital, so we moved her to a hospice. There's no life support in those places, you know. Only death support."

Jolene faltered, remembering how terrified she'd been to make the decision, how alone she'd felt as she watched her mother fade away. For the first time, she wondered whether Filippo would have stayed by her mother's side with her, comforting her and keeping vigil with her, if he'd been in her life then. Would he have considered her display of emotions disturbing? Would he have been scared off by her crying?

"I'm sorry," Lorenzo said. "That must have been very hard to handle."

"I had no idea how long it could take to die, Lorenzo. Day after day, all I could do was hold mom's hand and talk to her. All I could hope for was that she could hear me telling her how sorry I was that I found her too late to make a difference. All I could pray for was that she was not in pain. Sure, she was sedated, but for God's sake, we're better at putting our pets out of their misery when they reach the end. Watching her go like that, hour after hour, day after day, with no food, no water, no way to let me know if she was in agony, was sheer torture. Until you go through that, you have no idea. No idea."

Pausing, she glanced at Lorenzo. He nodded, his tired eyes shining with empathy, as if he had more than an idea; as if he'd been right there with her.

"She never opened her eyes again," Jolene continued. "She never imparted any final words of wisdom or gave my hand one last squeeze. One night I was at the hospice just listening to her breathing, wondering how much more it could slow down, how many more times it could stop and restart before stopping for good. It was then that I began praying that each breath would be her last, that God would have mercy on her and release her from her agony. When morning broke, I rested my head on my mom's tummy and starting singing to her. You see, we had this silly tune we used to sing when I was little and my mother took me out rowing. It used to make me feel strong when we sang together in the boat, as if I could go anywhere and do anything. I wanted to make her feel that way, too, wherever she was, wherever she was going. That probably sounds idiotic to you."

"No, not at all," Lorenzo said. "What song was it?"

"It starts out with 'row, row, row your boat, gently down the stream,' and that's the only verse she ever wanted to sing. So that's what I sang to her then, over and over, over and over, while I imagined Mom in that old rowboat of hers, always telling me to be strong, but always reminding me to be gentle. 'That's the only way to survive,' she used to tell me. My singing faded to a whisper as I imagined her rowing away from me on that lake, rowing gently, rowing incessantly, rowing farther and farther away until she faded from view. And then she was gone. She stopped breathing. I held her body tight as I cried, but I couldn't hold onto her life. Could she feel her spirit leaving her body, I wondered, the way she'd felt mine flicker to life inside her? I always wanted to ask whether she was happy to have a baby, and whether she would have wanted me anyway if she'd known that becoming a mother would ruin what she had with my father. I never did ask, though. I guess I was too afraid of the answer."

Jolene paused for a moment, recalling the fascinating stories her mother had told her about her and the Captain's early days together, making sure Jolene knew that there had been love there at one time; that there had been happiness.

"Flying was still glamorous back when my mother became a stewardess," she said. "And of course the most romantic thing she could do was fall in love with a pilot. They were always on the move, always studying ways to rendezvous in strange cities or finagle a layover at some airport hotel. Just like secret lovers, even after they were married. Until I came along."

But none of that had anything to do with Lorenzo's question, she realized, wrapping her hands around her cup to stop them from shaking.

"Sorry," she said. "I'm way off track. You spent all night listening to Monica, and now you get stuck listening to me."

"Hey, I like listening to you," Lorenzo said. "Tell me more about your parents."

"Maybe another time. Their story was like a fairy tale in reverse. Happy beginning, pathetic ending. I think I may be following in my mother's footsteps."

"Why do you say that?"

"I'm good at beginnings," she said. "But I mess up the endings."

"Until now," Lorenzo said. "Call me biased, but this time you're starting over in a corner of paradise. What we're going now through will pass, Jolene, and when it does, you'll still have your handsome prince to marry."

Jolene forced a smile. "Will I?" It had hurt Jolene that Filippo had not held her in his arms and consoled her, last night; granted, she had not wanted him to walk her back to her room for fear he would see the mess, but the fact that he hadn't insisted made her wonder why. Did he want to be with Luisa, or was it Windy he was worried about? Or maybe it was worse; maybe on some level, he actually held her responsible for what had happened. "I think he blames me for Vittorio's death."

"Now listen up, Jolene. It was only a question of where and when Pa's heart would give out and I can't tell you how sorry I am that it had to happen when he was with you. Please remember that you made him happy by going out on that boat with him, and don't let anyone tell you anything different."

"He was happy, you know?" Jolene said, recalling the sparkle in his eye, the joy in his chuckle. "And you know what? I even taught him the rowing song. Maybe my mother inspired me. Maybe she was waiting for him."

"Maybe," Lorenzo said. "It's a sweet thought, anyway."

"Getting back to your question," Jolene said. "My mother was a strong woman, but my father eventually wore her down. As she grew fearful of him over time, she seemed to physically shrink, as if she wanted to take up as little space as possible and be noticed as little as possible. It was January when she died, and she hated the cold and the dark so much I couldn't bear the thought of putting her in the ground. And I certainly didn't want her anywhere near my father's grave. Cremation felt like the right thing to do, but I still had a very hard time letting go of her. I wanted to hold on to what was left just a little longer, until I found the right place for her."

"So when Prince Filippo came along and swept you off your feet, you decided to bring her along to Italy?" Lorenzo said.

Jolene nodded. "For all her travels, she never made it over here. After my divorce, she talked about planning a trip one day together, but I kept putting her off. Unlike my parents, I really do hate flying."

"So do I," Lorenzo said, raising his hand to catch the attention of the man inside again.

"Lorenzo?" Jolene said. "Filippo still doesn't know about my mother. I mean, that I brought her ashes with me. I kept planning to talk to him about it, but I was afraid he would be against it. At this point, I'd rather not tell him."

Lorenzo placed his hand over hers. "It'll be our secret. I'm pretty sure our friends in uniform won't talk, either. They don't like looking foolish."

It felt good to have her hand held. It felt good to have someone to talk to. And when the man came to set another espresso and another cappuccino in front of them, it felt good to sip them together in silence, looking out at the sea, thinking that maybe, just maybe, she was where she should be after all.

TWENTY-SEVEN

Chiuso per lutto.

The sign taped to the window of the Locanda might have been posted exclusively for the benefit of tourists, had there been any, because it certainly wasn't discouraging the steady stream of villagers from walking right in. That the business was closed for mourning was irrelevant to the locals; they were like family, and no family worthy of the name would dream of leaving Luisa alone at a time like this. Respects must be paid (but maybe not the drinks), and with this craziness of holding the funeral that very afternoon, the dispensing of both must be crammed into the few remaining hours.

Entering, Jolene looked around, expecting to find Filippo running things after Lorenzo had been summoned to La Spezia to take care of the final formalities and Luisa, having received more respects than she could handle, had decided to hide out in her house with the aunties until it was time for the funeral.

"I'd like to know what the big rush is," a gaunt man with a cane was saying, leaning his ancient backbone against the bar as he spoke to a younger, heavyset man Jolene recognized from the previous evening, dressed in a blue jumpsuit that zippered up the front, of the kind favored by mechanics. Thinking it would be nice to greet him by name, she checked to see if it was stitched above his breast pocket but saw only an oval patch bearing the Esso logo. He smiled back at her when she passed them and said hello, but the gaunt man didn't deign her with as much as a glance.

"I'd like to know who put this cockamamie idea into Luisa's

head," the old man continued, his voice unnecessarily loud, his rheumy eyes fixed on the opposite wall, pretending not to notice Jolene as she slipped behind the bar and rolled up her sleeves. "I'd like to know if it's even legal!"

Whether people had been helping themselves the entire morning or someone had been serving them was not clear; what was clear was that no one was cleaning up after them. Tottering towers of espresso cups were stacked on the bar while the sink, clogged with scummy dishwater, was filled to the brim with dirty glasses. Jolene had never seen the place in such disorder, and she certainly couldn't allow Luisa to.

"Legal, it's legal," proclaimed the Esso man, talking too loud for a conversation with a person standing right next to him. "Twenty-four hours is all you have to wait. Just to make sure the dead person is really dead." He glanced at Jolene, now armed with a plunger, then leaned in close to the older man's left ear. "Unless there's suspicion of foul play."

"It smells pretty darn foul to me," the old man said, coughing into a crumpled handkerchief. "All I know is, I was standing right here in this very spot talking to Vitturin the day before he died, and he seemed fine to me."

"Ha! Just because he seemed fine doesn't mean he was fine. It's like when you're driving a car, and you're cruising down the road with a full tank, going wherever it is that you're going. The engine's running, the wheels are turning, and everything's fine then, too. Until the car breaks down. You just never know what's going on under the hood."

"You know perfectly well I don't drive. And I never owned a car," the oldster said. He had one of those mouths that didn't open very wide, making smiles more trouble than they were worth.

"That's beside the point," the Esso man said, catching Jolene's eye as the drain gurgled its relief at being freed. Holding up his empty tumbler, he graced her with a crooked smile to which Jolene responded by grabbing the liter-and-a-half bottle of bianco from the refrigerator and pouring him a glass. That much of the local language she understood.

"Well, Vitturin didn't drive either," the old man said, shaking his head. "And one day I was talking to him, and the next day he was dead." Like the Esso man, Jolene hated it when people made comments like that. She felt like saying that Vittorio had seemed fine to her, too, when they'd set off in the boat together, and when they were singing together, and when they were fishing together. He'd seemed perfectly fine all along. Until he was dead.

"At least Luisa's got her boys," the oldster continued in a voice loud enough for Jolene to hear over the running tap, despite the fact that his back was to her. "The young one came back from America just in time. I don't expect he'll stick around long though."

"Sure he will! Filippo's got all kinds of plans to fix this place up," Esso said, waving a pudgy hand through the air like a magic wand that could make the rickety chairs and scarred tables dance right out the door and off to the dump.

The old man shook his head, still staring straight ahead. "That boy's going places," he said. "Other places. Mark my word."

"But he's getting married," the pudgy guy said, lowering his voice slightly as he glanced at Jolene, up to her elbows in a soapy stack of cups.

"Speak up, for Jove's sake!" the old man cried, plunging a pinky into each of his ears and wiggling them around for several seconds. "Ah, that's better," he said, sniffing the wax trophies on the tips of his fingers before wiping them on his pants. "Now what did you say?"

"I said, Filippo's getting married!"

"I know that! Why are you shouting?"

The chubby man rolled his eyes, sighed, and drained his glass.

"I also know he's marrying a foreigner!" the old guy declared. "What was wrong with Gigi's granddaughter, Marina? Or Stevin's niece, Carolina? They're not good enough for him? No, no, if Filippo really wanted to live here, he'd marry a local girl. You'll see, that American will pester him into leaving as soon as they lay their hands on Vitturin's inheritance."

Each sentence uttered by the despicable man painted Jolene's face a deeper shade of pink. Who was this prophet, anyway, and on what information was he basing his foolish predictions? She'd been refraining from comment because she'd been trained to never let on that she heard what customers were saying to one another, let alone butt in, but he was making her furious. The fact that the man was elderly was no excuse for his unacceptable rudeness.

"Excuse me, sir?" she said, her voice terse as she addressed the back of his head, but the old geezer didn't even turn around! Pointing at the man's ear, the Esso guy extended his index finger and thumb like a pistol, rotating his wrist in the Italian gesture that meant many things, including "it doesn't work."

Well, so what? Being hard of hearing didn't give a person the right to badmouth people. Jolene wiped her hands on a dish towel, then tapped the old man on the shoulder. The man jumped, as if she'd been crouching in the dark, waiting for the right opportunity to pounce on him.

"Who's there?" he called out.

"I'm Jolene," she cried. "You know, that gold-digging American Filippo is going to marry?"

"Is someone talking?" the man said, cocking his head.

"That's not very nice of you!"Jolene said. "I don't see why you should say those things about me when you don't even know me. You don't even have the courage to look at me!"

The Esso guy took the old man by an elbow and turned him to face Jolene, but he stared right past her, as if she wasn't there. The nerve!

"You can't just act like I'm invisible when I'm standing right here!" she cried.

The Esso guy pointed at the man's eyes and made the "it doesn't work" gesture again.

"Oh!" Jolene gasped. "I didn't—"

"There you are, *Cara* Jo!" Filippo called as he breezed into the Locanda, trailed by Windy. "I've been looking all over for you!"

"I'm…um…just cleaning up here," she said, feeling as humiliated as if she'd been caught skimming cash from the till.

"Robertin!" Filippo called out in a loud, cheery voice. Setting his ever-present briefcase on the floor between his feet, he grabbed the old man by the shoulders. "It's Filippo!" he shouted into his left ear. "Good to see you still get out! Good for you!"

"Filippo!" the old man cried, turning his face to Filippo's. "We were just talking about you. Tell me this. Are you planning on staying or leaving after you marry that American girl?"

Filippo laughed in a way Jolene had never heard him laugh before. What did you call that exaggerated sort of chuckle, anyway? A chortle? Yes, that was it; Filippo chortled. He'd obviously been caught off guard by the question, and so had Windy, whose face was ashen. Although Filippo had certainly broken the news to her as delicately as possible, it still couldn't be easy for the girl to keep being reminded of it.

"My only thought right now is for Babbo, and of course Mamma," Filippo said, ably changing the subject and switching to a grave tone of voice, indicating that this was no time for frivolous chitchat about weddings or speculations about the future. "Will we see you at the funeral later?"

"Of course I'll be there to pay my respects to Vitturin. Pace all'anima sua."

The chubby man placed his empty glass on the bar, sliding it toward Jolene. He bowed his head when he made the sign of the cross, but his eyes were on Jolene, making certain she'd received his message. She poured him another half glass of wine, which he downed in a single gulp before taking the old man by the elbow and handing him his cane. "Andiamo, Robertin. Your lunch will be ready soon," he said.

As Jolene watched them toddle out the door, one man's gait dictated by girth and grape, the other's by age and infirmity, she doubted whether the old man had heard a word of what she'd said, or even realized who she was. Turning her attention to Filippo, she noticed him saying something to Windy. Nodding, the girl rolled up her sleeves, revealing a leaflike tattoo on her right forearm. While Windy made the rounds collecting dirty glasses, Filippo disappeared into the vacant dining room. Forgetting about the glasses piling up on the bar for a moment, Jolene took a clean one from the rack and poured herself two fingers of house bianco, downing it before she attacked another stack of dirty cups.

***

At last everyone went home for lunch and the Locanda fell silent. All the dishes were washed and dried and stacked, all the surfaces wiped down, the Cimbali machine cleaned, and the refrigerator restocked with mineral water, wine, and soft drinks. Windy, busy mopping the floor, looked up as Jolene walked toward her. It seemed as though she wanted to say something, but hesitated. Jolene continued on to the dining room.

"Phew! At least we're ready for the next round now," she said, collapsing into a chair across from Filippo.

Raising his eyes from the papers he was reviewing and dividing into stacks, Filippo rewarded her with the tight-lipped half-smile of one who does not wish to be impolite, but also does not want to be disturbed.

"I'm going to take a shower and change!" Windy called from the bar.

"Ciao, *Splendore!* Thanks!" Filippo called out. "Thanks for all your work, too, Jo," he added after the door slammed.

Jolene sighed, wondering exactly how many more "*Splendore*s" there were in his life besides herself, Luisa, Monica, and now Windy.

"I did what needed doing," she said. "I was surprised when I came in and saw that no one was running the place."

"I didn't mean to jump ship like that, but I absolutely had to dash up to the house and get these papers," he said, waving a sheaf in the air as proof. "And then I got held up by Wendy. She was feeling very sad and wanted to help out somehow, so I let her tag along. I hope you don't mind."

Jolene wanted to tell him that there were others things she minded more, like the fact that she'd come to Manarola at all, but didn't know how to phrase it without sounding more jealous than she actually was. "How did she find out about Vittorio so fast?" she asked.

"Well, I had to stop by the apartment while I was in Milan," Filippo said, lowering his gaze. "I needed to pick up the minutes of the last homeowners meeting, which of course I missed, and I had to talk to a neighbor about the new caretaker everyone is complaining about. I don't know whether it's because she's a woman, or because she's Ecuadorian, but everyone is all up in arms about her."

"Oh. I see," Jolene said, her irritation rising. "I was under the impression that you spent all morning running around taking care of important business at all those offices you're always talking about. And of course waving around my passport at the American consulate."

"I got an early start, as you know," Filippo said. "I went to the apartment after the Consulate."

"You saw Windy after we spoke? At her apartment?" she cried, her left eye twitching at the thought of Filippo hanging up on her, then rushing into Windy's arms after receiving the devastating news. While she was being harassed by the carabinieri, the two of them were crying and grieving together.

"Actually, it's my apartment," he said.

"That's not the point!" she replied.

"I didn't ask her to come, Jo. I didn't want her to. But she was genuinely fond of Babbo. And he was fond of her. What could I say?"

"You could have said that you didn't think it was appropriate, and that it might make me feel uncomfortable," Jolene said, but as soon as the words were out of her mouth, she realized how petty they sounded. The girl obviously cared about Vittorio. Who was she to deny her the right to attend his funeral? But still, he could have handled it better.

"Did you take the train down together?" she asked, not quite ready to let it go.

"I obviously wanted to catch the first train down, so I told her to sit tight until I knew when the funeral would be. That would have given me time to clear it with you in person."

"Yes, it would have been nice to have a little advance notice," she said, relieved that the thought had at least crossed his mind.

"She was so distraught, though, I didn't have the heart to leave her there all alone in that state. You saw how she was still crying when we got here."

Jolene nodded, battling an attack of resentment over the fact that while she was languishing all alone at the carabinieri headquarters in La Spezia, desperately trying to contact him, he was seated on a train, consoling, and being consoled by, his ex-girlfriend.

"Wendy has no family here," Filippo added, looking at Jolene with his brown saucer eyes. "You can't imagine what it's like for such a young woman to be so far away from home."

"Really, Filippo?" she cried. "Who am I? Where am I?"

"But you're older, *Splendore*," he said. "And you have me."

"Where did she sleep, anyway?" she asked.

Filippo looked back down at the table, all businesslike as he straightened his piles of papers, making her feel like she'd botched an interview with a prospective employer. She half-expected him to say, "We'll get back to you." Instead, he said, "Oh, we gave her one of the empty rooms in town. One of the ones that we couldn't even rent out this year because it's in such bad shape. You saw them. You know what I mean."

"Yes," she said.

"I can already envision what those rooms will look like after the renovations," he said. "Wait until you see the drawings Monica's working on now!"

"That's what I've been doing, Filippo," she said, her voice flat. "Waiting." Now that she was finally alone with him, she felt uncomfortable about the entire conversation; it all seemed so stilted and inappropriate, so devoid of emotion, on the day of his father's funeral, so off track and far removed from what they were both going through. "What are those papers? Do you really need to go over them now?"

"*Cara* Jo, please try to understand," he said, looking up at her. "I need to sort things out so I can present Mamma and Lorenzo with my plans as soon as this thing is over."

"Your plans? What happened to our plans, Filippo? But look, let's not get into that now!" she cried, struggling to stay focused on the main issue. "Do you realize that 'this thing' you're referring to is your own father's funeral? You need to stop and take some time to think about him. You need to mourn him. You need to process your grief."

"Look who's talking! You still haven't processed yours!" he shot back, his forehead as furrowed as a farmer's field. "If you weren't so obsessed with finding yourself a replacement father, you wouldn't have stolen mine! And now he's gone! For good!"

Jolene stared at him in disbelief. Filippo had never spoken to her in such a spiteful way. He'd expressed nothing but enthusiasm for how well she fit in with his family, but now he sounded jealous of her relationship with his father, the same way he'd sounded jealous of Lorenzo. But what hurt even more was hearing him finally admit that he blamed her for Vittorio's death. It didn't matter that the doctors said he would have died anyway; it didn't matter that Luisa and Lorenzo insisted that she was not at fault. In her heart, Jolene knew that she, and only she, had ushered Vittorio down the express lane to his Creator. And so did Filippo, and so did that old man, despite being blind and deaf. Tears sprang to her eyes. She wanted to tell Filippo that he was right, yet she wanted to defend herself. She wanted to run away, yet she wanted to sit right there in that straight-backed chair and let him punish her.

"I'm so sorry, Filippo!" she blurted, burying her face in her hands. Filippo rose so suddenly and with such force that his chair toppled over. "Jolene!" he cried, placing his hands on her shoulders. "Please don't!"

"No! You're right!" she sobbed. "It's all my fault!"

"Jolene, please! Look at me!"

Peeking up at him through her fingers, so tall and puffed-up as he loomed over her, Jolene was frightened that he'd leave her and frightened that he wouldn't.

"I'm sorry," he sighed. "I didn't mean for it to come out that way."

Jolene believed that he didn't want it to come out that way, but she also knew that if it did, there was a reason; that the voice of raw emotions rang truest.

Dropping to one knee, Filippo looked her in the eye. "Please understand. I'm under an enormous amount of stress. I needed Babbo to live just a little longer. Now everything is so much more complicated."

"What do you mean, Filippo? What's more complicated? How?"

"Not now, *Splendore*," he said, taking her hands in his. "You're right. This is not the time." He covered her hands with little kisses, starting with the backs, continuing down the fingers, then turning them over and kissing the palms. She hated that they were so rough and raw and blistered.

"Filippo, be honest with me," she said through her tears. "If you don't think you can forgive me for what happened, maybe we should reconsider everything. Maybe you'd be better off if—"

"Maybe you'd be better off if you just took this," he said, taking the heirloom ring from his pocket, and sliding it on her finger. "And this." He took her face in his hands and held it still, as he slowly moved closer, inch by inch, until his lips brushed against hers. Then he kissed her, the way he'd kissed her that day in the vineyards, when the grapes were ripe and the sun was shining, and she was bursting with the vitality of a teenager and joy at having finally found her place in a family. Now there was one person less in that family, and whether or not she bore any responsibility for the loss, she made a vow, right then and there, to do everything in her power to honor Vittorio's memory by making sure the rest of them remained united.

TWENTY-EIGHT

By mid-afternoon, the damp gusts and oppressive gloom had been chased away by the terse tramontana, just as Lorenzo had predicted on their way back from their early morning coffee. She liked learning the new word, and the way tramontana rolled off her tongue when she pronounced it. She also liked the fact that it was easy to remember because its name derived from its source, from "amid the mountains" to the north. But most of all, she liked the way it enlivened the air, disintegrating the depressing strata of gray and scrubbing the autumn sky to a brilliant azure.

It seemed suitable that the village's farewell to the head of the Garaventi family, whose very name suggested "competing winds" should be accompanied by a wind that was strong, that invigorated, that purified. And though such a splendid afternoon might have seemed squandered on a funeral, Jolene sensed that Vittorio would prefer to see his kin and cronies breathing in lungfuls of fresh air while soaking up the bright afternoon sunshine rather than crouching in misery under black umbrellas like the extras in virtually every film with a funeral scene. After her talks with Lorenzo and Filippo, Jolene felt as though she'd been relieved of a burden, and her spirits had lifted with the scattering clouds, encouraging her to believe that, given time, she might come to view her arrival in Manarola and her role in Vittorio's death as part of some master plan. Life for all those affected by the loss would change, but in which ways and to what extent she could not know. To start with, the Garaventis would have to make some decisions after losing the head of their family, meaning that Filippo's projects must be discussed more openly, eliminating the need for all his cloak-and-dagger dealings and allowing Jolene to take on a more active role in planning their future and that of the Locanda. Once he settled down, Filippo would certainly go back to being the attentive, romantic man she'd fallen in love with in Ithaca, the man whose professions of lasting love and loyalty had convinced her to follow him back to Italy. But first, it was time to mourn Vittorio, Babbo, Pa, Vitturin.

***

The chunky heels of Jolene's black boots clopped on the cobbles as she headed to the main road, where the extended family of Manarolans was to convene. Despite Filippo's complaint that black was depressing (hence gifts like the fluffy pink sweater), Jolene always felt her best in black. Black hid bulges and didn't show dirt; black made it a cinch to match trousers and tops, sweaters and skirts. Black made her feel protected by a shield of anonymity. Today, it also simplified the problem of what to wear to the funeral after the hours she'd put in at the Locanda had left her with precious little time to get ready, and absolutely no time to clean her room as planned. Clad in black slacks, black blouse, and black jacket, for once Jolene did not feel like the conspicuous foreigner as she joined the mourners gathered in clusters to await the hearse. Special permission had been granted for the vehicle to drive down the road so that family and friends could form a procession and accompany it the short distance back around the bend and up the hill to the church of San Lorenzo.

Walking toward Luisa, Jolene was saddened to see her petite frame burdened by the weight of widow's weeds. The black clothes seemed too shapeless and out of place, diminishing her in an unnatural way. Or maybe it was the fact that she'd only seen Luisa twice in the outside world: once on the day of Jolene's arrival by car with her returning son, and once on the day of Jolene's arrival by boat with her dead husband. Within the walls of her Locanda, Luisa seemed a larger woman, perhaps because her physical stature was boosted both at the bar, where she served her customers from a raised platform, and at the restaurant, where she presided over patrons who remained seated. But mostly, Jolene reflected, it was her role as proprietor that elevated to her a special standing within her realm. She looked uncomfortable in her new role as widow but stood up straight and held her head high as she gave Jolene a warm embrace, hugging her so tight and for so long that no onlooker could doubt her affection. That single gesture, in Jolene's misty eyes, made her the grandest woman in all of Italy.

After brushing her cheeks against the papery skin of Zia Matilda and Zia Marta, Jolene turned to greet Lorenzo, who kept his elbows close to his body as they hugged, possibly because he was unaccustomed to the restraint of the sports jacket Jolene noticed him wearing for the first time. She would have liked to gather him close in her arms to show her sincere affection and sympathy, and she would have liked to linger a moment longer with her nose in the hollow of his neck, where she detected the exotic scent of the patchouli she'd spotted in his bathroom the day before.

"Where's Filippo?" Monica asked, materializing next to them, smartly dressed for the funeral. Blushing, Jolene pulled back from Lorenzo, her left eye twitching as she greeted her with a close-lipped smile.

"He's already up at the church," Lorenzo said, clearing his throat. "He wanted to walk up alone."

"Alone?" Jolene asked, hoping her displeasure was not too evident. She was no expert on Italian funerals, but she assumed it would have been customary for Lorenzo and Filippo, together with Monica and her, to escort their widowed mother to the church as a family. If Filippo felt uncomfortable leading the procession of mourners, he should have talked to her about it, and they could have gone up to the church together.

"You know how he is," Monica said. "But of course if I were you, I'd feel—"

"I'm worried that I don't see Giobatta, either," Jolene said, unwilling to expose thoughts best kept private. "What did the doctor say?"

"He ordered him to spend a few days in the hospital," Lorenzo said, shaking his head. "Bronchitis at his age can be dangerous. The last thing we want is for it to progress to pneumonia."

"Pneumonia?" Jolene cried. She couldn't bear it if Giobatta's condition were to deteriorate. "I feel awful! He shouldn't have been out in the rain searching for us!"

"It's not your fault, Jolene," Lorenzo said. "He was with me. I tried to send him home, but he wouldn't listen. Besides, he's been suffering from chronic bronchitis for years."

"The men in this place are so damn stubborn," Monica said. "They refuse to take care of themselves. And then they die. Surprise, surprise."

Lorenzo glared at his wife. Jolene looked at the ground.

"Well, it's true!" Monica said, using her thumb and index finger to disentangle a stray hair from her thicket of eyelashes. Her nails were painted black, in that gel that seemed to be so popular lately.

"While we're taking attendance, where's Chiara?" Lorenzo asked, looking down at his wife's legs as if the child might be hiding in the folds of her mother's skirts, while completely overlooking the fact that the makers of Monica's skirts tended to skimp on the fabric. The stretchy black sheath she wore today was no exception.

"I left her with my parents in Monterosso, since they won't be coming," Monica said. "My father spent the whole weekend stringing nets from olive trees and now he's laid up with his back again. The men in Monterosso are just as hard-headed as the Manarolans."

"Your father is in Monterosso?" Jolene found herself asking, instead of minding her own business.

Monica stared at her. "Yeah, why?" Monica said. "You got something against Monterosso?"

"No, of course not, it's just that…well…never mind," Jolene said, realizing that this was neither the time nor the place to tell Monica she thought her father was dead and buried in the cemetery, where she'd found Chiara and Lorenzo visiting him.

"And?" Lorenzo asked his wife.

"And I didn't think it was appropriate for her to come," Monica said.

"You know how I feel about that, Monica," Lorenzo said. He didn't need to raise his voice for Jolene to detect the tension in it. "Chiara loved her Nonno. She needs to go through the process of saying goodbye."

"Really? By being exposed to all those moaning old people? By getting suffocated by their hugs?" Monica huffed. Fishing a pack of cigarettes from her bag, she shook one out and lit up. Jolene stepped aside to give the couple some privacy, focusing her attention on the crowd, trying to see how many faces she recognized, how many names she could remember. Anything that would prevent her from butting in again.

"It's healthy for children to learn about life—and death—-where and when it occurs," Lorenzo said. "They have to know it's natural."

"I'm sorry, Dr. Freud, but my daughter is only four years old. It is not healthy or natural for her to be exposed to death at that age. She's too sensitive. I'm her mother. I should know."

"Well, what you should know and what you think you know aren't always the same thing, are they?"

Monica looked away, too, as if to distance herself from the discussion, her gaze coming to rest on the slowly approaching hearse. She tossed her head back and exhaled, leaving the tramontana to dispose of her smoke.

"Phew! Thank God I made it in time!" Windy puffed, joining the three of them. She looked like a child coming in from the playground, her dewy face flushed a rosy pink, her eyes bright, her nose runny. Her bulky black sweater ballooned over leggings which disappeared into a pair of black suede booties, the flat-heeled soft-soled type a fairy might wear on a frolic. "I was waiting up at the church with Filippo, but he told me everyone would be here. I never seem to get things right," she added, rolling her eyes as if she'd exasperated herself once more.

Jolene nodded; she knew the feeling well, just like she knew the feeling of exclusion that assailed her every time Filippo and Windy were someplace she was not. But this was not the time for petty jealousies, she told herself, watching the massive black Mercedes maneuver into position for the procession up the hill. Wondering who'd sent the impressive wreath of chrysanthemums and carnations adorning the rear door of the hearse, she strained to read the writing on the ribbon hanging from the purple bow pinned to the arrangement. On one ribbon, handwritten in gold marker, were the words "*Al Mio Caro Babbo*" and on the other, "*Tuo Figlio Filippo*."

"To My Dear Daddy, Your Son Filippo," Monica pronounced the dedication aloud as Jolene read. "How positively sweet of him." Sucking a final drag from her cigarette, she tossed the butt to the side of the road and ground it out with the toe of her two-tone pump. Jolene wasn't certain whether Monica was simply being her usual ironic self or criticizing Filippo, but if it was the latter she was justified. Whatever would prompt Filippo to order flowers on his own, and not include at least Lorenzo's name?

"Pa didn't like cut flowers," Lorenzo said. "Once when I was about ten years old, he scolded me for picking a wild tiger lily for Mamma. He said flowers deserved to die on the ground they grew up on, not rot away in a stranger's vase. He hated the idea of rot."

"My mother felt the same way," Jolene said. "My father always sent her red roses after they fought. The fiercer the fight, the bigger the bouquet, but the flowers only made her cry more." If she'd been alone with Lorenzo, she might have explained that if her mother wasn't able to chuck the bouquet straight into the garbage, it was more out of respect for the flowers than for the man who'd given them to her, and that as soon as the first petals began to wilt her mother burned the whole bunch in the fireplace. Lorenzo would have understood.

Looking around at the dozens of people gathered to pay their respects, it saddened Jolene to think that both of her parents, neither of whom had siblings, had become alienated from so many of their old friends by the time they died that she didn't even know the names of the few people who had attended their funerals. They were strangers who had no regrets to express or anecdotes to share with her, offering only the word "condolences" as they shook her hand. In her father's case, morbid curiosity over his suicide had drawn a decent crowd, size-wise anyway. Her mother, on the other hand, had attracted about as much interest as one of those withered roses. One that Jolene could have never allowed to rot in the ground.

The atmosphere was quite different here among this Italian crowd arranging itself in choreographed movements like the cast of a long-running tragic opera. As she stepped into place behind the hearse, Luisa kissed her fingers then touched the back window through which the gleaming casket was visible. Zia Marta and Zia Matilde, equipped with canes for the occasion, hobbled to stand at Luisa's left. When Lorenzo stepped forward to take his mother's right arm, Monica fell in place behind him, and when Windy went to stand next to Monica, Jolene lined up next to the two of them. As the hearse inched forward, the rest of the mourners followed, the women locking arms, the men lacing their hands behind their backs or shoving them into their pockets. The church bell tolled slowly, resonating low and mournful as the villagers trudged up the hill, coming to a stop in the middle of the square. The driver, a skinny man in a baggy black suit, and his red-faced assistant grunted as they slid the casket onto a gurney. As they wheeled it into the church, hands fluttered to make the sign of the cross. There were no pallbearers.

Luisa and the aunties, followed by Lorenzo and Monica, then Windy and Jolene, filed into the church behind the casket, the pack of townsfolk at their heels. Filippo waited at the front of the church, his brow furrowed, his jaw clenched. He allowed himself the distraction of nodding to Jolene before turning his undivided attention to the positioning of the casket in front of the altar. Once he was satisfied with its placement, he hurried to usher the aunties and Luisa into the front row, where he took his place to the right of his mother, filling the short pew to capacity. When Lorenzo sidled into the pew behind them, Jolene stepped aside with the intention of allowing Monica to sit next to her husband, but when she turned around, she found that Monica was gone. Spotting her at the rear of the church, her face bathed in an otherworldly glow, Jolene concluded that unless she was being visited by the Holy Spirit, she'd stopped to read or answer a text message. Turning again to take her seat, Jolene found that Windy had slipped past her in the meantime and was already standing next to Lorenzo, clutching his arm while brushing a tear from her cheek. Feeling her charity toward the girl ebb to an all-time low, Jolene prayed for the music to begin in the hope it would inspire more spiritual thoughts, but the church's three organs remained silent. One person coughed; another sneezed. Filippo whispered something to the red-faced assistant, who returned a moment later with the wreath of flowers, placing it at the foot of the casket on a stand, the purple ribbons with their gold inscriptions hanging in plain view.

As the service commenced, Filippo, impeccable in one of his somber hotel manager suits, stood in front of Jolene with his back to her, Windy and Lorenzo. Standing just behind Luisa, Jolene was momentarily distracted by the woman's hair, in particular, by the visible regrowth of her roots. Jolene wished she'd offered to touch them up for the occasion; not that she was privy to that level of intimacy yet, and not that one's appearance was a priority at a time like this, but just the same, it would have been a small way for Jolene to help, the way a daughter would help, and no woman liked looking haggard when everyone's eyes were on her.

As Don Ludovico began performing the funeral rite, Jolene was touched to observe how attentive Filippo was when attending to his mother, sustaining her by the elbow when it was time to sit or stand, patting her arm, holding her hand, offering her a hanky. At one point, Jolene reached out and placed her hand on Filippo's back, a gesture meant to remind him of her presence and support, but his attempt to grasp her hand fell short, and he ended up patting himself on the back.

Jolene did her best to participate when the congregation mumbled its responses at Don Ludovico's prompting, but she knew none of the special prayers. While the senseless combinations of words swam around her, she said a prayer of her own as she stared at the casket, unable to fathom Vittorio lying inside it dressed in a suit she'd never seen, one he might feasibly have worn to his son's wedding. The only way she could picture him now was in the turtleneck sweater and coveralls he'd worn on the boat; chatting and smoking, baiting his line and laughing as he pulled squid upon squirming squid into the boat; refusing to breathe; dying.

Then Don Ludovico circled the casket, reciting a funeral blessing in Latin as he swung the thurible from its chain while wisps of incense snaked through the air. Jolene's stomach churned, nausea rising in a sudden, unstoppable wave, greater than all the waves she'd fought to bring Vittorio back home. The surge pushed her out of the pew, down the aisle, out the door, and across the square. Gripping the railing where tourists often gathered to watch the sunset, Jolene doubled over, vomiting into the void below. The retching had stopped by the time she felt a hand on her shoulder, but she was still too queasy to raise her head. Looking at the ground behind her feet, she expected to see the polished black leather of Filippo's Oxfords, but saw in their place a pair of well-oiled boots.

"Are you all right?" Lorenzo asked.

"I guess. Just a little overwhelmed," she said, glancing up at him, her voice thin, her mouth foul. "I'm already feeling better out here in the fresh air. You can go back inside."

"I think I'll stay here a minute too, if you don't mind. I was starting to suffocate myself." he said, raising his nose to the sky and taking a deep breath. "Ah, that's good."

"It's the *tramontana*," Jolene said.

"You remembered."

"Of course," she said, letting the fresh breeze fill her lungs as she gazed down at the village below. The days were growing shorter, and the sun was already dropping to the horizon, its orange glow glinting off the scraps of metal and glass and plastic strewn over the hill across from them.

"Filippo told me that a junk collector makes all those angels and shepherds and animals over there," Jolene said, wondering why she should talk about something so irrelevant to the current moment, before realizing that its irrelevance was precisely what made her want to talk about it.

"Is that all he told you about him?" Lorenzo asked.

"Well, he also told me that the guy is a little off his rocker."

"Why? Because he turns garbage into art?"

"Filippo says all those plastic tanks and broken bottles and scraps of metal are an eyesore. That they make Manarola look like a dump."

"And what does Jolene say?"

"Once in a while I wander up there to take a closer look. It's the most creative recycling project I've ever seen. All those figures standing around waiting for Christmas remind me of a theater cast waiting for the curtain to go up."

"For the record, Andreoli is not off his rocker," Lorenzo said. "He came up with the idea of building the nativity scene out of garbage a few decades ago in honor of his father."

"But there must be over a hundred of them," Jolene said. "How long did it take him?"

"He didn't build them all at once," Lorenzo said. "He adds new figures every year, and by the time he's done setting up, there'll be something like three hundred of them up there on Tre Croci. Opening night is a sight to behold, believe me. One minute it's dark, and everyone's holding their breath, and the next minute the whole hillside is lit up by thousands of light bulbs, and everyone's clapping and cheering.

"Thousands of light bulbs? Really?"

"Really. Something like seventeen thousand."

"Wow! Doesn't that cause a blackout?"

"Nope. The guy Filippo calls a crazy junk collector has set up a system to power the bulbs with solar energy."

"He sounds like a genius," Jolene said.

"He's just a regular guy who used to work for the railways. But he had a dream. And passion. And persistence. Without which, a dream stays just that."

Jolene glanced at him, but Lorenzo was staring off into the

distance; not at the hill, but at a place far beyond it. After a moment, he turned to look at her. "And now people come from all over Italy to see it," he said. "It's just, well, magical."

"I hope I get to see it," Jolene said, trying to imagine the entire hill lit up.

"Sure you will. They flip the switches on December 8th, the Feast of the Immaculate Conception. It's a huge event here, with fireworks and everything."

Jolene did want to see it, but that was still weeks away, and things seemed to change so quickly lately. A gust of tramontana whipped her hair into her face, blinding her.

"We'd better go back inside now," she said, shivering as she gathered her hair in her hand.

TWENTY-NINE

"How did you get here so fast?" Filippo called from the shadows of the dining room when Luisa entered the Locanda, followed by Jolene. Jumping up from the table he'd been crouched over, he hurried to greet his mother.

"Why, I walked!" Luisa said, her stature climbing to its habitual height the moment she entered her domain. She waved away her son's elbow but allowed him to catch her wrap as she shrugged it from her shoulders. "The church is only a stone's throw from here, and I'm not decrepit yet."

The door hadn't yet clicked shut when it opened again, admitting Lorenzo, Monica, and Windy, who slammed it tight, shutting out the gusting tramontana.

"But what about the cemetery?" Filippo asked his mother. "You can't have walked all the way up there and back already." He eyed the others as if he suspected them of cheating, or taking a secret shortcut they had never revealed to him.

"In fact, we didn't go to the cemetery," Luisa answered. "Honestly, though, Filippo, you could have made an effort to stay a few minutes longer. I know these things are difficult for you, but everyone wanted to offer their condolences to you. To you, of all people. You *were* his son, after all."

"I left because I assumed you were going straight to the cemetery. You know I never set foot in the cemetery." Filippo said, backing away from the others, who stood in a compact group in front of the bar. His eyes darted from frozen face to frozen face, as if trying to determine which might be the most likely to melt; only Jolene's softened around the edges before she dropped her gaze to the floor, noticing the gleaming tiles. Windy had done a thorough job mopping up after the crowd, she couldn't begrudge her that.

"*Va bene, va bene!*" Filippo cried, throwing up his hands in surrender. "I'm sorry, Ma. I apologize to all of you, all right? It's just that I can't handle all those weepy old people wanting to hug me and kiss me. I need to do this my way. In private."

"Then you'll be glad to know it'll just be us here this evening," Luisa said. "I told everyone that we'll be fine on our own and that tomorrow we'll open at our regular time."

"Thank God!" Filippo sighed, but it wasn't clear whether he was more relieved that they would have some time alone as a family, or that business would resume as usual so swiftly. Saying nothing more, he turned on his heels and headed back to the dining room, as if he'd already wasted too much time and must get back to whatever he'd been doing. He had only taken a few steps when he stopped in his tracks, pivoting to face the others again. "So where is he, then?"

"What do you mean?" Luisa asked. "Where is who?"

"Who do you think I mean? Babbo! My father!" Filippo cried. "Where is he?"

"He's in here, Filippo," Luisa said, pressing her open hand against her heart. "He's everywhere. But he's not in the body he left behind."

"*Aargh!* That's not what I mean and you know it!" Filippo was shouting now. "If you didn't take him to the cemetery, where the hell is he?"

At least he was finally venting some emotion, Jolene thought. Anger was good, although it disturbed her to see it directed at Luisa, whose words touched her. She would like to talk to her about her comment, but first she must try to get Filippo away from here before he further alienated himself from everyone. If only she could speak to him on his own, she might be able to provide some insight about grieving for a parent, having gone through it twice herself. Inspired by her idea, she hurried to his side and took his arm, but her affectionate squeeze was met with a flexed muscle, telling her to leave him alone. Fearing he would embarrass both of them by physically shaking her off, she let go, returning to stand by the others.

"They took him back to La Spezia," Lorenzo said, speaking up for the first time.

"Oh, that makes a lot of sense!" Filippo said. "I thought the idea was to get everything over with, to avoid carting him back and forth."

"It's not a question of getting anything over with, as you so elegantly put it, fratello," Lorenzo said. Though his voice was calm, he looked angrier than Jolene had ever seen him. "And there will be no more driving back and forth. La Spezia's the last stop. That's where he'll be cremated."

"Cremated?" Filippo cried. "Who the hell decided that? And why have I not heard about this before?"

"I just found out today," Lorenzo said. "You would have, too, if you hadn't cut yourself off from everyone else."

Filippo began pacing in circles around the group, panting like a rabid sheepdog penning his herd in by the bar. And that was where they stayed, standing so close together that their shoulders touched: Luisa, her eyes fluttering and her lips moving silently, as if she were lost in prayer; Lorenzo, his nostrils flaring and his eyes flashing, as if he were preparing for a face-off; and Monica, her foot tapping out her boredom; and Windy, her baby blues eyes flitting from face to face, in search of a safe place to alight; and Jolene, feeling as foreign as the dusty bottles of imported spirits she spotted on the top shelf, wishing she could pour herself a shot of liquid loyalty.

"I *detest* the idea of cremation," Filippo cried, his tone escalating from angry to anguished. "It's *awful!*"

Glancing at Lorenzo, Jolene wasn't surprised to find him already looking at her. He knew that she knew that this would be the perfect time to tell Filippo that there was nothing to be horrified about, that her own mother had been cremated. Instead, it was the moment when she realized that under no circumstances would she reveal to him that her mother's ashes were an unregistered guest of Suite 16.

"But you also hate the idea of cemeteries," Lorenzo said. "You just said you never set your foot inside them. So what does it matter to you?"

"What matters, is that my father would never have wanted that!"

"Yes, he would have," Lorenzo said.

"Since when do you know all about what he wanted or didn't want? What makes you such an expert?" Filippo cried.

"Your father wrote a letter," Luisa spoke out, stirring from her trance.

"He did? He wrote the letter?" Filippo said, his eyes widening, then squinting, scrutinizing his mother's face.

"*The* letter?" Lorenzo asked. "You knew about it?"

"Well, no, not all the details," Filippo said, throwing back his shoulders. "But there were a few matters that we discussed recently. He said he'd put them down in writing. It was *his* idea, really."

"And while you were talking things over, he didn't even mention his request to be cremated?" Lorenzo said.

"Well, we didn't really get into that," Filippo said, stroking his beard, straightening his tie.

"What did you get into, then?" Lorenzo asked.

"Other things. Properties and such. Projects," Filippo said, tracing lines in the air with his hand, as though he were sketching out a vision shared by himself and his father, but invisible to others. "In consideration of future plans. You know." He paused briefly, glancing at Monica, then Jolene, possibly encouraging them to speak up, possibly warning them not to. "So, where is it?"

"I have the letter," Luisa said. "And I think we can wait at least until tomorrow to discuss the rest of its contents. Enough said for now. You people do what you want. You can stay, or you can go. As for me, I'm having a glass of wine."

"I'm staying, of course," Lorenzo said, checking the time on his watch. "But first, I'm going to pick up Chiara."

"Why can't you just leave her where she is?" Monica said. "She's fine with my parents."

"That might be fine for you, and for your parents, and for everyone else. But I want my daughter with me tonight." Lorenzo hugged his mother, glared at Filippo, waved at the three younger women, and walked out the door.

Filippo stormed off into the dining room, returning a moment later with a sheaf of papers under his arm. "I'll be up at the house," he said. "I need a little time on my own." With that, he kissed his mother, he kissed Windy, he kissed Jolene, and he kissed Monica. All on the cheek, all with the same mixture of tolerance, affection, and a touch of what Jolene hoped was apology. The four women sighed, each experiencing her personal version of relief or exasperation or combination of both.

"You sit down, Luisa, I'll get the wine," Windy said, skipping off to the bar in her silent suede booties. "All of you ladies, please, sit down."

Luisa lowered herself into a chair and closed her eyes, placing her hands in her lap. Breathing in slowly through her nose, she made a humming sound, similar to a bumblebee, each time she exhaled through slightly parted lips. Not wanting to disturb whatever she was doing, Jolene eased herself into the chair across from her, where she sat in silence.

"I need a smoke," Monica muttered, her two-tone pumps practically pushing her out the door.

After a few moments, Luisa's eyes fluttered open. She looked more relaxed, but profoundly tired.

"You must be exhausted," Jolene said to her.

"I find dealing with life more exhausting than dealing with death," Luisa said. "The men in this family make it complicated."

Jolene wasn't quite sure what to say, or how to interpret the comment. She wondered whether Luisa really favored Lorenzo, as Filippo claimed. Or was it Filippo who made an effort to be less likable, just to prove himself right?

"I think all men are complicated," she said. "I've never had much luck making sense out of them." That was a good reply, she thought, if pathetically generic. At least it supported Luisa's statement, without sounding disloyal to Filippo.

"It's not so much that they're complicated," Luisa said. "Most of them are rather basic creatures, and their behavior is motivated by rather basic instincts. Life would be so much simpler if they were less selfish, less ambitious, less worried about always being in control. The one thing I appreciated most about Vittorio was his simplicity. I always knew where he stood. He was stable, and I knew I could rely on him. When we met, that was what I needed most."

Stability and reliability. These were the very same qualities that Jolene had appreciated in Filippo when they'd met. If his romanticism had attracted her, his steadfastness had convinced her that he was material for a serious relationship. If he said he would call on Saturday, he called on Saturday, not Sunday. If he said he would pick her up from work at four, he picked her up at four, not four-thirty, not even four fifteen. Whenever they saw each other his good humor could be relied upon to lift her spirits, while his determination motivated her to set new goals for her future. Had he changed since then, and since there, or had she? Or were they and their good intentions simply casualties of all the other circumstances that had changed in the space of a few short weeks? Time would tell, her mother used to say. Wait and see.

"The ring looks pretty on your finger, Jolene," Luisa said. "Unlike me, you have nice long fingers."

"Oh!" Jolene said, caught off guard by the compliment. She looked down at her scratched hands and inflamed finger; at the traces of squid ink still trapped beneath her nails despite her efforts to scrub them away with her toothbrush. "Thank you, but I'm afraid they're not at their best right now."

After studying her hands for another moment, Luisa looked up at her. "Do you play the piano?" she asked.

"A little. I can read music, and I took lessons at school, but we didn't have a piano at home. We moved around too much. The only thing I play now is my mother's recorder. It travels well."

"There's that baby grand up at the house you could play. I always wished someone in the family would."

"Didn't Vittorio play?" Jolene asked.

"Vittorio?" Luisa laughed, shaking her head. "You must be joking—with those stubby fish fingers of his?"

"I'm sorry, I thought Lorenzo mentioned that he played. I must have misunderstood."

"Oh, Lorenzo has always loved listening to piano music. As a baby, his bright little eyes would roll around in his head like a doll's when the piano was played, as if he were in ecstasy. After a bit, his little eyelids would get so heavy with sleep, but he would struggle to stay awake longer, to listen more." A faraway look crept into Luisa's eyes as she spoke, crossing her arms over her breast and rocking back and forth, as if she were still cradling that infant. When she laid her hands down on the table again, Jolene placed hers over them and gave them a gentle squeeze.

"That piano is the one possession I kept from my mother-in-law's old family home," Luisa said. "Filippo always complains that it just sits there collecting dust and hogging up half the room. He keeps insisting that I get rid of it, but just so you know, I've already told him that it's out of the question."

"Oh, of course!" Jolene couldn't imagine ever wanting to get rid of a piano, or how anyone could move one out of a place like this, even if they wanted to.

"The living room would look empty without it anyway, don't you think?" Luisa asked.

"Um…certainly…a piano adds so much to a house," Jolene stammered. "Generally speaking." Luisa didn't seem to be aware that she'd never been inside the Garaventi home, and how could she be? She spent every waking hour at the Locanda, mealtimes included. But Filippo had invented so many excuses for not bringing her over that Jolene had come to suspect that it was Luisa who didn't want her there.

"Well, you're more than welcome to play it whenever you're at the house," Luisa said.

"Thanks, but I'm not very good."

"You can't be much worse than Windy," she said, lowering her voice. "Last night she kept playing that dreadful "Für Elise" over and over again until she gave me a migraine. I finally had to beg her to stop. The beauty of that girl is that she never takes things personally."

Jolene tried to swallow, but her throat was too dry. She'd never even been to the house, yet Windy was there last night, pounding the hell out of the family piano? She'd probably spent the night there, too, while Jolene was tossing and turning and crying alone in her room. It would be easy enough to get Luisa to confirm her hunch, but she didn't want to ask, didn't need to ask. If she was right, Filippo hadn't hidden the truth from her this time; this time he'd lied right to her face.

"There's a retired music teacher from Milan who has a place here," Luisa continued. "We can ask her about lessons. I'll even have it tuned for you."

Jolene managed a nod and a smile, though she'd hardly heard the words moving Luisa's lips. She might have been talking to her from inside a fish tank.

"I hope I picked the right kind!" Windy chirped, bearing a stainless steel tray on which four glasses skated around a bottle, heedless of the peril. As she drew near, the combination of innocence in her open smile, gracefulness in her impish movements and freshness in her rosewater scent reminded Jolene of a spring breeze. As irritated as she was by the girl's presence, she still found it hard to dislike her.

After wrestling a few rounds with the corkscrew, Windy let out a cheer, declaring victory over the bottle. After pouring out three glasses, her smile suddenly gave way to a look of bewilderment, as if she had no idea how the cork crumbs bobbing to the surface of the pale gold liquid had gotten there. "Oh!" she exclaimed, but she was no longer looking at the wine. Her attention had been captured by the gem glittering on Jolene's hand.

"You're wearing that ring!" she gasped, falling into the vacant chair between the two women.

"Well, yes," Jolene said. "I am." Though she didn't want to hide the ring, she was neither the type nor in the mood to show it off. If anything, she felt a twinge of guilt that it was on her finger instead of Windy's. The girl shook her head vigorously, her blonde spikes stabbing the air as if to defend her from an onslaught of negative thoughts, then she placed her hands over Jolene's, which were still on top of Luisa's, and released a long, deep sigh.

"But hey!" she said after a pause, looking from one woman to the other. "How weird is that?"

Jolene was about to ask what she meant when Monica burst through the door. "It's damn cold out there now!" she said, dropping her phone on the table and huffing into her balled fists. She pulled out a chair and sat, the stink cloud of her recently smoked cigarette overpowering Windy's rosebud scent. "Oh good, wine!" she said, sliding a full glass in front of herself, then dipping a finger in to fish out bits of cork with her black nail. "I always enjoy a drop or two with my cork."

When no one laughed at her remark or acknowledged her presence in any way, Monica glanced around the table, noticing that the other women were too preoccupied with the pileup of hands on the table to pay her any attention. "Did I interrupt a séance or something?" she said.

"Of course not," Windy said, withdrawing her hands to pour a fourth glass of wine. "It's too early to contact Vittorio. He's still in transit. We were looking at the ring."

"The ring?" Monica said, leaning in to take a look. "Oh. That ring." Pushing her chair back from the table, she crossed her legs and hugged herself, tucking her hands under her armpits. "I told you to keep that thing away from me."

"For the last time, Monica," Luisa said. "You can't keep blaming what happened on a ring."

"Whatever you say," Monica muttered, rolling her eyes.

"Jolene, my wish is that this ring will bring you the happiness it brought to me," Luisa said, raising her glass.

"Thank you, I'll drink to happiness," Jolene said, searching the other women's faces for clues as to what she was missing, frustrated at not knowing what everyone else, including Windy, already knew. "And to you, Luisa, and to Vittorio, who brought such happiness to you." After clinking glasses with a shiny-eyed Luisa, an enigmatic Windy, and a reluctant Monica, Jolene took a long sip of wine. Bits of cork stuck to her tongue like her unasked questions; she picked them off in silence. Luisa looked down at the table, Windy up at the ceiling, Monica at her cell phone. The women sipped their wine, each lost in her own thoughts.

"Now!" Luisa said, springing to her feet so suddenly that Jolene nearly fell off her chair. "I feel inspired to cook us something to eat. And I would like to be left alone in Vittorio's kitchen while I do that. The rest of you can enjoy some girl time. I'll give you a shout if I need anything. Agreed?"

Jolene knew it would be pointless to object, and so did the others, who nodded as Luisa walked away, flicking on lights as she went, her crepe soles squishing, the kitchen doors creaking as they swung behind her. The room fell silent. Jolene fidgeted. She'd never been good at cultivating girl talk, girlfriends, or girlish behavior, and didn't feel like chitchatting with either Monica or Windy, least of all about herself. The best way to avoid that, she knew, was to be the one asking the questions. Most people jumped at the chance to talk about themselves; all you had to do was get them started.

"So, what are you doing with Luisa's ring?" Windy blurted before Jolene could open her mouth. "I don't get it."

Jolene's face grew warm. She took a sip of wine, cleared her throat. "It was given to me," she said.

"Luisa gave you that ring?" Windy said. "But you hardly know her."

"But I do know Filippo," Jolene said. "Luisa gave it to him, and he gave it to me. That about sums it up." The last thing she wanted to do was make a big deal out of the ring, or hurt the girl's feelings any more than they already were.

"Filippo?" Windy exclaimed. "*My* Filippo?"

"He's the only Filippo I know," Jolene said, determined to not lose her cool, though Windy was not making things any easier. She glanced at Monica on the off-chance she might be willing to provide some backup, but her future sister-in-law just leaned back in her chair, her dark eyes twinkling over the rim of her glass as she drank.

"But when did he give it to you?" Windy asked. "You weren't wearing it at dinner yesterday. I would have noticed."

Then it dawned on Jolene. With the excuse of not wanting her to damage the ring while she worked in the kitchen, Filippo had taken it from her, but what he really didn't want was for Windy to see it. He'd only given it back to her today as a peace offering, to placate her fears, to silence her doubts, and she'd fallen for it. And now he'd run off again, leaving her to deal with the fallout of his strategy.

"He gave it to me recently," she said. "But we've been engaged for a few months now."

"*Engaged?*" Windy asked, her long lashes batting. "You and Filippo are *engaged?*"

Jolene opened her mouth to answer but clamped it shut before it could get ahead of her and say more than she wanted it to. She glanced again at Monica, who stared back at her with raised eyebrows and a half-smile on her lips, then back at Windy. How could she not know about the engagement? The only possible answer was that Filippo hadn't told her. Was he that cowardly? That cruel? How could he stick Jolene with the job of breaking the news? She was furious with Filippo for putting her in this position, but she'd deal with him later. Her immediate concern was for poor, brokenhearted Windy.

"Look, I know how hard breakups can be, Windy," she said. "Believe me. I've been through it more than once. But if you're honest with yourself, you'll realize it's been over between you two for quite a while now, hasn't it? You really should try to accept it. You're young. You'll move on."

Throwing her head back, Windy burst out laughing, her tongue wiggling with amusement. "I would love to move on," she cried. "If he'd only let me!"

"What do you mean by that?" Jolene asked, her pulse quickening the way it did when she walked through the woods alone and heard a twig snap.

"What I mean, Jolene, is that Filippo is the one who won't accept the idea of breaking up," Windy said.

"Ha! This is getting good!" Monica cackled, replenishing everyone's wine.

Jolene blinked, dumbfounded. "That's not what Filippo told me. He told me you were hanging on, that you had no family and nowhere to go."

"I was hanging on, but only because he begged me not to go. He made me promise to wait in Milan while he was in America taking that course. He said that when he got back we could decide where we wanted to go live. Together. London, Paris—even Australia or back to New Zealand, if I wanted to."

"But that's crazy!" Jolene cried, nearly choking on her disbelief. "He couldn't have been serious!"

"That's exactly what I said! I said, 'You can't be serious!' Just like that. And that's when he gave me the ring."

"He gave you a ring? When?" Jolene asked, trying to ignore Monica's tittering.

"It was at the beginning of June, just before he left," Windy said. "And it was that ring." She pointed at the heirloom, quickly, withdrawing her finger rapidly, as if it might bite her. "But I wouldn't take it. First of all, I'm *totally* against diamonds. Millions of Africans have *died* mining diamonds! *Children* die mining diamonds! Wars are *financed* by blood diamonds!"

This whole story was growing more absurd by the minute. It was obvious that Windy was more than a little unbalanced, anyone could see that. Could jealousy be making her mind play tricks on her? Was this a last-ditch effort to hang onto Filippo, now that she realized she couldn't have him? Jolene had the urge to take the ring off and fling it at Windy, but with all those sacrificed lives and heinous crimes buried in each glinting facet, the stone seemed to weigh a million carats; she couldn't even lift her hand off the table.

"And so then he said, 'Fine, be like that.'" Windy continued, abandoning the woes of Africa and the horrors of the diamond trade. "And that was when he said he'd give the ring back to his mother for safekeeping. But he made me swear I'd stay on until he got back from America, when we'd talk about it some more."

Jolene's stomach churned, polluting her mouth with the sour taste of acid, but she must try to think straight, to reason through this. After Filippo had left Windy and Milan behind to go to America, things had changed in ways he couldn't have foreseen. The two of them had met, fallen in love, made plans. Now he was making Jolene do his dirty work by bringing Windy up to speed on the engagement, but what if there was more to it? What if he still couldn't let Windy go? Jolene needed someone to tell her how things stood, and if it meant looking like a fool, so be it.

"Filippo's back now. And you must have talked by now," Jolene said. "Why are you still here, Windy?"

"I know, right? I kept up my end of the deal, right? I waited, right? But whenever I bring up the subject of leaving he tells me I'd never be able to support myself with my English lessons. *Stay*, he says. He doesn't want any rent or money for the bills, he says. Of course I feel funny accepting that, right? But he says I might as well because it's a pity to leave the place sitting empty. He says I'm actually doing him a *favor* by keeping an eye on it. I was all ready to move out, I swear, but he's talked me out of it so many times in the past, he made me lazy. It's almost like he's *dependent* on my dependency, you know? And now I feel *stuck*, like I can't do anything on my own, you know? I wasn't like this before I met him."

Jolene shuddered. She knew the feeling. Was Filippo planning on holding her hostage in Manarola the way he was holding Windy hostage in Milan?

"Didn't you think it was strange that Filippo wanted you to stay, once he told you he'd met me?" Jolene asked.

Windy gave her a blank stare, pausing before she answered. "But he never mentioned you, Jolene. Not until yesterday, when we were on the train."

Jolene's head was reeling. Reaching for her glass, she took a gulp of wine, set the glass down, then picked it up again and drank some more. Monica held out the bottle, offering a refill; Jolene nodded.

"Yesterday, huh?" Jolene said, the balls of her feet anchoring her legs to the floor as they bounced up and down. "And what did he tell you yesterday?"

Draining her glass, Windy nodded at Monica, who obliged by pouring. "Not much," she said. "Just your name, you know, and that you were here."

"And that was it?"

"More or less," Windy said, shrugging.

"What else did he say, Windy?"

"I don't think the exact words matter, do they?"

"To me they do," Jolene said.

Windy inhaled, her breath catching on a sigh as she let it out.

"Okay, just remember, Filippo's a great guy, once you figure him out," she began. "But if you really wanna know, he told me he met this waitress who worked near where he was taking that course in New York. He said this woman was having a rough time after her parents died and her boyfriend dumped her and her business went belly-up. This lady—for some reason, I don't know if it was something Filippo said or what, but I pictured her a little older, maybe fiftyish?—wanted to come to Italy until she could pull herself together, so he offered her—I mean you, I guess—free room and board in exchange for helping out at the Locanda. It was all unofficial, he said, with no work permit or anything. Just a temporary arrangement. So, he told me, in case I was wondering, that was who the American lady I might run into at the Locanda was."

Jolene blinked several times, as if the up and down movement of her eyelids could wipe away Windy's words.

Monica snorted, but the hand she hid behind could not contain her mirth. "I'm sorry!" she roared. "This is just *too much*!"

"That's not nice!" Windy said. "You're hurting Jolene's feelings!"

"*Moi?*" Monica said, placing a hand on her décolletage. "You're the one dumping all this crap on her lap! I haven't said a goddamn word!"

"It's just the truth!" Windy cried. "I can't help it! What do you want me to do, lie?"

Jolene was shocked, as much at herself as at Filippo. Was she such an incompetent judge of character that she'd allowed him to dupe her? Or was she being gullible now, falling for Windy's cockamamie stories? If what she said was true, Filippo would never risk leaving them alone together, knowing his house of cards would come tumbling down at their first unsupervised conversation. Unless he had done it on purpose. Unless he was a master manipulator so lost in his own labyrinth of lies that he needed someone else to forge a path to reality. Jolene felt sick and disgusted and angry, but to her surprise, she didn't cry.

Windy reached out and placed a hand on Jolene's shoulder. Her touch was warm. "Don't worry, Jolene," she said. "I'll get out of the way now. The ring's all yours. Filippo's all yours."

Jolene looked at Windy. Her blue eyes were bright with empathy, her fair skin pink with emotion. She looked at Monica, her dark eyes flashing with expectation, her glistening lips thirsty for more juicy revelations. Jolene looked down at her finger, at the ring she'd never expected, never really wanted.

"All mine?" she said.

"Wine? Who asked for wine?" Monica giggled, divvying up the rest of the bottle.

Jolene brought the glass to her lips, but didn't drink. "No. I don't want to be like my father," she mumbled.

"Why?" Monica asked. "What's your father like?"

"Dead." Jolene said, setting the glass down with a thud.

"Geez! Why is that happening to everybody?" Windy said.

"In his case, because he was an alcoholic," Jolene said. "Among other unpleasant things."

"Well, then, I suppose we can take a break from the wine. Until dinner, anyway," Monica said, stretching an arm across the table to push aside the empty bottle and glasses like a croupier sweeping chips off a gaming table. After clearing the space she plopped her bulky leather satchel on the table. "But that doesn't mean our little party has to be over. Not when we still have so much to talk about." Rummaging around in her bag, she fished out a red cosmetic pouch.

Jolene shook her head, unable to conceal her dismay. No matter how deeply people disappointed her, they could always sink to an even lower level, couldn't they? Did Monica realize that Jolene's future had been demolished in the time it took to polish off a bottle of wine, while she just sat there giggling? Was she so insensitive and vain that she could worry about touching up her makeup now, while Jolene was dying inside?

"Ta-dah!" Monica cried, waving her hands in the air for the others to see. In one she held a sandwich-size version of the Ziploc bag which had caused Jolene so much trouble the previous day, and in the other, a packet of rolling papers. Before Jolene could realize what she was doing, she'd spread a chubby chunk of marijuana down the center of a paper, rolled it up, and sealed the joint with a quick flick of her bright pink tongue.

"But *Monica!*" Jolene whispered. "What if Luisa comes out?"

Shrugging, Monica lit up, sending pungent swirls of smoke in the air.

"We should at least open a window!" Jolene said, hopping to her feet. By the time she managed to separate the old casement from its frame, the joint had changed hands a few times. It was Windy's that held it out to Jolene when she sat back down.

"And now for the weather forecast!" Windy giggled. "A high Windy is expected in the Cinque Terre tonight! I'm free to fly at last!"

Oh, brother. Just what she needed, Jolene thought, staring at the joint, trying to decide whether to take a hit. She'd never been a fan of pot, really. She liked the taste of wine better, and also appreciated the fact that it came in a bottle with the name of the producer and the alcohol content right on the label. Who could trust pot?

"Trust." Jolene whispered the word, letting it sit on her tongue to see how it felt. "Trust," she repeated aloud, to hear how it sounded. It struck her as a pathetically outdated concept now, a remnant from a distant past, a game she used to play with a man she loved.

"What?" Windy said, sneaking in another hit while waiting for Jolene to make up her mind.

"Nothing," Jolene mumbled, accepting the joint and taking a toke before handing it over to Monica. By the time it came around to Jolene again, she remembered that another thing she didn't like about pot was that it seemed to have no effect on her— until it hammered her.

"So, what do you think?" Monica asked.

"I think that of all the things I imagined doing in Manarola, smoking pot with my fiancé's girlfriend and my fiancé's brother's wife in my fiancés's mother's restaurant wasn't one of them," Jolene said, snatching the joint from Monica's fingers before she could pass it to Windy. "Or killing my fiancé's father, for that matter," she added, inhaling and holding in the smoke for as long as she could. Gagging on the exhale, she grabbed her glass and downed the remaining wine, then banged the empty glass on the table. "Ha! Fiancé—that's another stupid word, isn't it? *Fi-an-cé, fi-an-cé, fi-an-cé*," she chanted, over and over, until she heard a noise, that creaky noise that came from the kitchen doors when they swung on their hinges. She fell silent, sitting bolt upright in her chair. "*Shhh!*" she whispered, the squishing of the crepe soles growing louder, closer. "Luisa's coming!" she cried. "We're gonna get caught! Let's hide!" Elbows on the table, Jolene propped her head in her hands, covered her face with her fingers and waited, remaining perfectly still and silent.

"I'll tell you ladies one thing, it smells way better out here than in there," Luisa said. That is, Jolene must have imagined Luisa saying. Peeking through her fingers, she watched Luisa sit down in her chair.

Her eyes were red and teary. "Just look at what those onions did to me!" she moaned. "Just as I was recovering!"

"Screw the onions," Windy tittered, waving the joint under Luisa's nose. "Try some of this." The girl had to be crazy, now she was sure of it.

"That's the best idea I've heard in a while," Luisa said, accepting the joint from Windy. If Jolene's hearing was shot, her vision must be playing tricks on her, too. Sliding her hands from her face, she gawked at Luisa as she took a deep drag, holding her breath for several seconds before tilting her head back and exhaling slowly through her nostrils. "My, what big eyes you have!" Luisa said, squinting against the sting of the smoke as she returned Jolene's stare.

"I'm sorry!" Jolene cried, embarrassed for looking so shocked. "I just never imagined, well, you know, that—"

"That an old Italian lady like me would smoke pot?" Luisa asked, raising just one eyebrow, the same way Lorenzo did, and Filippo sometimes did, too.

"You're not *old*." Jolene said, regretting the emphasis, knowing it made it sound like she meant "not *that* old."

"Well, I'm not in the habit of smoking pot, in case you're worried about what our dear Filippo would say if he found out," Luisa said, her expression indicating that she couldn't care less what Filippo would say. "Not nowadays, anyway. But I was young once too, you know. And I didn't always lead a sheltered life here in Manarola, either."

Jolene was confused; Filippo had told her, or at least she thought he'd told her, that Luisa had never budged from her hometown of Manarola.

"I was a high school student during the clashes of '68," Luisa continued. "We young people had our ideals and we stood up for them back them. We had our marches and our sit-ins and our voices. We made ourselves heard." Pausing, she looked around the table. "I was a little like each one of you girls. A little naive. A little daring. A little brazen. I had plans for my life. I was going to change the world. Then the world changed me."

Jolene accepted the joint again and took a toke, knowing that if she wasn't already a little high she would have felt way too self-conscious to smoke in front of Luisa, no matter how cool her attitude. Everything seemed so surreal, but she couldn't tell how much her constantly changing perceptions were influenced by the pot, and how much by the shifting of perspectives and uncovering of lies and rearranging of facts. She felt untethered, disoriented. She needed to find her bearings, figure out who these people really were, and whether she had a place among them. If she was sober enough to formulate a few questions, she was high enough to ask them.

"You said the world changed you," Jolene began. "Did getting married have anything to do with it?"

Luisa looked Jolene in the eye. "No, marriage had nothing to do with it," she said, shaking her head slowly, deliberately. "When I got pregnant with Lorenzo, his father and I were incredibly excited. This was our big chance to raise a kid the way we wished we'd been raised, by free-spirited, open-minded parents who were crazy in love with each other. We went to America when he was just a baby. We hitchhiked across the country. Sometimes we camped out under the stars, and sometimes we crashed in communes."

"I adore the story about that commune near San Francisco!" Windy said. "With all those leftover summer-of-love flower children. And you leading yoga practice in exchange for a meal! I thought Filippo was making it up when he told me!"

"*Wait*—you've heard about this before?" Jolene asked, flashing her eyes at Windy first, then Monica.

Both women giggled, but it was Monica who spoke. "Didn't you ever wonder why Lorenzo is so flaky?"

"You did all those things with a little baby?" Jolene asked Luisa. All three women nodded at her, as if it was the most natural thing in the world to imagine Luisa a hippy, and Vittorio, a car-hater who would not venture as far as Genoa, bumming rides across the United States of America.

"Once we were out on the west coast, we wanted to continue on to Hawaii to visit Lorenzo's only living grandparent, but we couldn't come up with the cash for a plane ticket, so we headed north. I'd always wanted to go to Alaska."

"Wait— a grandparent in Hawaii? And Alaska? You went to *Alaska*?" Jolene asked.

Luisa closed her eyes, inhaling and exhaling through her nose a few times before opening them again. They looked different now; more gray than blue; more Alaska than Hawaii. "No. We never made it."

"Why not? What happened?" Jolene asked, her throat burning, making her thirsty as hell. She wished Windy would go grab another bottle of wine.

"We were driving up the Pacific Coast Highway," Luisa continued, her gaze distant. "I'll never forget that inebriating sense of unlimited freedom and infinite horizons. We had this amazing, vast country to our east, and the immense Pacific Ocean to our west. I was young and in love with my man and our baby. We were in Oregon when a fellow headed to Portland offered us a ride in a VW bug. There wasn't much space, but we traveled light. I was curled up in the back seat with little Lorenzo in my arms. I'd just nursed him to sleep and was feeling the bliss big-time. Breastfeeding does that, you know?" She paused, looking at the women surrounding her. Monica grimaced; Windy beamed; Jolene shrugged, feeling a stab of regret that no, she didn't know.

"Anyway, the men were sitting in the front seat talking about Tricky Dick and LBJ and JFK and who was to blame for what. Colin, that was the driver's name, had served in the Marines and been shipped out to Vietnam in '65. He wouldn't get into details about what he saw or did over there, but you could tell it messed him up in a bad way."

"My father served in Vietnam, too," Jolene said. "He was a helicopter pilot." Her father refused to talk about his military experience, too. It didn't take a genius to link it to his drinking.

"How about passing me that joint again, please?" Luisa said, pausing to take another hit before continuing her story. "Anyway, we were driving along, nice and slow, because Colin freaked out when things moved too fast. We were approaching Cape Foulweather— how could you ever forget a name like that? One minute we were chilling out, just taking in the mind-blowing view, and the next minute a rusty old pickup came speeding straight at us from a side road, hit the front end of the car and slammed it into a tree. I saw it coming, but too late. The guy had fallen asleep at the wheel after a six-pack too many. He didn't even see the stop sign. Or us."

"Oh my God! How *horrible!*" Jolene cried. "It's a miracle you're alive to tell the story!"

"Yes, it is," Luisa said. A lone tear appeared at the corner of her right eye, swelling until it was so full of sadness that it could no longer hang on, and rolled down her cheek. "Lorenzo and I are still here. Thank God."

Luisa passed the joint to Jolene, but Jolene shook her head. Girl talk was far more educational than she'd ever imagined, but this pot smoking was turning out to be a real bummer.

THIRTY

The thing Jolene loved most about professional kitchens were the utensils: the oversize ladles and spatulas and spoons; the lineup of knives with their blades of various lengths and cutting edges; the battery of capacious pots and pans. Using both hands wrapped in a dish towel, she gripped the handle of the heavy-gauge aluminum skillet on the flame and tossed the al dente penne into the air with quick upward thrusts, circling back down to catch the pasta as it landed in the olive oil sauté of onions, garlic, porcini mushrooms, rapi, cauliflower, and other bits and pieces of autumn vegetables she'd found in the refrigerator.

If Windy's hurricane of revelations had left Jolene reeling, Luisa's poignant love story and tragic travelogue had stretched her mercifully altered mind beyond its limits of receptivity. Overwhelmed, she'd taken refuge in the kitchen, where nothing or no one could mess with her head, hoping that busy hands would clear the path to a lucid brain. Besides, she was starving and Luisa, who had resumed sitting with her eyes closed and her hands in her lap, seemed to have lost all interest in returning to Vittorio's haunt after her disastrous road trip down memory lane. As for the others, Windy had managed to uncork another bottle of wine without causing too much damage, while Monica rolled out another perfect joint. No one seemed to mind, assuming they'd even noticed, when Jolene left them sitting there without uttering a word about where she was going, or why.

Jolene wasn't fond of elaborate recipes. Measuring out exact quantities, manipulating cumbersome appliances, and forcing basic ingredients into complicated relationships with too many partners made her jittery. On the contrary, creating an appetizing dish based on what was available while following her instincts for the harmonious combinations of flavors and consistencies always gave her a sense of fulfillment. Cooking should be kept simple and natural, like love, she thought, drizzling a bit more olive oil over the pasta before tasting it. Finding it a bit bland, she added some crushed red *peperoncino*, worrying only in passing whether everyone would like it hot, then topped it all off with a flurry of grated Parmesan. Grabbing the skillet, she kicked open the swinging doors and headed to the bar area.

"It's ready!" she called as she approached the women. Though her mind was still reeling, preparing the food had calmed her down a bit, and all Jolene wanted now was to savor it with the others. She found the ladies slouched in their chairs, riding out a lull in their bizarre conversation, but their hooded eyes lit up when she set down the steaming skillet of pasta in the middle of the table.

"Oh, what the hell," Monica sighed, leaning forward as Jolene passed out the forks she'd grabbed along the way. "A bite or two won't kill me." She took one last toke from her joint, then wet the tips of her thumb and forefinger to snuff it out. Stabbing the pasta straight from the skillet, she brought a forkful to her puckered lips with the avidity of a woman who hadn't eaten in days.

"Hold on a sec, let me get some dishes!" Jolene said, but Windy latched onto her sleeve before she could walk away.

"Please sit down!" she begged. "We don't need to measure out *portions* onto individual plates. We don't need to *own* the food before we eat it. Let's *share* it from the common pan." Having made her point, Windy took a stab at the penne and vegetables. "Look at these *colors!*" she cooed, holding a loaded fork in front of her face and staring at the food with such intensity that Jolene feared she might stick it into her eye instead of her mouth. "This is so *beautiful,* Jolene! Thank you for this awesome creation! No wonder Filippo fell in love with you!" After safely delivering her food to the proper place, Windy began chewing, groaning with pleasure, her eyelids fluttering, her blonde spikes bobbing.

"Right on, sisters! Let's share!" Luisa said, suddenly alert and fisting the fork like a child, stabbing and chewing, stabbing and chewing, cramming five forkfuls of pasta into her mouth before stopping to speak again. "God, this is just what I was craving, Jolene. I was so damn sick of fish!"

Meanwhile, Monica's giggles filled the air, joyfully unencumbered by her usual cynical sneer as she stuffed forkful upon forkful of food into her mouth like a relapsed pasta addict.

"Hey, look who's eating carbs!" Luisa laughed, pointing her fork at her ravenous daughter-in-law, while Windy howled, nearly choking on her food.

"It went up my nose!" Windy sputtered. "I snorted and it went up my nose!"

Looking down at the women hunched over the skillet, Jolene felt as though she were floating over them, observing them from a different dimension. She liked the sensation of detachment, but at the same time, she wanted to be one of them, to partake of the food and laughter together with them. Sitting down in her chair, she grabbed a fork and was about to dig in when a blast of cold air chilled her spine, making her turn toward the door.

"*What the hell is going on here?*" Filippo demanded, loping toward them.

"Dinner!" Windy cried, bursting into laughter again as she chewed. Though she had sufficient manners to cover her mouth, her hand arrived an instant too late to prevent multicolored fragments of food from flying in Filippo's face.

"It doesn't smell like dinner to me!" Filippo said, his features distorted with disgust as he snatched a napkin from the table and brushed off his bristles. "It smells like *dope!*"

"I made vegetarian penne," Jolene said, amazed at how uncannily calm she felt. "Would you like some?" Her offer was automatic, and instantly regretted. Not because there wasn't enough, but because it was *their* pasta, and *their* table, and *their* conversation, and Filippo had no business being there.

"Sure, maybe I'll just dig in with my hands! Better yet, I'll stick my face right in the slop like a pig!" Filippo looked astonishingly tall as he towered over the table, much taller than Jolene remembered him. And his forehead! Oh, if only he could see the accusations written across that hypocritical brow!

"You'll do no such thing, young man!" Luisa chuckled, looking about as stern as a rubber duck in a tub.

Filippo did not appear to embrace their mellow mood, however, as he whipped out an envelope from his breast pocket, his cheeks aflame. Jolene couldn't help giggling when she fancied the fire spreading to his whiskers, the image so vivid in her mind that she could smell the singed hairs.

"You want to know what I *will* do though?" Filippo cried, waving the envelope in the air. "I'll tell you what I'll do. For starters, I'll rip this up, that's what!"

Since the day they met, Jolene had always perceived a certain current of electricity in the air whenever Filippo was near. He was like a live wire whose very presence caused that odd tingling of the skin, that instant acceleration of the heartbeat, that unmistakable fibrillation that comes with being in love. But this was different. Now the entire room crackled with tension as he loomed over them like a high voltage power tower. Good God, can't someone unplug him? Defuse him? Neutralize him? she was thinking, when another rush of cold air made her shiver.

"Hey, hey, what's going on here?" Lorenzo said, coming through the door to find the four women being held hostage by Filippo's fiery glare. He spoke in a calm voice, like a specially trained agent dispatched to negotiate with a psychopath.

"We were trying to relax a little until this lunatic came along!" Monica said, stuffing another forkful of pasta into her mouth before looking up at Lorenzo. "Hey, where's Chiara?" she asked, or at least that was what it sounded like through the chewing.

"I changed my mind," Lorenzo said. "After I got some fresh air, I started thinking that I was being selfish, that maybe she shouldn't be hanging out here tonight after all. It looks like I was right."

"Hey, everything's cool here. Except for Filippo," Monica said. "Anyway, listen, you gotta have some of this pasta. You like all this veggie shit and stuff."

"Could everyone just stop stuffing their faces and guzzling wine and getting high for five minutes?" Filippo yelled. Jolene wondered whether he'd inherited his father's predisposition for heart trouble because he sure looked like he was about to burst a coronary. For a second she imagined him keeling over, generously sparing her the dilemma of how to proceed in light of the latest developments. Her only choice would be to pack her bags and catch the first plane home. Wherever that was.

"We're all ears, Filippo," Lorenzo said, pouring himself a glass of wine.

"This letter that Babbo left is ridiculous!" Filippo pulled a single sheet of ruled paper out of the envelope and now waved that in the air.

"You took that from my desk without my permission!" Luisa cried, all giggles gone. "How *dare* you?"

"It says '*alla mia cara famiglia*' right on the envelope. I happen to be the *one* person who qualifies as his 'dear family!'"

"That's an *awful* thing to say, Filippo!" Jolene blurted, deeply ashamed of his behavior. Families weren't just a fact of common blood, families were supposed to share the bonds of loyalty and love. They were supposed to stand united and defend one another from the rest of the world, not attack one another from within.

"Well, that's because Babbo did an awful thing to me, *Cara* Jo," Filippo said. "He didn't keep his promise! He told me he was going to leave everything to his rightful heir. Who, as we all know, is *me*!"

"How can you say that?" Jolene asked. "What about your *mother*? And your *brother*?"

"My parents weren't even married! "She," he shouted, pointing a finger at Luisa, "wouldn't marry him!"

Luisa and Vittorio weren't married? How could that be, after living their lives together, raising a family together, and running a business together in this small Italian town together, under the vigilant eye of Don Ludovico?

"How incredibly annoying this is, Filippo. Really," Luisa said, shaking her head slowly, looking more disappointed than angry. "You young people need to learn how to think for yourselves, without the Church and the State cramming their rules down your throats, making you mold your lives according to their agenda. I don't happen to believe that a piece of paper is all that important to a relationship, and neither did your father. Honestly, sometimes it feels like we're regressing instead of progressing. But how could you understand something like that? You who are coercing Jolene to apply for a *sacra rota*, for God's sake!"

"Jolene wants to marry me in the Church!" Filippo cried. "Besides, what exactly have you contributed to progress, hiding out here in your hole-in-the-wall Locanda, sucking up to tourists, Ms. Antiestablishment?"

"What do you even know about my life, Filippo?" Luisa asked. "What do you care about me as a person?"

"What's there to know? Your life's here, it always has been and it always will be. Until the day you die."

"Filippo!" Jolene cried, springing to her feet with an uncontrollable urge to slap him in the face, not only for Luisa, but for herself, for Windy, for all of them, but Lorenzo caught her by the arm and sat her back down. She wondered how could he just stand there acting so calm, while Filippo spewed his venom.

"It's all right, Jolene," Luisa said, her voice even. "This is a good time to remind my son about a few things he may have conveniently forgotten. So, if you will oblige me, Filippo, sit down, shut up, and listen for once while I finish my story."

Filippo clenched his jaw, slapping the letter against his thigh. He didn't sit down, but he shut up.

"We came straight back to Italy after the accident," Luisa began, looking at Jolene. "I was devastated by what had happened. I had no family to fall back on, but I knew I could trust Lorenzo's father when he said Manarola was the place to raise our child. We'd been here for a short time right after Lorenzo was born, before going to America. That's when I first met Zia Marta and Zia Matilde. They were the ones who insisted on baptizing the baby Lorenzo before we left. Until then we'd been calling him Kamalani. That means 'heavenly child' in Hawaiian."

These Garaventis were hard to keep up with, but at least she'd learned about the accident already. What a horrific ordeal for a young couple to experience, especially with a little baby, in a foreign country.

"After landing in Rome we caught a northbound regionale train as far as Livorno, then a locale. When we pulled into this little two-track station, I was too paralyzed to get off, but there was a delay on the line, and I stuck my head out the window. After a few minutes of drinking in the briny air blowing in off the sea, the emotions balled up tight in my chest began to unravel, and for the first time since the accident, I felt like I could breathe again. 'Your daddy was right," I whispered, hugging my baby close to me as I gathered our belongings. "This is where we're supposed to be now."

Jolene was eager to learn more about Luisa's early days with Vittorio, and thought it would do her good to talk about them. Until now she'd been so stoic, absorbing the outpouring of everyone else's grief without releasing her own. The room fell silent while Luisa paused to drink, giving Jolene the chance to steal a glance at Filippo. Shifting his weight from one leg to the other, stroking his whiskers, rolling his eyes, tapping his foot, he looked like he couldn't wait for Luisa to finish so he could speak his piece and get out of there. The others remained immobile, their eyes focused on Luisa as they waited for her to resume her story, their expressions respectful but devoid of Jolene's fascination, as if they'd heard it all before, which they probably had.

"Your father was a fisherman who liked cooking and eating fish as much as he liked catching it," she said, looking at Filippo. "He was just starting out here, and said I could work for him in exchange for room and board. If he hadn't taken us in, your brother and I wouldn't have even had a home."

"'Your brother and I, your brother and I,'" Filippo cried, mimicking his mother's voice. "That's all you care about isn't it? The two of you. Babbo was the only one who ever gave a damn about me!"

"That's not fair and it's not true," Luisa said. "But I'm so sorry if my concern for your brother disturbed you. He was only a baby when he lost his father. You got to enjoy yours all those years growing up and well into adulthood. You should be grateful, not spiteful."

Jolene blinked dumbly, wondering how and when she could have lost the thread. Her mind, though not at its sharpest, had been struggling to keep up, and she thought she'd been doing pretty good up until now. But if she was processing what she'd heard correctly, it could only mean that: (1) Lorenzo and Filippo had two different fathers; (2) Filippo's father was Vittorio; (3) Lorenzo's father must have died in the crash! He must have been the part-Hawaiian hippy, not Vittorio. That made way more sense, Jolene thought, her mental image of Vittorio instantly reverting to its previous version while she flashed a look at Lorenzo's exotic almond eyes, thinking of all the other traits she'd noticed that made him so very different from Filippo.

"I can't believe I didn't know about any of this, Luisa!" she cried. "How could you not tell me these things, Filippo!"

"It's ancient history, Jo," Filippo said. "What does it matter to you?"

"It matters the world to me!" she replied, then turned to Luisa.

"What was his name?"

"My father's name was Lani," Lorenzo said. "It means 'heaven' in Hawaiian."

"That's beautiful. I'm so sorry for both of you," Jolene said, looking from Lorenzo to his mother, trying to remember where she'd heard that name before. "How did you meet Lani?" she asked Luisa.

"Lani came here fresh out of college to learn more about his mother's origins," Luisa said. "Ironic, isn't it, that a young woman born at home in 1920s Manarola could die giving birth in a modern American hospital?"

"Oh, so *she's* the grandmother who was born here?" Jolene asked, recalling bits and pieces of her conversations with Lorenzo the day of their hike.

"Yes. Lani's father—Lorenzo's grandfather—was an aspiring poet and translator of Italian literature. He'd studied in San Francisco, where he became a bit of an expert on Eugenio Montale. He came here as soon as the war was over to visit the place called the Cinque Terre that he'd read about in Montale's poems and interview Montale himself, who was living in Florence at the time."

"And that's how he met Lorenzo's grandmother?"

"Yes, she lived in Volastra. She was an older cousin of Zia Matilde and Zia Marta, and lived with their family after her own parents died. He was utterly enchanted with everything he saw in the Cinque Terre, especially her. They fell in love and he brought her back to America with him. Do you remember the land where you picked the grapes, Jolene?"

"Of course I do!"

"Well, she inherited that land when her parents died. It was a steep cliff covered with brambles and scrub at the time, but Zia Matilde and Zia Marta's family tended to it after she left, and planted the first vines."

"But how did you meet Lani?"

"Lani and I met in La Spezia in 1970, where I was attending a peace march. He was supposed to board a train for Rome, but we were blocking it, so he joined the demonstrators. Love at first sight must run in the family, because the same thing that happened to his parents happened to us. We were inseparable from the minute we laid eyes on each other."

"How amazing! Father and son both fell in love at first sight with an Italian woman. That's the same thing that happened to me and Filippo, only backward, when—" Jolene exclaimed, but stopped mid-sentence, swallowing the rest of her words.

"It's all about the energy," Windy said, her eyes wistful. "I could feel it in Volastra right away, just like Luisa felt it when she got off the train in Manarola. It's like this place picks the people it wants to live here, you know?"

"Come on, Wendy!" Filippo said. "Don't you start in on that metaphysical crap again, too!"

"She's right," Luisa said. "Lani knew it, too. That's why he made me promise to come here as he lay in agony. His mother was gone, but her land was still here. When Lani left his body, that land became ours, half mine and half Lorenzo's. Lani and I were married, you see. There was this group ceremony of love while we were in San Francisco, and we—"

"You call that a *marriage*?" Filippo cut in. "Some drug-induced hippie ceremony performed by a pseudo-guru on acid?"

"I'll have you know, Filippo, that if it wasn't for that hippie ceremony, which was perfectly legal in the State of California, I wouldn't have inherited half of that land. And if I hadn't inherited half of that land, I wouldn't have made the mistake of signing my part over to you when you turned eighteen! But Vittorio was so good to us that all I wanted was for you, our child, to have whatever Lorenzo had, just like Vittorio wanted Lorenzo to have whatever you had. We wanted to be fair to both of you! That land belonged to Lani's child, and you went and *sold* it!"

"That was years ago! Things change! People change!" Filippo spat, waving the paper in the air again. "You want to talk about fair? Well, this will is not my idea of fair! This will is my idea of a joke!"

"What are you talking about?" Lorenzo asked.

"This will!" Filippo said, fanning Lorenzo's face with the paper. "The last will and testament of Vittorio Garaventi! As if you didn't know!"

"Know what?" Lorenzo asked, looking perplexed.

"Pa left half of the property to Ma, when she's not even his wife. And the other half to you and me in equal shares, when you're not even his son! I'm his sole legitimate heir and all I get is a measly quarter of what he owned!"

Jolene stared at him, as stunned as if she'd been slapped by a person she'd never seen before.

"I have a good mind to contest this scrap of paper!" Filippo cried, throwing his hands up in the air as he paced back and forth, back and forth. "And I would!" he declared, stopping in his tracks, turning to look at the appalled faces of his spectators. "If I planned to stay in this shit-hole forever. But you know what? I'm not. Jolene and I have plans. Big plans. Once we're married, we're moving back to the U.S."

"We are?" Jolene cried, her eyes bulging.

"Did you really think I'd stay here forever, Jolene?" he said. "Did you really think I'd waste all my education and experience in Manarola, of all places?"

"But what about all of our plans? All of our projects?" she asked, so utterly confused that she was unable to funnel enough conviction into her voice to sound disappointed.

"Well, Pa screwed those up by dying. I was convincing him to fix up this dump enough to sell it. It would have been perfect for everyone. Pa could have spent his days fishing, Ma could have meditated herself into oblivion, and Lorenzo could have finally pissed off!"

Anger rose in Jolene like bile, poisoned by a disgust so profound that she couldn't bear to look at Filippo for fearing of vomiting. Her cheeks burned with humiliation as she searched the faces of the other women for some sign of support, some indication of what she should do or say. Luisa's eyes were closed, and she was breathing in and out of her nose again, her cupped hands resting in her lap. Windy sat with her elbows on the table, one hand still clutching her fork as she stared blankly at the penne congealing in the pan. Monica leaned back and lit up her half-smoked joint.

"You are way out of line, brother," Lorenzo said. "But hey, you can have my share, if that's what it takes to make you happy. I don't need to own this place, I just want to live here. But if you stay, you'll have to get used to having me around, because I'll never leave Manarola. I have history here. I have my roots here."

"What do mean you'll never leave Manarola?" Monica said, snapping to attention on that tight butt of hers. "We had a deal. When we got married, you said that—"

"Yes, and when we got married, you said that you'd love me and honor me, not that you'd start screwing around—or should I say *keep* screwing around?—with your old architecture professor. Is that the deal you're talking about?"

"I only married you because I was pregnant!"

"And I only married you because you were terrified of what your parents would do when they found out! The difference was, I loved you! I would have taken care of you and the baby whether we were married or not!"

"You took care of us all right! Exactly twenty-four hours after you put that cursed ring on my finger at City Hall, I lost my baby! If I had known that was going to happen, I would never have married you in the first place!"

"It was my baby, too!" Lorenzo said, his voice cracking.

"That's enough, Monica!" Luisa cried, her eyes popping open. "That ring is not cursed! Lorenzo's father gave it to me the day our beautiful baby boy was born, and that baby has grown up into a fine, healthy man!"

"Yeah, but did you notice what happened to the baby's father?" Monica spat, her words, like daggers, aimed straight at Luisa's heart.

Luisa stared at her daughter-in-law. "Any curse in your life comes from your negativity, my dear, not from the ring. I treasured it, and hoped you would do the same, precisely because it came from Lorenzo's father. The monetary value had nothing to do with it. They're not even real diamonds. And it's not even a real heirloom, at least not from our family. Lani bought it in Florence, at a stall near Ponte Vecchio, from a man who sold used trinkets."

"Oh great, you let Lorenzo give me a fake ring when we got married?" Monica asked. "No wonder it's all been such a farce!"

"I didn't know or care about the ring's value when I gave it to you," Lorenzo said. "I never even asked."

Monica turned to Luisa. "You should have kept the damn ring yourself, if it was so important to you," she said.

"Well, maybe, but it was a matter of sensitivity and respect, values you may not comprehend. Vittorio and I were friends for a long time before we became involved. I'd told him all about my great love for Lani, our travels, the accident, how I didn't think I could ever love another man again. Once we became a couple, I didn't feel right wearing the ring anymore."

"So that's how I was set up for giving a fake ring to my fiancée," Filippo said. "Thank you all very much for making me look like a fool!"

Jolene still couldn't bear to look at Filippo; she was mortified by his moral nudity, and ashamed of herself for all the times she'd looked the other way. If anyone should feel like a fool, it was her.

"One more thing, Filippo, just to refresh your memory," Luisa said. "When Monica miscarried, she gave the ring back to Lorenzo and he gave it back to me. When you found out I had it, you ranted on and on about how I always treated him better than you, and that, as my son, you had every bit as much right to an heirloom as Lorenzo. You may recall that I didn't think twice about giving it to you when you asked."

"Geez, I'm so glad I didn't want to accept that ring from Filippo when he proposed," Windy said. "This is way too complicated for me."

"Don't listen to her, Jolene," Filippo said, shooting Windy a threatening look before facing Jolene, for the first time, with eyes that conveyed some sort of unspoken apology. To whom and for what, was anyone's guess; there was such a backlog. "It's not the way it sounds."

"It is what it is, Filippo," Jolene said, holding his gaze. "Which, in my whole life, has never, ever been what I thought it would be. But *this*? This, Filippo?"

Monica snuffed out the joint and glanced at Jolene, her onyx eyes flat. Lorenzo looked at her, too, running his fingers through his curls, his lips pressed tightly together.

For all the yearnings this family roused in her, for all her burgeoning love of this tiny corner of Italy, Jolene could not say whether her need to belong was strong enough for these people and this place to want her here. But she did know where that ring belonged, and it wasn't on her finger. Without pausing to weigh the implications of her gesture, she slipped the jewel off and placed it in Luisa's hand, closing her fingers around it.

"You were lucky enough to know great love, Luisa," she said. "You should be reminded of it every single day of your life. Please wear this ring."

Luisa's eyes were bleary with memories of love and survival and grief, bloodshot with the sting of pot smoke and chopped onions and hurtful words as she looked into Jolene's. Yet they were lit with a flame that would never be extinguished, because she was a woman who loved, and who would always be loved by Manarola.

EPILOGUE

They came in droves, invading the town by train or trooping in on foot, armed with their artillery of cameras, tablets, and smartphones which, however technologically advanced, would fail to capture the full wonder of Manarola on the Feast of the Immaculate Conception. By mid-afternoon, the village was so crammed with day trippers that those wishing to stroll to Punta Bonfiglio to admire the sea or relax in the gardens, still lush with flowering succulents, date palms, and lemon trees even in December, were forced to crawl up the hill in single file. While some visitors ventured up the mountainside for a closer preview of Andreoli's fabled *presepe*, most hung around town to stake out a spot from which to admire the octogenarian's open-air installation. The day's events would culminate shortly after sunset, when the switches would be flipped and thousands of bulbs would light up the Nativity, heralding the Christmas season. Afterward, a spectacular pyrotechnic show would commemorate the event before people scrambled to catch their trains home.

Anticipation filled the air, as uncontainable as the enticing aromas of focaccia and fish, pesto and pizza, cakes and coffee wafting from the bakeries and bars and eateries roused from their November doldrums to throw open their doors—and cash registers—for the occasion. At Locanda Luisa, the last of the late lunchers had gone and Jolene was humming as she wiped down the countertops when she heard the door open. Prepared to tell whoever it was that she was closing up for the remainder of the day, she was delighted to see Luisa cross the threshold. Jolene's powers of persuasion met their match when Luisa was the object and skipping out on work the subject, but she had finally convinced her to go home and freshen up for the festivities. It made her happy to note the spring in her step and the smile on her face as she walked in, looking vibrant and youthful.

Luisa's new hairstyle, cut short and highlighted to ease the transition to gray, was the result of a trip to a tiny salon tucked away in the vicoli of Genoa's historic center where Jolene had discovered a silver-haired forty-five-year-old hailing from Feudenstadt, at the edge of Germany's Black Forest, who was a standard-bearer in the go-gray movement. Embracing one's natural look at any age empowered women, Helga sustained, with the added advantage of reducing the environmental damage caused by the rivers of dye being washed down the drain every day, an attitude shared by Luisa but which sparked criticism among her peers and a rupture in her sporadic relationship with the local hairdresser, who balked at such nonsense, predicting that Luisa would be back for the thirty-five euro color-and-set special before she could eat her Christmas panettone.

When Luisa had declared herself ready to sort through the closet she'd shared with Vittorio, Jolene had helped her, and when Vittorio's clothes were packed up and Luisa was faced with the dismal lineup of the practical skirts and plain blouses she had worn to work at the Locanda for so many years, Jolene had suggested making a clean sweep of the closet and buying a few new items to match her new look. The wide-leg trousers, turtleneck top and alpaca jacket she wore today flattered her still shapely figure, and now that she'd started practicing yoga again after a hiatus of some forty years, suppleness was being restored to her tired muscles and stiff joints. She and Jolene and Windy had even attended a hatha yoga seminar in Livorno together, on the same weekend Jolene had been slated for the pre-Cana conference in Asti, and since then they'd made it a habit of practicing together once a week. Luisa's goal was to spend more time standing on her head, and less on her feet.

"You look absolutely amazing!" Jolene commented. It still dismayed her to admit that she hadn't been able to see past the dutiful wife and mother slaving away at the Locanda to the adventurous, rebellious twenty-year-old who had been lurking there all along, waiting to make her comeback.

"Some say I'm losing my mind," Luisa said, tossing her head as she walked up to the bar. "But I'm warming up to the role of crazy lady. It gives you more freedom."

"Kind of like being a foreigner," Jolene said, smiling. "Coffee?"

"Why not have a cappuccino instead?" Luisa said, lacing her fingers as she gripped the edge of the bar, a giveaway that she was fighting the impulse to get behind the counter and make it herself. "I'd like mine with cinnamon, please."

"At this hour?" Jolene laughed, turning her attention to the Cimbali. When she set the cappuccinos down and looked at Luisa again, she saw that her gaze was distant, and that her restless hands were twirling the heirloom ring round and round on her finger. She hadn't taken the ring off since the day Jolene had given it back to her.

"You miss him, don't you?" Jolene said, sprinkling cinnamon over the foam.

"I miss both of them," Luisa sighed. "And I always will. They were two very different kinds of love. One was passionate and reckless, the other kind and comfortable. You know, every time the kitchen door swings open, I still expect to see Vittorio appear, wiping his fishy hands on his stained apron and grumbling about something." A wan smile turned up the corners of her lips as she raised her cup to drink.

"Give yourself time," Jolene said. She'd repeated the words to herself so often as she lay awake in bed, night after night, with faithful Fata by her side, that they'd become her mantra.

The kitchen doors swung on their squeaky hinges, sending a groan down the corridor. Both women started, holding their breath as the familiar footfall approached. When Lorenzo came to stand next to Jolene she noticed that even after hours in the kitchen, a faint scent of patchouli still lingered about him.

"You look fantastic, Ma!" Lorenzo said, bending over the bar to kiss his mother's cheek. "But are you sure you want to brave the crowds up at church?"

"Oh yes! Today I want to light a candle to our patron saint Lorenzo. And since Don Ludovico is always popping in to check on me when I'm working, it's my turn to go check on him. Zia Matilde and Zia Marta will be waiting for me, too. And besides, I love marching bands!"

"I'll walk you up then," Lorenzo said. "Do you want to come, Jolene? You've been stuck here all day."

"I wouldn't miss the marching band for the world!" she said. "I even have my recorder with me. I'd be tempted to play along if I knew some Italian tunes."

Leaving the quiet of the deserted Locanda behind them, the trio were caught up in the tide of tourists ascending the road to the church of San Lorenzo. A few shopkeepers greeted them along the way, but had time for no more than a wave. Jolene was happy to see that business was brisk for everyone, though she wouldn't recommend them all. By now she knew which places catered to tourists, which tended to take advantage of them, and which offered a friendly chat and affordable food for someone who wanted to get out for an hour or two. One of her favorites was the enoteca they had just passed, where she sometimes went with Windy to have a glass of wine, listen to some music, and munch on the crostini made from the exquisite bread baked up in Biassa, using the fresh spring water that ran so pure and sweet. Her stomach growled at the thought of sinking her teeth into a crispy chunk of toasted bread topped with gorgonzola and pears, or sheep cheese and figs, or tomato and mozzarella, or salted anchovies with butter, but today every crumb in town would be gobbled up by the greedy crowds.

By the time they reached the hub of activity in front of the church, where free fritters and mulled wine competed with the holy wafers being distributed inside by Don Ludovico, Jolene was so fed up with everyone elbowing her ribs and trampling her feet that she had to make a conscious effort to be tolerant of the invaders, reminding herself that she, too, was an outsider to the locals. Still, she wished she could chase away the hosts of amateur photographers poised like snipers, their expensive telephoto lenses aimed at Collina Tre Croci, their professional grade digital cameras balanced on long-legged tripods that tripped every person who passed.

"Giobatta!" Jolene called out, waving her hands above the crowd as she and Luisa and Lorenzo approached the entrance to the church. Her irritation dissolved in the flood of joy she felt at seeing him out and about again, wearing the Borsalino fedora she and Luisa had bought him in Genoa as a get-well gift. "You're looking quite dapper today!"

"Thank you kindly, *Americanina*!" he replied, touching a gnarled finger to his hat. Giobatta was a man who always held his head high, even when wearing a knit fisherman's cap, but judging by the slight tilt with which he sported the fedora, with one eye shadowed by its brim and the other free to catch the light, it seemed he'd already learned to appreciate the feel of fine felt against his scalp and the Leonard-Cohen-like dash it conferred to him.

"You can leave this young lady with me," he said to Lorenzo, taking Luisa's arm. "I'll look after her. I've already settled Matilde and Marta in their seats."

It was heartwarming to witness a friendship that dated back decades, surviving hard times and prosperity, floods and landslides, illnesses and deaths. When Luisa and Giobatta spoke to each other their words were sparse, almost unnecessary, and no cheek-kissing was required, or even desired, to confirm their longstanding affection. Jolene's smile turned wistful as she watched the pair disappear inside the church, realizing that she would have to hurry up and find a friend like that now, if she wanted one around later.

Neither she nor Lorenzo spoke as they stood under the portal observing the escalating frenzy. Members of the band milled about, the gangly boys with plumed hats checking the brass buttons of their jackets while pretending to ignore the girls in flared miniskirts tittering behind cupped hands. A pimply-faced trumpet player practiced scales, turning his back to the chubby-cheeked tuba player who sent an octave of lonely notes into the air in search of company. All the makings for gaiety were there, but Jolene never felt more alone than when she was in a crowd, preferring the Manarola of yesterday and tomorrow, when the only sounds echoing in the alleys were the rat-a-tat-tatting of jackhammers and the whirring of power saws broadcasting news of off-season renovations.

Though plans for drastic demolitions had been abandoned, some improvements were being made at the Locanda, too. Jolene filled in at the bar or restaurant whenever she was needed, and when she was at loose ends she often climbed the hundreds of stairs to Volastra to visit Windy and help out at the B&B she'd reopened, thanks to a loan from Luisa. On those days when she preferred to be alone to ponder over how she'd reached this point in her life and where she should go from here, she sometimes walked up to Punta Bonfiglio to play her recorder, sitting cross-legged in the grass by the graves where Lorenzo and Chiara had surprised her, or curling up by the water to read in the sunshine of the shortening days in a secluded spot she'd discovered between a wall of tall rocks. One day Lorenzo had turned up there, explaining that it had always been a favorite spot of his, too, and Jolene had offered to leave, but he'd said that there was plenty of solitude for both of them. They stumbled upon each other at that hideout now and then, always sitting and reading in silence. There were times when Jolene would have liked to talk to him, but not about the Locanda; she would have liked to ask him how he was coping, or ask what he thought she should do, but she didn't quite know where to begin. Maybe if they took another hike together, she thought, she would find the right words, but since Vittorio's death and the tumultuous times that had followed, she'd been wary of taking physical risks, preferring to stick close to what she'd come to think of as her home base, venturing only occasionally to Genoa with Luisa.

"How disappointed would you be if we got out of here?" she heard Lorenzo ask.

"Disappointed?" Jolene said, blinking at him, wondering why he was shouting, until she became aware of the ringing bells announcing the end of the special Mass; wondering why there were so many people around, until she saw even more spilling from the church into the square. "Um, not at all."

"Good!" Lorenzo said, taking her elbow, but the pressing throng made it impossible to walk side by side. "I'll go first to blaze the trail," he called over the din, leading her by the hand. By the time they reached the lower road, the marching band was striking the first notes of its opening number.

"But that's not Italian!" Jolene cried as they struggled against the wave of humanity seeking higher ground. "It's 'When the Saints Go Marching In!'"

Reaching the halfway point down the main road, they climbed the few steps to the square built back when the Groppo riverbed had been buried, where stalls had been set up for the sale of locally produced honey, cheese and Christmas crafts. As Jolene's eyes roamed over the wares, scores of stiff figures stared down at her from the hillside, still trapped in their flat forms of plastic and metal, anxiously awaiting their annual metamorphosis. On the road below, the conductor of the band raised his baton, parting the multitude like a Manarolan Moses to allow the safe passage of his band before launching into their rendition of "Jingle Bells."

"Dashing through the snow? *Here?*" Jolene said, trying to imagine a one-horse open sleigh careening over the steep mountain trails. The thought made her laugh, but the song made her homesick, though she couldn't say why, or for what. Not for the snow and ice of western New York; not for the home she no longer had there. "Can it really be December already?" she said. "Why am I still here?"

"Because I told you you would be," Lorenzo said.

"Yeah, well, a lot of people have told me a lot of things," she muttered, her voice too low for him to hear. "So, where's Chiara?" she asked, to shake off her melancholy.

"Windy's looking after her at home," Lorenzo said. "I didn't want her to miss this, but I was afraid she'd get trampled. They can watch from the window."

"Windy will be happier that way, too," Jolene said. "Crowds make her dizzy."

Dusk dropped from the sky suddenly, as it did in December, making the colored lights strung across the road blink to life, bumping the festive atmosphere up a notch. Spectators of all ages chattered like youngsters on Christmas morning, their eyes shiny, their excitement high.

"How long until they start?" Jolene asked.

"Here comes the *fiaccolata* now! See?" Lorenzo said, pointing to the east end of the dark hillside, where a procession of torches came into view.

"Oh!" Jolene exclaimed, instantly hypnotized by the fire-bearing shadows snaking along the dark, winding paths. Something stirred deep inside her on an instinctual level, as if she were witnessing an ancient ritual. She yearned to join those villagers on the hill, to walk with them, to carry a torch of her own, to belong to their tribe.

With no further warning, the legendary light bulbs she'd heard so much about were switched on, and the figures of the Nativity blazed with life, as if by magic, or miracle, or a bit of both. Italians and foreigners, fathers juggling children on their shoulders, couples snuggling against the chill, teenagers faking disinterest, and old folks taking it all in as if it were their last chance, all cried out and cheered. The applause had not yet died down when the fireworks began, eliciting more choruses of *oohs* and *aahs* as people stood shoulder-to-shoulder with their noses in the air, captivated by the wonder of the sky and sea and hillside flaring in the night. It irked Jolene to witness so many of those present sacrificing the vastness of the spectacle to view it through the tiny screens of the devices in their hands, determined to capture a moment in time that was unrepeatable, to replicate and distribute an experience that was unique.

"Now's the perfect time, Jolene," Lorenzo said, leaning in close to her, taking her hands in his. His nearness made her pulse race as it always did, whether they were peeling potatoes together or reading on the rocks together. It may have been the effect of the fireworks, but the look in his eyes was disarming.

"What do you mean?" she asked, flinching at the whistling of the rockets overhead. "The perfect time for what?"

"You know," Lorenzo said. "For that idea we talked about, after Pa's funeral."

"Oh," Jolene said, feeling slightly disappointed and very worried. His face flickered with the flashes of red, white and green shooting across the sky; his eyes glittered with the spangles and the sparkles bursting above as she stared into them. "But now, Lorenzo?" she asked. "In the dark? In the cold?"

"The moon is on the rise, and it won't take long. No one will notice if we go now," he said, giving her hands a squeeze. "Meet me in ten minutes?"

"I don't know if I'll be ready in ten minutes," Jolene said.

"We can make it fifteen."

"No, I mean, I don't know if I can be *ready*," Jolene said, freeing a hand and placing it on her chest. "Ready in *here*."

Lorenzo looked at her, his almond eyes soft in the brief lull that preceded the grand finale; not rushing her, or pleading with her, or pushing her. "I understand, Jolene. You decide."

"No, you're right," she said after a moment. "It is the perfect time."

Lorenzo nodded, then turned to pick his way through the spellbound crowd, while Jolene slipped off in the opposite direction. By the time she reached the harbor, Lorenzo had already pushed the small rowboat into the water and brought it alongside the jetty. He held a hand out to her, but Jolene hopped aboard without assistance, plopping down on the bench opposite him before her wobbly legs could give out on her. This was her first time aboard a boat since the day of Vittorio's death, and it made her nervous to venture out on the water in the dark. Yet at the same time, she knew this was something she had to do, sooner or later. It made sense that it should be now; that it should be here; that it should be with Lorenzo.

Neither of them spoke as Lorenzo rowed out of the harbor and along the coast, bringing them directly in front of Punta Bonfiglio, in alignment with the cemetery and Collina Tre Croci. The fireworks were over by now, but the entire hillside remained aglow with the lights of the Nativity, and the exclamations of the gratified crowd still buzzed in the distance. The sea seemed immensely dark and silent by contrast, the only light the silvery glitter of the moonbeam, the only sound the splashing of the oars dipping into the water.

"How's this?" Lorenzo asked at last.

"Fine, I guess," Jolene said, hugging herself as she looked up at the hills, then out to the sea, remembering how disoriented she'd felt when she'd first arrived in Manarola. But now she knew where north was, now she knew where the winds blew, now she knew where to take shelter.

"Do you want to go first, or do you want me to?" Lorenzo asked.

"I don't know. I don't really want to be first," she replied. She didn't really want to be last, either. She didn't really want to be there at all.

"How about if we do it together?" Lorenzo suggested.

"Good idea," Jolene said.

They both fumbled in the dark for a moment, then the rustling stopped.

"I feel like I should stand," Jolene said. "But I'm afraid I'll fall in."

"No standing while I'm captain of this ship," Lorenzo said. "We can do it sitting down. Face this way, though, or you'll be downwind."

Turning slightly, Jolene took a deep breath. "I'm ready whenever you are," she said.

When Lorenzo nodded they simultaneously raised their bags over the side of the boat and tilted them, letting their contents spill slowly into the water.

"This is where he'd want to be," Lorenzo said. "I knew Ma would agree."

"My mother would want to be here, too. She loved the freedom she felt out on the water," Jolene said. "No matter where I go, I'll always remember her here."

She considered saying a prayer, but silence seemed the highest form of respect as she and Lorenzo watched the ashes clump and bob on the surface of the water before being swallowed by the sea. Tears filled her eyes as she saw them dissolve, becoming one with the water, reconnecting her death to the great cycle of life. After a few moments, she wiped her eyes on a sleeve, reaching inside the pocket of her jacket to pull out her mother's recorder. As she began playing, the clear, pure notes drifted off in the night, bidding her mother farewell.

"That's the song you were playing the day we met in the cemetery," Lorenzo said when she finished.

"Yes. 'We Shall Overcome.' Chiara was with you."

"I thought you were a little strange."

"I thought you were a little strange, too."

"Has it ever occurred to you that it was everyone else who was strange?" Lorenzo asked.

"Everyone else and everything else," Jolene said. "Nothing went the way I expected. I couldn't have been less prepared."

"I've come to the conclusion that the only thing you can be prepared for in life is not being prepared," Lorenzo said.

"But how can I be here, scattering my mother's ashes in Filippo's birthplace of Manarola, while he's off managing a fancy hotel in my mother's birthplace of Atlanta? How do things like that happen? That's my big question."

"And here I am. Freed from a wife who never loved me but would never leave me, scattering my second father's ashes at sea," Lorenzo said. "And you know what my big question is?"

"What?" Jolene gazed into his eyes, transfixed by the pallor of his moonlit face.

"What would have happened if I'd kissed you that day on the beach?"

Jolene recalled it all: the feel of the autumn sun, strong but low on the horizon; the way it baked the seawater on her salty skin, making it tingle as it dried. She recalled the heightened awareness of her body, how tired her muscles had been after the exertion of the hike, how the invigorating swim had revived her, how relaxed she'd felt sipping the chilled wine on the beach. She recalled Lorenzo's closeness; their conversation; their silence. Yet if anyone were to ask about her injured ankle, she would have had difficulty recalling that she'd been in pain at all.

"None of this would have happened," she answered. "Or maybe

all of this."

"I really wanted to," Lorenzo said.

"I was terrified that you would."

"Are you still terrified?"

"I'm not prepared."

"We never are, as you know."

Jolene and Lorenzo rocked above the black velvet sea that moved beneath them and all around them, as they sat face to face on the peeling benches of the little rowboat. Lorenzo leaned toward her, coming so close that it was hard to focus on his eyes. The cold tips of their noses touched; their lips brushed. Lorenzo's mouth was warm and tasted of the fresh sage leaves she often saw him chewing. The gentleness of his kiss was excruciating. Then it was over, and it was enough.

Jolene looked away, staring up at the rising moon, wondering if her mother had somehow had a hand in introducing her to Filippo, just to get her over here. "Do you believe in angels?" she asked Lorenzo.

"I am the son of a man named Heaven," he said. "How could I not?"

Jolene trembled with a sudden shiver; she pulled her jacket tight.

"You're cold, we should go," Lorenzo said.

"Can I ask you one more thing first?" Jolene said.

"Sure."

"Can I row?"

"Sure."

They swapped seats, and when Jolene grabbed the oars, it seemed good to feel the aged wood in her palms again. She let the sea cradle them for a moment longer, wondering whether a rowboat could pass for an ark, and a kiss for a covenant, and whether instead of turning back she should row them along the silvery path of the moonbeam. Shaking her head at her fantasies, she tilted her face toward the mountains of Manarola looming in the night, admiring the one hillside glowing brightly with one man's dream, as if beckoning her to return. With a few strokes of the oar, she turned the boat around and set her course for the only place she wanted to be. Rowing slowly at first, her muscles responded to the familiar movement of her arms, setting their pace. She felt warm now, and alive, as she pushed herself harder, gaining momentum with each stroke. Jolene was a little girl again, showing off to her mother how strong her arms had grown.

"Gently, Jolene!" her mother reminded her. "And don't forget to sing!"

So Jolene sang their song, knowing that the time had finally come to add on the second verse.

"Row, row, row your boat, gently down the stream.
Merrily, merrily, merrily, merrily, life is but a dream."

ABOUT THE AUTHOR

A native of Rochester, New York, Angela Scipioni has made her home in the seaside village of Camogli, Italy.

Prior to writing *Gently, Jolene* she co-authored the bestselling novel series *Iris & Lily* with her sister, Julie Scipioni. A story of two sisters struggling to survive in a male-dominated world, it has been acclaimed as "a book every woman should read."

Reader praise for Iris & Lily

"Delightful, touching, deep and wise."
"Hard to put this book down!"
"I thoroughly enjoyed this gem."
"I laughed, I cried, I empathized."
"My new all-time favorite!"

Learn more at

www.AngelaScipioni.com
www.IrisandLilytheNovel.com